Echoes

Echoes

ROGER ARTHUR SMITH

BAOBAB PRESS

ISBN-13: 978-1-936097-09-8
ISBN-10: 1-936097-09-5

Library of Congress Control Number: 2016954297

Baobab Press
121 California Avenue
Reno, Nevada 89509
www.baobabpress.com

Cover Design by Travis Bennett

FIRST PRINTING
18   19   20   21   22   23
10   9   8   7   6   5   4   3   2   1

For Arthur F. Smith,
Who moved the family to Hawthorne and beyond.

One to make ready,
Two to show,
Three to make ready,
And four to g—o.
A hideous yell of more than mortal agony drowned the last word. A dull
reverberation followed . . . and then all was still.

—"Vanderlyn," American Monthly Magazine, 1837

Lisette sensed that this time she wouldn't just be hurt. It would be worse. Much worse. She had been afraid of this new country, this new city, but her mother counseled her to have courage, their lives would be immensely better. America, the land of the rich! Los Angeles, a city of movies and bright sun whose name, her mother told her, meant *angels*.

Lisette had tried. Even though she could not understand how people talked here, on a Saturday she went to the playground of what was to be her new primary school. Her mother had dressed her in her nicest red dress, because it went with her long, wavy auburn hair. She was at her prettiest. That was comforting. She sat on a swing made with a strap of black rubber and twisted its chains and then let the twists unwind, swinging her round and round, while waiting for some American children to come to the playground so she could make acquaintances. From playmates she could learn. She waited and waited for a young face to flash before her eyes as she spun.

An adult came instead. She never saw *that* face, but she believed from the strength of the hands and the odor that it was a man. She was grabbed up backwards from the swing, just as a last twist of the chain unwound. A hand clapped over her mouth, pinching her nose at the same time. He was very strong. She smelled an awful, hospital sort of odor, and a long, confusing, blurry time passed. Then, soon after he dropped her on a bare concrete floor in a chilly room, she knew for a certainty it was a man. He used her as a woman, just as her mother had warned her about bad men. And he hurt her—in so many ways—so now her insides throbbed with pain, a dull, pulsing pain if she lay still, and a piercing pain in her gut if she struggled to move. The struggle wasn't worth the effort. He left her with ropes on her hands and legs, tape on her mouth—only tears from her eyes moved freely. She felt sticky all over.

When he returned, even though it was again from behind, outside her peripheral vision, he came with another. Lisette could hear the distinct footfalls. In any case, when the shouting started, though she could understand none of it, the voice did not sound as if it belonged to a man. The man had been terrifyingly silent the whole time. In truth, the voice overshadowed anything she had ever recognized as human.

The tape was pulled from her face, Lisette began to scream, but a horrendous slap stunned her silent. As she tried to get a breath, she felt the knife inserted into the corner of her mouth. A jerk and ripping pain and then the gush of warm blood over her cheek brought a whimper, yet she recalled her mother's admonition to have courage, and thought, in sad surprise rather than resentment, *C'est ce que le courage m'a apporté en Amérique.* The knife was used elsewhere, again and again, and although the pain made Lisette howl once more and the fear was like a detonation inside her, this one soupçon of comfort came to her before the end. Her death would make a difference.

As life left her, a realization came—perhaps from the outside, perhaps from within. She didn't know. What she did know was that she was their fourth victim.

With that something awoke, something pure and evil, old as humankind itself. It was now aware of Lisette's tormentors. They were marked.

One

Mildred Warden did not hear the boy enter her library. That was because of the wind, she assumed. The spring zephyr had arrived the week before, the first part of May, 1960, and gathered strength until it was a bellowing, whistling wind, a hideous racket that had a scratchy sound to it because of the sand it carried. The wind scooped clouds off the desert, and from the naval ammunition depot nearby, whirled the sand into the air and flung it at Hawthorne. It was no wonder that commercial buildings, county buildings, and houses alike—everything—looked drab and poorly painted. The town received a yearly sandblasting. This was especially true for the Mineral County Library, because it stood far out along A Street on the edge of Hawthorne, as exposed to the central Nevada wastelands as a cast-off child.

Mildred was startled away from reading the *Saturday Evening Post*— the March 19, 1960, issue with the painting of downtown Manhattan on the cover. So colorful and so thrilling!

All at once, there the boy was, standing right in front of her desk, practically under her nose. She glanced outside the window—the sky was a pale, sandy blue—and back to the boy. A cold thrill made her shiver. How had he come in without ringing the bell on the door? If the door opened, it tinkled automatically. It had to have been because of the wind. It was too noisy—there was no other explanation. But then, Mildred wondered, why hadn't the wind sounded louder when the door opened? Why hadn't she felt its gritty breath rush in?

Mildred glared at the boy, who stared dumbly back. Her first impression was unfavorable. He was not a cute child. Barely presentable, in fact. It was impossible to see him and imagine a mother who found him to be adorable, who was proud of him. His head was large and blocky. He had stiff brown hair on his head pushed up in a coxcomb, no doubt by the wind. It made him look like a cartoon figure plummeting from a great height, or theatrically frightened. His skin was pallid except for brown freckles on his cheekbones and over the bridge of his nose. The nose was wide, the tip flat as if someone were pressing a finger against it. The mouth was likewise wide, and a half-inch scar running at an upward slant from the right corner gave him an ironic look, although there was nothing ironic in his eyes. They were a watery blue, hooded under heavy brows. Only his chin might lay claim to cuteness, in Mildred's opinion. It was a perky little dome of fat that jutted out and sported a small dimple. His body was stocky, and he held himself stiffly, hands fisted at his sides. He wore a long-sleeved shirt, checked blue and white, buttoned up all the way to his throat and tucked into jeans, the bottoms of which were turned up in four-inch cuffs. The black Keds, torn and sand-stained, were off-putting to Mildred.

He was not a child whose mother dressed him thoughtfully. He was a child dressed quickly and dismissed, gotten out of the house to play after school, so the mother could have time to herself. That was the way it looked.

Imagining motherhood. It was something that Mildred often did when there were no patrons in the library, which was the norm. She occasionally imagined how other women must feel about their children, but that was only for contrast. Her imagination more often conjured a child she herself would have one day. Sometimes it was a girl, whom Mildred could dress up and share confidences with. Sometimes a boy, whom she could prepare for college and brag about.

This boy was not her sort. Not at all. He was unpromising. Mildred understood that intelligence could hide behind all kinds of faces. Even so, he did not look very bright. He just stood there, lumpish as slag.

Nonetheless, Mildred put on a little smile for him. She always encouraged the young to read. It was part of her job as the county librarian, but beyond that she believed in the power of literacy to improve the young, believed in it more than anything, except maybe for her belief in marriage and children in her future. That was only a matter of time. For now, she relished introducing a child to books. This boy was obviously in need of it.

"Are you looking for a book?" Mildred asked the boy.

He took a long time before nodding, yes. His eyes stayed vacant, but they also stayed on Mildred, unwaveringly. She grew uneasy.

"Can you read?" she asked, a little sharply. The boy nodded again, but Mildred was unconvinced. "How old are you?" In a gesture too babyish for his age, the boy held up one hand, the fingers splayed. *Five*, thought Mildred, then, startled, did a double take. *No, four.*

It was a sickening shock. The hand had three fingers and a thumb. He raised his other hand, showing two fingers. He was six.

"What is your name?" she demanded, to cover her disquiet.

It was the only time that Mildred ever heard his voice. He emitted a throaty rasp, as if he were just getting over a bad cold or hadn't spoken in a long, long time. Mildred made out an *m*, *t*, *g*, *n*, and *s*, but it wasn't at all clear how they went together. She winced. Harshness aside, it did not seem to be a boy's voice, or not a pleasant boy's voice. Surprisingly deep for one so young, it was also dry and hollow, like the voice heard on TV in another room. She shivered again—once. A short, sharp clench.

When she asked him to repeat his name, he just gaped at her. She ran through the sounds in her mind, thinking now that the boy was simple and she would have to call the county juvenile officer to come and take care of him. She would need a name to give to the officer. *M-t-g-n-s*: Several people came to mind whose names had those consonants. She tried them out. He nodded, or appeared to, at the last, Matthew Gans.

It was all very frustrating.

Gans. She knew of the family, of course. Matt Gans was the new auto shop teacher at Mineral County High School, a position that automatically put him in the town's upper crust. The family had arrived the previous summer, but Mildred did not meet Mr. and Mrs. Gans until December.

It happened at a Christmas party. She was making her way round the crowded, cluttered, loud living room of Michael Callahan, the high school principal, when all of a sudden there they were, face to face, she and Mr. Gans. Immediately, he began chatting, asking about her job and family and prospects. Mildred was charmed. A fine figure of a man, open and dynamic. With an attractive wife, however, who allowed her husband only a short exchange. That was because, Mildred sensed, Mr. Gans displayed interest in her. She imagined the wife seeing a pretty younger woman captivating her husband and being a little jealous. It sent a pleasant warmth through Mildred. Titillating—she permitted herself that word only on rare occasions; the short conversation with Matt Gans was exactly that. About children of Matt and . . . Misty? . . . yes, Misty Gans, she could not recall having heard. Although of course a married male high school teacher would have children, she told herself. Didn't they always, though.

Her eyes refocused on the boy. "Is Matthew Gans your father or your name?"

Maddeningly, the boy nodded again. But it struck Mildred then: he could be Matthew Gans, Junior. With a speech impediment. And shy. Well, she couldn't hold those against him. A test, though, might establish his identity and whether he could in fact read at the same time. Mildred wrote out the four names she had pronounced to him and held it up for him to read.

"Which is you?" she asked.

Slowly, gently, he reached out and slipped the list from her fingers, and without looking it over held it at shoulder height. Mildred was taken aback. She dismissed the urge to order the boy away, however, or call the juvenile authorities right then and there. Every child deserved a chance. Instead, she became brisk.

A few more questions and a few more nods, and she established that he was not a library member, was willing to become one, and could write his own name on the small beige card with rounded edges that she set in front of him on the very edge of her desk. Hesitating, he laid the list beside it, took the pen that Mildred offered (she nearly lost patience), rested one forearm on the desktop, canted his head at a sharp angle in the opposite direction from his pen hand, and painstakingly filled in two blocky letters on the empty line below "Mineral County Library." *M* and *G*, widely spaced. The letters, if ungraceful, were the same size and on the line, exactly as Mildred liked. Yet as he wrote, the odd notion came to her that the boy was not writing them, but drawing them. Odd, too, that he should set down the capital letters first. She waited for him to fill in the rest of the names. He didn't, though. He set down the pen and stared at the capitals.

Sweeping the card away and reversing it, she added "atthew" to the *M* and "ans" to the *G*: Matthew Gans. After a hesitation, she put in "Jr.," then assigned him a member number, dated and signed the card herself, and handed it back to him explaining that he was allowed to check out one book for a week from the children's section. When she asked whether he knew what "check out" meant, he made no sign in response, so she explained how a lending library worked. It became evident to her, after a time, that she sounded high-handed, a little mean even, in giving a long explanation. And she was doing it because the boy was not likable, seemed slow. So she brought the library lecture to a sudden end by asking him what sort of book he would like to check out first.

Atop a low bookshelf next to her desk, the bookshelf she reserved for recent publications that she recommended to patrons, Mildred had propped several volumes for young adults and children. She pointed to the books on the shelf and prompted, "Do you like any of these?" The question made the boy appear suddenly closed, as if his eyes actually retreated into his head. It could have been a trick of the light. When the boy followed Mildred's gesture and looked at the books, he was also facing away from sunlight flooding in through the high window behind Mildred's desk and toward the comparatively shadowed area of the bookshelf; the pupils of his eyes dilated. Nothing so mundane and mechanical occurred to Mildred, though. The boy seemed, all of a sudden, furtive. Creepy.

He nodded slowly but did not point to any specific book. So Mildred removed the nearest and set it before him on the desk. However well the boy could read (if at all, Mildred wondered), the book was profusely, beautifully illustrated and would prove educational.

"Here," she said, trying to soften her voice some. "This is brand new and lovely and part of the famous Every Child's Omnibus series."

She stopped herself again. The name would mean nothing to the boy. In any case, he simply fixed his eyes on the book until she flipped open the cover, took out the checkout cards from their stiff paper pocket, stamped in the due date on each, and re-inserted one into the pocket, while laying aside the second for filing. When she picked up *Every Child's Omnibus of Wisdom* and held it out, he raised his hands to receive it readily enough. Just then the phone rang.

The phone stood on a half-size file cabinet behind Mildred and, still offering the book, she twisted round to reach for the receiver. The caller was not, as she hoped, Will Dubykky, whom Mildred dared think of as a *possibility*, but Deputy Sheriff Dodd. He wanted a book about Wyatt Earp, because he had heard that Wyatt Earp had actually served as a lawman in Mineral County. Mildred was familiar with the subject. She informed him crisply, because he was not a man she wanted to encourage through long conversation, that Wyatt Earp had indeed been a marshal in Nevada, but it was in Nye County, not Mineral County. In the course of her remarks, she felt a little tug at her extended hand, and released her hold on the book. The deputy's questions disposed of a minute later, she swiveled back. Matthew Gans, Jr., was gone.

Mildred looked around her library. It was a long single room of tables and wall shelves where there was nowhere to hide. The boy had vanished, and with him *Every Child's Omnibus of Wisdom*. He was the first to check it out. Mildred's smooth, powdered forehead creased. *And*, Mildred realized, the list of names was gone, too.

Did she smell something musty, like decay? She sniffed deeply. Yes . . . maybe, but she was startled out of that line of thought. A gust of wind swiped at the windows, scratching and rattling the panes. She pressed a palm to her heart to calm it.

That door bell, Mildred mused, disgruntled and more than a little spooked now, I'll have to get it replaced with something louder or people will be sneaking in on me all the time. Like that boy.

Now, what nice man should do it for her?

TO MILDRED'S DELIGHT, Will Dubykky did call later in the day. He was calling, he told her, simply to be sure that everything was all right with her. Such an attentive man! Of course, everything was all right, if a little lonely.

What else?

He took the hint. They agreed upon dinner in the restaurant of the El Capitan, the biggest casino in town. To Mildred, this was daring, just a little. The El Cap boasted the county's only fine dining and was beyond her means except for really special occasions. But not beyond Will's. Like her, he was of the professional class, yet unlike her he was a type of professional who actually made a lot of money. An attorney-at-law. Also, it was a Thursday night, not a day that Mildred normally allotted to dining out, yet again this was Will, and so the departure from her routine moved Mildred to romantic thoughts. Maybe Will was finally getting interested in being something more to her than an ersatz uncle.

On the way to the El Cap, after locking the library's front door, having carefully negotiated the three concrete steps to the sidewalk, she nearly toppled off her high heels. The wind was becoming especially fierce. One glance at the mountains to the west of town and it wasn't so hard to imagine a hurricane about to strike. The Wassuk Range rose straight up thousands of feet from the desert floor like gargantuan waves about to overwhelm the feeble human settlement, an illusion enhanced by the cap of snow on them, like foam on breaking surf.

Mildred hurried downtown, unable to stop herself reflecting on what a shame it was that Will was not more like Matt Gans, the teacher. Matt was handsome, lively. Dashing, even. Such a big wide smile he had, she had been all but blinded by the whiteness of his teeth. Will posed a contrast. Not that Will was a bad-looking man. Not at all! But where Matt was muscular-manly, Will was slender. Where Matt was animated, Will was impassive. Where Matt glowed with health, Will hinted of having some disability that diminished his vitality, perhaps related to wounds he had received in Korea. *Pizzazz* was not a word she could associate with him. *Unflappable*, maybe: the unflappable William Dubykky. Not so romantic, that.

Mildred sought the protection of the commercial buildings on Main Street, squinting against the grit in the air while gusts manhandled her. Once in front of the hardware store, she slowed her pace, enjoying the relative calm and the air's May softness. The snow in the mountains was beginning to melt. This meant that the winds carried some moisture with them, bringing an unusual fullness and tactile intimacy to the otherwise chalky high desert air.

She glanced at her watch, then checked it against the clock in the window of the jewelry store. She was a little early for the date, so she stopped and examined the rings and necklaces in the window display. She tried to keep her eyes off the earrings, especially the ones that were real earrings, the ones on slender posts, naked and silver, as opposed to the clasps. How her mother had ranted when Mildred returned home from the University of Nevada two years earlier. Pierced ears! Oh, horrors! The memory still made her blush. But it had been a little funny, too, when her mother, transported by rage, lost control of her syntax. "No daughter of mine—tricked out like a floozy—painted toes next—clasps like a good Lutheran woman—sitting on men's laps— hophead beatniks!" Overcome by the shame of it, her mother retreated to the recliner oppressed by a headache. Really, it was 1960. Tastes were changing. Couldn't she see that?

Mildred's only set of earrings, modest silver maple leaves on posts and not at all anything racy like gold hoops, disappeared from her dresser soon afterward. Mildred had not dared buy anything else like them. The piercings in her ears had all but closed up.

Still, she could—she thought of Misty Gans, Matt's wife. Misty had pierced ears and wore little garnet earrings. Very elegant. But of course the Ganses came from Los Angeles. They were sophisticated. The image of Matt came back to her, the twinkle of interest in his soft blue eyes.

Stop it, she chided herself, *just stop*. A married man! And they'd had only that one *rencontre*.

As for Will, his eyes were—well, there was certainly no twinkle to them. They were unreadable, usually. So dark brown that in all but the brightest light they seemed black. And that fact, against the habitual pallor of his face, gave them the appearance of bottomless depth. If Will hadn't had such an interesting, dry sense of humor, those eyes might be frightening. And if he hadn't been so caring. Since he had arrived in town after the Korean War, introducing himself as a friend of Mildred's father, who had not survived the conflict, Will regularly looked in on her and her mother. A good friend, and never an undertone of illegitimate interest, even though at sixteen she fancied herself pert as a poppy. Since then she had grown up, been to college, and matured in her interests, while Will, in the way of older men, remained simply older. She would welcome a little illegitimate interest from him now and less of the "old family friend." Still, he was only a *possibility*. There were other eligible men in Hawthorne of the right class and age, although, admittedly, far from a crowd of them.

Putting her hand over her pillbox hat, she bowed her head and dashed across Main Street, not easy to do on heels, exposed to wind and oncoming cars. Inside the El Cap, the air was blessedly still and cool, smelling of dust, cigarettes, lacquer, and alcohol. The penny and nickel slots already held up a solid wall of gamblers. Marge Dressler, an old high school classmate, hovered near to keep them stocked with change from the coin machine strapped over her groin. Marge's eyes rested on Mildred for an instant then moved away, her face contemptuous.

That didn't fool Mildred one bit. The coin machine wasn't the only money associated with Marge's crotch, a fact well known around town. It was simply spiteful envy on Marge's part. Mildred was a professional, and Marge had nothing but her hands and her sex to make a living. At twenty-four she had already been married and divorced twice, once out of obvious desperation to a sailor stationed at the navy depot. Mildred by contrast was determined to be patient and choosy about men. She had set her cap for Mr. Right. She had no patience with women who simply made do, although of course she would never tell them so. Not directly.

She was still early for dinner but nonetheless found Will waiting for her in the restaurant. The booths were screened off from the clamor of the gaming floor by wavy, orange glass. Yet Will's eyes were on her as soon as she came round the partition, as if he had somehow already seen her. She smiled at him. Then froze mid-step.

Sitting across from Will in the booth was a second man, a stranger. She inwardly said an unladylike word, the sort that never escaped the parentheses of her frankest feelings.

Several times previously Will had introduced young men to her, all of them of inelegant appearance, small prospects, limited education, and unappealing manners. Even seen from an oblique angle, on first glance this one appeared to be of the type. Although sitting, he was half a head taller than Dubykky. And hulking.

Probably loutish.

She paced her progress toward the booth to look him over. There was nothing to alter her first impression. His dark hair was crew-cut, a style she disliked as too square, too collegiate. His face was round and small, although the eyes were large and under brows surprisingly slender for a man. His ears stuck out. His lips were full to the point of babyishness, his nose unremarkable. Overall, he looked pleasantly plain, if immature. His expression was expectant, which made Mildred impatient. The nerve! Will was fixing her up again, and she wouldn't have it. She was perfectly capable of finding a man on her own. She hesitated at the front of the booth, then sat on Will's side.

"Hello, Milly," Will said easily and, as was characteristic of him, without smiling. "I'd like you to meet my new partner, Milton Cledge."

Partner? Another attorney in Will's practice? Mildred's attitude shifted. Brightened. She smiled shyly and, removing her gloves, extended her hand. Cledge's grip was warm and gently firm, his smile charming. But, she realized, even despite the charming smile Cledge was still homely and he had a surprisingly rough hand, like a working man's.

"I'm delighted to make your acquaintance," Cledge said.

Mildred's attitude dimmed once more. Not only was it a stilted greeting but his voice was too creamy. Large light-brown eyes, round head, creamy voice—Mildred thought of Guernsey cows. She let the smile relax from her face. She shot Will arch looks as the three of them went through the pleasantries and background inquiries typical upon meeting someone for the first time.

Cledge, a graduate of McGeorge School of Law in Sacramento, had just passed the bar, Will explained, and was joining the office to specialize in land and tax law. At that point Mildred, losing interest in the conversation, largely ceased paying attention. The men talked law and local politics, to which, out of politeness, she added vague murmurs now and then while reading the menu. Or pretending to. It was short, and she had long had it by heart. What she was really doing inwardly was deciding how much anger she should reveal to Will later. Somehow she would have to tell him never to try fixing her up again but do it without alienating him.

The waitress appeared, old blobby Bobbie Rooney, and Will ordered a martini and Milton a whiskey soda. "And Milly will have a glass of Chianti," Will told Mrs. Rooney. He winked at Mildred's astonishment. "I called Gladys," he assured her, "and it's all right if you have just one glass."

She was very pleased. She liked red wine. More than that she liked it that Will had gone to the trouble to make her feel at ease by getting permission from her mother first. Yet Mildred was also embarrassed. To say such a thing in front of a stranger! Milton Cledge couldn't have been above three years older than Mildred, and here she was being made to look like a teenager who had to check in with her mother over every little thing.

Mrs. Rooney huffed and informed them that there was no chicken or pork available that night, only lamb and beef. So a chop and two steaks were the orders, and Mrs. Rooney hobbled away wearily, as if the food were already weighing her down. Now that Hawthorne had passed two thousand population—again—there were more outsiders, like the two lawyers, for a local gal to make time with. Rooney had always liked silly Milly Warden, so good luck to her. Except it would be better if these two were the tipping type of lawyers rather than the skinflint type.

Dubykky and Cledge spoke of Hawthorne, the ammunition depot at Babbitt next door, and Mineral County, including the Paiute reservation twenty-five miles north of Hawthorne in an elbow of the Walker River at Schurz. All from the angle of legal work. Dubykky looked more at Mildred than at Cledge, even though the discussion was meant for him. He was expecting her to chip in information, such as historical tidbits or local color, about which she was an authority. But she wasn't having it. It was a bald ploy to make her be friendly to Cledge.

Finally, Dubykky said to her pointedly, "I talked to Dale Remus today, Milly." He waited.

Mildred could not help herself. She stifled a giggle and had to cover it by asking, "What now?"

Dubykky was deadpan, something he did superbly, but there was a merry crinkle by his eyes. "Dale said there was another test shot this morning."

Mildred replied airily, "Anybody would know that. It was announced in the papers." Then Dubykky and Mildred burst out laughing.

The test detonation of an atomic bomb at the Nevada Proving Grounds two hundred miles to the south was always announced beforehand as a public service. Some people in Las Vegas liked to climb on top the tallest casinos and watch the mushroom cloud billow up from the desert.

"What's so funny?" asked Cledge.

Mildred tried to keep a straight face as she replied, "Dale Remus forgot how to read almost as fast as he learned sixty years ago."

The answer brought an odd expression to Cledge, part perplexity, part admiration and a dose of wariness. To Mildred it was cute. Dubykky explained about the atomic explosions and how they were a great point of controversy locally. He pointed to a sign near the restaurant entrance. It read, "This air filtered for your protection." Some locals worried about atomic fallout, even though the government insisted there was no danger at all.

"I wondered about that," said Cledge. "Then why wouldn't this Remus fellow . . . ?"

"He's also deaf as a mule," Mildred interrupted and laughed again.

"Then how . . . ?"

Dubykky explained, "Dale claims he can feel the radiation pass through his body. That's the way he knows when there's been a test."

A strange expression flitted across Cledge's face. He suspected he was being made the butt of a joke. "No," he said uncertainly.

"Fact." Mildred grinned. "Oh, there are nuttier characters around here than Mr. Remus," she went on. "Odder, old and young," she added after a hesitation.

Dubykky eyed her curiously.

Noting it with satisfaction, Mildred began, "At the library today, well, you know how windy it's been? I hope it doesn't blow any radiation our way. Ha, ha. Well, there I was and . . . this was late afternoon . . ."

"Milly," Will interrupted, a touch of scolding in his voice.

"Yes, of course." Mildred had a tendency to wander. She concentrated. "There was this boy. I was reading the latest *Saturday Evening Post*, an article about Cocteau—no, wait, maybe that was two weeks ago in the March fifth issue. It really was a disappointing article, and all the disappointing articles sort of run together in my head, and I don't like the man's films at all anyway." At a look from Dubykky, she said hastily, "Oh, yes. Certainly. The boy. Imagine! The wind is so shrieky I can hardly hear over it, and I look up. There he is. Abracadabra! Smack in front of my desk. I didn't hear a whisper of him coming in. It was just like that, there he is, and, oh, Will, he was such an odd little boy."

Mildred described the boy minutely, dwelling especially on the four-digit hand he held up when Mildred asked his age. The reactions of the two men could hardly have contrasted more. Dubykky appeared distracted, as if his mind had drifted off. Cledge grimaced. Mildred couldn't blame him. Disfigurement in a child so young was difficult to accept.

"Well, I assumed he came to get a book, naturally, though I couldn't get anything from him in reply to my questions except nods and blank stares. When I asked his name, all I got was garbled sounds, like chalk on a blackboard, but I think I figured it out finally. So I filled out a child's membership card for him."

"What name?" Dubykky asked, a perfunctory politeness, as though he were simply chipping in to keep the conversation rolling.

"Oh, yes. What a surprise! Matthew Gans. Or so I think. I named people with similar sounds: Matilda Gosse, Mitchell Garrison, Manuel Gonzales, Matthew Gans. He seemed to react to the last, especially when I wrote them all down.

"You know, Will—that Matt Gans who teaches shop at the high. The boy seems to be his kid. Matt Gans, Junior."

A furrow appeared between Dubykky's brows at the admiring tone she used when pronouncing the father's name.

Mildred was poised to continue elaborating the incident, the only noteworthy one of her day, but Dubykky, despite his apparent lack of interest, surprised her, asking, "Did this Matthew Gans, Junior, check out a book?"

"Why, yes."

"Which book?"

Mildred did not expect such curiosity on the subject of children's literature and was a little unsettled. Dubykky was staring at her. "*Every Child's Omnibus of Wisdom*. It's brand new, part of a well-thought-of series. *Every Child's Omnibus of Sports, Every Child's Omnibus of Science*—have you heard of those? Anyway, this one's a very interesting volume, full of rhymes and riddles and fables, all with clear moral lessons. Just what a young boy like him needs."

While Milton Cledge struggled not to look confused and uninterested at the same time, Dubykky's stare was positively disturbing. Mildred didn't know how to describe it, or what to make of it. It compelled her to continue without his evincing any pleasure from what she said. So she explained how the book was a Beginner Book, one meeting the publisher's policy to introduce new readers to a basic vocabulary of 350 words. She admitted that the contents were quirky and that the book probably did not adhere to that policy strictly, but then she stumbled to a halt.

Dubykky had turned and was looking out the window, which presented a view of Highway 95. Mildred did so, too. A long-haul truck was moving past, but when it was out of the way, a boy was revealed standing in front of Simpson's Jewelers. He wore the very same kind of checked shirt as had Matthew Gans, Junior. Mildred looked at him more carefully. Tucked under one arm was a thin strip of color. With a start, Mildred realized it was the spine of *Every Child's Omnibus of Wisdom*. The series' book covers had a shade of burnt orange instantly recognizable, even from a distance.

"It's him!" she exclaimed, practically squeaking.

Dubykky neither said anything in reply nor moved, but Cledge, following their eyes, squinted, then reaching inside his suit jacket took out a pair of glasses with heavy black rims. A small part of Mildred's mind registered this disapprovingly as Cledge unfolded them and put them on. Even with the glasses on, he squinted.

"Where?" he asked, scanning the street.

"There." Mildred pointed. "Across Main."

"I don't see anybody across the street at all," he said in a cross tone, because he again suspected that he was being made the dupe for an obscure joke.

Mildred turned to him, impatient. "You don't see the boy? He's straight across the street. There." But when Mildred looked back, the boy was not there. She swung her head, searching. Nobody at all was out on the sidewalks. "Huh," she admitted after a moment, "how strange. I'm sure I saw him. Now he's gone and he seemed to be looking right at us. He certainly moves fast! Didn't he move fast, Will?" Despite herself, she coughed a short, nervous laugh.

Mrs. Rooney arrived with their salads right then, settling them on the table with much clattering. Right behind her was the bartender, dressed immaculately in black and white like Mrs. Rooney, but looking spruce where Mrs. Rooney was dowdy—but also blank-faced while Mrs. Rooney's eyes darted among her customers, shrewdly assessing the gossip value of Cledge, the newcomer. The bartender set out the drinks. At this Cledge frowned, an indication of restaurant savoir-faire that pleased Mildred. As swanky as the El Cap purported to be, the staff didn't know to bring the alcohol before the salad course. The three ate in silence, a silence that continued after her lamb chop and their two steaks were served. Though he dug into his food, Cledge seemed vaguely uncomfortable, whether because of the silence or the food quality Mildred could not divine, but it evoked a twinge of sympathy. Poor man, she thought, Will Dubykky and Mildred Warden must seem strange sorts for first acquaintances way out here in lonely Hawthorne.

She smiled reassuringly at him when he glanced up, then uncertain about the boldness of that, studied the level of wine in her glass. It had declined a little too quickly to last through the meal, so when Mrs. Rooney returned to check on their progress, Mildred glanced at the wine glass and then at Dubykky. He shook his head minutely. He himself had not touched his martini, so she felt reproved. Instead, Mildred ordered coffee and no ice cream for dessert. Cledge had ordered ice cream, but she had a figure to maintain.

Conversation resumed with the dessert. By then Cledge had forgotten about the boy and queried Dubykky and Mildred about local politicians. Mildred barely responded, which seemed to distress him. But Mildred did not have a problem with Cledge. It was just that nothing would fix in her mind except the sight of that strange boy across Main Street, his eyes trained right their way. Uncanny.

Cledge left first, shaking her hand and again assuming a stilted style of address to profess great pleasure in meeting her and sharing a meal. Watching him leave, she was interested to find him a sturdy figure and tallish, maybe five eleven, but a little ungainly in gait. Large feet. The soles of his wingtips, canted back at her as he stepped, were clean, hardly scuffed. She approved.

"Well, Milly," said Dubykky, and Mildred snapped her eyes away from the retreating figure. Dubykky had a little smile, the one with just the very corners of his mouth turned up that he used to tease her sometimes. "What do you think of your future husband?"

Mildred flushed and spluttered protests. He just shook his head once and turned to watch out the window. Mildred was glad of the opportunity to switch the subject. Sometimes Will Dubykky just—she had been going to say to herself "went too far," but the words didn't suit her, and she balked. Her frank, inner voice finished the sentence with, acts like a weirdo. She compressed her whole face, which was how she got rid of unpleasantness in her mind. Back to the subject: "You saw him, didn't you? The odd-looking boy?"

Dubykky nodded, almost imperceptibly.

"Wasn't it strange, though? I mean, there he was across the street. And looking right at us. Will?"

Dubykky continued to stare out the window. Mildred kept her eyes on his ear while she spoke, because with the approaching dusk she felt a compulsion not to look where he was looking. "Don't you wonder why he was there? I do. Maybe he wanted something from me. But how would he know I was here in the restaurant? Will? And what could he possibly want from me now that the library is closed? Will? Say something!"

Dubykky sighed, which astonished Mildred. She had not heard such a sound from him before, a sigh that said something like, All right, there it is, I'll have to attend to it. Or so it seemed to her.

At last he replied and did so in a tone hardly more than a murmur, but a tone nonetheless firm and clear, the tone he used when he told her something that she was absolutely supposed to take to heart. Sometimes, on the infrequent occasions when she heard that particular tone from him, Mildred wondered whether Dubykky regarded himself as a replacement father to her.

"It's a warning," he said.

Ridiculous as the remark sounded, a chill swept through Mildred.

"Nonsense," she managed to say, prim and steady despite the frisson. "What warning would a boy want to give me?"

Now Dubykky took his eyes away from Main Street and directed them hard at her. The little teasing smile played on his lips for a moment, yet the fatherly tone was still there when he said, "A warning not to let yourself get interested in Matthew Gans, Senior."

"William Dubykky! I never—"

But he cut her off, and playfully. "Milly, Milly. A married man. Really! What would Gladys say?"

That brought him exactly what Mildred expected he wanted: flurried protestations of surprise and dismay at the very idea. Of course, she would never, ever entertain . . . But even as Mildred was running through her denials, her absolute assurances of propriety, even then she understood that Dubykky had not been teasing her. The warning, whether the boy's or just Dubykky's or from them both, was genuine. After they parted, Mildred did not tarry to enjoy the sensuous evening air, now that the wind had slackened. The sky was darkening. Mildred wanted nothing more than to hurry home before night set in.

Nevada was the state of endurance and defiance. Nevadans endured nature and happily defied each other; they happily defied nature and endured each other. But no one with a grain of sense tempted the desert night, not without cause, not without trepidation. Outside the busy lights, boundless and bare, it mocked humanity.

Two

All the next day, Will Dubykky had the fey boy, "Matthew Gans, Jr.," on his mind. He suspected what the boy really was. Not a boy. Not a human, but a related, though darkly distinct, creature. He intended to find out for sure. Duty required it, in fact.

After work he returned home and got into his '51 Ford pickup, venerably battered and covered with lumpy pea-green enamel by its previous owner. Perched on his shoulder, clutching so hard that the claws dug into Dubykky, was a new friend, a young crow. Together they drove out of town looking for obscure back roads where they might come across abandoned shacks. In some such place, Dubykky expected, they would find the boylike creature.

The crow and Dubykky had met only hours earlier. He was walking home from his office, as he liked to do on a fine spring day, and on a whim diverted to the Mineral County Courthouse park to enjoy the sunlight filtering through its cottonwood trees. He felt an affinity for trees, difficult to satisfy in Hawthorne. It was a lucky whim.

He had cocked back his fedora and was just settling himself onto a bench to have a careful, undisturbed think about the creature when a plaintive, anxious squawk rang out nearby. He searched among the middle branches of a cottonwood until he spotted the squawker, a crow.

Dubykky liked crows and was immediately entranced. It looked like a fledgling. Even when they reached more or less full size, the juveniles were distinct from their elders. Their feathers were finer, fluffier around the neck, and had a subtle gray overtone; their bills showed faint red streaks at the back. In the nest, when an adult arrived the chicks crooned a low, harsh, breathy sound, like wax paper being crumpled slowly, and the adults crooned back in kind. These were identification sounds, Dubykky supposed. There was something so intimate and comfortable and trusting about crows when they were together that Dubykky was almost envious. They belonged to each other. Belonging —it was a mysterious concept to him, but recently, an appealing one.

The crow was looking downward intently and shifting its weight from claw to claw. Dubykky followed its gaze, and as he did so, he heard a disorderly flapping of wings in the lower limbs of a nearby tree. There he spotted a second fledgling, this one hanging upside down, thoroughly flummoxed. It flapped its wings to right itself but failed. The limbs were too close together. It tried and tried. Finally, it let go and dropped to the next limb. But it missed its grasp and ended hanging again, this time by one claw.

Dubykky's first impulse was to go to its aid. The bird was easily within reach. He didn't dare, though. Crows were rightly shy of humans, and the first crow might call in others to mob him and drive him away. Then he would not get to watch how things turned out for the youngster. Instead, he called out for it to drop to the ground and get its bearings there.

Dubykky was half in earnest, too, yet he did not expect the crow to take the advice. Whether by chance or choice, though, it did. It let go again, landing in a heap on the grass, and for a moment lay there stunned. Finally, it struggled up on its claws and looked around, then waddled seemingly at random over the lawn in a side-to-side roll, tail wagging to balance, shoulders hunched, the head jutting forward with each step. This fledgling had not yet mastered the crow walk. It stumbled once and had to flare its wings. Dubykky chuckled in an appreciative way. The kid had gumption!

Maintaining a respectful distance, Dubykky got up and followed the bird as it ambled along. Its sibling was cawing aggressively now. Still, he considered catching the bird. Crows were smart, great mimics of human words if cared for and educated properly. And they were companionable. While Dubykky was mulling the idea, the fledgling came to its own decision. It hunched down, jumped up with wings outstretched and, flapping like a feather-duster in a whirlwind, made it atop the park's lone picnic table. For a long time it perched there, looking by turns confused and bored, yawning wide its beak, then probing among its wing feathers. When Dubykky paced a few more steps forward, it canted its head to keep an eye trained on him, the whitish membrane blinking rhythmically over the black bulge, but it did not flee.

And so there the two stood, eying each other, only a dozen feet apart. Suddenly aware that the cawing had stopped, Dubykky glanced upward. The sibling was gone.

Then something happened that Dubykky had never before experienced, not ever in his long observation of crows and their cousins. The youngster crooned to him. Not only that, but it gathered itself and leapt into the air once more, windmilling its wings for all it was worth until it came to rest on Dubykky's shoulder, knocking off his hat.

Terrifically pleased, Dubykky left the hat on the ground and made his way slowly homeward, assuring the young crow of his respect and goodwill in a polite, careful voice. There was no one about to goggle at the outlandish sight, a prominent local attorney with a crow on his shoulder. Dinnertime, the town's central daily ritual, kept people indoors.

It was all a very good omen and irresistibly flattering. Befriending him, the fledgling clearly perceived that Dubykky was fundamentally different. That Dubykky could be a friend.

Dubykky decided to call him Jurgen, for he was male. He caressed feathers under the crow's beak and spoke the name aloud each time. Jurgen remained rooted to Dubykky's shoulder all the way home. The bird sometimes gurgled gently in response but seemed on the whole content to listen to whatever Dubykky said, and he had a lot to say, because he had a specific purpose in mind for Jurgen. It required, first, that Dubykky teach the vocabulary of his own existence: of destiny, crime and retribution, evil and duty, pursuit and punishment, vengeance and death. Dubykky took care to repeat important words in as many contexts as possible.

His house lay at the end of English Street at the town's edge, a half mile from the park, single-story, flat-roofed, pale ochre, and tidy as a new deck of cards. Inside, he set Jurgen on the back of a dining table chair. A quick survey of his refrigerator, and he laid out a plate of raw hamburger. For himself, Dubykky grilled a pork chop and heated up canned spinach. He didn't really care what he ate.

They sat companionably together, Jurgen mostly quiet after the excited outburst of screeching that came with his first taste of hamburger. In the slanting light through the tiny kitchen window above the sink, his black eyes glinted like ebony. When he finished, he hopped back onto Dubykky's shoulder and pecked affectionately at his earlobe. At that point, Dubykky's fondness for him was cemented. Yet it would not be his to enjoy for long, and Dubykky felt a pang of regret.

He squelched it. The boylike creature would benefit far more from a boon companion like Jurgen. The creature was far needier.

NOW IN THE PICKUP, Jurgen might have been having second thoughts about his new acquaintance. When Dubykky had turned the key in the ignition and the engine ground and fired, Jurgen flared his wings, uttering a censorious hiccoughing sound. Dubykky murmured soothing words as they backed out. "Grawp," Jurgen objected after Dubykky shifted into first gear and the truck lurched forward down English Street. It seemed wrong to him that while he was standing still the world moved past, and at a steadily increasing pace.

Matthew Gans, Jr.—if that was indeed the correct name, which Dubykky had no reason yet to believe—might be lurking anywhere. Miles upon miles of sand and scrub, mountains, gullies, and lake shore all lay within the walking range of a sturdy boy. And, if Dubykky's suspicions proved correct, the creature was more than merely sturdy. This could mean days of searching. Yet Dubykky's experience told him that the creature would seek to conceal himself until he was ready to strike. That gave Dubykky the idea where to look.

"I'll call you Junior," he said aloud, just to get the feel of the name, "whether you're Matthew Gans or not." Jurgen took a small step sideways and peeped around at him, curious.

Hawthorne was one of those high desert towns that had always seen better days. It was surrounded by a halo of neglect. From its outskirts, dirt roads cut through the sand flats and into and out of ravines and around little knolls of rock and greasewood, where invariably stood trailers or tarpaper shacks at irregular intervals, most empty, at least temporarily, companions to scavenged automobiles and jumbled appliances. If Nevada's highways linked its far-flung towns into a state, it was the dirt roads that lashed a town to the landscape. Where the sandy ruts ultimately led revealed what the community cared about, past and present—a mine, a ranch, a reservoir, a fossil bed, a hunting range, a campground, a field cabin, a hot spring, a graveyard, a lake, an inexplicable pasture, or, as was sometimes the endpoint, a petering out, an idea abandoned.

Dubykky started down three of the roads until each time he came upon a shack leaking light from behind a sheet-curtained window, then turned back. A deserted road was what he sought. The fourth he explored proved to be just that. He followed its ruts until they dwindled away and put the Ford into reverse. It was too risky to turn around in the soft sand, so he stayed in reverse until he returned to the last of the shacks he had passed.

He stopped nearby, letting the truck idle while he emptied his mind of every thought and sense impression. It was an old familiar practice of his, and the nighttime desert produced nothing to distract him. The last thing he noted before he achieved complete blankness was the faint susurrus of Jurgen's even breathing. The crow had fallen asleep.

Nothing from the first shack intruded on his inner void, not the least whisper. He was wearing a wool sweater and heavy corduroy trousers against the intensifying night chill. Even so, cold soon penetrated, and he realized it, a mentation that ended the trance. He tried to re-enter it but shivered. Strange, that. So slight a chill had never distracted him. It was one more instance, if a small one, of change creeping into his long, errant life, a life in which change, if it came at all, came for a reason, foreseeably.

That had not been the case recently. That very morning Dubykky had experienced something nearly unprecedented: a gush of warmth for a human. This unaccustomed emotion arose while he was standing behind his desk at Dubykky & Cledge, Esq., Attorneys at Law. It was evoked, in fact, by his brand-new partner.

Dubykky and Milton Cledge could not have been more dissimilar, even discounting that Cledge was a twenty-six-year-old human and Dubykky had lived more than half a millennium as something that only looked human. It was their here-and-now temperamental differences that mattered, and they did not put Dubykky off. He got along with humans just fine when he needed to. But Milt was proving to be almost superhuman in a modest, inadvertent way. The exceptional thing about him was his face. Not its appearance, which was somewhat adolescent and doughy. Its expressions. Milt could not control them— did not even realize he couldn't. That ought to have simply been ridiculous, yet the first time they met, Dubykky perceived at once that there was much more to Milt's expressions than mannerism. They were the emotional eruptions of a decent person. The perfect antithesis of Dubykky.

He had been interviewing applicants to become his partner in the Hawthorne law practice, until then a solo concern. Cledge was among them. He walked into the interview looking determined but wary. It took place in Reno because that was Nevada's largest city and conveniently near the California border. Nevada had no law school of its own, so most fledgling lawyers came from those in California, McGeorge above all. Dubykky rented a Mapes Hotel conference room for the purpose, the tinny jingle-jangle of slot machines just audible in the distance, the air scented by tobacco smoke, nervous sweat, greasy food, and hair oil. How better to make a Nevada newcomer antsy?

Yet Cledge surprised Dubykky. He did not fidget or perspire. He sat still and straight in his chair, hands on his lap. He met Dubykky's eyes expectantly. His smile, if tentative, was pleasant, unassuming. Dubykky was charmed despite himself. For that reason, he skipped the usual opening pleasantries. He asked straight off, "What would you do if you discovered I was cheating our clients out of their money?"

The bluntness was rewarded. Cledge's grimace of revulsion was pure reflex. "Tell them," he answered tightly.

"Tell them? Really? Not ask me about it first?" Dubykky pretended to be affronted.

Bewilderment wrinkled Cledge's brow. "No. If I knew it to be true, you'd be untrustworthy. It would be best to warn off clients."

"So you'd favor clients over our partnership."

A moue of offense, then a squint of craftiness, and Cledge replied, "There would be no law practice without clients." His eyes widened. He evidently realized the answer was evasive.

It amused Dubykky, both the evasion and the telltale expression. If principled, Cledge was yet eager for the job.

Dubykky pressed, "I suppose you'd report me to the Bar. Or would it be the police?"

Cledge's eyebrows leapt in astonishment, then came rushing back down from indignation. "Not right off! Of course not. I'd confront you first." He shifted in his chair while his eyes wandered uncertainly. When he continued, he tried to sound reasonable, and it was wonderfully stilted. "Sometimes there are mitigating circumstances. Defrauding, that is to say mulcting, may be redressed privately."

Honest, unsubtle, labored, naïve. Dubykky was content.

"Do you gamble, philander, or patronize brothels?"

Cledge reddened. His chin lifted, and he put his hands on the chair arms to hoist himself to his feet. Dubykky waved for him to remain seated.

"I take it that means no to all three."

Incredulous outrage distorted Cledge's whole face. "I'm a Catholic, and a devout one."

Earnest, sensitive, upright. At that point Dubykky ceased evaluating Cledge simply as a prospective partner. He began considering him as a husband for Mildred. As the interview progressed, Cledge proved himself to be sensible and intelligent as well, if only reasonably so. He was also reasonably slow to recognize humor, reasonably strong in physique, and reasonably homely in appearance. As such he was the sort of man who would feel lucky winning the hand of a lovely, educated young woman like Mildred and temperamentally mild enough to put up with her waywardness. Best of all, he was completely unable to dissemble. Even someone as self-absorbed as Mildred could read his heart. Nothing would be so

conducive to a solid, functional marriage for her than actually recognizing what her husband was thinking at any given time, rather
than imputing to him what she wanted him to be thinking. Dubykky
hired Cledge on the spot.

Seated in the pickup pondering his unexpected affection for Cledge
and the uneasy sense that his own nature was somehow changing,
Dubykky thought back to when his partner had walked into his office
earlier that day.

"Were you talking to yourself?" Cledge inquired.

Dubykky had been venting to himself about Mildred's inattention
during a phone call he had just ended. Cledge's expression was jocu-
lar, yet perplexity also lurked there. He must have already come to the
conclusion that Dubykky was eccentric, perhaps even downright odd,
and was trying to define its extent. Cledge had the lawyer's propensity
to gather information. That Dubykky talked to himself interested him,
and it wasn't an idle, finicky interest. Only sensible. Cledge needed to
understand his partner if they were to work together effectively.

"That's right," Dubykky lied straight-faced. "I was exclaiming to
myself how much violence, turmoil, and misery there is in the world."
He gestured open-handed at the *Nevada State Journal,* the Reno morning paper, lying open on his desk. Cledge knit his brow. The headline
only involved celebrities: "Lucille Ball Divorced from Desi Arnaz." But
he took the point. The day before, the headline had announced the
electrocution of the author Caryl Chessman, which was controversial
worldwide, and there was a nearly constant drumbeat of impending
war with the Soviet Union, or the Warsaw Pact, or China, or North
Korea, or any combination of them. News was bad news, and it was
frequently bad for the very reasons that Dubykky mentioned.

Yet too, news was just news. To Cledge, it was born old and quickly
faded. What truly occupied his mind was more immediate and dura-
ble: working during the work week and during free time pursuing his
true passion. That passion had come as a second surprise to Dubykky

during the job interview. After satisfying himself that Cledge was well trained in family and property law, he asked about hobbies, as if an afterthought. It was most definitely not that. A man's hobby expressed how he attached himself to the world around him. A useful thing for Dubykky to know.

"I'm a rockhound," Cledge replied, showing pleasure, pride, wistfulness.

Dubykky was delighted. A collector's mentality was acceptable because it was simple to manipulate. More than that, Cledge's hobby revealed his brand of good sense. For a rockhound, the west-central Great Basin was like Hollywood to a film buff. Everything that glittered, or could glitter with a bit of polish, was here, from amethysts to zeolites. Though not a native Nevadan, that rare breed, Cledge was in his natural habitat, for Mineral County was well named. It could not have a more appreciative, knowledgeable immigrant.

Any collector of rare beauty like Cledge yearned to show off his discoveries. If Mildred were to display interest—Dubykky tucked the thought away for now and laid out the contract that Cledge had come to ask about. It involved water rights. A ticklish issue in Nevada, water. There was so little of it.

"Oh, Milt?" he said as, their discussion concluded, Cledge was turning for the door. "Do you remember Mildred Warden? We had dinner with her at the El Capitan."

The question was disingenuous. Dubykky knew that Mildred would be remembered. Cledge's face told him that was so: remembered and with keen interest. Mildred had that effect on men.

He continued, "She and her mother, Gladys, would like you to join them for dinner tomorrow night. I'll be there too—I'm practically a member of the family—and I took the liberty of accepting on your behalf. Does that suit you?"

It did. Cledge's expression of gratitude was far more restrained than the eager anticipation his face broadcast.

ALTHOUGH THESE RECOLLECTIONS sped through Dubykky's mind as he sat in the dark, he was by now thoroughly chilled, and deeply put out with himself for drifting from his trance. He gently transferred Jurgen to the seat and put on a jacket he had brought.

Backing the truck onto the yard's hardpan, he turned around and moved on to the next hovel, a gray travel trailer propped on railroad ties, a quarter-mile farther downslope. There, stopped and in his trance, he sensed a faint vibration, like a velvet puff of air in his mind. This was not the right place either, though. The source of the sensation remained distant. He moved on.

At the next shack Dubykky had hardly stilled himself when evil irritated him like a mote in his inner eye. Turning off the engine, he removed a flashlight from the glove compartment and slid out of the cab. He did not switch it on, not wanting to startle Jurgen, who was now awake. Jurgen delicately sidestepped up his arm and onto his shoulder, and Dubykky picked his way by starlight through the junk-strewn yard.

The shack's door, made out of mortar-shell crates, hung on rubber strap hinges. The shack proper, under the tarpaper, comprised walls of pallets on end, buttressed by vertical and horizontal two-by-fours, the whole structure about ten feet square. Dubykky wondered that the wind had not already leveled it, yet when he grasped the door frame and gave it a shake, the structure barely shuddered, flimsy as it looked. He nudged in the door with his foot. It swung open easily, silent except for a clack when it struck a milk crate behind it. On his shoulder, Jurgen started, then moaned a low, dry, drowsy *nhrr* in complaint.

Dubykky ducked through the doorway, clicking on the flashlight but keeping it trained straight at his feet. The roof was on a slant, the highest end over the entrance, only inches above his head. There was just one small window, curtained with a yellow terrycloth rag, to his left. Seated in that corner, legs splayed out on the rough plank floor, was the boy. He turned his head slowly at Dubykky. His features were pools of black.

Dubykky shifted the light cone so that the faint edge illuminated the boy's whole figure. A lumpish body, a chunky head, heavy eyebrows, wild brown hair, and a blank expression. Or almost blank. A little twitch of the eyebrows hinted interest. Even a measure of recognition. Perhaps the boy sensed something about Dubykky. In any case, it was not the way a human boy would react if an adult found him alone in a dark shack.

Lying in the boy's lap was the book that Mildred had checked out to him, *Every Child's Omnibus of Wisdom*.

"Speak the name," Dubykky commanded. If the boy was indeed the type of creature that Dubykky suspected, the command compelled a reply.

And so it was. As Mildred had described, a series of sounds like *m*, *t*, *g*, *n*, and *s* came in response, a slow, harsh garble. They formed no recognizable word or name.

"Matthew Gans?" asked Dubykky.

"Matthew Gans," the boy pronounced precisely.

Dubykky regretted that Mildred had spoken names to the boy, although he could not fault her for trying to do her job. It was only that the creature would absorb and repeat everything indiscriminately.

"Mitchell Garrison?" he asked again.

"Mitchell Garrison."

"Matilda Gosse?"

"Matilda Gosse."

"Manuel Gonzales?"

"Manuel Gonzales."

The boy enunciated each name, reacting to none more than the others. How would Dubykky find out which, if any, was the right name? It was best, he decided, not to worry about it for now.

He shook his head in an exaggerated manner. "No. You are *not* Matthew Gans or Mitchell Garrison or Matilda Gosse or Manuel Gonzales," he said. "You are Junior. Say 'Junior.'"

"Junior," echoed the boy.

Following a long pause, during which neither the man nor the boy made a sound, Dubykky went to his side and crouched. He set the flashlight on the narrow ledge under the window so that the light shone against the back wall and revealed him to the boy as much as the boy to him. Dubykky looked long into his eyes, which did not waver. The few times Junior blinked, he did so with unnatural slowness. Dubykky picked up and studied the hand that had so disturbed Mildred. It indeed had only three fingers and a thumb. There was no indication that it had been mangled, though. Where the pinkie should have been there was no hint of a stump. Not even a metacarpal to support a finger. The sensible, human conclusion would be that Junior had a birth defect.

Dubykky knew better. It was a sign. A crucial sign. The mark of four. Its presence provided final confirmation of what Dubykky had surmised. The creature seated before him was an echo of evil like all the other echoes he had encountered. Every one had the mark of four somewhere on the body. Reflexively, his hand went to his own mark, the perfect diamond of moles at the base of the neck.

The sight of Junior seated there moved Dubykky. Another echo, another monster on the loose, another confrontation, more death. He had seen so many of them. He was suddenly weary, wishing Junior could be a . . . departure. Somehow.

He shook his head to clear it. What was going on with him? It was not his place to feel such things, only to watch and support evil's procedures. He forced a smile, expecting, and getting, no response from Junior.

"Do you know why you are here?" he asked gently, circumspectly, spreading his arms to indicate the world.

Junior slid his hands over the cover of *Every Child's Omnibus of Wisdom* and lifted it straight up. Then he repeated the movement with one leaf after another until five stood vertical, and page six was exposed. He rested his hand by the illustration there. It showed three boys. One was dark-haired, his face rugged, his eyes slitted, and his mouth set in a wicked grin. He was shoving a second boy, who had yellow hair, rosy cheeks, and an expression halfway between a smile and astonishment. He was falling backwards over a third boy, pinched, meager, mouse-haired, and scared, who was on hands and knees. Below was a nursery rhyme:

> This little boy is the good little boy.
> He smiles on all he sees.
> This little boy is the bad little boy.
> He does but as he please.
> This little boy is the fool of a boy.
> He gets down on his knees
> That the bad little boy
> The good little boy
> Shall sorely trick and tease.

Junior put his finger on the bad boy's head.

"Yes." Dubykky spoke slowly, kneeling. "But you're not here about little boys." He rested his forefinger under the *T* of the rhyme's third line and drew it across as he read, "'This little boy is the bad little boy.' And so are some adults."

"And so are some adults," repeated Junior. He pronounced the words exactly but in a dead, flat tone.

Dubykky settled into a cross-legged position, a movement that made Jurgen spread his wings to keep balance. Junior's eyes shifted to the bird and remained there until Dubykky reached over and turned the pages back to the very beginning of the book. He put his finger under the text's first word, which began a short rhyme centered in a page-filling illustration: a broad meadow bordered by forest and split by a brook, rounded mountains in the background, in the sky a smiling sun shooting out thick golden rays.

"'For every evil,'" he prompted, pointing. After a hesitation, Junior looked at the words and repeated them. Dubykky slid his finger to the second half of the line, "under the sun." Junior repeated again. And so on:

> There is a remedy or there is none.
>
> If there is one, seek to find it;
>
> If there is none, never mind it.

In this way, Dubykky led the boy through the entire book. On occasion, Jurgen perked up at one or another of the words, even a phrase, and croaked out an imitation. Then Junior would shift his attention to the crow until Dubykky softly encouraged him to return to the lesson. After they read all fifty-four pages, Dubykky closed the cover and told Junior to recite. He did so, flawlessly, every rhyme and fable, in an uninflected, leisurely, whispery voice, ending,

> Come when you're called,
>
> Do what you're bid,
>
> Shut the door after you,
>
> And never be chid.

"Why are you here?" Dubykky asked once more.

"This little boy is the bad little boy. And so are some adults," Junior told him.

"Where is the bad one?"

It was the all-important question. How much did the echo already know? Only a little, it seemed. Junior held out his palm in the direction of Hawthorne.

"Who is the bad one?"

Junior did not reply. Jurgen shifted uneasily on Dubykky's shoulder as the silence lengthened.

Who had caused the boy to appear in a desert town, a wind-blown valley, four thousand feet above sea level? Because someone had. After a human exploited and then murdered four others, purely for self-satisfaction, the lingering malevolence created a disturbance in that small portion of nature that was exclusively human, and rebounded. An echo. The echo of evil assumed a human form. Dubykky could not tell Junior who his target was. It was for the boy, not him, to follow the spoor; the mission was to tempt, lure, and trap the human monster. The echo killed that human and, if all went in accordance with evil's intent, died in the process. The rules of evil, which bound Dubykky as much as Junior, recognized no other outcome, lamentable as that might be.

Dubykky's role? That was more delicate. He would watch, certainly. He might teach, he might guard against error and inhibiting injury, but above all it was for him to ensure a clear, neat, final vengeance.

For the rest of the night—Dubykky could get by on almost no sleep—he taught Junior words and how to put them together and the rudiments of ideas and reasoning.

Before leaving, he mulled what his parting words ought to be. He might not get the chance to speak to Junior again. He could not predict how the events would play out. Except at the very end.

"When the time comes for you to kill," he said carefully, touching Junior's chest, "you will feel it here, and it will feel right."

The boy blinked at him but gave no sign of comprehending. Dubykky did not expect it. But he did hope that when Junior fulfilled his destiny, his own role would be simply as a witness, not as an executioner. For Dubykky's duty was just that. If either survived the echo-human encounter, he would complete the killing.

An echo's existence was lonely and brief, sprung from violent death and ending in violent death. Whatever happened to Junior in between, Dubykky did not wish the boy to be companionless. And this did not have to be so. While Junior had taken in the dismal tutelage placidly, his eyes never wavering, he did show a flicker of interest whenever Jurgen repeated something. The young crow sparked emotion in the young echo. It pleased Dubykky, for that was exactly as he had hoped.

"Now I have someone I want you to get acquainted with."

It was early on in the morning but before the eastern mountains developed a pale border of light, the little shack still dark beyond the yellow glow of the flashlight. Dubykky roused Jurgen, who was beginning to doze again, and guided him onto his wrist. Smiling at the crow, he pointed to his mouth and then said to Junior, "Smile." The boy repeated the word dutifully. Dubykky pointed to Jurgen and spoke his name.

"Jurgen," Junior repeated.

"Smile at Jurgen," Dubykky told him, and Jurgen, grouchy from being awakened before dawn, also enunciated, "Smile," if in a discontented scrape.

Junior made an attempt to imitate Dubykky's broad smile, faltering at first so that his unexercised lips looked wormy, but then managing it. Slowly, crooning to the young crow all the while, Dubykky extended his arm until his wrist was right by Junior's shoulder. He shook his hand lightly. The bird stepped across, then daintily lifting his claws turned himself around until he faced Dubykky again. As he did, his tail feathers brushed Junior's cheek. The boy smiled once more, and it was unforced, natural. With the neck flexibility equivalent to a newborn infant's, he swiveled his head ninety degrees and directed the smile at the bird. He crooned to it, emulating Dubykky meticulously.

He left boy, bird, and book in that sad cobbled-together shack feeling at odds with himself. Homely as he was, Junior had a winning smile, attractive because it was unworldly. Already, Dubykky was growing fond of him. Such a nice smile was typical for creatures like Junior, though, and made no difference in the long run. Only the fated dark, cruel end awaited him. It had been a lucky chance, then, that Dubykky had found Jurgen so that Junior could share what life was allotted him.

Yet something was awry this time. Always before, an echo came into being knowing the name of its target human. Junior had only a jumble of sounds to guide him.

That was one reason Dubykky was moved to teach Junior. It was not strictly out of necessity. Junior would follow his destiny one way or another, eventually. Dubykky taught nonetheless. To smooth the boy's path in part and in part to discover why there was a muddle with the human name. That was not the entire truth of it either, though. Dubykky also taught for his own sake. Junior's haziness about his destined human made Dubykky wonder about his own blighted, obscure origin in medieval Hungary. That was the real heart of it. At some point before memory, Dubykky must have been like Junior. He felt fellowship.

Three

For hours after the slender man left, the man who belonged to the sounds *Dubykky*, the boy-creature practiced words with the crow, Jurgen. In the course of it, he discovered in himself a new state of mind, which desired the bird to remain close, required it even. So most of all he practiced his new self-sounds, *Junior*. He pointed at himself, widened his mouth as Dubykky had taught, and spoke "Junior" over and over. Now perched on the shoe tip of the boy's right foot, the bird paid strict attention. When he finally said, "Junior," in return, the boy switched to a new instruction. He pointed at Jurgen and began to repeat, still smiling, "You are Jurgen." Eventually the crow repeated the phrase exactly.

Too exactly. Junior sensed something wrong. He checked the book, thought over what Dubykky had taught him, and realized that he had used the wrong words. He should have taught the bird to say, "I am Jurgen." But if he, who was called Junior, said that, it would also be incorrect. "I am Jurgen" and "You are Jurgen" meant different things. It would be like teaching the crow to say, "I am Junior." That would be equally wrong for the crow to repeat because Jurgen was Jurgen, not Junior. Thinking further, Junior considered saying, "I am Junior, and you are Jurgen." But if the crow learned to say that, it would be twice wrong. Possibly he should instruct, "I am Jurgen, and you are Junior." But the boy couldn't say that. It was not correct that he was Jurgen. He sat wordlessly a long while, puzzled.

An idea came to him from nowhere. He recognized it as an idea because it fit the description of ideas that Dubykky had given him. Junior pointed at himself and smiled. "Junior," he said, and the crow said so too. Then Junior pointed at the bird, smiling, and said, "Jurgen." "Jurgen," agreed the crow. Junior dropped his hand, relaxed the smile from his face, waited a minute, never taking his eyes off the bird, and then pointed once again without smiling or speaking. After a lengthy pause, the crow said in a diffident rasp, "Jurgen." Junior pointed at himself. "Junior," said the bird with a shade more assurance. "I am" and "you are" turned out not to be necessary, despite the examples given by the book and Dubykky. It was confusing that language contained unnecessary words.

Nevertheless, an agreeable satisfaction spread through Junior and with it a strengthened will. The boy liked the bird, wanted him near, wanted to hear him speak, and was glad that Dubykky had left him. He understood that *Jurgen*, *Junior*, and *Dubykky* fit the idea *name*, although in different ways. There was no similar agreeable sensation attached to the name *Junior*, no sensation at all in fact, yet there was to *Jurgen*. And the name *Dubykky*? Junior repeated it, pondering. He found he wanted to be in Dubykky's presence again even though the name evoked a different sensation, a mixture of agreeableness and something else. Something that suggested Dubykky would not stand next to him and speak to him as did Jurgen. More than that, there was something that hinted Junior should not want him to. A basic difference divided Jurgen and Dubykky, besides shape.

Junior paged through the book considering the different animals in it and the words describing them—fat, clever, white, bold-faced, dreary, gay, sweet—until he came to a page showing an angular, black bat:

Bat, Bat,

Come under my hat,

And I'll give you a slice of bacon.

And when I bake

I'll give you a cake

If I am not mistaken.

The bat reminded him of Jurgen. It was smiling happily as it hovered over the head of a boy doffing a high-crowned cap and holding a rasher. At that point Junior perceived a truth entirely on his own, a truth that Dubykky had not discussed, and the power of it pierced Junior. It made his whole body vibrate. The truth was that Junior liked to have a bird; Dubykky liked to have a bird; and Dubykky had given him the bird, and the bird was happy on his shoulder. Dubykky had given him the bird to like, which is to say, passed on the agreeable sensations of having a bird and having a happy bird. That put Dubykky in a perspective. It was as if the man were still nearby, albeit not physically. Junior liked having something to like from the man who had liked it. Junior concluded that Dubykky liked him, and so he felt likewise.

Next the sound sequence *Matthew Gans* sprang to mind, which the book lady had assigned him. Dubykky had used it. Junior sensed that it too was a name. What sensation did its sounds carry? He let his mind wrap around *Matthew Gans*, drift among the sounds, pry them apart to feel out each, rearrange them, and then steep in them, while staring fixedly at Jurgen, who fell asleep in the silence. The sounds did evoke something. It lurked at the very edge of his mind as in a haze, and what there was of it did not seem agreeable. Not Dubykky-like. Definitely not Jurgen-like. Nor were the names Gosse, Gonzales, and Garrison.

When morning was well advanced, Junior decided that he and Jurgen should find food and water. These things he understood even before Dubykky had explained. Junior's body was now asking for nutrition. As for the crow, he answered Junior's inquiry about food with "Junior!" From that, the boy surmised that the crow was like him. Hungry. Dubykky had taught him to use his breathing to find food and water. He was to breathe in through his nose. If his body liked an odor, Junior could eat or drink from its source. With Jurgen on his left shoulder, Junior left the shack and walked away from the dirt road and through the sagebrush flats, stopping occasionally to inhale deeply. The day was warm but not hot. Light gusts blew by from time to time, causing Jurgen to tighten his claws on Junior's shoulder, which produced a mixture of prickling and tickling that the boy found, on balance, agreeable.

"I like Jurgen," he declared.

The crow cocked his head and answered, "Hickory dickory dock!"

The Hawthorne dump lay just a mile away from the shack over a long slow rise and down a steep slope into a wide ravine. It was one of the innumerable ravines in Nevada, the primordial relics of deluges, windstorms, and the relentless shifting of sand and rock. Junior paused at the top of the slope and inspected the dump. A gravel road led to it from town and stopped at a turnaround. Along its edge rose hillocks of garbage. Even a hundred yards away the stench was strong. Junior didn't mind. One smell was much the same to him as another, providing that he didn't put the source of some into his mouth. Off one side of the turnaround in a small clearing of its own was parked an old shepherd's trailer. Painted white with blue trim, both colors faded, the trailer had a rounded roof and flat ends, at each of which was a small curtained window. Another window, even tinier, was on the narrow door at the right-hand end. At the other end a rusty stovepipe stuck up.

An old man was sitting on his usual chair by the door in a little parallelogram of shade. His arm resting on a folding card table, he did not move. His chin was on his chest. He wore dark glasses.

Junior waited a full five minutes for the man to move. In that time, Jurgen roused himself, ruffling his neck feathers. He murmured a polite caw to Junior, spread his wings, and glided to the ground. Two adult crows were nearby, standing in the shadow of a large sagebrush and pecking listlessly at the carcass of a lizard. Jurgen hop-walked over to them, squeaking obligingly, but they were unfamiliar and not welcoming. He stopped five feet away and cawed, hoping for an invitation. They ignored him. Jurgen was not discouraged. He was experienced enough to expect strange crows to respond from a limited repertoire: chase him away, flap around him to play, settle next to him to caw in his ear, or let him join them. Eventually. They would not ignore him for long.

As for the old man, his name was Hans Berger, and he was the watchman at the garbage dump. Mineral County paid him by the week to check for fires and illegal ejecta, such as goods, especially munitions cases, from the navy base.

The county commission wanted to charge a fee to leave garbage at the dump, but even though collecting it would mean a little more in wages for him, Berger was against it. He dreaded contact with people. At fifty-five he looked seventy. Wizened with yellowish gray hair and a long head, he wore a pointed beard of the same hue. It added to his aura of elderly peculiarity. That put people off, kept them away. Which was fine with him. It reduced the chances that they would ask about his thick accent.

Explaining! He always shook his head at the idea. How should he explain? He had sunk to nothing more than a junkyard denizen and wanted nothing from others.

Berger was not asleep. On the contrary, he was fully aware of the boy on the ridge and watched him from under his eyebrows, just over the rims of his Wehrmacht-issue smoked glasses. "Go away," he said quietly, to himself. The boy, thankfully, was too far away to hear. Berger's accent, his rich Bavarian consonants, tended to attract children. That, he did not want in the least.

He detested children, especially the boys. They taunted him, calling him Hamburger from a safe distance. *Die kleine Scheissen!* They knew they could stand just ten feet away, and he would be powerless to catch them and give them the beating they deserved.

Taunt *him!* Feldwebel Hans Berger, tank commander during Germany's glorious drive for Moscow, until the disaster at the Kursk salient. Then fleeing on foot among infantry, his tank having lost its track to a mine, a piece of Soviet shrapnel slashed open his knee to the bone. For two days he crawled along the muddy ground, hiding in every stinking hole he could find to evade the Soviet advanced guard as his roughly bandaged wound festered. Finally, a German counterattack brought paratrooper units close enough for him to find help. He was bundled off to the rear for medical treatment and then on to Warsaw for surgery. But it had been bungled or it was too late or the damage was just too great. It left him crippled. Now his leg was stiff as a crutch, a crutch he could not set aside. Or throw at the little monsters.

While he was recovering from the leg surgery, the Germans retreated, and conditions became hectic, nearly chaotic, for the splendid Wehrmacht. Berger took advantage. He deserted, hitching rides to Danzig and then to Rostock and across to Denmark under forged orders. He lighted in Sweden for the duration of the war and then took a berth as a cook on a cargo ship. He deserted it in Maracaibo. Every change of country, every painful movement along the way, was driven by his overwhelming fear of the Russians. Get away, as far as possible—that was his destination. And as far as possible, physically and politically, meant the United States. Well, he had finally made it, only to be called a hamburger by ignorant, undisciplined American brats.

The boy waited a long time without moving. Berger also did not move. Perhaps this one he would lure close and catch. Then he would work out his vengeance against them all at one time. He would wait to see.

With no discernible trigger, the boy was suddenly descending the slope in modest strides that left long projectile-shaped footsteps behind him and sent small fans of dirt sliding before. At the bottom he

stopped just outside the turnaround and drew in a deep breath. Looking sidelong in the direction of Berger's trailer, the boy veered and
continued, although not straight for the trailer. Instead, he headed for
the shack that stood to one side.

This is a first, Berger thought disgustedly. Now one is to go so far as
to steal my food! The shack held the icebox where Hans stored his per-
ishables, mostly meat. He curled his fingers around the long-handled,
three-prong pitchfork that was propped next to him against the trailer.
It was his only weapon, but it would be enough. No one would blame
him for protecting his property, even if a boy was hurt by it. Or perhaps not just hurt. The boy had wild hair, coarse features, and cheap
clothing. A poverty child, Hans saw. Someone no parent cared much
for, if there even were parents. Probably unloved, cast off, feral. Hans
could focus half a lifetime of disappointment, pain, and abuse from
others on this one unneeded boy. Who would ever know?

The intensity of Hans's desire for blood vengeance made his heart
thump. A long-dormant warmth came to his face. So strong, so profoundly vicious was the desire that it took Hans aback. He was surprised to find himself already on his feet, using the pitchfork, tines
upward, as a staff, and on course to head off the boy. Hans had to struggle with dizziness to remain aware of what he was doing. It was almost
as if the boy were drawing him, compelling him to his vengeance.

Junior halted in the middle of the turnaround. The old man
approached, dragging one leg over the dirt, jabbing the pitchfork handle in the ground and pulling himself forward. His face was twisted in
an odd way. Junior had no experience in reading human expressions.
A normal person, however, would have recognized the conflict in the
old man's face, two overwhelming emotions battling for supremacy:
utter hatred and terrified shame. To Junior the old man seemed merely
mistaken. He was not the one destined for Junior. The old man had
done nothing to attract him.

Junior held up his hand at the old man, reciting from the book,

"Better to starve free than be a fat slave." The man stiffened in place. He blinked as if coming fully awake from a dream. Neither budged.

On the ridge above the dump Jurgen was finally invited to peck at the dead lizard, although little was left but bone. The strangers hopped backwards to let him in, and he approached ducking his head in thanks. But the strangers did not stick around. With a parting squawk each, they took to the air. Watching them go, Jurgen felt abandoned, and when he looked around for Junior, the boy was not in sight. Jurgen, never wholly alone in his life before, was suddenly forlorn. For a moment he spread his wingtips to the ground and shivered, bleating and rolling his eyes at the sky. Then he pulled himself together at last and tucked in his wings. He hop-flew to the top of the steep slope, casting his eyes over the smoking knolls and dales of the dump.

There in the clearing below was Junior. Jurgen recognized the brown hair sticking up from Junior's head like a dark crest. At the same time Jurgen sensed trouble. Another figure was poised near Junior, holding a stick with three sharp points. Between Junior and this other one there was palpable tension. It frightened Jurgen as keenly as had the loneliness. Gathering all his strength, he stepped, bounded up, and flapped as the earth sloped away, then glided downward in a sweeping 270-degree arc. The heads below faced upward.

Berger spied the shadow as it slid by the boy and looked up to see the crow itself swing around, rear back flaring its wings, and land on the boy's shoulder. For a second it looked remarkably like a symbol from his past, the black Nazi eagle. He squeezed his eyes shut, then peered between the lashes. Everything was too bright.

Off. Garish. Spooky. The light, the tousled, ill-featured child before him, the bird. Hans had never seen a crow land on a human, except on a corpse to tear out flesh. This one alighted, ruffled, settled in as if it belonged. It was all too *schaurig. Seltsam.* Hans struggled for English: infernal.

The boy said, "He is Jurgen."

The crow emitted a two-part squawk-caw that sounded so like the name *Jurgen* that Hans nearly fumbled the pitchfork while taking a half step backwards.

"Heigh-ho, hi-ding-do," said the boy, beaming hideously at the bird.

"Junior," the bird replied.

To the old man the boy said, "I am Junior."

Hans was now thoroughly fuddled and alarmed. Though there was no overt threat from the boy, or even a hint of taunting, he felt the urge to run. Run in any way that he could manage, however painful and perilous. But at the height of this panic, just when he was about to give in to it, the boy's stomach gurgled loudly, protractedly, like the very last water in a bathtub as the drain sucks it down.

Hans relaxed.

The orphan was hungry. Of course he was! That was why he had come to the dump. That was why he was on his way to break into the shack. Scavenging. A empty-headed orphan, a gleaner at his dump. Han's intense hatred and shame abruptly dissipated, although not the encounter's surreal mood.

Hesitantly, Hans beckoned to the boy with his free hand. He pointed at his card table. "I have food, child," he said.

Junior recognized the change and supposed that it meant the old man understood now. Junior had not come for him. So when the old man pointed to the table, Junior complied and went there to sit. Talking nearly constantly, producing long strings of incomprehensible words, the old man left Junior and entered the shed. He reappeared with a small white package in his hand. He unwrapped it to reveal a length of sausage. This he took into his trailer. When he came out again, he had the sausage cut up on a tin plate along with a piece of buttered bread. He set the plate on the table as well as a glass of tepid tea. Then he hobbled around the side of the trailer and came back with a packing crate, which he set down across from Junior and sat on.

Junior watched all these movements impassively. When the old man, who called himself Hans, urged him to eat the food, Junior picked up a piece of sausage, which was firm and cool and slippery with grease, and offered it to Jurgen. Jurgen took it in his beak but held it there while Junior ate. The old man, still uttering harsh words, such as *Krieg* and *Flüchtling*, followed his every move, helplessly fascinated. When Junior finished the food, Jurgen glided to the ground, dropped his sausage chunk, put a claw on it, and set to tearing it into bite-size bits. These he consumed, trilling delightedly. With another flurry of activity, the old man assembled a second plate of sausage and bread for Junior and set a piece of sausage on the ground near Jurgen. In the course of it, Junior heard in English about Germany, Russia, Sweden, explosions, dead people, snowbound landscapes, ships, trains, the mountains of Mexico, the seamy wharves of San Francisco, and the pitilessness of Americans who learned of the old man's background.

Junior understood little and cared not at all. Still, he perceived that there was something deeply unpleasant in the man, something the man did not want to remember but could not stop himself from talking about.

The boy wished Dubykky were there to explain. The old man's evil seemed but a wisp. Hardly anything. It bothered no one but himself. So why the fussing?

When at last the old man paused to catch his breath, the boy smiled at him and said, "One story is good until another is told."

To Hans the smile seemed hideous, veritably demonic. The words seemed a goodbye. He had done his best to placate this strange apparition of a boy with food, then with the one precious offering he had left in life, a confession. Although his degradation and sin had come out fast and hard and dry, at long last it was out. The boy, however, seemed mysteriously unmoved. Why? Was there nothing he could do for expiation?

Hans suddenly felt panicky again. The inexplicably bright sunlight intensified. It penetrated his body like a drumbeat.

Pounding-blinding.

His body seized up so he could not move. He struggled with himself, but his muscles would not obey. He couldn't even close his eyes, still fixed on the smiling boy. "You are death," he tried to say. Though all that came out were strangled sounds, the boy shook his head no as if he had heard clearly.

"Tisha. Tisha. We all fall down," the boy mumbled around the sausage in his mouth.

A horrible pressure built in Berger's head, as though it were inflating. Larger, larger, and impossibly larger it felt. He struggled again to move and couldn't. He could not raise a hand to protect his left ear from the siren sound that had begun skirling there: no modulation, just a keening that steadily rose in pitch and volume until he felt he would burst.

He didn't, though. Instead there came a sharp, short, steely twang, and the pressure disappeared. The drumroll of sunlight faded away. The perimeter of his vision shrank until only the boy's face remained visible, a blurry round image. Fog blanched it, then obscured it, and finally conquered it. Junior watched the life go out of the old man's eyes. All the bad memories, all the fear and resentment, went with it. Slowly the body slumped, as if some final defeat had ended Berger's most cherished hopes. He toppled sideways when his good leg buckled. The impact with the ground did not even disturb the dirt.

It was no affair of Junior's. He called to Jurgen. When the crow resumed his shoulder perch, they walked away from the body and the faded trailer and the smoldering dump. The sky gathered plump, white clouds.

MILDRED TIMED HER ARRIVAL PRECISELY. Matt Gans, Senior, was just stepping up to the cash register at the Five and Dime, a spool of medical tape in his hand, when she emerged from the toy aisle. He could not help but see her. At first he seemed unable to place her. They hadn't been in each other's company since Christmastime, after all, but then he did, made a lopsided grin, and waved. In return Mildred smiled broadly and dipped one shoulder just a little, an inch and no more, as she had seen pretty actresses do in the movies about the same time that they batted their eyes. As for that, Will Dubykky had absolutely forbidden it. He was vehement: eye fluttering was obvious, silly, ostentatious, affected, juvenile, and repulsive. In a word, cheap. Maybe so. She had discovered, anyway, that she didn't need to bat, whatever the movies showed. It was enough for her to smile at a man. Such an attractive man! Matt Gans looked like a movie star, like Dana Andrews, except broader in the chest. When her smile inspired his grin to widen into a full show-the-teeth smile, she liked what she saw very much. It was the sort of smile that caused something in the pit of her stomach to warm up and her hips to feel agreeably loose.

Not all smiles, or all men, had that effect. The man whom Will had introduced to her last week, Cledge, the one invited to dinner the coming evening, had not produced such a sensation. Invited, she groused to herself parenthetically, by Will and her mother. Further, she could not imagine Cledge producing a deep sensation in her, however brilliant his smile or animated his eyes. Matt Gans was the handsomer. Definitely. An alluring man. Mildred's mind unexpectedly produced the image of the other Matt Gans, the junior, the boy. How the boy could come from the man was impossible to perceive. Mildred thought of Misty Gans then and couldn't derive the boy's features from her clearly, either. She was a good-looking woman. Good-looking but somewhat sour and severe the only times Mildred had caught sight of her. Not really the woman to have a hold on a handsome man like Matt. Matty. Nice sounding. She might someday call him that.

But that odd boy—maybe he was *not* the son of Matt Gans. Maybe only Misty's child. A love child. The delicious odor of hidden scandal, of marital betrayal and infelicity, made Mildred grin wickedly, but only inside. On the outside, her smile broadened, because if Matt was not exactly free, he might be free-able.

"Hi," she said in the bright drawl that Will always frowned at. "Remember me from the Callahans' Christmas party? Mildred Warden." She held out her hand, fingers loose and on a downward bias. When he took the hand in his, she squared her shoulders and breathed in deep. Her breasts were not very big (more's the pity, that) but big enough to cause men to glance down willy-nilly and then look glad that they did.

He shook her hand delicately, replying, "Callahans' Christmas? Was that the name of the party?"

Mildred's laugh was tinkling, although the remark struck her as peculiar rather than funny. He released her hand, and she held it across her tummy, grasping her other arm halfway between elbow and wrist. She dropped her eyes demurely and said, "Was it your son who was in my library last Saturday?" As she intended, that required her explaining exactly what her library was and where.

When she finished, Gans knitted his brows, puzzled. "My boys were at the track meet with Lowry High School." After Mildred told him of making out a brand-new library card for a Matthew Gans, age six, his face showed nothing but amazement. There was no mistaking the sincerity.

He told her, "Can't be. My youngest is eight. To think that another Gans family lives here in tiny Hawthorne! I had no idea."

The "tiny" put Mildred off a little bit. Hawthorne was not that small. It was bigger than Yerington, Fallon, Fernley, and Winnemucca. Nearly the size of Ely. She was prepared to tell him so, yet didn't. Telling off a man about facts introduced the wrong tone.

Anyhow, Mildred did not get the chance. The door to the Five and Dime swung open, its bell clanged, and Will Dubykky walked through. Mildred's heart sank. Caught again. He came directly to them, greeting Gans politely. The two shook hands, and Mildred noted that they both shook firmly. There was nothing delicate about Matt Gans when dealing with another male. He was manly.

"What are you up to, Milly?" Dubykky asked. His manner was cordial, not a hint of censure in the tone, but Mildred recognized the look in his eye and was embarrassed. He read her so easily.

"Shopping," she answered. The pout in her voice was obvious even to her. She was tempted to add, "for feminine napkins," but decided not to. The moment to be naughty had passed. It would only sound vulgar. Besides, however Matt Gans might react to the risqué, Will was impossible to provoke. Gans paid for his tape, nodded goodbye, and left them at the counter.

"Milly, Milly," began Dubykky and paused, squinting one eye. "Fifteen years older, married, three children—is there anything else you require before accepting that a man is not right for you?"

She folded her arms and pouted openly. The clerk behind the cash register, the widow Eschenbaugh, put her hand to her mouth, pretending to hide a smile. (The hag!) Mildred thrust her chin forward and walked away.

"See you at six," Dubykky called behind her. "Don't forget about the rocks."

Really, why she ever, sometimes, bothered to think of William Dubykky as a possibility! He only liked to ruin her fun, which he did with an accuracy and persistence that almost seemed supernatural. For a husband he would never do.

As for Dubykky, watching her walk away and, despite sulking, sway her hips sultrily, he reflected on the time, the one brief time, when out of deep aggravation he had actually considered marrying her as the least troublesome measure. It would satisfy his debt to the family. He could watch her behavior and protect her directly. Their first meeting, Mildred's dreadfully coquettish behavior, had goaded him into an overreaction.

It happened in 1953 when he was fresh out of military service. He realized he was facing a unique challenge as soon as the front door opened on the Warden house and he introduced himself.

"Ma'am," he started when Gladys stood before him. Then he faltered. The words he had rehearsed suddenly seemed stilted, vapid— My name is Will Dubykky, an army buddy of your husband. I'm setting up law practice in town and thought I'd look you up. If there's any way I can be of help, just ask. For Victor's sake. Here's my card.

Gladys had smiled wanly at his silence. Then behind her Mildred appeared, and her budding beauty took him by surprise, even though Victor Warden had shown him a photograph of his wife and daughter. She might have passed for a teenage Audrey Hepburn, almost. Mildred's face was a tad longer, her upper lip more bowed, and her eyes dulled with daydreams, but she was no less winsome.

"Ma'am," he said again, "Victor sent me. I'm Will Dubykky, and he was the best friend I ever had."

"Oh, my Victor," Gladys breathed. Her eyes rounded, brimming with tears.

Weepiness left Dubykky cold, but what happened next provoked an unaccustomed emotion, and powerful: astonished distaste. Mildred stepped forward, pointed her shoulder at him, peered over it, tucked one knee behind the other, and purred, "Hello there, William." The worse part was how long she took pronouncing his name. It was but a foretaste of his dealings with silly Milly Warden.

Gladys offered her hand shyly and invited him in. He went

reluctantly, yet during the ensuing, often uncomfortable hour his initial reaction to Mildred evolved. There was enough of her father in her that he felt a twinge of affection. At the same time her simpering and posing exasperated him.

"I owe this to Victor," he sighed to himself once he was outside the house again, free of lugubrious Gladys and flirty Mildred. But marry Milly, or worse, Gladys? The prospect made him shudder. He would watch over them, nothing more.

Now seven years later, though he had grown used to being a member of the family, standing in the Five and Dime, he repeated to himself wearily, "I owe this to Victor."

He had done what he could. Mildred, who was bright, had matured. Some. But not without taxing his patience so much that sometimes it seemed bankrupt. He would not have put up with her had not his fondness deepened and the distaste at her silliness turned to worry about her future.

More than that, he could not regret his obligation to Gladys and Mildred because it arose from his own decision. Disregarding his accustomed solitary life, he had befriended Victor. Even though his duty to evil forbade attachments, he enjoyed the friendship. He could not abandon it by ignoring Victor's last request.

It amounted to the biggest of the changes to have come upon him. A complex of fondness, friendship, and loyalty. Why would such sentiments master him, a factotum of evil? Now, after centuries and centuries? He did not know. He had come to recognize one thing, however: that very same evil made friendship with Victor tempting. It made being Mildred's protector a compulsion.

He stepped up to the store's wide display window, but not to watch Milly walking away. To check on Gans. Something about the man troubled him. Gans was just a little too smooth, too sharp-eyed. That on its own meant nothing. Yet if Gans was lurking outside to spy on Milly, that did mean something.

Gans was nowhere in sight, but Dubykky felt no less troubled. The image of Junior sitting in the hovel came to mind. Dubykky's misgivings intensified.

DUBYKKY ARRIVED EARLY for dinner at the Warden house, which lay only two blocks away from his own. Under his arm was a picture frame wrapped in brown paper. Gladys eyed it warily as she let him in. Her house was full of Dubykky's odd gifts. She wasn't at all sure she wanted another. But she changed her attitude after he laid it on the living room coffee table and unwrapped it. She even forgot about the headache that had been tormenting her all afternoon.

"Oh, Will," she breathed, entranced. "It's beautiful." Then, "What are they?"

Dubykky explained. The mahogany frame contained four rows of rock slices, each highly polished. Some were agates; others were ores, like malachite and cinnabar. The rows were arranged by colors: shades of red, blue/purple, green, and yellow/gold. There was a neatly hand-lettered label beneath each gleaming piece.

On the way home from work, Dubykky had stopped off at Pastor's Rock and Mineral. Ralph Pastor owed him for past legal work, most of it involving deserted prospecting claims that he wanted to take over. Dubykky convinced him to satisfy part of the debt by handing over one of the most striking displays in his shop, which Pastor had made himself. He was a capable artist, if a poor businessman. It was Mildred who was supposed, by Dubykky's order, to arrange for rock art to be on hand in the living room, but Mildred was Mildred, flighty and forgetful. Dubykky decided at the last minute not to leave the task to her.

When Mildred glided in and beheld the rock display, she was as full of praise as her mother. She ran a forefinger over each one, pronouncing the name underneath it. Suddenly she straightened and said, "Oh!

I was supposed to bring rocks too, wasn't I, Will!" She hustled from the room.

When she returned, it was with a big, knowing smile on her face. She was carrying a thick encyclopedia volume on top of a black frame. "I'll bet you thought I forgot, but I didn't. Remember after we talked to Mr. Gans, the high school shop teacher? You said—I must say, you weren't very nice to me about it. It was just a casual encounter, and he was so pleasant."

"Mr. Gans?" cut in Gladys. "You were talking to Mr. Gans?"

Mildred nodded enthusiastically. "A very manly sort of man."

Gladys agreed, "I've seen him at the market. He looks like that movie star. What's his name . . . ?"

"Dana Andrews?" suggested Mildred.

"No, the other one."

Dubykky, long used to the ricocheting conversations of Gladys and Mildred and well aware they might continue indefinitely, interrupted by asking Mildred what was in her hands.

"I told you I didn't forget!" She lifted one shoulder, turned her chin over it, lowered her eyelids, and smiled knowingly again. Then she set down her burden beside the frame of mineral samples. "Here's the Britannica volume with the article on minerals. I can read about each one of the ones here. And—" She lifted the volume and set it aside on the coffee table. "Voilá!" she exclaimed. Under the book was not, as Dubykky expected, another rock display but a collection of small arrowheads arrayed point outward in three concentric circles.

"Close," he said. He had, after all, simply asked her to get some interesting rocks.

Mildred tossed her head at him. "They're so perfect!"

Too perfect, Dubykky suspected but didn't say so. He asked where Mildred had found them. When she answered that it had been at Boudreau's Gifts and Desert Antiques, his suspicions were settled. But it didn't matter. That Mildred had even remembered something he'd asked of her was a positive sign. And the collection of arrowheads, even if counterfeit, would serve the purpose well enough, he supposed. He looked forward to watching Cledge react to it.

While Gladys sat in the easy chair, picked up the heating pad, stuffed it behind her neck, and resumed her headache, Dubykky and Mildred took down a landscape painting from the wall and replaced it with the rock slices. Both she and her mother gave simultaneous advice to ensure that the frame hung level. Dubykky then cast around for another spot on the wall to hang the arrowheads. He reached for a prewar photograph portrait of Victor Warden, as approximately the same size.

"No, not Daddy!" cried Mildred, affronted.

At the same time her mother cried, "No, not Victor!"

"Oh, Will, how could you?"

Dubykky, his back to them, didn't know which had spoken, they sounded so much alike when complaining, but it didn't matter. He sighed to himself. Victor Warden's features were ever fresh in his memory. Only nine years had gone by since Victor's death. His lamentable but necessary death. And here he was, smiling mildly out of the frame just as he had habitually smiled in life. It was such a waste that Victor had to go. Mildred's face was so much like her father's that they were nearly interchangeable, except for Victor's pencil mustache and Mildred's thick, wavy brown hair, which was like Gladys's. Victor's was as matte-black as coal. And whereas Mildred was constantly mimicking the expressions of actresses, to Dubykky's disgust, Victor's face had always been mild and pleasant.

Victor Warden, his friend and victim. How Dubykky regretted having to kill him.

The doorbell jolted Dubykky from the reverie. There was a hesitation while Mildred looked to Gladys as head of the household to answer the door, but her mother pressed a hand to her temple and grimaced gingerly. So Mildred went instead. Dubykky removed a framed crochet of Home Sweet Home and hung the arrowheads. The ceiling light reflected from them in oily bronze glimmers.

To Milton Cledge, when he was welcomed by Mildred into the Warden home, it was as if he were entering a television program. First of all, everyone was so darned photogenic. Mildred's beauty dazzled him.

She had on an airy blue-and-white dress of thick, wavy horizontal stripes and blue high heels, both of which served to give her figure animation. Gladys, by contrast, was sedentary and dressed in a nondescript rose dress but also possessed elegant, fragile good looks. His senior law partner, Cledge realized, fit the tableau as well, even dressed in his workaday gray three-piece suit and dark gray tie. It was a funny thing to Cledge that out of Dubykky's presence he could never recall precisely what the man looked like, and even in his presence Dubykky did not draw attention to himself. Yet, here with these two attractive women, his dark hair and darker eyes, his slightly sallow complexion, and his slender, straight posture made him seem mysteriously aristocratic, or perhaps aristocratically mysterious. Cledge had no experience with either dark mysteries or aristocracy.

Gladys smiled wanly, apologized for not feeling well, and still sitting, offered him a limp hand to shake. Cledge astonished himself then. Maybe it was Mildred's bedazzling effect. Or maybe, in front of her and Dubykky, he felt on stage in a way, as if whatever he did right then would set the tone for the evening. In any case, he wasn't the type for witticisms or the offhand pretty remark. Yet out it tumbled.

He said to Gladys, smiling, "I'm feeling overcome, too, just being among such lovely people in such a lovely setting."

Everyone beamed back at him, Gladys proudly, Mildred interestedly, and Dubykky with amusement. To underscore his appreciation, particularly of the room's collection of assorted Queen Anne-style furnishings, Cledge turned in a slow circle. His eyes passed over the large frame of rock slices and bounced back. He stepped closer to study them.

"Pretty, aren't they," said Mildred. Her regard, however, went to Dubykky. Her expression told him she was about to be jealous of Cledge's interest in the pretty rocks instead of her arrowheads, and this fretted him a little. Mildred could be fractious if she felt upstaged.

"Magnificent," Cledge agreed, to which Mildred shrugged. He studied the collection minutely.

It gave Mildred the opportunity to glance covertly at the Britannica article. She said, a little artificially, "Don't you just love malachite? Who'd believe that two copper atoms, three carbon dioxide molecules, and a hydroxide could create such brilliant hues of green? And that jasper! It's like a picture of the earth's rock strata itself!"

Cledge gave her a strange glance, while Dubykky walked to his side.

"Mildred can't help herself," he explained. "She's a librarian through and through."

Mildred's face was beginning to darken at that when Cledge, still gazing at the rocks, exclaimed, "And one with exceptional taste. What an amazing lapis lazuli!"

Behind Cledge's back Mildred stuck out her tongue at Dubykky, then said, "Do you like arrowheads? We have a collection of those, too."

Cledge betrayed no especial interest in arrowheads and only reluctantly let Mildred lead him away from the rocks. But when he saw them up close, he sucked in his breath and breathed out a slow "ah." He said, "They're so perfect."

It sounded forced to Dubykky, but not to Mildred. And it struck home. She was capable of many gradations of smile—part of her armamentarium of calculated expressions—but only one that wasn't calculated. It was her innocent, unselfconscious smile of pleasure, and on the rare occasions it broke loose (unlike the others, it was never planned), it infused all who saw it with a pleasure as genuine and intense as hers. It burst out now, brilliantly. Cledge, turning toward her, caught the full force of it. He was dumbstruck.

Well, one down, thought Dubykky, watching Cledge. Now for Mildred.

Gladys, her headache again forgotten, broke the brief silence. "Milly," she said. "Check on the meatloaf, won't you. I'll get the salad together. And Will, shame on you. Offer Mr. Cledge a drink. What do you like, Mr. Cledge?"

"Above all, I'd like you to call me Milt, and I'd welcome a scotch and water," he answered a little breathlessly.

Gladys, pleased, followed her daughter through the narrow passageway into the kitchen-dining room. Cledge lowered himself into an easy chair a bit unsteadily. Dubykky reached behind and flipped closed the Britannica, then went to the liquor cabinet and poured out a stiff measure of Cutty Sark and a drop of water. He handed the glass to Cledge, who took a sip at once. When he looked back up at Dubykky, his eyes were wide and watery.

"Good," he croaked.

Gladys was only a passable cook. Mildred was talented. Completely uninterested in food for its own sake, Dubykky never inquired about her methods. He knew from experience that the most talented cooks were somehow touched by evil, as Mildred was. Yet he recognized full well how proud she was of her skill. For this reason, he expressly asked her to make meatloaf. Hers was universally admired. Its effect on Cledge nearly equaled the effect of her smile. What's more, Dubykky saw Mildred seeing its effect on Cledge. But it got better.

"Very tasty, dear," Gladys said, as a matter of course. Like Dubykky, she was apathetic about food so long as it didn't make her ill.

"Tasty?" Cledge replied in a tone of astonishment. "Why, this is far and away the best meatloaf I've ever had. This is the Supreme Court of meat loaf!"

Gladys was displeased at being overspoken at her own table, which Mildred noted gleefully. She noted with yet more pleasure that Milt Cledge was too occupied by the meatloaf to pay any attention to her mother. He was a man who truly appreciated how well she cooked. At that, she experienced a deep warmth spread through her, different from the warmth that handsome Matt Gans caused, higher up in her body and not so exciting, but still enjoyable.

So. A start for Mildred, Dubykky thought.

But as he knew that any compliment given or hinted from one man automatically brought to her mind some other man, whose appearance or past courtesy would divert her into making comparisons, Dubykky carefully steered the conversation to focus her strictly on Cledge. At the same time, he ensured that Cledge did not begin talking shop. Not that the law bored Gladys and Mildred so much as that they did not understand it and often expressed outrage at aspects of legal procedure that were simply a matter of course for lawyers. Dubykky did not want to fill the evening with the explanations necessary to make them see Cledge's profession in the same light that he did. That would be dull.

So they spoke of minerals, locations for finding them, local mines like the Lucky Boy, incidents related to local mines, the Nevada Paiute, Washoe, and Shoshone, arrowheads, antique weapons, Boudreau's store, Hawthorne merchants in general, people who can be encountered in the shops—from gnarled prospectors to fresh-faced sailors—the atomic proving grounds, the local danger of war with the Soviet Union because the proving grounds and Nellis Air Force Base near Las Vegas were sure to be prime targets, not to mention Hawthorne itself because it lay smack beside the Babbitt naval ammunition depot, and, because the core material of atomic weapons—uranium—was to be found in Nevada, back to minerals.

All participated, although primarily Cledge and Mildred. Cledge's views on topics tended to be settled, definite, whereas Mildred's, however vehemently expressed, were contingent on appearances. When the presidential race came up, as a tangent to atomic warfare, from the field of candidates, Republican or Democrat, Mildred immediately picked out John F. Kennedy as her choice.

A handsome man had to be a good leader. She could not be talked out of that view, though Cledge tried. He was a Lyndon Johnson man.

Dubykky only had to toss in an observation or fact now and then to keep the talk lively and away from unsuitable topics—unsuitable in that they might start a rupture. The closest it came to that occurred when Mildred, flush with satisfaction in herself, suggested to Cledge that he might be more comfortable with his tie removed. It was a thin, solid royal-blue tie over a stark white shirt and gave the unfortunate impression that his head was a balloon on a string. Dubykky agreed he would look more comfortable with it off but said nothing. The suggestion made Cledge blush, endearing in itself, but Mildred did not like to be balked. Cledge looked meaningfully to Dubykky, who was also wearing a tie, but he declined to take the hint and offer support. Mildred frowned. Gladys's interest in the conversation, not very great until then, freshened.

Sensing that he had upset Mildred, Cledge asked the table in general about the photo portrait of a man that he had noticed on the living room wall. The man, he averred, bore a striking resemblance to Mildred. Was he a brother? Gladys perked up even more.

"That is Victor Warden, my husband and Mildred's father," she said to Cledge in a pedantic tone. Her husband was the dearest topic in the world to her. She never tired of speaking of him. "He died in that awful war in Korea while serving in the army with Will. That's how we know Will." She expanded on Victor's background and virtues.

While Cledge assumed a small, fixed approximation of a smile and Mildred looked down at her hands, folded in her lap, and Gladys prosed on, Dubykky let his mind wander into the past: to Victor's death, then back further to their first meeting in Fort Bragg, North Carolina, and to what he knew of Victor's early life.

In fact, he knew a lot more than Gladys. Even the dinner reminded him of that fact, starting with the table service. The plates, silver-rimmed and gleaming white, though now smeared with food, were Japanese-made china, which Dubykky had brought home and presented to Gladys soon after he met them. He claimed it was a set that Warden had already bought for them. That was a white lie. Likewise the silver cutlery and candlesticks, all bought at a PX in Japan. A way to ingratiate himself. A way to assuage his regret. Regret not just because he was responsible for Warden's death but also because what he knew of the man could not be shared.

Mildred got up to get dessert, a rice pudding, while Gladys reflected on the mystery of her husband's background. Victor, she told Cledge sadly, had never been specific about his family or childhood home. Really, it never concerned her enough to press him about until it was too late. Now it added piquancy to her nostalgia. Her eyes grew moist.

She didn't know because her husband had little to tell, and even then, he understood little about the context of his first days. Dubykky had turned up a few facts through his own research, as well as some probabilities. But even those small, available histories were dismal.

Victor Warden was the product of multiple lynchings.

Based on what Warden told Dubykky, the lynchings occurred sometime late in World War I or shortly thereafter somewhere in the Deep South. From old news stories and magazine articles, almost all from northern periodicals, Dubykky identified three clusters of lynchings, of which one seemed most probably related to Warden. But the paucity of specific information and Warden's ignorance of the circumstances made it impossible to pin down for sure.

Even in outline, the sequence of events was unspeakably foul. A white woman complained to her brother that a black man had molested her. The brother had the man arrested and put in a small-town jail. Then he got drunk. The drink stoked his rage. He gathered friends and went to the jail. The lawman stood aside while the mob beat the black man, who was then dragged by his feet from his cell into the street. A noose was displayed to the gathering crowd. The brother tied a rope to the prisoner's feet, intending to hitch the opposite end to a horse's halter so the prisoner could be dragged to a suitable tree outside the town, when a second mob arrived to stop the lynching.

One member of the incoming mob, a veteran just returned from the Great War, tackled the brother to stop him tying the prisoner to the horse. For his efforts, the veteran was wrestled to the ground and his hands tied. A brawl started, only to be stopped when the lawman fired his pistol into the air. The rescuing mob was chased away under threat from the gun.

The hanging took place within the hour. A week later, another lynching occurred, this one after the same woman accused the black veteran of assaulting her to avenge his friend. Early in the following month, a dual lynching dispatched the brothers of the original victim. The white woman was again the accuser; again she claimed to have been molested for the sake of vengeance. In all cases, her brother was the leader of the lynch mobs. Not long after, he disappeared; she was shut away in a hospital for the insane after sustaining disfiguring burns in a fire.

Victor Warden's version of the events was more intimate, singular, and sinister, even though he could say little about the time or location. No lapse of memory or psychological block hindered him. It was simply not in him to remember.

Though fully grown, he was new, very nearly a blank slate. He came to life because of a failure of humanity in others—the woman and her brother, specifically—the first a vindictive liar, the second a sadist. Their homicidal selfishness was as deeply inhumane as evil ever got. Yet the local authorities would not punish them for it. The lynchings were not treated as criminal. A greater force was required to wreak the just punishment. Like Junior, Victor Warden was an echo of evil.

"When I first came to myself, there was only one bit of knowledge about the world in my mind. A name," Warden told Dubykky early in 1951. By then, Dubykky was convinced that Warden was an echo. Dubykky recognized the tell-tale signs: thoroughgoing lack of sophistication about people; earnestness and absence of selfish regard;

vagueness about background; guilelessness; a slow, spare, flat manner of talking.

Dubykky drew out the tale slowly, only after convincing Warden that he was uniquely able to appreciate the story—was in fact much like him. Which was true as far as it went.

Warden had spent his first weeks hiding in the woods near the town where the lynchings had taken place. He passed some nights perched high in the branches of the lynching tree itself, an enormous white oak. Like Frankenstein's monster, he listened in on people talking. But he was not eavesdropping to learn speech. He listened until he heard the name Sophia Nichols. This did not take long.

The lynchings were the talk of the county. But it did require patience before he tracked a person who had used the name to the name's owner.

Sophia Nichols and her brother Stanton lived alone in a tidy country cottage on the outskirts of a farming town, Warden told Dubykky, a cottage surrounded by flowers, more flowers and in greater variety than he ever met with afterwards outside a florist. Even after so many years, the odor still clung to his memory, aromatic and lulling. By the time he had climbed to the stoop and stood at the door, his thoughts were dulled, floating, cloaked in fragrance, a batting of voluptuous air. For this reason, he hesitated. Sophia spotted him through the stoop window and, rushing to the door, opened it, a naughty smile on her lips and conquest in her eyes. She drew him inside. She guided one of his hands to her breast. Her free hand reached up behind his neck to pull him close. Still, he hesitated. He knew he should end her existence, and at once, but her lips grew closer to his, her voice murmured what a bad man he was while her body pressed against him, lean and yielding to his at the same time. The heavy floral aroma, which was also her aroma, befuddled him. He couldn't act.

Their lips were only a pant away from brushing together when an enraged bellow erupted. Warden broke away from Sophia to face her brother charging at him from a bedroom. He was naked. More bewildered, Warden barely managed to face Stanton in time.

When Dubykky heard the story, just before he and Warden went into combat together for the first time in Korea, he supposed that Warden had not been the first man ambushed in that cottage. Stanton Nichols had a powerful physique. So why did he simply push Warden, still frozen in surprise, against a wall instead of doing him real damage? Perhaps the brother and sister wanted nothing more than that, to entice and then terrify, a kind of brutal, sexual game. Or perhaps the naked Stanton had designs on his victim that required an uninjured body. Warden didn't find out. The attack cleared his head and reminded him of his purpose. Moreover, his strength was beyond Stanton's.

He broke Stanton's neck. And then he realized that one leg of his pants was on fire. How this happened was never clear. Maybe Sophia threw a lamp at him, although why the Nicholses would have a lamp lit at midday was another puzzle. He threw himself to the floor reflexively, rolling and tearing off his clothing. Extinguishing the fire on him set fire to a rag rug, soaked with spilled kerosene, then furniture, then curtains, and smoke filled the cottage.

He rolled to his feet again in time to see Sophia throw him a look so terrified, and at once so full of craving, that it bespoke a mind plummeting into insanity. Still looking back, she made to run from him out the front door but tripped over her brother's body. When she struggled back to her feet, her dress, a flimsy cotton shift, was on fire, as was her hair. Shrieking, she flew out of the cottage, and that's the last Warden ever saw of her, a human torch framed in the doorway, glimpses of flowers visible in the yard beyond.

After he picked his way around the burning rug to the front door, it was already too late to follow. Neighbors were visible coming down the lane, drawn by the smoke. And Sophia had disappeared into the woods. Finding an exit through the kitchen window, he ran to the river behind the cottage and floated down it and away. He stole clothes, hovered around the town, but never could get close to Sophia again. Badly burned, she lay in a hospital for months, then was transferred to an insane asylum. Her brother's body apparently was burned to ashes and leached into the earth when heavy rains fell the next day.

Growing ever more accustomed to human ways, Warden gave up then. Sophia Nichols would never entrap an innocent man through false witness again. Her wits were gone. So he left the South, following a random path of part-time jobs and patchwork schooling until he ended up, as if inevitably, in Hawthorne. He got a job as assistant undertaker in the town's only funeral parlor. He met a pretty, sweet girl who was as opposite Sophia Nichols as was possible and still be human: open, loving, unquestioning, artless, and a bit sickly. He married Gladys in utter amazement and gratitude. Then, a greater delight even, Mildred was born, physically every bit as beautiful as her mother. And—what Dubykky understood and Victor did not—she bore the blemish of her father's evil origin, a reckless naïveté that would only lead to ruin unless her behavior was safeguarded.

To his intense regret, Dubykky had failed to ask Warden a crucial question. Which name had been in his head when he first became conscious? Stanton's or Sophia's? Or just Nichols? At the time Warden told him the story, Dubykky assumed it was Stanton, the lyncher, who was the target of vengeance, and that thereby Warden had fulfilled his destiny. He assumed further that Sophia had been a loony bystander, nothing more, and he assumed it because in his experience human abuser-serial killers were loners. But what if . . . ?

Dubykky was roused from Warden's story when Gladys asked him why he wasn't eating his rice pudding. Didn't he like it? He liked it fine, he assured her, but was too full from gorging on the transcendent meatloaf. He had no room left. He beamed at Gladys and Mildred, and long familiar with his distracted ways, they smiled back. It was a chummy, confidential, familylike moment.

Cledge recognized it and was envious. Then he felt like an outsider and was jealous. How could he not be?

Directing himself at first one then another, he began thanking them for the wonderful evening, but thanking Mildred most of all. She was pleased. And when he offered to bring over some of his mineral collection to show her, because already knowing so much about mineralogy she would surely appreciate it, the merest flicker of amusement came to Mildred's eyes before she wholeheartedly encouraged him to do just that.

He left much satisfied, escorted out by Mildred, who returned humming to herself. Dubykky, however, was diffident. Although his plans for the two were advancing well enough, the recollection of her father weighed on him. He helped Gladys clear the table and wash the dishes, their longstanding routine, without really fixing his mind on anything, except this one truth: Warden had been the only real friend he had ever had.

Later, as was also their routine, the three of them had nightcaps together. Dubykky, also as usual, only pretended to touch his, mostly water that it was. No conversation was necessary, so content were they just to relax in each other's presence, but Dubykky nevertheless took the opportunity to comment on Cledge's promising future as a lawyer—and, he dared venture, eventually something grander. Mildred listened with half her mind, and Gladys with practically none whatsoever because she was feeling her old nemesis the backache setting in and devoted herself to the proper positioning in her easy chair and the adjustment of the heating pad.

Still, at one point Mildred remarked, a little dreamily, "I like a sturdy, tall man."

Four

The next night Dubykky chose to break the law. He had a mystery on his hands—three mysteries, really, all interwoven—and there should be none. Evil might be obscure, it might hide, it might even disguise itself as good, but evil did not create red herrings, not the sort of evil that Dubykky understood. An echo awakes knowing the name of the human responsible for its existence. Junior did not. Why not? Mystery number one. Junior had only a string of sounds. Did they even point to a name? Which name? Dubykky knew of four so far. Mystery number two. Mystery number three was even bigger, and darker. An echo awoke after four grisly crimes, no more, no fewer. There had been no such string of crimes in Hawthorne, or even northern Nevada. Dubykky would know if there had been. It was his duty to know.

So something seriously odd was going on. The mystery irritated Dubykky because five centuries of habit, unfailingly effective, balked at accepting mystery. It tempted him to do more than instruct and watch over Junior, and he gave in to the temptation. It was not that he shied from breaking the law. Human laws broke so easily. But he disliked complications.

Nonetheless, he set out to spy, which is to say, be a peeping Tom. He was perfectly suited to it by temperament. Watching humans behave at home, unselfconsciously, exposed their inclinations. He enjoyed seeing them remove the masks they put when out among other people. But the important point was that he needed to see the true faces of people if he were to track down a monster among them.

And he was suited to spying by ability. He could do it without ever being detected. Invisibility was the key, and it came naturally to him, among his few truly inhuman talents. All he had to do was go perfectly still. No tics, no breathing, no blinking, no eye movement, not even a pulse. When he did that, no one could see him. The best part was that he remained aware of everything in view even more keenly than when he was in motion.

There were drawbacks, to be sure. He had to stay put. The least twitch, and he would snap back into visibility. He had to take care to position himself where someone would not bump into him. Some few humans—they had to be especially perceptive and free of self-absorption—could sense his presence, although without recognizing exactly what they were sensing or where. Most, though, immediately forgot about him even if he had been standing right in front of them, talking to them.

Very useful.

As for Matt and Misty Gans, they puzzled Dubykky. If the husband was responsible for Junior's appearance, how could the wife not know? And if she understood even only a little of what he was, why was she silent about it? Possibly, he acknowledged, Matt could tyrannize Misty into silence. He doubted it, though. On the few occasions he had met Misty she did not strike Dubykky as the submissive type. If evil conspired in their marriage, who knew what, and who did what? If Gans was not the evildoer, his behavior should make it plain.

DUBYKKY LURKED next to a ragged lilac, just a little taller than he was. Behind it was a lighted window in the Gans house. The window was open a crack, for the night air was still pleasant. Through it came a muddle of voices, glasses clinking, chairs creaking, and cards snapping as they were shuffled. He took a quick peep through the limbs. A haze of tobacco smoke hung over the living room. At each of three fold-away card tables sat four people. Focusing on the nearest he heard a voice call out, "Four diamonds." Another countered, "Double!" and the voice of Misty Gans retorted, swiftly and sharply, "Redouble!" She and her husband were hosting a bridge party.

Dubykky enjoyed card games of all varieties and always accepted an invitation to play. The play itself didn't interest him. How the other players behaved did. Card games concentrated attention, fired up the competitive spirit, and bypassed normal social restraints, all in pursuit of clear goals. The way people reacted to setbacks and lucky breaks, mistakes from partners, aggression and bluffing, and most of all, triumph spurred on traits that they reined in under other circumstances.

He crept round to the back entrance. Luck was with him. Only the screen door was closed. Listening carefully, he awaited his chance and then slipped in. The kitchen was empty, and the door to the living room afforded a partial view of the players. Dubykky paused behind the frame until their racket suddenly ramped up. Then stepping into the living room he stilled into his statue mode and went invisible.

Engrossed in changing partners and tables, no one glimpsed him coming in. The twelve players, high school faculty and their spouses, appeared to be having a fine time. The new round had Matt and Misty seated at different tables, diagonal to each other.

He focused first on Misty. Her partner was Agnes Evans, the English teacher. They bid and played the tricks efficiently, shrewdly, and Evans was clearly enjoying herself. At the end of the first hand, gathering the cards to shuffle while Evans started dealing, Misty briskly critiqued their opponents' use of trump. The know-it-all undertone did not upset them. They seemed accustomed to it.

Matt caught her eye and winked, but Misty did not respond. As for him, he had Principal Callahan for a partner, and the two played in a slapdash style, quick to take risks, on the whole unsuccessfully. It was a lively table and—Matt so easy-going and affable, disarming others with sunny smiles and trite jokes—a merry one.

A comfortable, congenial party. Dubykky was disappointed. What had he learned? Matt didn't care much about the game, just at being the center of fun; Misty played to win, especially pleased when she out-smarted male opponents. He relished attention; she liked prevailing. That wasn't out of the ordinary. Or significant.

A half hour later he was about to sneak away when a rapping came at the front door. The bridge crowd made no sign of hearing. Almost at once Dougie Gans, the youngest son, darted out of the hallway to the door. That attracted his parents' attention. They watched, eyes hard, as he opened it.

A girl approximately Dougie's age stood on the step. She spoke a quick word of hello and ran to one of the tables. Her mother was the home-ec teacher, Matilda Gosse. They had a quick exchange, the girl breathless, her mother annoyed. It was trivial, some errand that the girl's older sister had sent her on, possibly just a practical joke, and the girl was out the door again in less than a minute.

But Dubykky learned two things about the Ganses. It became apparent that the girl and her sister, age twelve, had no babysitter—and that prompted a reaction from Matt Gans. Before he could disguise it, his eyes narrowed and he smirked. Nobody else noticed, except Misty. That was the second significant thing. She locked eyes with her hus-band. Her expression revealed weary contempt. But was that about her husband or the girl?

Unfortunately, there was a third matter. Watching her daughter leave, Mathilda Gosse pressed her lips together until they were white, a hard, cruel look. There would be trouble for the daughters when their mother got home. Was that just maternal embarrassment and irrita-tion? It was more than a passing question. Gosse was another of the names Mildred had tried on Junior. Walking home, Dubykky replayed the incident in his mind. As was his long-standing rule, he took care not to overinterpret. A card game, an interruption, a long history of husband-wife private telegraphing, a shorter but intense history of mother-daughter relations: it was all too easy for an outsider to mis-read. But Dubykky could not let it go. The emotions had looked too raw, too rabid.

"NEATO. GREEN M&MS!" Dubykky heard Mildred exclaim with feigned enthusiasm.

It was two days after the dinner party. He was walking with Cledge from a restaurant back to their office after lunch and just passing the Chevrolet dealership. The day was a warm, high-blue-sky day, so the front entrance of the dealership's wide-windowed façade stood open to admit the air. That was where Mildred's voice came from. It wasn't far away, but Dubykky could have picked it out of a crowd from five times the distance when, as now, it carried with it the overtone of coy frivolity, Mildred-style. Dubykky turned on his heels and walked in. Cledge hesi-tated, confused because he hadn't heard Mildred, then followed several steps behind. He had come almost to expect such behavior from his partner, however perplexing. And that there was usually a serious pur-pose to it.

Mildred was standing by a gold Impala, talking to two sailors. They were junior officers wearing blue jackets that had two gold stripes on each sleeve and holding white peaked caps tucked under an arm. One of the men, dark-haired, oily, and burly, was looking ill at ease, while the other, tall, also dark-haired but tanned and slightly stooped, was openly leering at Mildred while holding out a hand, five green discs on the palm. It tickled Dubykky that when he caught Mildred flirting, which was all too frequently, she looked both peeved and guilty. She did so now. A glance up at him, a tightening of her mouth, a wrinkling at the brow, and a wash of red on her cheeks.

"Oh, hello, Will." Chirpy, forced innocence sharpened her voice. The naval officers turned round to him then, the short one seeming even more ill at ease and the other distinctly galled.

"Milly, Milly, haven't I warned you never to take candy from sailors?" Dubykky composed his face to seem amused but did not smile. Neither did the officers. He nodded to them, "Lieutenant Parselknapp, Lieutenant DeVrees."

Lieutenant Parselknapp was nonplussed because he could not at once place Dubykky. Lieutenant DeVrees scowled self-importantly. Dubykky continued, "Don't recognize me? I was introduced to you a year ago March in Captain Glay's office when I was advising him about the groundwater contamination litigation."

Cledge, who had been hanging back, stepped beside Dubykky just then. Mildred smiled shyly but wouldn't meet his eye. It was a good sign, Dubykky told himself. True embarrassment.

Parselknapp, a phlegmatic man known derisively among his subordinates as Partial Nap, recalled Dubykky then, and his face showed relief. He offered his hand. The scowl on DeVrees's face remained. Closing the M&Ms into his fist, he crossed his arms. He didn't like lawyers, he didn't like people who interrupted him when he was coming on to a pretty girl, and even if Dubykky had been neither of these, he still didn't like Dubykky. Dubykky gestured behind him and added, "And this is my new partner, Milt Cledge." He and Parselknapp shook hands.

DeVrees said in a steely military voice, "Miss Warden and I were having a private conversation."

"Yes," Dubykky agreed pleasantly. "About green M&Ms." Dubykky knew how to provoke men of DeVrees's caliber without seeming to: stand just a little too close and fix unwavering eyes on the forehead. He did so. After a minute DeVrees lost track of how he intended to give Dubykky and Cledge the brush-off. His tan darkened.

Mildred tried to explain in a small voice, "I was just on my way back—" But she trailed off too, sensing the tension in the air.

Both Parselknapp and Cledge roused themselves to action at that point. The lieutenant began, "Well, we really must be—" as Cledge, showing sudden inspiration, said to the surprise of them all, "How about a picnic?"

Parselknapp fell silent, dumbfounded. Everyone turned to Cledge.

He continued, "I was just on my way to invite Mildred and her mother to a picnic at Walker Lake this Saturday. They had me to dinner, you see, and it's only decent to return the kindness, don't you think? Anyway, why don't you come as well? Bring some of your fellow officers. We'll have a nice, big party."

Well played, thought Dubykky. There was more to Cledge than the plodding legal mind with a hobbyist's obsession, it seemed. Cledge's face betrayed a flash of cunning. Dubykky doubted the officers noticed, but it was enough to tell him that his partner was bluffing them away in order to keep Mildred to himself.

Dubykky chipped in, "A fine idea! Lieutenant DeVrees, you could bring your wife and children."

This had the desired affect all round. Mildred's jaw dropped, Parselknapp clasped his hands behind his back and looked away, and Cledge forgot his jealousy at seeing Mildred with two navy officers. He slitted his eyes.

DeVrees blustered. He had better things to do with his time, he tried to say. But he stumbled and said "better duties" inadvertently. His tongue tangled over "than picnicking" and he spluttered. His scowl turned into a sneer.

After the naval officers left them—Lieutenant Parselknapp with an apologetic nod and his comrade with a furious glance at Mildred— Dubykky observed, "A lecher really ought to be more eloquent than that, don't you think?"

Flustered, Mildred denied that any lechery was involved, no

impropriety at all, but she ended by wringing her hands and casting miserable glances Cledge's way.

Cledge pretended to be innocent of Dubykky's meaning, yet he lacked the capacity to pretend. The amusement written on his face was unmistakable. Even Mildred took note of it. When she attempted a quick, abashed grin, Cledge grinned back.

"What do you think, then?" he asked her.

"Commander DeVrees is probably not a very nice man," she admitted, a little sullenly.

"He said he was a commander? He's only a lieutenant, Milly," Dubykky was happy to point out. He wanted to rub her nose in her foolishness a little more.

"He told me he just got promoted," Mildred said, pointing her chin upward. On the verge of anger, she needed to be recognized as in the right.

"Then he's a lieutenant commander, not a full commander. That's the next step up from lieutenant."

Vexed that she hadn't known that, Mildred still took the main point. She had been lied to, however she looked at it. She felt affronted in that special way that those who are perfectly willing to lie to others feel when they discover themselves victims of deception. Her anger shifted to disgust at the lieutenant.

Dubykky saw her diverted and pressed on. "Anyway, Milly, Milt was asking what you thought about going on a picnic Saturday."

Mildred's moods were like alcohol fires: a blue flash, then gone, leaving no heat behind. She smiled her unfeigned-delight smile at Cledge and agreed it was a wonderful idea. The date was made, Dubykky included at the urging of them both.

"Now, Milt, do you mind my talking to Mildred alone for a minute? I have a librarian favor to ask of her."

Cledge did mind. Failing to suppress a frown of hurt puzzlement, he said goodbye to them.

"Milt has such animated features, don't you think," Mildred said confidentially and giggled. "You can almost see what's going on in his head! He's like that guy on television. What's his name? You know, the one with shiny black hair—"

"Milly, I want you to do a little research for me. I'll be glad to pay you."

But Mildred would never dream of accepting money from Will Dubykky for something she loved to do anyway and could do while at her job. Looking things up was part of her duties as county librarian. The very idea! Dubykky cut her off, explaining what he needed.

BACK IN HIS OFFICE, Dubykky found the latest issue of the *Mineral County Independent-News* on his desk. He pursed his lips. Not at the newspaper itself, which he not only enjoyed reading but found useful to his law practice. He was in fact the paper's attorney, in the sense that when the publisher was worried about some legal matter he asked Dubykky for free advice. In return, his subscription was on the house. And in it. There was no need to deliver the paper. The offices of Dubykky & Cledge, Esq., occupied the story above the newspaper offices and pressroom in a building on the corner of D Street and 5th Street, just a block from the junction of US 95 and Nevada 395, the center of town. Every publication day, an issue was left atop his mailbox on the ground floor.

He liked the paper, but its unexpected presence on his desk meant trouble. Somebody had carried it up to him during lunchtime. That somebody was most likely Loretta Lurie. And that could mean either of two things. She wanted a favor, or she wanted a date. Or both.

It was a sticky matter for Dubykky. He liked Loretta well enough, but that wasn't the problem. Part of it was that she liked him, too. Not loved, or even had a crush on, but liked, which was enough. She was thirty, and since he appeared to be somewhere in the vicinity of that age himself, he was eligible as husband material. From her point of view, the pool of eligible men in Mineral County was too small to be choosy, which is to say, romantic. After twelve years as a reporter, which began straight out of Mineral County High School, Lurie was getting fed up going it alone. And she was finding that being a reporter put off more men than it attracted, a fact certainly worsened by the reputation of her stepfather, the newspaper's owner-publisher, as a fire-breathing, shotgun-wielding, youth-detesting, McCarthy Republican, patriarchal son of a bitch. It was said of Charlton O'Faelan that he was the most evenhanded newspaperman in the state: he despised everyone equally.

Dubykky rather liked and admired O'Faelan, an adamantine scoundrel of the old school, and wasn't afraid of him. The problem about Loretta wasn't her stepfather either. The problem was making sure that he didn't in any way encourage her marital interest while still remaining friends. She was a good reporter, a good source of information, a handy person for a lawyer to be friendly with. She covered some hard news and most of the feature and cultural stories for the paper. And she had a popular regular column, "Mineral County Nuggets," that Dubykky sometimes wrote for her when it suited his purpose.

He picked up the paper. Below the fold, Loretta had circled an article in pencil. The headline read, "Dump Head Found Dead."

Dubykky made an unhappy face. Whoever wrote that header was in for a chewing out. O'Faelan hated cutesy headlines, especially those that rhymed. And when O'Faelan chewed someone out, that person had permanent tooth marks on his soul. But what Dubykky reacted to was not the rhyme. It was the big question mark in pencil next to the article. He tucked the paper under his arm and headed for the editorial office below, sticking his head into Cledge's office on the way out to let him know he was leaving. Their receptionist, Angie Ottergol, was at lunch.

He was amused to find practically the whole newsroom staff, four of them plus the advertising manager, huddled at a desk by the door. The managing editor, Dale Atkinson, looked up and nodded hello, then ducked his head back into the discussion. Dubykky paused to listen in, only to listen harder, then suppress a chuckle. The five men were pointing and nodding and shrugging to each other while speaking total nonsense. One, in fact, was just making random whispery noises while maintaining an expression of deep concentration and concern.

Hiding in plain sight. Something was up, all right.

The newsroom was one large space that extended through half of the ground floor after the tiny foyer, which held the mailboxes. Near the opposite wall was the reason for their pretend huddle. Charlton O'Faelan himself, as erect, thick, hairless, and tall as a bollard, stood beside his stepdaughter's desk, his back to the huddle. Dubykky walked straight there.

"Hello, Loretta. Hello, General," he sang out.

O'Faelan turned around and glowered. "Don't start sassing me, young fella. I have something serious to discuss."

Lurie winked at Dubykky. Her relationship with her stepfather was a strange one. O'Faelan had married her widowed mother when Loretta was still a babe in arms and her mother was barely out of her teens. He was seventeen years her mother's senior. There was already the breath of scandal in the county because of that, and so the righteous among O'Faelan's enemies saw what happened a year or so later as divine retribution. At an Eastertide after-church dinner party, Rebecca O'Faelan said sharply to her husband, "Charlie, I don't like sweet potatoes, and you damn well know it!" She pushed back her chair, stood up from the table, and collapsed, dying minutes later from a burst aneurysm.

Loretta was a toddler by then and sitting on a chair of her own, boosted by a *Webster's New International Dictionary*, Second Edition. She hopped down, went to her mother, bent down to peer into her face, and then walked to her stepfather and tugged at his sleeve. "Da?" she said.

This lit a fire under the gossip. Loretta was in fact O'Faelan's natural daughter, said his enemies, and born out of an adulterous affair. The first husband, a pressman who had died in a car accident, was "disposed of." No such thing! cried O'Faelan's supporters and those who feared him, but they all said it nervously, uncertainly. Loretta was taller than her stepfather by the time she was thirteen, then grew another four inches. Her brow was flat, her eyebrows thick and dark for a woman, whereas his forehead was rounded and his hair, what remained from his distant days as a redhead, was wispy rust; likewise, frizzy black hair to smooth pate; brown eyes to blue eyes; long, slightly hooked nose to a blue-veined walnut; full lips to mouth-slit. Yet the belief persisted that she was his natural daughter. In any case, O'Faelan watched over Loretta with mental guns cocked and rhetorical grenades at the ready. She still lived in his house, a further disincentive to suitors, and kept the name of the long-dead pressman, her father of record.

Of all the people in Hawthorne, Lurie was one of only two who could josh O'Faelan and get away with it. Dubykky was the other. Sometimes. He liked to address O'Faelan as General, but not because of the old man's military record. His only service came during World War I as a lieutenant in the Quartermaster Corps. Instead, the nickname derived from his bluster. When in a good mood, O'Faelan's favorite expression was *generally speaking*, which he used even when talking about things that weren't general.

O'Faelan wasn't in a good mood. He plucked the newspaper from under Dubykky's arm and tapping the circled article with his forefinger demanded, "What do you know about this?"

"I have an alibi. I was upstairs at work for the last ninety-six hours straight."

O'Faelan sniffed. "Have you read it? Then do so." He handed back the paper, gave Dubykky about ten seconds and then barked, "Well?"

"Interesting," Dubykky had to admit.

"'Interesting'? That's all you have to say? Eight years that man has been running the dump, a county employee, and nobody noticed he was a war criminal? That's what you call 'interesting'?"

"War criminal?"

Lurie turned a superior smile on Dubykky and explained, "I did some research—you know, a few calls here, a little rifling of personal papers there. Hans Heinrich Berger, which seems to be his real name, was born in Germany."

"He was a goddamn Nazi," broke in O'Faelan, who pronounced it as though it rhymed with *patsy*. "An SS bastard to boot."

Dubykky couldn't help himself. "Waffen SS or Death's Head SS?" he asked.

They stared at him blankly. "Never mind," he said.

"No, no, William. You have information? I knew it." O'Faelan slapped his thigh with a palm. Loretta regarded Dubykky quizzically.

He asked her what military organization Hans Berger had belonged to. When told it was a Panzer division, he nodded to himself then explained the difference. The Waffen SS, for the most part, provided elite units for the Wehrmacht, the German army. It was the SS-Totenkopfverbände that had the true Nazi fanatics, those who enforced racial policies and ran the concentration camps. Berger, he told them, was probably just a patriotic German who liked the distinction of being in an elite corps, not a war criminal. It was likely the truth, up to a point. O'Faelan humphed.

Dubykky said seriously, "Mr. O'Faelan, sir, I served in the U.S. Army Airborne during the Korean War, an elite unit by any standard. That doesn't mean I'm a Democrat."

O'Faelan humphed again, then chortled. "All right, wiseacre, I get the point. Sure I do, but generally speaking Nazis and Commies are our enemies, whatever shade of bad they are. I want Lorie here to write a follow-up feature about infiltrators in Nevada. Including Berger, even if he was only Nazi fool's gold. Do you have anything else you can contribute on that score? No? Well, I have another question for you."

Loretta frowned sourly and looked away.

"As an attorney, do you think I have a basis for suing the county for negligence in hiring Berger?"

"No. None," Dubykky answered with lawyerly finality.

O'Faelan looked annoyed. "Then how about the Feds? How did that Kraut get into this country in the first place?"

"Probably with forged papers. Which you cannot blame the State Department for. If you brought suit in federal court, you'd either be ignored or laughed at. Neither of which would be good for the paper."

Suspecting as much, O'Faelan didn't reply.

"There's the other matter, Dad," Lurie prompted.

O'Faelan worked his tongue round in his mouth. "Odd thing," he said finally. "When Berger was found, he was lying next to his hovel."

"The article says he died of a stroke," Dubykky said.

"*Apparent* stroke," Lurie corrected.

"Apparent stroke. It happens."

O'Faelan said, "Yes, well, he hadn't been sitting in his regular chair. Ever go to the dump, William?" Dubykky nodded. He'd seen and wondered about Berger on several occasions. "Then you know that Kraut always sat in the same place. Same chair, same position, with a pitchfork at hand. So he could watch over his Fourth Reich." Dubykky waited. "That chair was empty, and he was sprawled next to a crate on the other side of the table."

"What's more," Loretta added, seeing the amused look come over Dubykky's face, "there was a plate with scraps of sausage and bread on it right on the table where Berger usually sat. There were scraps of sausage on the ground, too."

Dubykky went absolutely still. Junior and Jurgen? Couldn't be. Could it?

O'Faelan, whose eyes had strayed from him, glanced at Lurie

questioningly, as if he had forgotten what they were talking about. Meanwhile, she stared past Dubykky, perplexed. He roused. "I don't suppose there was anything else strange about the scene."

O'Faelan snapped his eyes on him, startled, then recollected himself. "Yes. Bird droppings, fresh ones. I tell you, William, it sounds like some bizarre Nazi ritual to me, some mystic Aryan claptrap. Do you know of anything like it?"

Dubykky forced a skeptical grin and shrugged. Normally, such a response would have sent O'Faelan into a tirade, but he liked Dubykky, despite the Slavic-sounding name, and nurtured a suspicion that his stepdaughter did too. So he simply clapped Dubykky on the shoulder, saying, "You and Lorie thresh out something for a feature, will you? I'm going to bullyrag some local politicians about it anyway. Generally speaking, things have been too quiet around town."

He left them, spotted the knot of employees in the far corner, and shouted, "What are you know-nothing shirkers up to? We have a paper to put out. Get to it!"

As he strode toward them, Atkinson held up a folio sheet of paper with a political cartoon on it. O'Faelan grabbed it and held it at arm's length. Then he barked a loud, nasal laugh. He said to Atkinson, "Masterful. Put it in. Now, you all, get busy with something else."

Lurie smiled vaguely at her stepfather, glanced at Dubykky, and directed herself again to her copy of the Berger article. She was suspicious about the food scraps, she told him, expecting agreement.

And he did agree, but under no possible circumstance would he ever tell her about Junior, much less Jurgen, Berger's probable last visitors. He surmised also that they had indirectly precipitated the stroke. Berger was frail and susceptible. Junior might—*might*—have somehow stressed his cerebral vasculature by frightening or enraging him. To Loretta, however, he offered a number of possible and uncheckable speculations. She couldn't use them, was unsurprised at them, but still a little disappointed.

They discussed what form a follow-up feature might take. Only half Dubykky's attention was engaged. He wondered about the presence of Junior-Jurgen, which led him to think of Mildred. Lurie and Mildred did not much care for each other. It was nothing poisonous. In fact, it was quite possible that he was the reason for their mutual coolness, nothing more. They could spend time together without a spat breaking out, yet whatever Lurie was interested in Mildred was likely to covet. It gave Dubykky an idea.

"I have a favor to ask of you," he said.

"What? You want to write another 'Nuggets' column luring in new clients?"

Dubykky *tsked*. "I'd like you to come to a picnic at Walker Lake Saturday with Gladys and Mildred and me. My new partner, too. I'd like you to meet him."

Loretta, who perked up at the first part of the request, glared when he mentioned Mildred. "I've met Milt Cledge, Will. You already introduced us. Remember?"

"That was professionally. Meet him at a party! Relax and have fun. He's an interesting fellow. An expert on geology."

She rolled her eyes. "What joy! What are you really up to?" Dubykky put his finger next to his nose. Lurie thought a moment. "Oh! I get it. You want Mildred to attach herself to Cledge, and you think my showing interest in him will help that along. Right?"

"As always, Loretta, you jump to devious conclusions."

"Only because you give me a shove. But okay. Swell. Making Mildred Warden jealous sounds like fun. Next best thing to a date."

THAT NIGHT, Dubykky went out spying again, under cover of gauzy clouds. The weakness of any mystery—and this Dubykky already knew well—was that it inevitably splashed suspiciously vivid colors over dull behavior. Even dullness came to seem threatening, innocence sinister.

Manuel Gonzales, for instance. Dubykky knew him slightly because, as the mechanic at Bowser's Texaco station, Gonzales worked on his Edsel. A moon-faced, quiet man of forty, a bachelor immigrant from Oaxaca, a competent mechanic, even with an Edsel.

Peering through the window of Gonzales's one-bedroom house south of town, Dubykky found him reading. Unexpected. Binoculars brought Dubykky the title. Even more unexpected—*Azul* by Rubén Darío. So, a mild-mannered, frustrated intellectual in a foreign land who nurtured a taste for modernist Latin poetry. What did that tell Dubykky?

Or Mitchell Garrison: retired mailman, Mormon, duck hunter, diabetic, and collector of girlie magazines. Dubykky caught sight of him reading a dirty magazine, then laughing and leaning over on his couch to point out something in it to his deaf wife, sitting beside him. She laughed, too. Hmmm.

And last, Matilda Gosse. It was a source of wonder in Hawthorne how much she and Mike, her husband, were alike. Early forties, medium height, medium build, milky blue eyes, bright blond hair, button noses, cheek dimples, flappy ears. Inevitably, the rumor spread— they were really brother and sister, or cousins, or something incestuous. Dubykky didn't see it, not that it mattered.

He observed Matilda, seated at the kitchen table, patiently explaining to Mike how smoking was bad for him, no matter what the commercials claimed. Meanwhile, Mike looked at the cigar in his hand, looked at the ashtray in front of him, looked at Matilda across the table, looked at his cigar, looked at the ashtray, looked at Matilda . . . until Dubykky marveled at how complacently humans could trudge through life. But then, boring did not mean non-evil.

Dubykky returned home hoping that Mildred's research proved more illuminating.

Five

If at the end of the last ice age a satellite had looked down on north-western Nevada, it would have seen an inland sea spread over the landscape like a tumbler of ice water spilled across a crumpled sheet. This was ancient Lake Lahontan. And if over the next ten millennia the satellite had snapped one photo every century, those photos, assembled into a video, would have shown the mountain glaciers vanish, the once-wide, rain-swollen rivers thinning to threads, and Lake Lahontan drying up like a puddle in the hot sun until only three disconnected wet spots remained.

Walker Lake was one of them. Shaped like an elongated hatchet, about twenty miles in length and up to eight miles in width, it was shrinking steadily. Beginning in the previous century, settlers had diverted its source water to irrigation and reservoirs. Since 1920, its volume had reduced by half, and its depth fell one hundred feet. This served to concentrate minerals already in the lake, making life difficult for fish and waterfowl but giving the water bizarre, striking hues. Depending on the degree of cloud cover, time of year, wind speed, and inflow from the Walker River, the lake could shift through a green-blue palette that cast it as a vast, flat, shimmering gem among the desert mountains, hues such as turquoise, malachite, Tiffany blue, and Persian blue.

To the indigenous Agai Ticcatta, the lake had been for millennia both a sacred place and a refrigerator. It kept their favorite food fresh all year round. That food was the flesh of the local cutthroat trout, for which they called themselves the Trout Eaters of Trout Lake.

No longer. They had recently been renamed the Walker River Paiute. Their traditional food fish was growing scarcer year by year, and on average smaller.

Like the one at Junior's feet.

The exhausted fish flapped its tail one last time. Jurgen hopped backwards, then stepped close again and pecked at its eye. He pecked again, and out it came in his beak. He flew away to enjoy it alone. Meanwhile, the trout's eye socket welled blood. Junior had seen blood several times now and leaned forward to sniff at it. It smelled different from rabbit blood, lizard blood, or snake blood, but acceptable. He did not reach for the fish right then, though, as he had intended to. He felt a human nearby.

She was Sarah Muni, a girl of eight. She stood on the ridge of a sagebrush-dotted dune twenty yards behind, watching him. Was the strange boy a Paiute like she was? She couldn't tell. When he suddenly turned her way, as if he sensed her, his face was full but the skin white and the hair brown. Maybe he was one of the kids her father told her about, the kids who were both Paiute and white. She started down the dune for a closer look, stepping delicately in order not to slide on the shifting sand and to avoid the coarse webs of spotted orb spiders. The boy stood up as she descended. He was stocky. And unlike any boy she had ever met before. He watched her approach without any expression whatsoever. How strange! That was what made others so fascinating to her. Everyone was different.

"Hi," Sarah said, neutrally. When he failed to answer, and didn't even blink his large, dark eyes, she was not afraid. She was seldom afraid of others, however odd. Even the ugly scar by his mouth did not scare her. She said in a bolder tone, "I'm Sarah Muni."

"I am Junior." The depth of his voice took her by surprise. It almost sounded like a grown-up's voice. It reminded her a little of the voices of men living on the reservation at Schurz. They did not make the sound of words rise and fall so much as white people and sometimes stressed different parts of words. It made the boy sound friendlier.

She pointed at the eyeless fish by Junior's feet and said, "That's an agai." It was practically the only Paiute word that her father had taught her. He avoided using the language because he believed Sarah had to learn to live in the white man's world, yet he disliked the English *cutthroat* and never used it, not even at his job with Nevada Fish and Game. He usually referred to it as the black-spotted trout.

Junior looked in the direction her hand pointed and considered the fish for a long moment, then said,

> I sent a message to the fish:
> I told them "This is what I wish."
> The little fishes of the sea,
> They sent an answer back to me.
> The little fishes' answer was
> "We cannot do it, Sir, because—"

Sarah waited for more, then laughed. She loved poetry, especially funny poetry. "That's a nice one. Did you make that up?" she asked, adding on second thought, "Or is it from a book?"

Junior didn't answer. He searched the sky. He made a gurgling noise in his throat that unsettled Sarah a little, it was so eerie.

"You're an odd little boy," she said. She began looking around, too.

Then with a dry, whispery fluttering, a crow circled just behind Sarah's head and landed on Junior's shoulders. She was startled and, at first, scared.

The crow produced something that sounded like "dickory dock"

—right at Junior's ear—and did it quietly, familiarly, as if it were muttering in crow. Sarah forgot her fear. She was intrigued.

"Is it yours?" she asked, taking a step closer to them.

To Junior, the girl was an unexpected creature. She was no larger than he was but imposing. Her long black hair, whipped by the wind, was blown in strands across her face, which she was constantly flipping away with a toss of the head and a brush of fingers. Her skin was browner than Hans Berger's, her cheeks round and her mouth small. Her eyes were particularly novel. They lacked the steadiness and dark shine of Dubykky's eyes, but they danced from Junior to the fish and from Junior to Jurgen so swiftly and frequently that they made Junior want to speak. They were wide open, too, unlike Hans Berger's, which had been hooded, lusterless, and fixed.

Junior felt glad the girl had approached. It was a relief that he could now say, correctly, "You are not Junior. You are not Jurgen. This is Jurgen."

The crow spoke his name then, too: "YRRRGIN."

Sarah smiled broadly, "Wow! Your own crow! How did you get it?"

"I have a bird. He has me. That's the best way we can be."

"Sure, but—"

A call came from behind. "Sa-*rah*!" It was her father's voice. He was waving for her to follow him back from the beach. She waved in return and then beckoned him to join her. He shook his head and called, "Time for lunch. Mom says now, no dawdling."

"Can my friend come too?" To Junior she said, "Want to have lunch with us?"

Again Junior did not answer. He picked up the fish by the tail and set off down the beach. She thought she heard him say, "Birds of a feather flock together." How rude! Still, she was about to repeat the invitation but was forestalled.

"Sarah. Now!"

"What were you doing going off by yourself like that?" Paul Muni asked after his daughter labored up the slope to his side.

She looked at him strangely. "Talking to that boy." She pointed.

To Muni there was no one within sight, nor had there been. "You were talking to yourself, Sarah. You shouldn't do that. People will think you're not right in the head."

"I was talking to him. His name is Junior, and he knows poems. And he had an agai, and a crow landed on his shoulder. The crow could say its name."

Muni chuckled uneasily. He often worried about his daughter. She was smart in school but daydreamed a lot. Imagined things. And was very open with people. Too much so. Maybe, he thought, it had been unwise to raise her in Hawthorne among the whites. The other children liked her. So did the parents, even those who turned up their noses at the reservation children.

He took her hand in his, and together they made their way through the brush to their picnic table. All the while she insisted the daydream was real. She asked him if the boy might be a lost spirit, a magical being. He coughed and refused to answer, wondering resentfully who was putting tribal lore into her head.

OVER A SHARP RISE, across a dirt parking lot, and beyond the sign for Sportsman Beach Boat Access was a broader, sandier, shallower beach by the lake. Around three picnic tables on its verge the Saturday beach party was getting underway.

Midday, the air was warm despite a playful breeze. The few clouds were high, flat, and smeared. The partiers were dressed for sun and water. Mildred wore a white two-piece bathing suit that could not be called a bikini by any stretch of the imagination, although Gladys had scowled at it earlier that morning and insisted her daughter wear the matching white beach jacket. The jacket had been tossed aside minutes after Mildred set down the Warden picnic basket on a table. Mildred's lustrous smooth skin, the clean lines of the bathing suit, and a hint of cleavage attracted every one of the males as they arrived.

These were many more than expected. In addition to Milt Cledge and Dubykky, who drove out together, a navy contingent was there. Lieutenant Parselknapp had taken Cledge's invitation seriously. Free of his uniform, he looked a transformed man. Wearing long red, white and blue-banded swimming trunks, he was barrel-chested and hirsute, and his hair was wet and clean of hair oil, because the first thing he did upon arriving was to plunge in for a swim. With him was an assortment of petty officers and enlisted men from his administrative unit at the base, and no Lieutenant DeVrees.

Loretta Lurie brought a photographer from the *Independent-News* with her, Donny Wainbright, and his eleven-year-old daughter, Betsy. The girl had her father's easy smile, freckled oval face, and powdery brown hair. Mature for her age, she rose above the shoulder of her father, nearly a six-footer himself, but the frilly one-piece pink swimming suit hid her figure. To Lurie's wry amusement, Donny immediately toted his big Hasselblad over to snap some shots of Mildred striking poses, laughing with the navy men, and handing out cans of beer. The Dubykky & Cledge receptionist, Angie Ottergol, arrived soon after, bringing yet more beer and enough hot dogs and hamburger patties for the crew of a destroyer.

Last to arrive was a carload of Dubykky's legal colleagues. They weren't exactly invited, but that meant little. In Hawthorne, parties, unless specifically restricted, were usually understood to be open to all, provided that the uninvited contributed something. These did: more beer. One of the latecomers, an assistant county prosecutor, had heard Cledge mention the beach party and that was enough. He brought two other lawyers with him and, to Dubykky's surprise, Judge Younger.

Dorothy Banning Younger was not a fun-in-the-sun type. The first woman to be a circuit judge in Mineral County, she preferred events that were contained, formal, and controllable—cocktail parties, card parties, Toastmasters, charity boards, and fund-raisers. She was widowed, forty-five, upright, severe, interested in becoming a state senator, and occasionally, when she tired of rectitude and rubbers of bridge, Dubykky's lover. Secret lover. Above all, secret when Loretta Lurie was in attendance. The last thing Judge Younger wanted was for the casual affair to become known to the *Mineral County Independent-News*. That would spell disaster. She had a love-hate relation with Charlton O'Faelan, in that she hated his guts and would love to see him humiliated. He returned the sentiment.

In her youth, she had been a beauty, a classic Collier-girl type: auburn hair, green eyes, high arched eyebrows, full lips, narrow nose, elegant heart-shaped face. But living in the high desert, constantly exposed to its dry air, had evaporated her youthful freshness quickly, and although she was still striking and statuesque, her face was now lined, her eyes had the desert squint, and her slenderness seemed ascetic. She wore white shorts and a dark red sleeveless blouse, exposing a lot of pale skin, harsh in the sunlight. And she was tall, taller even than Lurie. They were cordially wary of each other but not enemies in their own right. About Gladys and Mildred, the judge allowed herself a condescending fondness, because she knew they were projects of Dubykky's. They were afraid of her.

So the party held promise to be a success, in local terms: a knot of sailors hoping to get drunk and to get lucky, four out of five women whose mutual regard was potentially volatile, and an assortment of local lawyers for whom the occasion was as political as it was recreational. Dubykky sat down at a picnic table and settled into his statue mode with keen anticipation.

Invisible, he listened:

Lieutenant Parselknapp in response to Mildred's question: "DeVrees a lieutenant commander? Not yet he's not. He's only in the promotion zone, and not very high. Ha ha! Oh, by that I mean—"

Judge Younger to Lurie: "I trust your father is in rapidly failing health, Loretta."

Lurie: "No such luck for you. You should have married him when he proposed and hastened him to his deathbed."

Younger: "I want to thank you for that lovely piece you did on the Wannamacher trial. It was accurate and complete. Except that you misspelled the defendant's first name again."

Lurie in a snappish tone: "Thank you, Your Honor. As always, it's informative to be in your company."

Younger in a tone intended to be dismissive but also sounding troubled despite herself: "Where has Will got to?"

Lurie: "He was right here a moment ago." Then, knowingly, "Is there some message you'd like passed on to him?"

To Dubykky, the undertone of interest in Younger's voice explained her unexpected attendance at the party. She was here because she wanted to invite him to pay her a visit. Fine by him. What troubled him, though, was that Lurie was regarding the judge with a degree of speculation that hinted she too had divined something more in the question of his whereabouts than casual interest. Like his friendship with O'Faelan, his affair with Younger was first and foremost camouflage. Quite apart from their value as information sources, he always cultivated the movers and shakers of any community he moved into. It made him seem human to them. But if the affair became known, or even rumored, it would attract attention to him and so lose some of its value. Secrecy was a costume that could not be changed.

Mildred in an impatient, lecturing voice to Parselknapp and his coterie: "No, I didn't mean sea serpent literally. It's just called that. *Lake* serpent if you want to be picky. But the legend is very old. It comes from the Paiutes. The serpent has swum in the deep waters since time out of mind and goes to the surface only rarely. There's some real evidence for it, too. A long time ago a kind of swimming dinosaur, the ichthyosaur, lived in the prehistoric sea that covered this land. The high school takes its mascot from the legend."

Cledge's voice: "The high school is called the Ichthyosaurs?"

Mildred, laughing: "No, silly. The Serpents."

Cledge's voice already had the sound of a couple of beers in it. Dubykky made a note to get a hamburger into his partner at once and keep him away from the cooler.

Gladys: "Oh, you. I'm not nearly as pretty as Milly. Why would you want to take a picture of *me*?"

A sailor: "Before I came to the ammunition depot I was in UDT."

The voice of the lawyer for the county auditor: "You were what?"

Sailor (clearly fibbing): "You know, a frogman."

Lawyer (sounding amused): "Hello there, froggy."

The same sailor, clearly referring to Betsy Wainbright to change the subject: "Look at that slinky little number. Wouldn't you just like to put your flippers on that!"

The lawyer, uneasily: "Uh, no."

Dubykky didn't like the sound of it either, but he had to put it out of his mind because he became aware of a small black shape sitting on an awning by the beach parking lot a hundred yards away. Wings flared out to keep it steady in a gust. Dubykky unfroze himself and stood up. *Jurgen*? He started to walk toward the awning.

"Oh, there you are, Will," called out Younger. He swerved toward her and Lurie. He gave each a peck on the cheek in greeting. Neither approved of it, a foreign affectation. It made them stiffen. That gave Dubykky the opportunity to talk fast. He claimed to have forgotten his sunglasses in his car and would return at once; he encouraged them to watch over Mildred and Angie so they didn't overcook the burgers and asked Lurie specifically to maneuver Cledge away from the beer, which drew a questioning glance from Younger. Then he was past them.

It *was* Jurgen.

The crow saw Dubykky approach and recognized him as the human who had given him Junior for a nest mate. Like Junior, Dubykky was clearer, easier to sense, than other people. Different. Humans existed in a shimmering nimbus because they were warmer than Dubykky and Junior, and smelled disagreeable. Repellant. All crows fled when a nimbus-figure got close enough to offend their senses. The lack of such offending emanations was what initially had made Jurgen curious about Dubykky. He was cool and gave off a faintly herbal odor. Junior was even better—also cool but he smelled strongly of good, black, moist earth and rich sage.

Jurgen waited until Dubykky was within six hard flaps and then launched himself into the air, turning away northward along the lake shore and keeping just high enough for Dubykky to see him. Heading into the gusty wind, it was easy to fly slow enough for the man to follow. Jurgen was enjoying himself. His stomach was full of fish entrails.

Dubykky kept his eye on Jurgen as he clambered up a steep hillside, down into a fold, and up the opposite slope. From its top, he could just make out Jurgen dipping behind a large tufa rock shaped like a fist. Here, upslope, unhindered by ridges, the wind was livelier, sometimes gusty enough to buffet him and turn walking into something like a drunkard's stagger—a condition he had no interest in. Alcohol nauseated him.

Just beyond the tufa was a second, smaller formation, a rounded, dented knurl. Junior squatted by it, protected from the breeze. As Dubykky approached, the echo stood up, and the wide smile spread across his face. He looked like a shell-shocked Howdy Doody. Dubykky made a note to himself to teach the boy not to open his eyes so wide, or spread his lips quite so much.

"I am Junior, kind sir."

Kind sir? Where did that come from? What jumble of sources provided Junior new bits of language and knowledge of the world? Dubykky could only speculate.

"Hello, Junior. How are you getting along?"

The boy paused for so long that Dubykky was tempted to amend the question. It had been too idiomatic. But he forbore. It was best to let the boy analyze it and respond on his own.

"I like Jurgen," he said quietly and then gestured downward. "I sent a message to the fish." The tail, spine, and mutilated head of a cutthroat lay on the ground, speckled with sand. Dubykky knitted his brow.

He took out his Zippo—he didn't smoke but many of his clients did—and flicking open the top produced a dancing flame. Junior was immediately entranced. Extinguishing it and handing the lighter to Junior, he explained how to produce a flame, then a fire, then a means of cooking. It took a while, but Dubykky finally communicated that cooked food was better to eat than raw food. Dubykky peeled back a flap of cheek skin on the trout, dug out the little oval of flesh behind it, and stuck it on the end of a sagebrush twig. He had Junior light the Zippo. Dubykky put the flesh over the flame, rotating it slowly. After a minute, he held up the stick to Junior and told him to eat the morsel. Junior chewed slowly. His eyebrows shot up. He stopped for a minute, sliding the masticated fish around in his mouth. Then he smiled. This time it was not eerie at all. It was like his very first smile back in the shed, an unforced, pleased smile that made him look like a real boy. Almost.

"I like agai."

"What?"

Junior pointed to the fish bits on his tongue and then to the carcass on the ground. Dubykky didn't know the word, and so it made him suspicious. He sat down cross-legged on the sand and had Junior do likewise, so that they touched knee to knee. Meanwhile, Jurgen inspected the cutthroat again, jabbing his beak at the skin that Dubykky had peeled back, thinking how clever and dexterous the man was to have flayed so neatly.

"Tell me about agai." With careful questioning, Dubykky coaxed out the story. Meeting the girl Sarah Muni. Muni—Dubykky recognized it as a Paiute family name. He was meticulous in getting everything about the encounter from Junior, every word and gesture. When the adult had called to Sarah from the top of the dune, he asked, had the man also seen him? Junior fell silent.

"I hungered," he explained at last.

That was new, an explanation that was not a quotation.

Dubykky waited

"One, two, three, four, five, once I caught a fish alive," the boy explained further.

The adult Muni had not seen Junior, Dubykky surmised. But his daughter definitely had. He filed that away to ponder later and asked what other humans Junior had met. He soon confirmed his suspicion that the boy had been with Hans Berger when he died. "Jack fell down and broke his crown," Junior told him. "With my little eye I saw him die."

So Berger had seen and talked to Junior, too. It was understandable. That old German had been around a lot of wartime evil. Enough had seeped into him that he could perceive an echo of evil like Junior. Experience had taught Dubykky not to assume too much, however. When an echo appeared, unpredictable, uncanny things happened. Not always, but frequently enough that every time he dealt with an echo he allowed for surprises.

There was no real norm, in fact, no set method to handling them. Still, a few qualities recurred in all cases. First, echoes were *likable*. The initial affection Dubykky felt for Junior was deepening. He was so open, so steady, so accepting, so undemanding that he was irresistible. And tragic. Echoes were always like that, early on, innocent and tragic. Tragic because it was an echo's fate to offer itself as the sacrificial fifth victim of a human monster. Innocent because it had no choice but to kill and die. Yet Junior seemed particularly sweet in undertaking his strange, brief life.

Second, only someone touched by evil could see a new echo.

Touched covered a lot of possibilities, however. It was difficult to draw conclusions from any single instance.

For Berger, though, it was fairly obvious. War had stained his soul. For Mildred it was also obvious. Mildred's father was an echo. She was marked by evil through heritage. And without Dubykky's care and guidance, it would have destroyed her by now. It still could. Free will might be the most precious part of human life, but for someone like Mildred it was a naked flame in a powder magazine.

About Sarah Muni, though, Dubykky could not be sure. Except for one thing: it was not a good sign.

Because third . . . no, Dubykky didn't want to have to think about third right then. Too grim. And time would tell.

He stood up, warning Junior to be wary around humans. It was best to avoid them. He promised to talk to Junior again soon, and feeling too much time had passed to accord with the excuse for his absence, he hurried away, making yet another note to himself: bring Junior some other source of knowledge than *Every Child's Omnibus of Wisdom*.

Instead of going straight back to the beach party, however, he detoured to get a glimpse of the Muni family. There were five of them seated at a picnic table: father, whom Dubykky recognized as a state employee, mother, two preteen boys, and a daughter, the youngest. Sarah. Dubykky waited until he got a clear view of her face, memorized it, and then continued on his way. He stopped by his car and took the sunglasses from their leather sleeve clipped to the sun shade and put them on.

The party had divided into three clumps. As he neared the closest, Angie Ottergol split from the cluster gathered around the barbecue and ran giggling into the water, pursued by Lieutenant Parselknapp. They splashed each other until Angie, thoroughly soaked, realized that the thin cotton blouse she wore might have been rendered too revealing. She wrapped her arms around her chest, dodged the lieutenant, who fell backwards guffawing into shallow water, and returned to her cooking post. Angie's curly red hair was plastered to her head and her freckled face shone in the sun. Not subdued by her secretarial job, for once, she looked radiant.

All faces had turned to watch the cavorting. Dubykky rejoined Dorothy Younger just as she said, put out, "Angie should act her age." Gladys looked away primly and remained silent. The lawyer contingent smiled at one another, relishing the judge's censure.

"Oh, I don't know, Dottie," Dubykky said brightly. "She can't be more than ten years older than Parselknapp." Startled, Younger turned round. He explained, "She ought to take what fun she finds. Don't you think so? Men of a certain age are rare in these parts." Younger glowered at him, the thrust about age having hit home.

"Don't call me Dottie, Counselor."

Dubykky smiled innocently, while the others in the cluster found something else to engage their attention.

She snapped, "Well, I certainly don't approve of *that*!" She pointed at the beach. "Do something, Will."

The sailor who had ogled Betsy Wainbright was pulling her by the hand down the beach to the water. She allowed herself to be led but cast doubtful glances at him. Dubykky didn't like the look of it either. He set off to intercept but didn't get far before her father trotted toward them, dropped to one knee, raised his camera, and shouted, "Look this way and smile, Bet!" She did. The sailor dropped her hand and turned away before the camera clicked.

Dubykky returned to Younger. A troubled silence fell until she rallied and said, "You certainly took your own sweet time just to fetch a pair of sunglasses."

Dubykky explained that he had run into a friend and chatted. He suggested that Younger have a plunge in the lake before the wind blew up more.

"Me? Right after I've eaten. Certainly not!"

"You might enjoy it." Dubykky stared at her levelly and waited. They had their code.

"Maybe later. Anyway, William, I want to have a serious conversation with you sometime soon."

"How about the fifth?"

"No, I'd rather the sixth." Younger squeezed shut her eyes and shook her head as a finger of wind curled round her hair and pulled it behind her, turning her normally severe face truly fierce. "It's already too windy for a swim." She walked away to dig a scarf out of her purse, but everything had already been said. He was to go to her house at six the next morning. He sighed. Conversation? Not precisely the exchange Younger had in mind. So much hiding and deceit in Hawthorne! Yet in his experience small towns were like that.

Angie and Gladys had taken over fixing the hot dogs and hamburgers. Lieutenant Parselknapp was putting them in buns and on plates, handing them out to the navy men and the lawyers. Cledge sat at a picnic table, sandwiched between Lurie and Mildred, beaming from one to the other. Lurie looked to be flirting, and Mildred was on the verge of exploding. So Dubykky walked over to them.

"Oh, hello, Will," Cledge sang out in a four-beer voice.

Dubykky nodded and sat down opposite. The women regarded him with differing expectations. Mildred was simmering, Lurie mischievous. They waited for him to diffuse the situation.

He would have preferred watching them get into a first-rate brawl over Cledge, just to see how it would play out. Most of all to watch the emotions clutch and contort his partner's face. But he knew that wouldn't do. Cledge might get scared off. Mildred would have to be talked out of her anger and then comforted when she burst into tears, as she would. Loretta would have to be managed so that she remained a friend. All that did sound more amusing than sitting under a fierce sun, battered by breezes, while those around him got increasingly silly. It just wouldn't do, though. Dubykky couldn't indulge in personal fun. His first concern was Mildred.

Cledge asked him, "Did you get a burger yet? Here, have a beer."

He pulled a can from a cooler behind, used a church key to open two triangles into the lid, and slid it across the table to Dubykky. He used only his forefinger to slide it, watching with exaggerated care to make sure beer didn't slosh out. Seeing that, Mildred and Lurie both scooted closer to him so he couldn't reach back for another.

Dubykky accepted the can but didn't drink. The prospect of eating either a hot dog or a hamburger revolted him. He grabbed a handful of potato chips from a bag on the table, anchored with a rock, and popped one in his mouth. After swallowing and suppressing a grimace at its greasy saltiness, he said to Lurie, "Can you get Donny over here? I want him to take some shots of us."

By us he meant Cledge and Mildred and him. Lurie took the hint. She rose from the table saying Wainbright had gone with Betsy to snap some sea gulls swooping over the chops. The lake had turned a little rough, changing from topaz to gun metal blue because of it. She walked away. His left arm free, Cledge reached around for another beer.

"Milt, don't you think you should have another hot dog first?" Mildred asked. "I'll get it for you." Cledge smiled happily and nodded.

He watched Mildred's rear sway toward the barbecue. Then his face tensed—worried shame. He glanced at Dubykky. "Am I drinking too fast?"

"Well, let's put that to a test, shall we?" Dubykky noticed that a pair of sailors was already flanking Mildred at the barbecue, pointing at the hot dogs and laughing naughty laughs. One of them was the same sailor who had led away Betsy. Clearly, a man who was not discouraged for long.

"So, Milt, do you think a hot dog is like a penis?"

Cledge reacted with a look of such utter horror that Dubykky couldn't help snickering. "So you don't. Right? No. It's a very good sign that you've not yet had too many beers. But it sounds as though not everyone here has held off." He pivoted his head slowly and pointedly toward Mildred. The sleazy sailor had a hand on the small of her back.

Jealousy battled with indignation on Cledge's countenance. He stood up, flushing vehemently, and strode toward the barbecue. "See here, now," he bellowed, "are you taking liberties with my friend?"

Dubykky could imagine what the two sailors saw when, caught off guard, they faced Cledge: an enraged bull of a man, half a head taller than either of them and wider, approaching with his arms out like a wrestler ready to grapple. They took simultaneous sidesteps. Cledge's tone had penetrated the freshening breeze to alert the other sailors. Led by Lieutenant Parselknapp, they converged.

For a glorious moment, there was dead calm. The brief calm before a storm, or a donnybrook. The faces showed surprise, alarm, calculation, belligerence, and in Cledge's case deepening wrath. Judge Younger, a dozen feet away, folded her arms and bit her lip, as if calculating whether it was better for her to intervene or walk away. The lawyers who had been talking to her turned to watch, hoping for conflict. Gladys, on the opposite side of the barbecue from her daughter, reached out a hand to calm Cledge and then hastily withdrew it because of the heat. But it was Wainbright who saved the situation. Again. A loud click startled both the sailors and Cledge. Wainbright had gotten a good photo this time and was immensely pleased with himself.

"See here," Cledge began.

But the lieutenant lay a hand on his elbow and said, "No harm was intended, Mr. Cledge. Just the boys having a gab."

Cledge peered down at him as if from an awful height, not responding at first. Mildred turned toward him holding a paper plate with a bare, well-browned, and blistered hot dog on it. "Here, Milt, I cooked it just for you," she said, a little plaintively. She felt guilty that he was upset.

His frown faltered, and a grin spread slowly. Then, when he saw the bare dog, uncertainty. He glanced at Lieutenant Parselknapp and nodded, then slid his free arm around Mildred's and brought her back to the table. Cledge's color quickly moderated. The two were smiling shyly at each other and then looking away.

Dubykky picked up his beer and left the table to them. He drew the lieutenant aside. "That sailor needs a talking to. Who is he?"

To his credit, Lieutenant Parselknapp did not pretend incomprehension. "Machinist Mate First Class McGinnis."

Dubykky groaned inwardly. Another string of *M*s, *T*s, *G*s, *N*s, and *S*s in a name.

"He gets kind of . . . free-handed when he's drunk," the lieutenant went on.

"Where's he from?"

Parselknapp was surprised at the question. "Baltimore. Why?"

Dubykky only shrugged in reply, and the lieutenant assured him, "We'll be getting back to base soon. I'll make sure he doesn't grope anybody until then." And he walked off.

Dubykky studied the sun and sky. It was getting on to midafternoon, and the wind was starting to protest in earnest. It clawed at their eyes with fine sprays of salty sand; it groped under their clothing for something, anything; it danced on their food and fire, ecstatic in its lust to level all frail things, in league with the desert to bury them.

It was indeed about time to leave, since more of the navy party were getting the worse of alcohol than just McGinnis. Lieutenant Parselknapp, who had not skimped on beer himself, began herding them toward the two cars they had come in.

A stack of paper plates suddenly lifted in the air, separated, and spun away like frightened snow geese. Gladys said something snappish to Angie, who looked hurt. They began jamming the rest of the lunch into baskets.

The only ones who didn't notice that the picnic was over were Cledge and Mildred. Lurie came over to Dubykky, trailed by Younger. Lurie said, "Well done, Will. Looks like your plans are panning out."

"As always," Younger chipped in. "By the way, Loretta, can I have a look at Donny's photographs before you print any of them?"

"Interfering with freedom of the press, Your Honor?"

Younger forced a laugh. "Of course! I may need a good campaign photo. If you publish it first, it'll ruin the surprise element."

Lurie regarded her for a moment, then made a Chaplinesque, back-and-forth movement with her mouth. "Let's go find Donny then." She headed away. After a significant glance at Dubykky, Younger followed.

A few moments later an engine roared, followed immediately by a second. Then came the sound of gravel kicked up by tires. The first car full of navy men raced up out of the parking lot, jerked as the tires gripped the pavement, squealing, and rocketed down the highway. The second car, which had been pelted with gravel from the first, followed, fists shaking from the windows. Lieutenant Parselknapp was back at the picnic tables, talking to Angie. He watched, aghast, took two steps to run after the cars, realized the futility, and stopped, throwing up his arms in exasperation. Angie went to him and put a hand on his shoulder, saying something. He bowed his head once, looking grateful. They headed for Angie's car, the lieutenant hoisting a cooler.

Lurie had found the Wainbrights and was heading for the parking lot, as was Younger, trailed by the three lawyers. Gladys told Mildred that it was time to leave, and had to say it twice to get noticed.

"Thank you for being so attentive, Milt," Mildred was saying. Cledge was puppyish when he replied, "Thank you for . . . nice food." The hot dog lay uneaten in front of him.

Good, thought Dubykky, *mutually inarticulate*.

Mildred glanced up just then, narrowed her eyes, widened them, and waved. "Oh, Will! I just saw that strange little boy again. I think. Yes, over there." Her eyes focusing well past Dubykky, she waved again and hallooed. Cledge bobbed his head trying to see and squinted. He couldn't make out anything.

"Oh, he's gone! I'm sure it was the same boy. You know, the Gans boy. I want to know how he likes the book. Come on, Milt." She started to get up, but Gladys put a hand on her arm.

"No gallivanting off, Milly," she ordered. "I need you and Milt to help me carry all this stuff to the car." Mildred was disappointed, Cledge relieved, Gladys no-nonsense.

Good, again. Gladys has accepted Cledge, Dubykky thought, checking the sky. Jurgen was north of him in a hover, rising on the wind. Dubykky jogged over the nearby rise. Junior squatted on the sand, waiting. He stood up and held out the cigarette lighter on his palm.

"This I know and know full well. I do not like this, Dr. Fell." There was a blister along the outside of Junior's thumb where he had burned himself.

Dubykky showed him again how to light the Zippo safely and handed it back, encouraging him to use it to start fires for cooking and keeping warm. Junior received it unwillingly and shoved it into a jeans pocket, then walked off. Ten feet away, he stopped to look back over his shoulder. "Sarah Muni? M, N, O, to play let us go?"

"No, Junior. She has to be with her family. I'll find you soon and we'll talk some more. Now, goodbye." The boy trudged away. Jurgen followed, riding the wind above him.

Junior had revealed himself to Mildred again, and that troubled Dubykky. He would have to concoct some lie about it to her so she would forget about the boy, but the encounter did remind him about Sarah and the Munis. He caught up with them as they were loading up their picnic things into their car, a battered '52 Olds Rocket 88 parked on the shoulder of the highway.

As he approached, Paul Muni faced him unmoving, his expression blank. Even though he was a college-educated state employee, Muni retained his stoniness to whites. Muni did, however, incline his head in recognition. They had met once or twice before. Dubykky explained that he was looking for a lost little boy and described Junior. What he really wanted was to get a better look at the daughter.

Sarah Muni stuck her head out the rear window of the Olds and was about to say something but, seeing her father shake his head subtly, closed her mouth. Muni replied that there had been no strange child around their picnic site.

Dubykky handed Muni one of his business cards. "If you see anybody like him, please give me a call." Then he swung away in case an explanation should be asked. As he did so, he glanced at Sarah. Hers was a chubby, sweet face, a little dreamy-looking.

Why had she seen Junior? How could she? Should Dubykky be worried about her, too? Evil draws victims as much as it attracts other evil.

When he reached the parking lot, Gladys, Mildred, and Cledge were standing by Dubykky's car, their clothes flapping lustily.

"Why do you keep sneaking off like that, Will?" Gladys groused, looking put-upon. Mildred and Cledge were subdued and stood apart. Which Dubykky assumed was because of Gladys. Had Mildred been flirting too openly with Cledge? Probably, and Gladys intervened. She pointed for her daughter to get in their car, then climbed behind the steering wheel and set off. Dubykky, with Cledge, followed in the Edsel.

They didn't get far. About five miles down the road, past the Walker Lake Resort, was a sweeping bend. Cars were parked at all angles along the approach to it on both sides of the highway. In the distance a siren was skirling, a Highway Patrol cruiser speeding near. Dubykky pulled over just as Gladys did and got out.

The bend was on a shallow slope down to a hollow. When Dubykky reached the elbow of the curve, it was obvious what had happened. Black rubber tracks arced off the road, continuing as grooves on the shoulder that veered into deep trenches in the soft dirt. The '57 Chevy Bel Air must have hit the shoulder, swerved sideways, and rolled down the embankment. It was the first of the two cars jammed with sailors, now perched upside down on the front windshield among the sagebrush, its rear canted into the air. The sailors from the second car were clustered around, pulling at the doors and windows, tearing away chunks of crazed glass and yanking at handles. Most of the people from the other cars stood above them on the roadside, Judge Younger and the lawyers among them. By them Lurie was scribbling in a notebook. Wainbright was crouched near the car snapping photos. Lieutenant Parselknapp, feet bare, was trying to pick his way down to the car through rocks and sage. One of the sailors knelt to stick his head and shoulders into the driver's side window of the wreck and then pulled slowly back. In his grasp were the bloody arms and upper body of the driver, his head flopped down on his chest at an ugly angle.

When Mildred stepped up behind Dubykky and stood on tiptoes to see over his shoulder, the bloody man was completely out of the car. Both of his legs bent the wrong way. She drew in a sharp breath and felt her stomach heave. She thought she recognized him as one of the sailors Cledge had gotten mad at. "He's a goner," she heard a voice, carried on the wind, say emphatically. She had to gulp to keep the hamburger in her stomach. Then Cledge's hands were on her shoulders, tugging gently. "Come away, Milly. You don't want to see this."

But she did, just a little, and resisted. Cledge urged, "Please, Milly, you're getting sunburnt." With that she let herself be led away. They got into the front seat of the Wardens' '56 Studebaker sedan, where Gladys had been sitting stiffly behind the wheel the whole time.

Dubykky watched their frightened faces through the windshield, the whispering back and forth, then turned back to the wreck. A second body had been pulled from it, and the patrolman was on his way down the slope, waving his hands for everyone to leave things be.

A fast car, drunken young men in high spirits, a windy day, an unfamiliar highway—what but a wreck could be expected? It would be called an accident, of course. Such mishaps, however inevitable, always were. This one, it could be said, was an accident that served an end. As much as anything that had happened at the picnic, the sight of the bodies pushed Mildred and Milt closer.

Some die that others may love, mused Dubykky. Human life seemed a terrible muddle.

IMMEDIATELY TO THE WEST rose the Wassuk Range, a titanic stone rampart, snow still clinging to its battlements, from whose vantage humanity was frantic rather than muddled. The mountains had stood witnessing their arrival. Humans flitted across the valley floor in small bands. Then came larger groups, and more frequently. Some stayed. Permanently. Next little cubic mounds came springing up that the humans flew into and out of with unnatural regularity. Soon the lake and river, recent acquaintances of the Wassuk, shrank and shrank. And still the humans came, poking into the mountain flanks, littering the flats with nasty, unfamiliar chemicals, drawing long thin lines over the desert by which they conveyed themselves in tiny packets over the blue, toothy horizon.

The minuscule hoopla made little impression on the Wassuks. Together with their coevals across the Great Basin, they were busily engaged in an eons-long advance. It would soon destroy the valley below and everything in it, by the mountains' reckoning. Humans did not know. They could not know. They dwelt in the near distance, ardent in their frenzy, careless of the long view.

Six

Death always made Gladys nostalgic. She couldn't face getting out of the Studebaker to look at the wreck herself. She had never actually seen a corpse. Her husband's body was not returned from Korea. But to hear Cledge and her daughter discussing the dead sailors was enough to send Gladys into the past and the memory of Victor.

He had been such a strange and handsome man! And just right for her. Never an angry word, never an impatient gesture out of him. Never a fib or excuse to get away for a night out with the boys. Always so solicitous of her. And of Mildred. When their daughter arrived, exactly nine months to the day after their wedding, Victor was immediately besotted, and unlike so many husbands of Gladys's friends he wanted to participate in her care—hands-on participation: comforting, getting up in the night to check, dressing, even diapers. Once he wished out loud that he had a breast so he could feed her. Gladys giggled until she had a hiccoughing fit.

Gladys let Mildred and Cledge whisper about the dead. He was trying to comfort her, which was good, since Mildred could be frightened into hysteria. Yet, too, Mildred was allowing herself to be comforted, which was a bit troubling. Though Gladys liked Cledge, she was uneasy about how rapidly he had grown close to her. A daughter was a daughter, after all. She couldn't really focus her mind on the problem, though. As she drove them home, her thoughts returned to Victor. She did not even—as she otherwise might have—refuse Mildred's request that Milt stay to dinner.

Instead, she led them into the house, told Milt to mix himself a drink, vaguely noted Mildred shake her head no to him, and went straight for the closet and the photo albums. There were three of them: the first was titled in neat block letters on the cover *We Two*. Their wedding album. The cover of the second had a happy loopy cursive, *We Three*. The addition of Mildred in 1937. The last had no title, because Gladys could not bear using something like *Two Again* after Victor died. Sometimes she was tempted to put *We Four* on the cover, because strange as it seemed, when Dubykky was around, it felt almost to her as if Victor were still alive and present. Anyway, that album held photos of Dubykky. She lay all three on the living room coffee table and sat on the sofa. They joined her on either side, Milly explaining to Milt the meaning of the titles.

Gladys remained silent. Emotion was choking her up and threatening to spill over in tears. One thing she particularly remembered about Victor was that the sight of tears alarmed and then saddened him, so she had learned not to show them. She was determined never to forget that.

As she was just lifting the cover to *We Two*, a knock came on the front door, and Dubykky let himself in. Gladys was able to show him a small, bleary smile. Now that he was here with them, everything seemed perfect, and her heart swelled, and she wondered for the millionth time why she and William Dubykky had never had a romance. He was always so nice to her and Mildred. Really, though, it didn't matter. He drew up a chair so he could also enjoy the photos, although upside down.

Victor wore the sort of pencil mustache so popular in the 1920s and '30s. It gave his dark good looks a mysterious air, though in their wedding photo, the overall impression of his face was that he was pleasantly astonished. As always, Mildred, seeing the formal wedding shot, which occupied the whole first page of the folio album, exclaimed at how young Gladys was. Really, though, seventeen wasn't so very young to be married, not for 1936, not to a man who could give her a comfortable life, the Great Depression notwithstanding. Victor was only a couple of years older, he claimed, and had been working at the Hawthorne Funeral Haven for eight months, or maybe nine. He always was somewhat vague about time.

As Gladys slowly turned the pages, Mildred provided most of the commentary. Dubykky said nothing, but Cledge was quick to remark at the bride's beauty or, in the next volume, the baby's absolute, adorable cuteness. Mildred stayed her mother's hand after she turned the leaf to one photo. It was a snapshot of her with her father in 1942, just before he left for army training and then was sent to the European Theater.

"I remember just when that was taken. I had turned five the week before, and Daddy took you and me to Reno to see that movie, something about a boy and a jungle. Wait." She thought a moment. "*The Jungle Book*! It was such a long day! You took the picture, Mama." Gladys nodded, and Mildred sighed. "He was so nice to us." Cledge commented on how pretty little Milly was in her white and pink pinafore.

This was all usual to Dubykky, who had been through the albums several times already with Gladys when she succumbed to a nostalgia fit. As she lifted the third album to set it in front for their inspection, however, a photo slipped out onto the floor. Dubykky picked it up.

"Oh, that one!" said Gladys, perking up. "You haven't seen it, Will. I found it tucked away in an box of old letters. It's you and Victor."

Dubykky saw that. He recalled exactly when it was taken, though he'd never laid eyes on the photo before. It was a close-up from a picture of two dozen men who, like them, had undergone reindoctrination training to prepare World War II veterans for deployment to

Korea in the 187th Airborne Regimental Combat Team. As veterans, Warden was made a corporal, Dubykky a buck sergeant. Having met at the school two weeks earlier, they were already buddies.

Dubykky suspected that no matter how endlessly his inhuman existence was prolonged he would never again come across anyone so easy to befriend or so admirable. A small noise of sadness escaped him willy-nilly.

"Will?" Gladys watched him, concerned.

"Tell us about Daddy in Korea," Mildred urged. Gladys's eyes told him that she wanted to hear the story again, too, and Cledge's face shone his interest like an opening-night marquee.

"We met during training camp," he began. "Everybody respected him, but he and I especially hit it off right away."

A lie. Warden attracted a lot of resentment. He trained hard, never complained, and volunteered for just about everything. He made others look bad. Worse, he did not join in on the raucous bluster of those who expected to kill some Commies and get home by Christmas. Dubykky had to take Warden aside and urge him not to make everything look so effortless, to blend in with the others, to be their pal. Warden had been so completely, ingenuously uncomprehending that Dubykky wondered about it. Humans simply did not respond that way.

"In fact," he continued, "Victor finished first in the school. Then he and I were assigned to the same company and shipped to Japan."

It had to be that way. Dubykky manipulated his officers and regimental admin to make sure he was with Warden, because despite Dubykky's attempt to restrain him, Warden stood out too much. He needed protection from the other men, who like Dubykky sensed something odd. In the military to be a standoffish oddball is to make yourself a target. Victor's first enlistment apparently taught him little —reasonably enough—he had spent most of it as part of a graves-registration detachment. He saw direct combat only briefly when he was transferred to a rifle company as a replacement during the height of the Battle of the Bulge.

"It was then I really got close to Victor. He showed me that photo." He pointed to a photo of Warden together with Gladys and little Milly.

A half lie. Dubykky's suspicions had been steadily mounting. Warden was never apprehensive, never nervous, never upset, even during the most dangerous training. Because Dubykky hung around him so much, Warden came to trust him and want his approval. So in a DC-3 on the way to a practice combat parachute drop in Japan, managing to whisper into Dubykky's ear despite the racket in the plane, he took out the treasured photo and described his family. And he did so with such dazzled, happy pride that it touched Dubykky. More than he had thought possible, in truth.

"On our first mission, he saved my life."

An outright lie. Part of Operation Tomahawk, their regiment parachuted into the Musan-ni Valley in North Korea to act as a blocking force to a Chinese advance. He and Warden were in the second wave. They dropped into a large, disorderly firefight and ended up assaulting lightly fortified positions on nearby hills. All the while, Warden showed complete disregard of enemy fire, no fear, standing out in the open, plain as day, even exposed on ridge lines. Finally, Dubykky gave up pulling him out of danger. It simply didn't matter. The enemy couldn't hit him.

"Victor was given a medal and a promotion. The whole company did so well that we were rewarded with two weeks furlough in Japan."

True only if the context were ignored. Dubykky again pestered his superiors. The Silver Star was an easy sell. Warden had fought heroically, although whether it was possible to truly be a hero when you could not experience fear was a question he never bothered them with. But wrangling the sergeant's stripes was harder. Men were uneasy about following Warden, for an obvious reason. He was a magnet for enemy fire but never got shot himself, only those around him.

While in Japan, Dubykky had to drag Warden away from camp. Warden was still apt to volunteer for anything. They toured the country, visiting temples, watching Noh theater, learning simple Japanese phrases, observing a tea ceremony, attending kendo and sumo matches, and in the process becoming true friends. For Dubykky, it was the strangest sort of torture he could imagine. The more he was with Warden, the more he liked him. He had never had such a friend before. It was exhilarating. Yet the more he was with Warden, the more his suspicion was confirmed. Evil had delivered Warden into the world, not a human mother. He was an echo—now rogue. Like Dubykky himself. To his dismay.

Dubykky's last shred of doubt vanished when they visited a Zen monastery in Kyoto. An American poet who was a student there gave them a tour. At first, the poet was condescending, flippant about Warden's expressions of interest. Soon, though, Warden's calm, earnest questions overcame the intellectual's disdain of soldiers, and the poet grew friendlier. He demonstrated za-zen and introduced them to his master. That proved to be a bad mistake. The master reacted to Warden and Dubykky with profound disquiet and peremptorily ordered them away. Warden was downcast, mystified, but for the first time not completely unself-conscious. He admitted to having caused such reactions before. Then, as if in explanation, he related the tale of his coming to awareness, how he had killed the lyncher and caused the siren sister to be disfigured and deranged.

Dubykky's heart plummeted. He mourned that the last wisp of uncertainty was now dispelled. He could not ignore his obligation to evil. He could not keep his friend. He could not let him live. But he also could not deceive him. It was only then, at long last, that Dubykky told Warden what they both were, echoes of evil committed by ordinary humans. Beings who themselves must not continue living after killing the evildoer.

"To the last, Victor was the bravest, most active man in the company. The best person I've ever known. He got shot during our second combat parachute drop. He probably didn't even feel what hit him."

An outrageous lie. Warden knew beforehand exactly what caused his death. And who. Dubykky. His buddy.

Dubykky was the drop master for the C-117. Scheduling Warden to be the last to jump, except for himself, he unhooked Warden's static line, which was meant to deploy his primary parachute automatically; Dubykky had already sabotaged the secondary chute. And when Warden stood at the door, Dubykky handed the unhooked static line to him. He hesitated just a second, looking Dubykky in the eye, and said, "Help them." Then Dubykky shoved. The impact with the ground was what killed Warden.

There was never any question about "them." Dubykky recognized his obligation at once. Even had Warden said nothing, Dubykky would still have gone to Hawthorne after his discharge.

Mildred and Gladys sobbed openly, happily, at the heroic version of the story that he always told them, and Cledge's eyes brimmed as well. Mildred got up and hugged him for it.

Dubykky let the weepy moment lengthen, pondering the single most important question that Warden had asked him after the monastery incident, perhaps the biggest question of all. One for which he had no answer. How come Dubykky, once an echo, was still alive?

Why, indeed. Dubykky had escaped the echo's fate somehow. He could not remember the circumstances that had created him, but he survived. Or had he truly escaped? The unending cycle of retribution and death still ruled him, albeit not exactly as an echo. Instead, he brought an end to the existence of echoes who did not die with their human creators, echoes who became rogues. None had lived a twentieth as long as he. So perhaps longevity had endowed him with the mission to make sure he was the only rogue. But was he the only one? Perhaps an even older rogue existed who eventually would track down Dubykky and perform the chore on him. Survival of the eldest, a kind of feed-back mechanism. Evil was so devious, who could understand its machinations?

Whatever evil was, it had never been separate from humanity. Of that Dubykky was positive. That was how it could be so devious, so various. Evil was a consequence of human social life. It emerged in many forms, some that had no public impact and a few that had sweeping effects on humanity as a whole. As for instruments of vengeance like Dubykky, Warden, or Junior, their target was a local sort of evildoer, vicious but limited, and thereby exposed.

Thus did evil beget evil, calling forth its own countermeasure. When Dubykky first read *The Origin of the Species*, just after it was published, it occurred to him that evil might be a means of natural selection. It culled humanity of those who were harmful to societal survival. Yet whenever Dubykky tried applying the theory to individual cases, such as a serial rapist or a tyrant, it didn't fit well. Rape, repression, brainwashing, and slavery never died out of human culture. To the contrary.

Then what exactly was evil's function? Dubykky could not bear believing that it, and he, had none. After five centuries, he wasn't anywhere nearer an answer than the time in Podolia, Hungary, when he became aware of a man, a priest, flinging holy water at him and shouting, "Vade retro, Satana."

Pitiless old fool, Dubykky grumbled to himself. Whatever had he done? Nothing specific, probably. Priests were just too perceptive of evil in the Middle Ages. Moreover, from that priest's point of view the exorcism had succeeded. Dubykky made himself scarce.

His ears perked up. Mildred was saying, "I'm sure it was the same boy. Didn't you see him, too, Will?" She pointed to the snapshot of her and Gladys in front of the Reno movie theater. "Remember when Daddy took us to see *The Jungle Book*? It had Joseph Cotton in it."

"No, Milly, Joseph Calleia," said Dubykky in a bid to divert her.

"Are you sure? Joseph Cotton is such a striking man. He looks a little like Tony Curtis. Only older."

"Maybe you're thinking of *The Magnificent Ambersons*, dear. We saw it that same year." Looking at the photo, tears came to Gladys once more. Dubykky grumbled silently because Gladys's remark was likely to put Mildred back on her original subject. And so it did.

"No, I'm sure it was *The Jungle Book*. Because of Mowgli, you see. I *loved* Mowgli. Still do! And *that's* what made me think of the strange boy. Don't you see?" She looked around at the others, whose faces told her that they did not see. She sighed at their obtuseness. "Maybe he's a lost boy, too."

"The lost boys were in *Peter Pan*, Milly," Dubykky said. Gladys and Milt laughed. Mildred glared.

"Okay, then, a feral child, Mr. Picky Dubykky. My *point* is that the boy needs someone to take him in." She glanced at her mother and Milt, daring them to deny it. "Don't you think so, too?"

They didn't think so and said nothing. Mildred read their silence as simple reluctance. "No, no, I don't mean us. Not necessarily. I'd certainly be willing to help now and then. Of course I would! But I'm sure others would chip in to find the boy a steady home. Like Judge Younger, for instance."

Dubykky was startled. "Dorothy Younger? You're joking."

"Oh, Will, the judge isn't nearly so much a clothespin as you think. She asked about the boy, too."

"She saw him? When did she see him?"

"At the beach. Weren't you paying attention?"

Not enough, apparently, Dubykky chided himself. But Dorothy Younger? It was a disturbing development, if true. It could only mean one of two things: that Junior was becoming visible to humans much faster than typical for an echo, or that Younger was somehow marked by evil. It troubled him to think either was possible.

He wondered: had he misconstrued so much? Exactly what had Gans and his wife been thinking about the girl who interrupted the bridge party? Had he missed something while spying on Gosse, Gonzales, and Garrison? Was Younger implicated with Junior? Suddenly a deep uneasiness gripped Dubykky. What looked like a nice, straight-forward punishment-execution was growing complicated. More complicated than it ought to be. He longed for his once rock-steady patience.

But he said in a tone of confident finality, "As for the kid, leave that to me. I'll track him down and find out who his family is. Now to other matters. Milly, did you do that research I asked for?"

She immediately forgot that she was cross with him. "Yes!" she breathed. "Was it interesting? And how!" Mildred left them in a rush and returned from her room with a manila file full of papers. She moved aside the photo albums on the coffee table and spread out newspaper clips and pages of notes.

"Okay," she said happily. "You wanted me to check back five years, right? So, first Mitchell Garrison. He moved to Hawthorne after the war—I mean the world war—and carried the mail. Nothing interesting about him at all. Same for Matilda Gosse, the home-ec teacher. She's from Carson City. She and her husband came here when the high school hired her eight years ago. There're rumors about trouble between her and Mike—that's her husband—because she makes more money and he's a lush, but nothing more. Now Manny Gonzales, he's an interesting case. You know him, don't you, Will? He works for Pete Bowser at the Texaco."

Dubykky nodded. For once he did not want to divert Milly from tangents. They might contain useful information.

"Thought so. Well, he claims to have been raised in Oaxaca, Mexico, but I couldn't verify that. I did find this, though." Mildred paused for effect. "He was arrested in San Diego and deported as an undesirable alien."

"That usually means Communist," Cledge pointed out. "But isn't Manuel Gonzales a common Mexican name?"

Mildred shrugged, a little deflated. She admitted, vaguely, "Maybe. Anyhow he somehow snuck back in, if it's him."

"Did he ever live in Los Angeles?" Dubykky asked.

"Oh, Los Angeles! You were right about that, Will. I only had to check back two years in the *L.A. Times*, and there were thirteen murders of children in the city and seven reports of children gone missing. And look at *that* name. Oh, Will, those poor people!"

Gladys and Cledge, flummoxed by the switch to a gruesome topic and Mildred's enthusiasm, waited uncomfortably for an explanation. Dubykky wasn't ready to give it. There was still too much that he did not understand. Incomplete explanations were as deceptive as false-hoods. He simply told them, "Just following up on an odd hunch I had the other day."

"Oh, no, Will. Remember you told me about—"

"Look, Milly, on the back here there's an article about that book you liked so much, *Lolita*. It's been banned in Boston."

Mildred seized up the page and read angrily. "Idiots," she hissed. But she wasn't about to be sidetracked. Yet, too, she had recognized Dubykky's reluctance to discuss the horrifying material in front of her mother. Her face clouded, then she said finally, "Milt, will you help me fix a little something to eat? It'll do us all good."

Cledge followed Mildred into the kitchen. Gladys sat in her easy chair with a cloth over her eyes, expecting that her headache would return because, she wholeheartedly believed, the strain of the struggle against weeping had left her tense. Dubykky read through Mildred's file.

He discounted Gosse and Garrison, one a nag and the other a dirty old man. Not killers. It was the murders he concentrated on first. All had been solved, most of them immediately, because parents or rela-tives were the murderers. Then he studied the missing children. Three were eventually tracked down. Again, almost immediately, because one or other of the parents was the kidnapper. Two of these children were found dead. That left four unaccounted for, one of whom had a tell-tale name.

Four. It was a number that immediately alarmed Dubykky. Finding a four at the heart of any matter put him on guard, but above all if that matter involved unexplained deaths.

Four wasn't the essence of evil. No number was. Yet four was asso-ciated with evil. Why that should be, he had no idea, yet it was a sinis-ter number, somehow woven into the structure of existence, whether considered from the viewpoint of religion, such as the Four Horsemen of the Apocalypse, or from modern science, the fundamental forces of physics, for instance.

The occurrence of four, the existence of Junior, and the presence of Gans, who hailed from Los Angeles—and possibly Gonzales, too—were compelling evidence of connection, too much to be mere coincidence. He was coming to believe that Gans was the perpetrator. One of the four missing children in the article had that name. Far too much coincidence. Yet he couldn't be positive, because what about Gonzales? Could he have been the killer? And Gans somehow followed him here?

Speculation, no hard evidence for it. He needed more, if he was to help Junior and protect Mildred. If there was in fact a serial killer in Hawthorne, which Junior's presence signaled, he would strike again. Dubykky needed to have some notion of when, where, and how. That would point to who. He drew Milly aside just before dinner and asked her to pursue two more lines of research. Serial killings in San Diego, for one. He asked her to go back ten years this time. And he wanted any information she could find on Machinist Mate First Class McGinnis.

"Oh, you mean that friendly sailor at the party today?"

He shot her a hard look. Pouting, she turned away immediately for the dinner table. Mildred was going to need a greater degree of protection, it seemed. Her evil heritage drew her to the wicked. Almost like Junior. Would he be able to protect the boy, too?

The thought was not even complete when he lost patience with himself. What are you thinking? he rebuked silently. Junior's not a boy. He's an echo. He exists, he kills, he dies. That's all there is to it.

That was straight, time-tested truth, and it left him uncharacteristically disconsolate.

After a light dinner of sandwiches composed of Velveeta and Mildred's homemade sausage, with a side of coleslaw, Dubykky said good night to the three of them and left. In leaving, he noted that Milt appeared to enjoy the meal, eating two whole sandwiches. Dubykky found his too disgusting to venture beyond a single bite. Milt must be so in love already he'll eat anything Mildred sets before him, he marveled. Or have an iron stomach. Maybe, he mused, that's all love is, an antidote for nausea. He wouldn't know. Romantic love had no chance with him.

He walked home in the warm evening air, relishing the stillness and pure light of the stars overhead. There was a crescent moon, but it hovered just above the horizon. Its light did not outshine the constellations. Most prominent among them, Orion leaned down toward Earth, portent-bright, his mighty club raised as if he were about to smite lowly earthlings.

After the long, macabre day, the thought cheered Dubykky. He chose to take it as a sign that he was on the right track. A serial killer was hiding in Hawthorne. Whether it was Gonzales or Gans, or even McGinnis, he would expose him. At the same time, the temperature was falling rapidly. When Dubykky got home, he changed into dark canvas trousers and a thick gray shirt, then drank a glass of orange juice to cleanse the taste of Mildred's sandwich from his mouth.

He wanted to speak with Junior, but when he checked the shack where he had first found the boy, it was empty, no sign left of its having been used. It meant Junior had shifted his nest. Why? It was hard to say, and didn't much matter. As echoes aged and reacted to experience, they acquired little preferences, almost as a human would. So out beyond Hawthorne somewhere, Junior had resettled. Dubykky set off in his pickup to find where. First, he estimated Junior's range. If he had walked all afternoon, he could cross about five miles of desert and hills. Then Dubykky worked backward from the picnic area, assuming that Junior's nest was near Hawthorne. He assumed further that he would keep away from settlements but yet needed access to water. After skirting the southern tip of Walker Lake all the way to the old Schurz Road by the eastern shore, he returned to US 95 and began searching dirt roads that led west into the mountains.

Junior had exceeded Dubykky's estimate. Well after midnight, he found the boy at the Rose Creek Reservoir, more than six miles from the picnic area and thousands of feet higher.

Junior had collected remnants of discarded army shelter halves to erect a ragged tent. It was placed out of sight of the dirt access road, tucked into a copse of bushy pines on a rise about a hundred yards from the reservoir. Dubykky sensed Junior nearby and stopped the truck even before he spotted the dim point of light in the tent. A satchel slung over his shoulder, he made his way up toward it, making sure to advertise his approach by shining a flashlight in front of his feet.

Junior was waiting for him. On a pine bough hanging over the tent's entrance perched Jurgen, asleep.

"Kind sir." Junior held back a flap so Dubykky could crawl into the tent. They sat cross-legged on either side of a battered old camp lantern and for several moments neither spoke.

Dubykky opened the satchel. From it he took out a transistor radio with fresh batteries. Explaining how to operate it took only minutes, but explaining what it did and how it was useful to Junior required many more. When Junior grasped that the small, scratchy, tinny voices coming from the radio were people talking and singing from far away, he immediately understood why Dubykky brought it.

"Words may be deeds," he said solemnly, "deeds may be words."

Dubykky let that go and took out cans of vegetables and baked beans for Junior, as well as an opener. At once Junior left the tent with a can and started a small cooking fire. He punched two triangular holes into the lid of the baked beans and carefully placed the can on a cradle of wood at the fire's center. "Brown within and red without and all of it round about," he muttered to himself while doing it.

Meanwhile, after turning up the lantern and hooking its handle over a tent strut, Dubykky took the time to search through the assortment of things that littered the floor. There were several old books, their spines cracked and covers warped, in addition to the *Omnibus*; an ammunition box half full of iron pyrite shards and other minerals; a dimpled yellow rubber ball; a Prince Albert tobacco tin holding an assortment of nails, most bent; a collection of ragged clothes, more or less neatly folded, on which Junior slept; several cats-eye marbles in a porcelain cup with a baby's face painted on it; the tail from a coonskin cap; and two small stacks, one of magazines and one of newspapers. On top the last was a page from the *Independent-News*, yellowed and brittle. It contained a photograph of Matthew Gans shaking hands with another man as they stood by a car engine resting on a metal stand.

The caption caught Dubykky's eye. He recognized the second man as the owner of a car dealership who had donated the engine to the high school. Jethro Gundersen of Gundersen's Chevrolet.

Then Dubykky read again. Obscenities revolted him, and he would never use them, a human vice, especially near so innocent a creature as Junior, but one nearly escaped him this time. The caption actually referred to "Hawthorne High Automotive Shop teacher Matthew Gans and Martin 'Jethro' Gundersen." Jethro was a nickname. Dubykky hadn't known that.

Was there no end to people in Hawthorne with names containing Junior's mysterious string of *M*, *G*, and *S* sounds? Now he was going to have to ask Mildred to look into Gundersen's background, too.

Junior crawled back into the tent, holding the hot can wrapped in the tail of his shirt. When he was settled, Dubykky pointed at the newspaper picture, at Matt Gans. Junior busied himself prying open the can all the way, then began spooning beans into his mouth. He chewed slowly, methodically, eyes on the picture. After a moment, he pointed the spoon at the photo and then at his own heart, "I am here." Again he pointed at the picture. "I am there."

"Do you know who that man is, Junior?"

The boy shook his head and resumed eating his beans.

"But you are connected to him?"

Junior nodded, then mumbled around his food, "I do not like him, Dr. Fell. The reason why I cannot tell."

Well then, thought Dubykky, somewhat relieved. Maybe that simplifies things for me. Junior believes Gans is his creator. Then he wasn't so relieved. Still, still, still—could it only be because Mildred put the name into his head?

Echoes were not omniscient because evil itself was not especially clear-sighted. It reacted to inner depravity, not social identity, and identity is easily disguised. Echoes could make mistakes. That said, Junior's perception that Gans was connected to him could not be ignored. It underscored Dubykky's own misgivings about the man. Nevertheless, misgivings and perceptions were not enough, and a mistaken killing was intolerable. Innocent humans must not die. So he told Junior more about Matthew Gans and described his wife and his sons, but he refrained from giving Junior their address. If Gans was indeed the evildoer, Junior would be drawn to him sooner or later. What would happen then was difficult to foresee. Dubykky carefully explained the need for caution.

The boy made no sign of comprehending. Instead, he told Dubykky where he had found each item in the tent and why he kept it. He kept the yellow ball that he had found on a lawn in Babbitt because Jurgen liked to peck at it. That was plain; there were divots all over. He kept the lantern, found behind an antique store in a pile of rubbish, for light. He kept *Every Child's Omnibus of Wisdom*, which the book lady had given him, for knowledge and for the pictures. Junior liked the colors in the book because they were like no other colors in his world. He kept the marbles that he found on the grade school playground. He had watched boys playing marbles, and the game appealed to him. He kept the lighter that Dubykky had given him so he could make the metallic clicking when the top flipped open.

Pointing, Junior explained every single item in the same lifeless tone until he returned to the newspaper photograph of Gans at the car dealership. For the first time, emotion colored his voice—a washed-out watercolor sort of emotion, but emotion all the same. Staring at the photo and again pointing to his own chest, he said, "Needles and pins, kind sir, pins and needles."

Dubykky was moved. The boy was experiencing an exceptional variety of feelings for an echo so new. Junior loved the crow, had the desire to play a boy's game, admired a little girl enough to talk with her, appreciated the *Omnibus*'s artwork, and reacted to Gans with a mixture of shame and anxiety. Extraordinary. Junior was on a course to grow as complex and compassionate as Victor Warden, and more swiftly. If he were to survive. If.

Dubykky turned on the transistor radio again, moving the little serrated wheel controlling the frequency. Static suddenly gave way to the sound of human voices and then returned. Junior leaned toward the radio, fascinated. He gently pushed Dubykky's hand away and turned the dial himself. At first too fast, so that radio station signals went *wheet* as he passed them by. But he quickly learned to turn it slowly and at last produced a clear sound. A popular song was playing. The two listened, Junior putting his ear right by the speaker. It was Lloyd Price singing "Stagger Lee." Dubykky knew the lyrics from earlier versions of the song, and when Price started the next-to-last verse, he sang, too.

> Stagger Lee, cried Billy,
> Oh, please don't take my life.
> I've three little children,
> And a very sickly wife.

Junior looked up at him in utter astonishment. Dubykky sang through the next two songs, "Wonderful World" and "Shimmy Shimmy Ko-Ko-Bop," encouraging Junior to join in on the choruses. Junior's attempts at singing were impossibly flat and lacked rhythm, yet the astonishment on his face quickly transformed to wonder. They continued to listen to music. Junior, totally absorbed, occasionally uttered a tuneless phrase in accompaniment. When at last Dubykky said goodbye to him and crawled out of the tent, Junior followed.

"Kind sir," he said, and touched Dubykky's lips with a forefinger, then broke into his wide smile.

Disturbed from his sleep, Jurgen ruffed and irritably burbled *rrrgwk*. Junior gazed on his crow fondly and then surprised Dubykky yet again. He repeated a sound they had heard in a teen love song on the radio. In the song, it was meant to be a laugh of wild, nearly demonic glee. Junior's version was tamer, flattening away the wildness, but almost doleful in timbre. It was unlike anything Dubykky had ever heard before, from human or echo. Deeply plaintive, it chilled him to the bone.

Later, as he drove downhill, it occurred to Dubykky that when Junior had pointed to the newspaper photo, his gesture with the spoon was ambiguous. He did not touch Gans's image. Could he have in fact been pointing to Gundersen? It hadn't seemed so—but there it was again, a mere perception. Too late to make sure which man Junior meant. This time Dubykky did not stop the obscenity from escaping his lips, nor regretted it.

There simply should not have been so much confusion surrounding the echo. It had never happened before. He had to be missing something important, Dubykky felt. What was going on?

He continued out of the mountains and through the desert toward town under the first leavening of dawn, oppressed by foreboding.

Seven

Dawn was well advanced when Dubykky parked his truck in his carport and walked the ten blocks to the house of Judge Dorothy Younger. The air was cold, still, and very dry, so much so that it confounded normal perspective. Snowy Mount Grant, 11,239 feet high and more than ten miles away, seemed as close as the American flag on the high school flagpole.

It was Sunday, well before church services, and nobody was on the street. Hawthorne looked fragile, as if Walker Lake or the mountains or even the scrubby desert floor might rise up at any moment and flick it away. So very old as he was, Dubykky lacked the furious human communal self-absorption. He could sense something of the wider, more diffuse, nonhuman presences all around. The desert, for instance—it was biding its time, imperturbable, remorseless. Anything living sank away into it. In the long run. As was only right. Deserts challenged, and won.

For this reason Dubykky enjoyed the sensation that he was not so much walking in a high desert town as in an elaborate mirage. It put in mind an experience he had at a photography exhibition once. The exhibitors framed the photographs, which were of city scenes, behind glass, and as he studied each, the glass reflected him and people moving behind him: liquid, distorted, oversized shapes gliding over still streets.

The memory fit the morning. As one Nevada writer said of Hawthorne, it was a ghost town just waiting for its residents to realize it. An ungenerous comment, perhaps, but not baseless. Beginning as a railroad siding, Hawthorne had nearly dried up when the railroad was redirected elsewhere. Then came mining, which was fickle. A good mine lasted twenty years, too little to give a town much stability. Then came the military and its ammunition depot, thanks to a governor who grew up in Hawthorne. But even during the long, menacing Cold War, Hawthorne could not hitch itself to the military wagon forever.

Dubykky let himself in Younger's back door, left unlocked for him. She preferred to make love in the morning. After spending a couple of nights with her in bed, he did too. Dorothy was a restless sleeper, but in a specific way. She frequently roused herself from sleep by laughing. Awake, her sense of humor was arid and sardonic. But she was hilarious to herself asleep, and she continued to appreciate her genius while waking. One morning she recounted a dream in broken gasps, laughing while tears streamed from her eyes: she was on a stage during her University of Washington graduation ceremony; the dean was presenting an award to her for excellence in English; it was the Straw-Buttress Award, with a $1,762 grant that she had to collect personally in Fargo, North Dakota. To Dubykky, the dream sounded mildly amusing, but Dorothy became another person, giggling, snuffling, and guffawing. It was not the sort of behavior that Dubykky, who seldom slept much anyway, wanted to endure through a night.

That said, and beyond her value as camouflage, Dubykky actually liked Younger, disturbing though that was. He had no business letting himself be attracted to a human for any reason at all. At the same time, it amused him that she should choose a lover who, at least to all appearances, was half her age. She was an interesting oddity.

So they had their infrequent Sunday mornings. This time, after the lovemaking, catching their breath and facing the ceiling side by side, she spoke of the picnic the day before and the car wreck afterward. It had dawned on Dubykky months earlier that this was really Younger's favorite part of sex—conversation afterward. She could sound, for her, almost languorous then, and her face relaxed so that her features regained some of their youthful beauty. He was content to watch and listen, murmuring sounds of interest whenever she paused.

Today, however, she destroyed his pleasant torpor. "Will, I've made up my mind. I'm running for the Mineral County senate seat, starting tomorrow. I'll file and announce my candidacy. And I have an issue that will get attention."

Dubykky moaned inwardly. Younger would expect him to participate in her campaign, if not directly then at least as an intermediary to win over political opponents. He did not look forward to it.

But it got a lot worse when she explained her pet issue. "Childhood poverty," she said, then turned her head to stare at him expectantly.

"I assume you're against it."

"Don't be inane."

"Okay . . . hmmm. People are generally afraid of poverty and kind-hearted about children, at least in the abstract."

"There are children living in deprivation and poverty right here in Hawthorne, Will! You see them if you just look around. Badly dressed, badly nourished, sometimes bruised by drunken parents, left to run wild. Why, just the other day I saw a young boy—he couldn't have been seven—rummaging through garbage cans. That's intolerable." She thought a moment. "You know, I believe it was the same boy that Mildred and I spotted near our picnic ground Saturday. What?"

Dubykky realized that he had grimaced reflexively. *So it's true. Junior is appearing to normal humans.* Then he thought again, *or is he? Oh, oh.*

"Tell me about your family background."

"My family? What has that got to do with childhood poverty?"

"Humor me. If I'm going to be of any help to you at all for the senate run, then I need to know more about you."

The tacit offer pleased Younger. She turned toward the ceiling again, collecting her thoughts.

She came from fine English stock, she told him, dating back to before the Revolution. Her branch of the family moved from Hartford, Connecticut, to Seattle, Washington, in the 1880s and ran a successful lumber shipping business for decades. She herself graduated from the university and law school there and married after her first year of practice as a divorce attorney. Her husband was another lawyer, Colton Younger (no relation to Cole Younger or any other desperado, she assured him), and they soon moved to Reno, where Younger's family lived. Her husband's political connections eventually got him an interim appointment as district judge in Mineral County, while she set up a general private practice. When he died of a heart attack playing golf in Carson City, she was appointed to replace him temporarily on the bench. Her tenure was approved by voters at the next election. She was now serving her sixth year as a judge. She told him a couple of stories about prominent relatives until Dubykky, bored, had to interrupt.

"Has the family ever had any black sheep or eccentrics?" Her expression became closed, so he elaborated, "Having a maverick or two in an otherwise sterling family could be an advantage. After all, this is Nevada."

"Well, as a matter of fact—" She hesitated and smiled impishly, an unusual expression for her. "There was Grandmother May, my maternal grandmother. Hortense May. There must have been something fishy in her background, because she never told anybody, grandfather included, exactly where she was from, but that didn't matter. It was that she was such a fierce and dictatorial presence. With a flare for ominous emotional drama. Everything had to be done her way, and she was always right. Or so I heard. I never met her. She disappeared when Mother was fifteen. Just walked out the door one day and was never seen again. Another strange thing about her was her looks. She was striking in the dark French way, and according to Mother she never seemed to age. She was famous for—"

Dubykky interrupted again. "Disappeared? Didn't your grandfather report her missing?"

Younger laughed dryly. "No. Probably he knew she was going to leave. More probably, he and Mother were relieved to have her gone. She was harsh, very much so with Mother."

"Tell me about your mother. Was she a handful as a girl?"

She pursed her lips, nodding. "Grandfather claimed that every silly fad was her obsession just as soon as she found out about it, even as a grown woman. She was crazy about clothes, and men. Since she was even prettier than Grandmother May, there was always a lot of those around until Daddy arrived, married her, and took her in hand."

Dubykky squeezed shut his eyes. There was little room for doubt. Younger could see Junior because she herself belonged to a lineage of evil. Her grandmother was a rogue echo. Even more disturbing, she had produced a child with a human. Though possible, it was a great rarity. Dubykky only knew of Milly, Younger's mother, and one other.

And the grandmother was still on the loose. That had to be his assumption. Rogues were very hard for humans to kill.

"Nobody ever heard from your grandmother again, at all?" he asked without any real hope.

She shook her head. "And she only left one possession to Mother as a remembrance."

Dubykky leaned up on his elbow to make eye contact. "A memento? What was it?"

"I'll show you." Younger sat up, swinging her feet to the floor in one smooth motion. She padded to a chest of drawers and took out a parquet box the size of a cigar box. She raised the lid slowly, reverently, then removed a small bag. When she held it out to show him, she said, "I don't know why, but I always feel a touch of comfort holding it. Mother hated the thing. She gave it to me when I was twelve, going through puberty."

She grinned with one side of her mouth. "It made me feel as if I belonged. Silly, isn't it?"

Dubykky wanted to shy away from the bag but hid his reaction. It was made of white leather, cracked with age, the top tied with a thin braid of black human hair. It smelled faintly of an anise-like herb.

He knew exactly what it was. A gris-gris bag, a voodoo protection against hexes and spells. Dubykky disliked touching such things because they reeked of malevolent fear. Fear that was misdirected and misconceived. Spells were worthless in warding off true evil. Things like gris-gris bags only encouraged fool's comfort.

Younger's eyes weren't on Dubykky but on her little bag, and with a faraway look.

"Did your grandmother speak French?"

She glanced up at him in surprise. "As a matter of fact, yes. How did you guess?" When he didn't answer, she asked, "Do you know what this is?"

"Perhaps. When do you estimate your grandmother was born?"

"What does that have to do with it? Okay, okay, don't give me that look. I'd say somewhere about 1870 to 1875. Now explain."

"Hortense May probably grew up in southern Louisiana. That's a voodoo amulet you have there." Younger's brows arched, so Dubykky explained, "It's supposed to protect against evil."

Younger laughed. "Sounds like Grandmother May." She didn't elaborate, and in any case Dubykky had heard enough. He feigned lack of interest and diverted the conversation to Younger's campaign for the state senate.

But he only half listened to Younger unfolding her plans. He was considering Hortense May. She could be practically anywhere now, living under who-knows-what name. But . . . an echo from mid-nineteenth-century Louisiana with some connection to local voodoo —that couldn't be so difficult to track down. He would have a place to start looking, at least, and it would give him something to think about. After Junior, anyway. He would have to leave Hawthorne then. The prospect both saddened and consoled him.

AFTER TELEPHONING to ask Mildred's help digging up information on Jethro Gundersen's background, Dubykky set off to do some more digging of his own. Where exactly in Los Angeles had the Gans family lived? Dubykky could not just go up to Matthew Gans and ask him, and the question felt too urgent to wait on Mildred. Gans still seemed the most likely of the *MGS* crowd to be the evildoer. So he went to Mineral County High School first thing Monday morning.

Dubykky was well known to the high school staff. For a lawyer, it was a good idea to have friends in all prominent local institutions, and few were more central to the life of a small Nevada town than its high school. It provided, in order of importance to townspeople in general: entertainment (sports, plays, gossip); things to argue about (sex education, waste of tax dollars, declining standards, teen clothing styles and delinquency); and opportunity in the form of college prep and vocational training. Accordingly, Dubykky maintained membership in the booster club and donated money regularly for things like the homecoming parade and new sports equipment. When he walked into the high school main office, he was greeted warmly.

"Would you like to see Mr. Callahan?" asked Penny Worthington, the principal's secretary and overall mastermind of school operations. She was a rail-thin woman of fifty with carroty hair of a suspiciously intense hue. She was notorious for singing loudly and badly in the Lutheran Our Shepherd's Church and railing against the stinginess of voters and the legislature in providing for her school.

He thanked her, she pressed an intercom button on a desk console, Callahan appeared from his private office, he and Dubykky shook hands, and they chatted for a couple of minutes. As soon as the principal and his secretary glanced away from him for the first time, Dubykky went absolutely still.

Callahan looked upward, pinching the bridge of his nose, as if he had forgotten why he had come out of his office, while Worthington took up a balance sheet to read. Callahan returned to his sanctum. Dubykky waited like a statue for a full five minutes before some errand took Worthington out of the room as well, then he went straight for the file cabinet holding faculty information. It was a matter of a few seconds to locate Gans's personnel file and in it his application for the position of industrial arts instructor. Dubykky jotted down the address from which Gans had applied and returned the file.

He was just leaving the main office when Worthington returned. She asked if he had seen Mr. Callahan, to which he said yes and thanked her. Then to take her mind off his presence, he mentioned that Judge Younger was rumored to be planning a run for the state senate. She was known to be supportive of education, so maybe Worthington and Callahan might want to think about ways to get behind her candidacy. Worthington looked thoughtful. That seed planted, Dubykky left.

And nearly ran into Gans himself. He was walking toward the office surrounded by boys. Dubykky resumed his statue pose just in time. He wasn't seen, though the group passed within a foot of him. They were discussing the virtues of straight-eight automobile engines, but what immediately intrigued Dubykky was the chumminess that Gans had incited among the group of boys, one of whom was a young black man.

Hawthorne had the tensest race relations in Nevada, unsurprisingly. Of the white population, many families hailed from the South, a large proportion of them conservative Southern Baptists—in fact, Southern attitudes persisted. When black servicemen were stationed at the navy base, they found themselves objects of curiosity, not a lot of it friendly. Many had grown up in eastern cities and were unused to Nevadan mores and manners. Only a handful of African Americans had lived in the county before black servicemen began arriving, so locals did not know what to expect either. Factor into that the national desegregation movement, which struck locals as simply misbehavior, and friction was bound to occur. Some restaurants would not serve the black sailors, including the largest in town, the El Capitan. They could not use the town's pharmacy. If they went into the wrong bar, well . . . .

Matt Gans did not seem to differentiate. He spoke to the black student exactly as he did to the others: encouraging, engaging, friendly. An enthusiastic teacher.

Huh, thought Dubykky grudgingly, whatever Gans is, he's not a bigot. Or hides it superbly.

BACK AT THE FIRM, Cledge was waiting for him. Alight with nervous curiosity, he emerged from his office as soon as Dubykky walked past. Without even a greeting, he began, "Why did you have Mildred look into deaths and disappearances in Los Angeles County? Of children."

Dubykky raised an eyebrow, and Cledge flushed. "I'm your law partner, Will. Shouldn't I know what's going on?" It delighted Dubykky to see the lie so plain on Cledge's face. The law practice wasn't behind the question. Mildred was. Because he was so deeply smitten, he worried over everything that might affect her. Even a mysterious research project.

Dubykky patted his partner's shoulder and made a snap decision. "Sure. Let's go into my office."

Up until that moment he hadn't decided whether to lie to Cledge or reveal his findings. Before coming to the office, he had reviewed Mildred's file in light of what he had just learned about Gans. It was all but decisive, yet his conclusions would surely seem too outrageous to be swallowed whole. Telling Cledge anything, of course, would be like painting it on the side of his office building, so little was the man capable of hiding his feelings. Yet again, Cledge was a lawyer. If anything could make him careful, it was fear of causing an embarrassing scandal. It seemed, on balance, that it was more sensible to shock Cledge into caution.

"You know Matt Gans, the shop teacher?"

Cledge nodded, jealousy flaring. "Milly speaks well of him."

"Well, she shouldn't. Gans may be a serial murderer. And I aim to find out if I'm right about that."

Cledge's face was a wonder to watch. Horror, relief, disbelief, skepticism, smugness, outrage, moral indignation, and anxiety conducted a battle royal.

"Serial murderer? How do you know?"

"Milt, I'm being as open with you as I can. Exactly what raised my suspicion is a thing I cannot tell you. It's a matter of a professional confidence." Dubykky held up a hand to check Cledge's objection that as a partner they could share such information. "And to protect you in case I'm wrong. And Mildred." That confused Cledge. So Dubykky hastened on, speaking in a brisk courtroom manner. "What Milly found only supports my theory, however. Look."

Dubykky spread out a map of Los Angeles that he had picked up that morning from the Texaco station. Beside it he lay the articles that Mildred had collected about children gone missing in L.A. during the preceeding years. One by one he read off their names and their families' street addresses and made a corresponding circle on the map. The first three formed a triangle in West Los Angeles. The fourth fit almost exactly into its center.

"Wait a sec, Will. You didn't give the name of the first missing child."

Dubykky paused. "Lucy Gans."

Cledge looked stricken. He straightened and said, "No. The Ganses have three boys. There's been no mention of a girl."

"Would they chat about a missing child, Milt? One who's been gone two years? Now, look over these newspaper stories. Notice anything interesting?"

As Cledge read, Dubykky came to another decision. It would be best not to leave his partner on his own in Hawthorne while he was away. The decision was reinforced when Cledge pointed to one article and grinned. "Boyden Smoot! An assistant county D.A.? So soon! Who would have thought!"

"What are you talking about, Milt?"

"Boyden Smoot. Oh, yes, of course. You wouldn't know him. Boyden was my classmate at McGeorge. We were co-editors of the law review. He's a good friend."

That was potentially useful, but Dubykky hardened his voice. "Look again at the articles. Look at them like an investigator."

Cledge found it in seconds. "Lucy Gans has been missing the longest."

The two men exchanged a significant look, but then Cledge shook his head. "It's not conclusive evidence, Will. Except that Gans suffered a tragedy."

"Or caused it. But you're right. I only have surmises based on circumstantial evidence, far from enough to raise an alarm that we have a child-killer living among us."

"Then—"

"Then we need to find hard evidence, and quickly."

"Quickly?"

"Look at the intervals between those articles."

Cledge leafed through them reading the datelines. "Six to nine months." He paused and stared off into space. "The Ganses have been in Hawthorne since August, I believe. Nine months. Yes, I see. *If* you're right."

Dubykky nodded. "*If* I'm right. My instincts are screaming at me that I am. So we have to go to L.A. and find the hard evidence."

"We?"

"I can't do this alone. Just the driving would be too much. I'm going to take Mildred along. She can be trusted to drive on country highways, and despite her . . . idiosyncrasies, she's good at dredging up information."

"But you can't drag her along!" Cledge blurted.

"And I'd like you to come with us. To keep an eye on Mildred, if nothing else."

Cledge shifted from foot to foot—anticipation, worry, fear, determination. The prospect of being near Mildred for four days straight won him over. "But what about the office?"

"We'll close for a long weekend. Angie's overdue for some time off anyway. We'll leave Thursday morning at the crack of dawn. What do you say?"

Before Cledge could answer, Angie's buzzer sounded on Dubykky's phone. He lifted the receiver, looking his question at Cledge, who nodded yes and left while Dubykky said, "I didn't want to be disturbed, Angie."

"I know, I know," she replied, upset. "But Judge Younger is on the line and in a rage. She insists on speaking with you right *now*!"

Dubykky humphed and was about to tell his secretary to make the connection when a click sounded and Younger's voice, impatient and angry, said, "Will, you there? Well, finally. Have you seen this morning's *Independent-News*?"

Dubykky hadn't. "I've just got to the office after running errands." He picked up his copy from where he'd tossed it on his desk walking in. "Here it is. Oh. Oh-oh. Yow!"

"That's all you can say?" Younger read aloud as Dubykky's eye tracked across the above-the-fold headline. "'Local Judge at Wild Beach Party Ending in Sailors' Deaths.' I could kill that bastard O'Faelan. He's making me out to be a beach bunny."

While Younger ranted on, Dubykky skimmed the article, which was bland enough, although it did refer to the picnic as a "beer bust." The accompanying pictures showed the wreck of the car and sailors attempting to extract the injured. One was snapped at the beach: Younger standing next to Mildred and Lieutenant Parselknapp—she and the lieutenant were holding cans of Pabst; Mildred was offering the lieutenant a hamburger.

"Now I'm going to have to put my campaign on hold."

"Don't be ridiculous, Dorothy. Announce your candidacy right now. No, wait. I'll do it. I've already started spreading the word at the high school."

"But look at that story. O'Faelan's ruining me!"

"Your Honor, get a hold of yourself. I'll type up an announcement about the senate run and take it down to O'Faelan. You wanted me to be liaison with your political enemies, didn't you? Well, my job starts now. This will turn to your advantage."

"How?" Her tone was caustic, disbelieving.

"I'm not going to tell you. Just phone your regrets about the sailors to the base commander. Oh, and I'll be out of town this coming weekend. Would you do me a favor?"

"Why won't you tell me? I have a right to know."

"Put this under the heading 'what a politician doesn't know about, she doesn't have to pretend she doesn't know,' and leave everything to me. I'm going to twist some arms."

"Whose?"

Dubykky didn't answer.

"All right, all right, I get it. What was this favor you wanted?"

When Dubykky told her, she was bemused. "You want me to drive up to the reservoir and leave cans of beans and franks by it. *That's* the favor? It's bizarre. You'll have to tell me why."

"Just do it as a favor." It was a test, but he could hardly tell her that without ruining it. "And don't forget to call Captain Glay. Right after you hang up from me. Hear? Now I'm going to make you a few friends against their will."

He hung up, chuckling to himself. What would happen if Younger and Junior met face to face? Whatever, it would be good for both of them. He hoped. At the very least, the cans of food would make it unnecessary for Junior to scrounge in town. That would keep him from being seen.

Dorothy and Mildred, scions of evil living in such a small, remote town? As well as a brand-new echo? It was like finding three 1955 Lincoln penny double-dies in pocket change. Maybe something about Hawthorne attracted evil. Dubykky doubted it, but there was no use taking chances. Who knew what else might lurk in town? It was better if Junior stayed away.

As Dubykky walked into the news room, people turned away from the door and bent over their work. Typewriters started clattering. At the far end of the long room, a door shut softly to O'Faelan's office. Dubykky could see his silhouette behind the shade over the plate glass window. The old man lurked there, almost certainly peeking out.

Loretta Lurie was at her desk, waiting for him, the only one in the room who would meet his eye.

"Howdy, Loretta."

"That headline wasn't my idea, Will."

"Never said it was. That photo, though. Judge Younger sure looks fetching in a swimming suit with a can of beer in her hand."

Lurie glowered. Dubykky winked. "Look, I just came in to give you this announcement to publish." He lay the sheet of legal paper on her desk.

Lurie snatched it up and read it through, much slower than necessary. Finally, she let out a faint razz and said, "I suppose you expect us to run this as is."

"On the front page."

"I can't do that."

"You can so, Loretta. You're as much the publisher here as your father. Dale Atkinson is not about to nix anything you insist on. But if you'd rather I talk to Charlton—"

She squinted. "I'd *love* that."

Dubykky pulled the sheet out of her hands. "Fine. Loretta, it's time for you to step forward here, or go to a larger paper. First of all, your father has become too crotchety and hot-tempered to run daily operations. Being a colorful old troublemaker is one thing. It's quite another to oversee responsible journalism. That headline wasn't responsible. If he was just trying to get a rise out of the judge, he's succeeded. She's on the warpath. And to what purpose? Vindictiveness, and nothing else. It's not good for the paper or the county.

"Second of all, this feud between the judge and Charlton has to end. Now. They belong to the same party, for pity's sake. They don't have to like each other, but they do have to stop the petty mischief. Dorothy Younger is going to be the next Mineral County state senator, and I can tell you exactly why."

Lurie didn't disagree. She just looked away and said, "Tell Father, not me."

"I intend to. But remember what I just said. And think how much better it would be to have the judge, or senator, as a friend."

Dubykky walked straight into Charlton O'Faelan's office. The old man had scuttled around behind his desk and seated himself by the time Dubykky was fully inside.

"Young fellow," the old man said. "That door is made to be knocked on. This isn't your boudoir."

"It's time we had a serious talk, General."

"It most certainly is not. Now get out."

Dubykky put the candidacy announcement before him on the desk. "Dorothy Younger is running for Cal Donovan's senate seat. I wrote up an announcement, and I want you to run it on the front page, next issue."

O'Faelan brayed a harsh, sarcastic laugh. "Are there any other orders for me today? For instance, to fill your skinny butt full of buckshot as you run for your life?" He leaned sideways, pulled open the bottom drawer of his desk, and drew out a sawed-off shotgun.

"Put that away, and stop acting like an old fool. Younger is going to defeat Donovan in November, and there's nothing you can to do to stop her."

O'Faelan lay the shotgun on his desk and leaned forward belliger-ently. "You want to place a bet on that, Counselor?"

"Do you remember that little ranch house out by the reservation that you sold to Dwayne Nyquist two years ago?" Dubykky had handled the legal work for the sale, which involved twenty acres of mostly use-less land set back from the highway two miles.

"What has that got to do with anything?"

"Nyquist is Donovan's brother-in-law."

O'Faelan had been drawing in a breath to bellow at Dubykky but instead sat back, looking suddenly cagy. "What of it?"

"Nyquist refurbished the place and turned it into a brothel."

"So? Good business decision. There's a lot of sailors who need to blow off steam around here, or hadn't you noticed?" O'Faelan beamed slyly.

"General, I fully appreciate that prostitution is legal in Nevada, pro-vided two very important things."

O'Faelan raised his eyebrows and tried to look uninterested, but Dubykky could see him tense.

"First, that you get the proper licensing. Which Nyquist forgot to do. Second, and by far the most important, you absolutely do not try to protect yourself from legal problems by photographing the license plates on the cars of your patrons."

O'Faelan went rigid and exploded, "He didn't!"

A light tapping came at the office door. Lurie stuck in her head. "Father, are you all right?" she asked, anxious.

"Get out!"

"No, Loretta, come on in. I want you to hear this, too." At the end of five minutes, despite loud, profane, threatening objections from O'Faelan, Dubykky had them both convinced.

Nyquist, who was hardly the shiniest cartwheel in the cashbox, had deposited the photos, taken with his Polaroid Land camera, with his attorney for safekeeping. Dubykky was that attorney.

Lurie was quivering with rage. "Father, I cannot believe you would

. . . soil yourself like that. *And* put us at risk." She stopped and turned away, folding her arms when O'Faelan at last managed to pout contritely. But he wasn't the only man in the newspaper office right then whose quick trips to the brothel would be exposed in the photographs. And far from the only prominent local civic leader. Certain married politicians would be embarrassed as well.

She said, "This is blackmail."

"For a good purpose. And as a gesture of good faith, here." Dubykky took out the bundle of photos from his coat pocket and tossed them in front of O'Faelan.

"What about copies?" he asked, suspicious of a trick.

"Oh, for Pete's sake, General. Those are Polaroids. Keep up with technology. The negatives only work once."

Lurie was unconvinced. "Is that true?"

"Ask Donny Wainbright. I'm not here to ruin reputations but to stop them from being ruined. Specifically, Judge Younger's and yours. You see? You have the actionable evidence now, not me. In return, all I want you to do is quit smearing Younger. Sure, she rejected you as a suitor. Get over it. You're just plain too old for her anyway." Lurie nodded agreement. "Instead, be her political partner, where a partnership will really count for something."

O'Faelan was unsure whether to be insulted.

Dubykky plunged on. "Publish that announcement, don't back either candidate until late in the campaign, and then run an editorial suggesting that Donovan has been feeding from the public trough too long and that the county needs to switch from Democratic to Republican representation. Make it sound like you're not saying everything you could. Such as—" Dubykky pointed at the photos.

"General, you're good at this sort of bullying. Do what you're good at for someone who can actually be an honest senator with good ideas." He described Younger's intention to emphasize child welfare and education, until bona fide lack of interest glazed O'Faelan's eyes.

He waved his hands vaguely and said to his stepdaughter, "Lorie, you want to take charge of this?"

Her eyes were on Dubykky, who held them steadily. He was impressed how quickly she got over her outrage at her father and philandering men in general.

She nodded acceptance. "And to make sure everything gets done right, Father, the *News* needs a new position of responsibility, right below you. Executive editor. With me filling it."

O'Faelan started to object, but the fight had gone out of him. One pointed look from his daughter stopped him cold. To Dubykky he said, "I assume the judge doesn't know about these photographs." Dubykky shook his head. "Good. Then you'll arrange a kiss-and-make-up, William?"

He nodded. Then O'Faelan bellowed for him to get himself off the newspaper premises before an accident occurred with the shotgun anyway.

"First Mildred, now my father," Lurie said with dangerous sweetness outside her father's office. "Next time you use me to manipulate others, there'd better be a wedding band on my finger first."

Dubykky left without answering, but with all due speed.

Eight

They took Cledge's 1959 Buick LeSabre, the newest and roomiest of their cars. Leaving at 6:30 Thursday morning, Cledge drove them down US 95 to Nevada 360 and then US 6, past the ghost town of Basalt and a casino on the border, and over Montgomery Pass into California.

The day was cloudy and unseasonably cold. Large, flat, widely spaced, dry snowflakes were falling when they reached the pass, barren except for sagebrush and telephone poles in the flats and the stunted pines of Inyo National Forest on the hillsides. To the south, glimpsed through broken clouds, rose snowy Boundary Peak, the highest point in Nevada at 13,146 feet. They cruised through, hardly having to slow down. Nevadans and Californians, even law-abiders like Cledge, disliked slowing down on rural highways for any reason, weather particularly, so long and lonely were the distances. They observed the two-skids rule. Lose control twice and a driver might consider easing up. That did not happen. Cledge plowed on.

Meanwhile, Mildred brought Dubykky up to date on her research. Machinist Mate First Class Percival McGinnis, she told him, was currently in the brig. Dubykky crossed him off the *MGS* list even before Mildred continued that the man had spent most of the previous ten years stationed in the Philippines or aboard some ship. Martin Gundersen was born in Yerington, went to university, and moved to Hawthorne in 1940 to open the Chevy dealership, which was actually an extension of the family-owned dealership in Yerington. Gundersen dropped from the list, too.

Most important, Mildred had found no indication of serial child killers in San Diego. Negative evidence, it settled nothing. Gonzales remained on the list, after Gans.

An hour and a quarter later they were entering Bishop and got onto US 395. There Mildred replaced Cledge. It was still cloudy over the Owens Valley, but dry. The town was surrounded by wide agricultural fields, green with alfalfa, but soon they were back into the desert.

Mildred, who had never been so far south before, was in high, chatty spirits. She kept Cledge deep in conversation. He had the delight of pointing out the tallest mountains of the Sierra Escarpment immediately to the west and naming them, North Palisade, Mount Williamson, Mount Whitney. He told of the area's famous water wars, which ended with much of the Owens Lake drained to a chalky basin in the 1920s just so Los Angeles could have water. She in turn had the pleasure of informing him of the area's Indian tribes and settlers, most now long gone from the once-verdant valley. Old West history was among her favorite topics.

Seated in the back seat, Dubykky did not join in. He went into his statue state so that they forgot about him. Besides, he was tired from spending the previous few nights watching Matthew Gans's house. Nothing unusual had occurred. The family's habits were regular and simple and typical for a small-town teacher. After a 6:30 dinner, the three boys went to their rooms. Misty cleaned up. Matt read the Reno newspaper. The boys reappeared about eight o'clock, and all of them watched television for an hour. Then the boys went back to their rooms for the night, although the light in the eldest's room stayed on until ten.

By then, the parents were also finished with television. All lights were out by 10:30.

Very boring, very regular. But not, apparently, a cozy life. Dubykky noted that the two younger sons were a subdued pair. He expected signs of rambunctiousness from three strapping lads, and sass, if only among each other. There was none of it. He asked Dale Atkinson to ask his boy, who was sixteen, about the Gans brothers. The report came back that all three of them got on well enough with other students, given that they were newcomers, but yet there was something in their manner that was closed, guarded. It kept them from being popular even though they were good athletes. The oldest boy had a reputation for rough play and was scary to girls.

Mildred continued on US 395 through Lone Pine and Olancha, where they had lunch, then took the west fork at Indian Wells onto California 14. It skirted Edwards Air Force Base after the Mojave. Cledge took over driving again at Palmdale. Mildred was growing increasingly distracted as they approached the suburbs and agitated that other drivers were rude. Even Cledge realized she might slip into a tantrum after she shouted "California driver" at a man who cut her off. Cledge drove them to the new Interstate 5 so they could zoom the rest of the way into the city. They reached the Musketeer Motel in Anaheim after a little more than eleven hours on the road. By then, catnapping through the day, Dubykky was well rested. Not Mildred and Cledge. They were both weary and jaded. Even seeing the fairy kingdom spires of Disneyland, just across the boulevard, did not revive Mildred for long.

They had a quick dinner at a nearby pancake house and returned to their separate rooms. By then it was past eight. Dubykky waited two hours, reading the copy of Albert Camus's *La Peste* that he had brought along, and then checked outside. The lights in Mildred's room and Cledge's room were off. Having sneaked the keys from Cledge's jacket pocket at the restaurant, Dubykky drove the Buick north to West Lost Angeles. It had been a long time since he had been in L.A., but it was no problem to find the campus of UCLA, and from there he located Gans's former house with little trouble. It was halfway down a quiet street of bungalows, each set back behind uniformly flat green lawns. What trees there were stood in back yards, leaving the view of the front yards open the street's whole length, which disappointed Dubykky. Worse, street lamps shone at each corner, spreading light evenly. The Gans house was not covered in gloom as he had hoped.

Dubykky parked the car across the street and waited three hours, until well after midnight. Only two cars passed him the whole time. There were no late-night strollers. It was a quiet neighborhood.

He had arrived too late to be absolutely sure, but no one seemed to be living in the Gans house. It was totally dark. The left-hand neighbor across a shared driveway had a porch light on. The house also had a light on in the front corner room, which Dubykky took to be the kitchen because of its frilly curtains. It was one of only three houses in the entire block with a porch light and the only one to have an interior light on.

On first consideration, the light in the neighbor's kitchen *probably* meant nothing important. Probability was a tricky thing to trust, though, and Dubykky did not. The light was worth investigating.

But not in the middle of the night. Dubykky got out of the car, careful to make no noise. He walked slowly and evenly down the street, turning at the corner and doubling back the next street over, sauntering along like someone unable to sleep and out in the pleasant night air before returning to bed. He noted that the house directly behind Gans's also had a porch light on.

When he got back to his car he deliberately closed the door with a sharp *tick*, then listened closely. No barking. Either it was not a pet-loving area, which tended to indicate older residents, or all the dogs were complacent. He hoped for complacent dogs. It meant a peaceful neighborhood.

SLEEP reinvigorated Mildred and Cledge. At the pancake house the next morning, they sat side by side, heads together. They were eager to be at their task and could hardly sit through breakfast without blurting something or other about how they should go about it. Dubykky had to rein in their enthusiasm before Mildred got completely out of hand and before Cledge turned into a neon billboard advertising skullduggery.

So he tightened his features into their most severe glower. "Get a hold of yourselves," he said. It was a quiet tone, correctly serrated, that cowed people the most. Dubykky had centuries of practice employing it. Mildred and Cledge not only responded with identical gapes but drew yet closer to one another.

"You're being silly," he went on, moderating a little. "*You* two are not doing any investigating this morning. I have some inquiries to make, and neither of you would be of any help. Just the reverse. So, Milt, you're taking Milly across the street for a morning at Disneyland. How does that sound?"

They brightened at the prospect. "I'll need to use your car." At that Cledge rummaged in his jacket pockets, then frowned and tried his pants pockets. Dubykky watched, amused, until Mildred realized what was going on and scowled at him. "Never mind, Milt. I have them. They fell out of your pocket last night."

"You might have told me straight off." Cledge, no longer intimidated, showed his annoyance.

Dubykky nodded but said nothing. It was enough that Mildred had correctly read his mischievous expression and become irked on Cledge's behalf. They were swiftly becoming a pair, those two. Such a sympathetic reaction from Mildred was far from enough to cement her affection, of course, but every little thing helped. Dubykky believed in inflicting love by a thousand glues. He slid out of the booth, instructing them to meet him back at the Musketeer Motel at three o'clock.

First he went to the home offices of California Commercial Bank, which were downtown. From his safety deposit box there, opened in 1910, he took a cherry-wood ring box, a deed, and a stack of stock certificates, one of them indicating his shares in California Commercial Bank. The deed showed that he owned the property the bank was built on.

Brandishing the stocks and the deed at the head teller got him an unscheduled appointment with the bank president. By threatening to raise the bank's rent, while also offering a little cumshaw, he persuaded the president to convert the stock shares to ten thousand dollars cash and five times that in negotiable bearer bonds—without the usual legal formalities and tax assessment.

It was amusing and pleasant to own part of a bank *and* its land. Handy, too. The United States of America was an agreeable country, providing a person had plentiful resources—the means to coerce and corrupt. Otherwise, simple transactions took far too long. Dubykky did not have time to squander. When he left Hawthorne to take up a new identity, it would have to be fast and with plenty of money.

From the bank, Dubykky drove directly to Gans's old house, parking in the driveway. He made a show of knocking on the front door, then looking in through the windows and going round to peer over the fence into the back yard. By then, he was sure, a snoopy neighbor would have registered his presence.

He was right. In the house across the shared driveway an elderly man was peering at him through the kitchen curtains. Dubykky smiled, waved, and went to the man's front door. It was opened before he could knock.

Dressed in a V-neck teeshirt and dungarees, the man had a sickly yellowish cast to his skin, which sagged from him as if he had lost a lot of weight quickly. A gush of stale cigarette smoke wafted out from behind him. Dubykky suppressed the urge to gag and smiled fatuously as the old man scowled.

"Mr. Gainor?" Dubykky asked.

"What?" The man cupped a hand behind an ear.

"Mr. Gainor?" Dubykky bellowed.

"No. The name's Sanderman. If you're looking for the Gaylords, they're the fifth house down. There's no Gainors hereabouts." He coughed. It was deep and dry.

"Sir, the realtor sent me. I'm interested in buying a house like your neighbor's. He said you would have the key."

"Who?"

"The realtor."

"Well, I don't know anything about it. You want to buy the Gans place?"

Dubykky nodded.

"Good. You're not a pinko, are you?"

Dubykky grinned. "Up to no good, were they?"

Sanderman coughed again and spat, but little came out. "Pair of Communist softies if I ever saw one. Do you know the first thing they did when they bought it . . . oh, four years ago? Bricked up the door to their fallout shelter. That's what they did."

Dubykky waited, broadcasting puzzled surprise.

The old man went on, "Either stupid as they come or expect the Commies will save them when they invade. What did you say your name was?"

"Joseph Stalin."

"What? I don't hear so well."

"Were they trouble to you personally?" Dubykky raised his voice again.

"Not trouble. They were sneaky. Always skulking in and out at odd hours. That's the way I knew. Fifth columnists. I reported them to the FBI, too, but it's full of Commies just like the rest of the government, despite Hoover. You look like a pinko. Are you?"

"What do *you* care? Cancer's going to kill you within six months."

"Why, you young bastard, I heard that. I fought in the war to keep snot-noses like you free, and this is the thanks I get." Sanderman threw the door shut with a shuddering crash. Hacking coughs came from the other side.

Dubykky wasn't particularly pleased with the exchange. Only two useful tidbits, both tainted by the old gasper's venomous resentment at the world. Useless fallout shelter. Secretiveness. And he didn't even get to the questions he most wanted answered. He was about to leave when the door was jerked open again. Sanderman was holding a Colt automatic. Dubykky had already gone absolutely still. Sanderman wheezed, then leaned over the jamb, looking up and down the street, his line of sight sweeping through Dubykky. "Goddamned bastard shit-ass faggot," he muttered before stepping back in and slamming the door.

Dubykky walked quickly round to the adjacent block and to the back-fence neighbor. He knocked at the front door of that house, too. Or rather the screen door, which was firmly latched. A television set was droning inside the house. He knocked more vigorously, making the screen rattle. It was five minutes before he roused a response.

The girl who inched the door open was in her early teens. She peered through the crack, her face flushed and dotted with brighter red blemishes. All that was visible was half her head and hair, which was mussed. She seemed to be trying not to pant. With the door open, Dubykky recognized the television program playing in the background, *American Bandstand*, from the slangy heartiness of Dick Clark's voice.

He smiled his best dazzler smile. "Sorry to interrupt your dancing. I was wondering whether you knew the Gans children who used to live behind you."

She pouted at that—how did he know? He glanced over her head into the house. Behind her a hall mirror was partially visible, and in it he saw the reason she was only peeking out from behind the door. She was naked. Dubykky rocked to one side so he wouldn't have to see it.

"Why?" she asked. Her voice was both sullen and amused. She wanted to be able to laugh at him because he was an adult and didn't understand how she'd been dancing. But she didn't dare.

Dubykky explained, "I'm an investigator for the Boy Scouts." Her eyes narrowed. "And George Gans is trying to qualify to be an Eagle Scout. Part of the process is getting reports about his character from friends, neighbors, teachers, and religious leaders."

"George is a Boy Scout? Huh. I didn't know that."

Dubykky nodded.

The girl got a faraway expression, then asked, "Do I have to give my name or anything. 'Cause I don't want to."

"No, nothing like that. All the testimonials are anonymous. So is George a good guy, do you think?"

"He's a creep. I liked the other three okay. I babysat them sometimes."

Dubykky asked, as casually as he could, "Was George nice to his sister?"

"I guess. But I didn't like him. Or his parents. The way they looked at you—And then something happened to Lucy—Look, don't say that I said anything, okay. I gotta go now," she said abruptly. She shut the door on him.

Dubykky took his time walking back to the car, going the long way around to avoid passing Sanderman's house. He considered the girl's expressions. She evidently didn't care for the eldest son, George, but the parents spooked her. He hadn't seen fear in her eyes so much as revulsion—until she mentioned Lucy.

Thanks to traffic, Dubykky was a little late getting back to the Musketeer Motel. Neither Cledge nor Mildred was perturbed. They were sitting in metal chairs in front of Cledge's room watching the stream of cars rumbling by on West Katella Avenue and chatting. He asked Cledge to call his law school classmate at the Los Angeles County District Attorney's office, just a keeping-in-touch-call, and while his partner was at it, he took the chair beside Mildred. She was glowing. He doubted she was in love with Cledge yet, but the signs were encouraging.

She leaned toward him confidentially. "Oh, Will, you can't imagine what a pleasure it is to do things with Milt. We went to the World of Tomorrow and Huck Finn's Island and the Jungle River Cruise and saw the Hundred Acre Wood. The whole time he was such a gentleman, so interesting. And *interested*. He spoke to me as though I were a real person." She hesitated, trying to look bashful. "I mean, you know that I'm good looking." Dubykky nodded. "Well, most men, they only see that. They only think of the . . . the sexual aspect. But Milt listens to what I have to say. He pays attention when I explain something. It's so refreshing to speak my mind."

"Milton Cledge is a good man, Milly. You haven't seen the depths of that yet."

Caught up in her own thoughts, she wasn't paying close attention. "Still," she faltered, "he wears his heart on his sleeve. You know?" Dubykky grinned, winking. Mildred giggled. "Sometimes I catch him looking at me like other men do. But he never acts on it." A tone of disquiet entered her voice. "I wonder. Is there something wrong?" She was troubled in a wistful way.

Dubykky didn't have the opportunity to reassure her because Cledge emerged from his room. He hovered near Mildred, glancing down at her uncertainly, while recounting the short phone call. He and Smoot made plans to meet for a cocktail on Saturday. Dubykky in turn told them what he had uncovered in his interviews with Gans's former neighbors: precious little. They were disappointed.

"What's next?" Cledge asked.

Dubykky regarded them evenly. "How would you feel about a little breaking and entering?"

MATT GANS'S FAVORITE GAME was Maybe You. He played it whenever it was his turn to pick up his youngest son, Douglas Mac-Arthur Gans, from Hawthorne Elementary, which he did each Monday and Friday right after his own last class of the day.

He parked his car across Sixth Street from the old concrete building and watched the children spill out its twin entrances. Then, until his son reached the car, he could look random kids in the face and say to himself, "Maybe you," and imagine how the child would react. Girls were best because they regularly displayed the most interesting emotions. Yet it all depended on the individual.

For instance, that boy there. Pinched face, unruly black hair, dark shifty eyes. The kind of boy who stole from friends' lunch bags and cheated at marbles. Gans pictured it: that boy, tied up nice and painfully, might show anger, curse, and then finally resort to promises and offers through his tears of helplessness. Or that sweet-faced girl in the crisp white blouse and blue skirt: she would scream for her mother but then, because she was probably spoiled, grow quiet in expectation that her fear and desire would be attended to, until the very end. Of the two, he preferred the latter, the cosseted innocent.

Or *that* one. A girl with a round, open, brown face caught his eye as she skipped out the door. She was obviously a local Paiute, which was somewhat unusual because the Paiute children went to the reservation school in Schurz. Unless her parents were trying to live as white. Gans grinned to himself. That meant she might be taught to respect but not resent men like him. Her horror in learning the error of that would be delicious. He rolled down the door window as she reached the sidewalk and waved to her. Seeing it, she stopped, shy rather than wary.

Gans stuck his head out the window. "Have you seen my son? Dougie Gans?"

She skittered across the street to the car. Hers was a broad, guileless, trusting face whose black eyes were pools that he would gladly reach deeply into. You're the winner of today's Maybe You, he thought.

"You're Dougie's dad?"

Gans nodded. "He hasn't left the schoolyard yet, has he? What's your name?"

"Sarah Muni. No, Miss Bailey kept him inside because he talked out in class today. But Dougie's nice. I like him."

Gans smiled. He liked to hear his sons praised. There was something so perversely incongruous about it. Sarah Muni smiled happily in response, for Mr. Gans's smile was inviting, sunny.

"How old are you, Sarah?"

"Eight."

Perfect. Old enough to experience despair. It was the sweetest part of his adventures.

Just then, to his disappointment, Dougie came running out the school door and hurtled across the street. He called out to Sarah, startling her. She flashed a small, self-conscious smile at him and then walked quickly away.

After Dougie climbed into the back seat and closed the door, he said to his father, quietly, "She's a nice girl, Dad. She helps others with their stuff."

Gans grinned in the rearview mirror. "That's jim-dandy."

Avoiding his father's eyes, Dougie opened a library book and buried himself in it.

JURGEN LIKED TO PRETEND he was a hawk. He soared over the barren ridges, maintaining station in the fluctuating air to keep the reservoir within sight. It was difficult. His wings were not well suited to hovering. The feathers splayed too readily and slipped him sideways, so he had to flap a lot, which spoiled the fun. He was about three hundred feet up and being steadily lofted higher and backwards when he spied a rooster tail of road dust winding up from a fold in the mountains. Moving his beak to the side, he pivoted and started gliding downward.

A car was responsible for the rooster tail, and cars, Jurgen knew, carried humans. He understood too that humans could pose a danger, so he needed to see into the car in case there was danger for his friend Junior. What he might be able to do about it was immaterial. Corkscrewing downward, he swooped in front of the car, ten feet out from the windshield. Jurgen did not recognize the person inside and did not expect to. What mattered was that there was only one. Less danger from a singleton. He flapped away, keeping low to avoid the full force of the wind, toward his friend.

To Dorothy Younger the crow's sudden appearance was very nearly the last straw. She was already cursing Dubykky for sending her on this nonsensical errand. First of all, her Chrysler was ill-suited for the rugged mountain road. She tried to go slowly enough to be safe but not so slow that she would be all day about it. That meant she sometimes bounced and actually was lifted from her seat. Second, she was not even absolutely sure she was on the right road. There were forks, and each time she took the one that Dubykky had described, but what if he had remembered wrong? Younger vastly preferred being sure about things. She did not hanker for adventure. So when the crow frightened her out of her wits—a sudden frumpy streak of blue-black, seemingly inches away—she made up her mind to turn back at the next opportunity. To hell with Will Dubykky.

But after a bend, the road angled up away from the wash and over a ridge. The reservoir came into view when she topped it, a hundred feet below and a quarter mile away. There was a well-packed semicircle of gravel by the flood gate. Younger drove there and turned the car so it was pointing back the way she came, then turned off the engine. It quit with a steamy sigh.

She got out, went to the passenger side, and opened the door. The cans of food had spilled from the bag because of all the bumping, so she gathered them back, considering what to do. Dubykky had told her to leave the cans by the reservoir, but where precisely? This was all so nebulous! The reservoir was a couple of hundred yards across. The road hugged its eastern side before climbing higher into the mountains. There was no obvious place to leave anything, nothing like the campground or tool shack she had expected. The only really distinctive feature was the floodgate. It would have to do. Beans and franks—a repellant concoction to Younger. So she had departed from Dubykky's instructions and included cans of ravioli and spaghetti. He had refused to tell her precisely why she was leaving the food here. When she pressed him about it, he had merely gotten that damnably adorable twinkle in his eye and changed the subject. Yet Younger had her theory. Carrying the bag to the small concrete-and-steel sluice, she scanned the slopes around. The image of the strange, square-faced boy came to her, the one she had spotted raiding a garbage can. He could be anywhere in these hills, a thought that suddenly made her apprehensive.

To think there were children left to roam in the desert like wild animals. Poor thing! Was he the reason Dubykky had sent her here? She thought so. How he knew the boy would be here was beyond her, but Dubykky had always demonstrated a remarkable knack for knowing peculiar things.

The bag placed securely on the gate's concrete housing, where it could be seen easily, Younger sat beside it. The day was hot and breezy, mountainous clouds scudding overhead, their shadows undulating across the hillsides. Younger had her hair up in a scarf, which was a good choice, because left loose it would be in and out of her eyes. She wore Levis neatly rolled up a couple of inches at the ankles, a plaid shirt, and canvas shoes.

It felt good wearing coarse casual clothes, a nice change of pace from a dress and judicial robes, although the bra itched as the hard sunlight brought her close to sweating. She leaned to face up to it, closing her eyes, enjoying the heat and the bright, veined red glare behind her eyelids.

The weather was one of the things she most enjoyed about central Nevada. Hawthorne was not a place she would ever have settled in on her own. Nor had she expected to stay. It had grown on her nevertheless, and the changeable, dry, dramatic weather was part of the reason. Just think, two days before, snow had fallen on the passes, while in Hawthorne a thundershower left the pavement on the streets smelling overpoweringly of ozone and pebbled with hail. Now today, sun, heat, breezes, and clouds like something out of a Maxfield Parrish painting. Newcomers always said that the desert was drab. Younger had thought so herself at first. But, oh, what lack of discrimination! The intense green-blue of Walker Lake, the pale, ragged, marbled ranges, the green haze of new plant life all around, the dome of azure overhead, the pastel yellows and browns and grays of lichen, the matte green of piñon pines . . . She drifted into a reverie.

What?

Suddenly, Younger perceived, rather than felt, heard, or smelled, a presence near. For a second she was afraid to open her eyes.

A puff of wind carried an odor to her, the rankness of an unwashed body. Her eyes opened exactly level with those of the strange young, box-headed boy. His face was expressionless, which struck her as disturbingly wrong, yet she wasn't put off, not really. There was innocent comedy in his appearance that belied the face. His brown hair stood out in hanks at odd angles, his top shirt button was done up, one collar tip curled upwards, and grains of sand stuck to his cheek, as if he had slept on the ground. Probably did, poor child, she told herself. The clothing was filthy.

The crow was another matter. Younger had never heard of a pet crow, yet sitting right there on the left shoulder, it seemed almost part of the boy's body, or self. One crow was just like another to her. Still, she recalled the one that had zoomed past her windshield only a half

hour earlier and wondered. It swung its head from left to right, training its black eyes her way, as if intent on identifying her.

"Hello," Younger said in the voice she reserved for dealing with a
child who had to be on the witness stand and was scared. "My name
is Dorothy Younger. What's yours, little boy?" She expected shyness,
reticence, so was completely unprepared when he spoke.

Jurgen and Junior recognized Younger as a woman. Junior compared the appearance with his memory of the lady who had given him
the learning-book. This person was thinner and crinklier but otherwise
sufficiently like the book lady to be a woman. And unlike Sarah Muni,
who was small and fresh and had white teeth. This Dorothy Younger
had interesting eyes, though, also unlike Muni but like the book lady.
Junior saw in them some quality that he recognized in Kind Sir as well,
though less intensely. After Jurgen's warning of a stranger in an angry
machine, he felt reassured.

"Who am I? I am Junior." He pointed to the crow. "Jurgen is Jurgen."

"Who do you belong to? Where do you come from?"

Junior thought over the questions. He had heard many things on
Kind Sir's radio, but nothing fit well as an answer, and singing a song,
in his experience, was not good. His singing upset Jurgen. In any case,
he preferred the book. His mind's eye leafed through the pages until he
came upon words that sounded right.

"I come from haunts of coot and hern."

The strange remark, articulated in a flat tone by an unexpectedly
deep voice, made Younger wonder if she was being made fun of. But
no. That couldn't be. The boy's expression never changed. What a very
strange child, she mused. Why is it that he seems both ghastly and
compelling?

She took a can out of the bag and showed it to him, saying, "A friend
of mine, Mr. Dubykky, told me to bring these cans for you. Are you
hungry?"

That was a lot for Junior to mull over. The can held up before him contained beans and franks, like the can that Kind Sir had brought. "Dubykky" was another name for Kind Sir, and the woman claimed to be a friend of Dubykky, too. It puzzled him why Kind Sir wanted Dorothy Younger to bring him food. Stranger yet, why would the woman want to know if he were hungry?

"Why?" Junior asked.

Younger did not know what the boy was asking about, yet her experience told her that with children it didn't much matter. She could select what she wanted to explain and that would set the course of the conversation. "I don't know exactly why Mr. Dubykky sent me here. I suppose he worries that you're hungry. Are you?"

Stranger and stranger. Like him, the woman did not know Kind Sir's reason and was forced to guess. Junior wasn't hungry just then but refrained from saying so. There was no reason to answer until he understood more. Maybe, Junior considered, every adult in the world worried about his hunger. The idea pleased him vaguely. He smiled.

Younger's first impulse was to recoil at the boy's expression. He bared his teeth, which were perfectly shaped, large, and white, although bits of food were stuck between. Yet it was exaggerated, eerie because of the scar in the corner of his mouth and because his eyes did not change. He continued to stare. Younger checked the impulse to shy away, however.

Maybe not so blank, those eyes, she thought upon reconsideration. There was a certain glimmer. Something that drew her. Inexplicably, the image of her mother came to mind. But that was nonsense.

"Do you live here all by yourself?"

Junior recognized that *live* covered a wide range of meanings but that the most likely, given its usage in songs, concerned where he was staying over an extended period. He decided he could answer. "I live with Jurgen."

The crow stretched out its wings and twitched them. Jurgen enjoyed hearing the boy speak his name. "Junior," it crooned.

This is like a dream, Younger thought. But that was nonsense as well. Everything about the day, the hour, the place, and boy's appearance felt real, except his behavior. Well, the crow's, too.

And yet, nothing the boy said accorded with what she expected from his age. The logical conclusion was that he was defective in some way. But she had seen simple-minded children before. This boy didn't look like one. On the contrary, his eyes were steady, possessing some secret intelligence. One thing was obvious, though. The boy was defective in upbringing. Left to run wild or abandoned entirely, he had not been civilized.

At that point, Younger gave in to an impulse even though she feared it would change her life. "Junior," she asked, "how would you and Jurgen like to come home with me?"

After a long pause, Junior intoned,

> Let us leave the confusion
> and all disillusion behind.
> Just like birds of a feather
> a rainbow together we'll find.
> Volare.

THE DRIVE from Anaheim to West Los Angeles was silent. Mildred exhibited her muddle of fear and keenness by fidgeting constantly but did not speak. Cledge, who disapproved of their plans to break into Gans's old house, kept quiet out of worry that anything he said would make him seem squeamish to Mildred. Dubykky didn't speak because he didn't have to.

Instead, he was thinking about fallout shelters. Personally, he believed them to be a waste of money. In a principal U.S. city like Los Angeles, should nuclear war break out, a fallout shelter would simply ensure that the people in it were buried alive, or pillaged by marauding looters if they survived.

He dismissed the thought. About Gans, though, what could his motivation have been? Why bother to seal up the entrance to the shelter? Did he have a similar view about fallout shelters? Dubykky had met Gans only a few times and had no idea about his politics. His impression, though, was that Gans was not the type to concern himself. There had to be another reason. The most obvious and reasonable explanation was that he wanted to keep his children from getting into the shelter and creating mischief. That *was* most obvious and reasonable, and Dubykky rejected it. If, as he was now all but convinced, Gans was a serial child murderer, the shelter should be the target of his investigation. A secret, concealed place reused for an antithetical purpose, a place not to protect but to maltreat—that was what evil adored. He had to get into it somehow or other.

He parked the car at the end of the block on the cross street, out of old man Sanderman's sight. There was a brief argument about whether Mildred should wait in the car. The prospect of being left out infuriated her. She was well on her way to a tantrum when Dubykky gave in. Right afterward Cledge did too, grudgingly. The three of them walked to the Gans house in a sour mood.

It was three o'clock in the morning. The street was empty as an unplugged television. They cut across the neighbor's yard to the western corner of the Gans house because light was spilling out of Sanderman's kitchen. Dubykky waved for Mildred and Cledge to wait while he ran over at a crouch and peered in the window. Sanderman was nowhere in sight, so Dubykky judged that, as on the previous night, the light was just for the bathroom visits. He rejoined the others.

While Mildred and Cledge disputed in whispers the best way to break into the house, Dubykky got on his hands and knees and searched northward along the concrete stem wall below the siding until he came upon a small basement window. He took out a dinner knife that he had stolen from the pancake house and worked it between the sill and frame below the barrel latch. With enough pressure the serrations dug into the bronze bolt to gain purchase. Dubykky slowly pushed it inward until the bolt rotated, freeing it from its recess, and then used a short, diagonal sawing motion to work the bolt back from the latch. He pushed the window inward and wiggled through feet first. It took three *pssts* to get the others' attention. Finally, Mildred's legs slid through, and Dubykky helped her down, glad that he had convinced her to wear stirrup pants rather than a skirt. Then came Cledge, who briefly got hung up because he was thicker.

Except for the rectangle of dim light from the window, the basement was black. Cledge clicked on a small flashlight toward the opposite wall and slowly scanned the room clockwise: furnace, water heater, cleaning closet, vertical struts, utility sink, door frame, old-fashioned agitator-and-wringer washing machine, and pile of assorted wood scraps all slid in and out of view. The basement was otherwise empty, from its ugly brown linoleum floor to the overhead joists. With Mildred holding on to Cledge and Dubykky an inch behind her, the three edged along the west wall and then turned along the north wall, searching for anything out of the ordinary. They reached a narrow door that led up through a concrete slot to the backyard. Mildred unbolted it, and Dubykky went through first.

The near yard was nothing but grass bordered in arborvitae. Behind it was a wood fence five feet high. Dubykky shone the flashlight around once and handed it back to Cledge. The low mound of the fallout shelter took up a good half of the far yard. Its entrance had originally been a concrete slot on the east end, like the one from the basement. He went to it and knelt down. The entire slot was filled with bricks. He ran his hand along the seam between bricks and concrete, then over the mortar between brick rows. It was all solid. He pushed on bricks, rapped on several listening for a hollow space underneath, and finally ran the dinner knife between the concrete and grass. Absolutely nothing. The entrance was blocked up, and good.

Frustrated, Dubykky crept over the yard in search of a hatch, or anything. Cledge and Mildred did likewise with the help of the pale moonlight and the general city glow. It was Cledge who found something. He stumbled and grunted. The three of them froze, fearing the noise. After a moment they relaxed. There was no indication that a neighbor had heard.

Dubykky began feeling around with his hands. It was an air vent that had tripped Cledge. He twisted off its cover and put his nose to it. There was a stale smell, but not the odor of earth. Rather, it was the odor of a closed-off room and a faintly sick-sweet aroma of decay. He found a pebble and dropped it down the pipe. A small click sounded when it landed in the air trap and a more distant tinkle of an echo. Although bricked closed, the shelter was not filled in.

But how to get into it? Dubykky sat awhile thinking while Cledge and then Mildred sniffed at and listened at the pipe. Dubykky considered the basement. Along the wall facing the backyard were the washing machine and utility sink, logically enough. That was where the main water line entered the house. But there was no clothes drier next to the washer and no clotheslines in the yard. Who would use a wringer-washer without clotheslines? Dubykky bet himself that there was a new washer-drier set on the house's main floor. The wringer-washer was not intended to be used.

Tugging at the others to follow, Dubykky returned to the basement, pointing to Cledge to light the way. Inside, he motioned toward the wringer-washer and Cledge trained the beam on it. Dubykky put his hand on the hose to the cold-water spout. It was so loosely screwed on that it immediately fell off. Likewise, the hot-water hose, and he noticed that the electrical plug lay unattached on the floor. Crouching, he felt around the machine's base just outside where it was bolted down.

There! His fingers detected a wider gap between one seam separating rows of linoleum than between the others. Beside him, Mildred found it too and traced it around to the side of the washer. He whispered for her to take the flashlight. With Cledge, he pushed against one side, then the opposite, before their pulling forward succeeded in toppling the washer over and opening a trapdoor in the process.

The flashlight revealed a three-by-three shaft and a row of metal rungs below the hinge. Mildred pointed the light at the bottom and up and down the shaft's sides. It was about twelve feet deep. At the bottom was an opening in the direction of the backyard. "That's it!" Mildred whispered and sitting down put her legs into the shaft. Both men immediately placed hands on her shoulders to restrain her.

Why is it, Dubykky asked himself, that darkness attracts evil? Even the little that lurks in an echo's daughter? Mildred didn't hesitate, was in fact eager to see where the opening led while Cledge stood rigid, uncertain, unhappy. Yet they faced the same unknown.

"Me first," Dubykky said, "in case there are demons and dragons at the end." Mildred tittered quietly at that, but Cledge's frown deepened. He wanted to stop them and was shocked at Mildred's eagerness. He couldn't understand it. Mildred might be a beauty, but a confounding one. To him, no good could come from rushing into a dark tunnel.

Dubykky grabbed the top rung, slid forward until his feet rested on the fourth, and started down, ordering Mildred and Cledge to wait until he whistled. But Mildred was already positioning herself to follow him by the time he reached the bottom.

The light from Cledge's flashlight cast rays over Dubykky's shoulder and into the passageway behind the opening. There, the faint light reflected from the concrete floor was sufficient to reveal that it was clear of debris or obstructions. The opening was only about five feet high, so he would have to walk bent double. Telling Mildred to stay put, he shuffled in. Behind him came the voices of Mildred and Cledge, whispering urgently to each other. It quickly faded, though, and Dubykky could see why. The floor of the passageway sloped gently upwards, and acoustic tiles lined every surface except the floor.

Even despite the stray light from Cledge's flashlight behind him, Dubykky soon could make out nothing ahead at all and had to extend one hand in front while running the other along the wall. He wished he had his Zippo with him, a thought that reminded him of Junior. What was the young echo doing just then? Dubykky stopped, displeased that his mind was wandering. He felt through his pockets until he found a book of matches. He opened the flap, twisted off a match, felt for the scratch pad, and struck it. At the flare of light the voices behind him, just audible, fell silent. Mildred began inching into the passageway.

The match burned for six seconds before Dubykky waved it out. Its light revealed the end of the passageway, twenty feet ahead and three feet upslope. Beyond it was the fallout shelter, but nothing was discernible there yet. He continued forward, feeling along the wall until it cornered. He lit a second match and found himself standing at the step-down entrance. The door opened easily, silently, into the side of a room.

Even in the match's flickering light, it was obvious the shelter was spacious, bigger than a one-car garage. He noted that while searching for a light switch. It was right next to the entrance, in a metal box at the end of conduit. Flipping the switch had no effect, however. He dropped the match just as he felt Mildred's hand on his back.

"Is Milt coming?" he asked, lighting another match and holding it up to her. Mildred just shrugged, knitting her brows in puzzlement. Though she couldn't, he understood Cledge's hesitation. Even if the prospect of crawling through a narrow tunnel into an unknown room wasn't daunting, that they were also breaking a host of laws made him too apprehensive.

Handing back the book of matches to her, he said, "Look for candles. There should be some near the door." To the left was a small chest of drawers, to the right a steamer trunk. Dubykky opened the trunk and held the match over it. And immediately closed it. At the bottom lay a jumble of knives, bars, hooks, rags, and sheets. All bloody.

Mildred found a candle and lit it. Dripping wax on a small ledge at shoulder height, she affixed it. She lit a second candle and held it up, scanning the room. In addition to the trunk and chest of drawers it held only two plain wooden chairs. Halfway around, she stopped and sucked in her breath. A wide reddish-brown stain, big as a bathtub, fanned out from the center of the north wall. Or rather, from the door that was there. Dubykky took the candle from Mildred and squatted. It looked as if several stains overlapped.

"You'd better go back," he said.

Mildred ignored him. "That's a lot of blood." It was in the tone of stating a fact. But lit upward by the candle her face seemed taut and eyeless. Why was she so calm? Though tense, she appeared almost to be enjoying herself. Did evil have too strong a pull on her? Should he worry? Or should he be pleased that she showed such spine? He decided on worry.

"Go check on Milt."

"He's fine," she said automatically.

But he wasn't. They heard a distant crash. Mildred started and looked away from the blood in alarm. They turned toward the passageway together. The glow from Cledge's flashlight disappeared as a clank and heavy thud sounded.

An instant later, air whooshed up the passageway and made the candle in Dubykky's hand gutter.

"Milt's closed us in! That was the washing machine falling back into place." Mildred was incredulous rather than frightened, but he shushed her nonetheless, passing her the candle.

"Aren't you—" Dubykky shushed her more violently and shot her a warning look, then motioned her aside. Getting the other candle and holding it behind a cupped hand, he stepped away from the passageway, too. The candlelight probably was too feeble to illuminate the cracks around the trapdoor, but there was no use taking chances.

Pantomiming for her to suck in a deep breath and hold it, he stilled himself completely, reaching out with his senses. He shut his eyes. At first the silence was complete, except for Mildred's heartbeat and a gurgle from her stomach. Slowly, though muted almost to nothing by the surrounding concrete and earth, two disturbances reached him.

The first was auditory. From down the passageway and beyond the trapdoor he heard voices. Dubykky could make out nothing of what was being said but enough of the tone to know that one voice, or set of voices, was commanding, a second appeasing, and that was information enough. The import was obvious. The commanding voices, probably belonging to police, were taking control of Cledge. He was the appeasing one, probably reassuring them that, in the timeless phrase, "this is all a mistake."

But still—interesting! Cledge had had the presence of mind to shut the trapdoor before the police got into the basement, thus saving Mildred and him from being caught, too.

Good man, Dubykky cheered. Now can you keep your face from revealing us under questioning? He was dubious about that and so was surprised and relieved when the voices faded out entirely without the trapdoor being reopened. I knew it, he thought with satisfaction. There *was* more to his partner than the soul of a rockhound and the face of a mime.

The second disturbance was entirely different. It brought nothing having to do with the five senses. Rather, it was a whiff in the mind, a gray mist of despair. And it sickened Dubykky. It came from behind the closed door, not the passageway. It came like the last air molecule vibrating from an old, old scream.

"Will? *Will*?" Mildred's hiss was desperate.

When he opened his eyes, she was squinting frantically in his direction, holding her candle up high. He moved his hand away from his own candle, and she focused on him. "I looked away from you just once, and you turned into a ghost! For a second there, I couldn't see you. Gosh, it was spooky."

She gazed around the shelter in fright for the first time. "This place—well, I don't understand the feel of it, Will. It's like—a tomb or something."

Finally, Dubykky thought, she's having a proper human reaction. But his relief ended when she stepped toward the door behind the blood stain.

Dubykky moved fast to place himself between it and her. "It's just the candlelight," he said in his best offhand tone. "Makes everything look like a cheap horror movie." She smiled wanly at that. "Maybe we ought to get that trapdoor open again and see what happened to Milt. I thought I heard voices."

It was a disingenuous remark, and they both knew it. For now Cledge was on his own. Her concern for him was not about to displace her curiosity. They had to open the door. They had to see what lay behind it. There was no turning back.

Yet too, Dubykky recognized a tone of genuine worry for Milt when Mildred replied, "Don't be ridiculous." Then, "Something bad happened here. This is exactly what we came here for. Blood, Will—*blood* in the Gans house. Evidence, Will. But you're right that we should hurry. What if it was the police you heard? That means Milt's on his way to jail. We can't leave him on his own."

Blocking her view, he turned the door handle. It turned, but the door did not open at once. He tugged and tugged until with a sucking inrush of air, it swung outward.

The stench that flowed out made them both stagger back. Mildred swayed, then went down on hands and knees and vomited by the wall. But when he went to her, she waved him back, speaking through clenched teeth. "I'm fine. Just took me by surprise."

"Breathe shallowly. Through your mouth," he advised. She only grimaced and pushed herself up the wall to her feet.

It was the odor of decomposed human bodies, tacky-sweet, cloying, damply rancid. The final adieus of the flesh. Dubykky recognized it all too well. He had smelled the worst of smells: abattoirs, lutefisk, the corpse plant, garbage dumps, sulfur works, open city sewers on a torrid day. None of them came close to the visceral disgust that a long-dead corpse provokes.

He stepped to the threshold and thrust his candle inside. Mildred rested her chin on his shoulder to get a clear view, too. Originally, the space had been meant to be the shelter's larder. It was about eight feet wide by four feet deep. On the back wall were brackets that must have once supported shelving. What they now supported was too grisly even for Mildred. She uttered a strangled cry.

Four bodies, in different stages of decay, hung from the wall. Even naked, they were not obviously the remains of girls except by size. They appeared to be hung from left to right in order of death. The leftmost one looked like a paper bag that had once held fish and chips and was misshapen because of the grease. Skins sloughed downward, pulling away from the collarbone in a scalloped pattern and bunched at the ankles and one wrist. Some of it was dry and papery, some deep brown, especially around areas of the gut where gas had burst through the skin, which opened a view into the trunk. Ribs were visible and the glutinous remnants of unidentifiable organs. On the floor below was a pool of oily liquid, partly dried into a chalky substance, and a nearly fleshless arm. The head hung down on the chest, barely attached, the yellow hair stained brown and tangled. Dubykky was glad he couldn't see the face.

The next two bodies, although in firmer shape, were marred by so many cuts and tears that they were like Raggedy Ann dolls. He held the candle closer. Through the tangled curtain of black curly hair on one, half of the mouth was visible. A chill ran through Dubykky, and Mildred finally backed away, hastily. From the corner of the mouth ran a two-inch-long cut similar to the scar beside Junior's mouth. The last corpse, the only one that was indisputably female, had a matching cut.

Probable sexual abuse, certain torture and mutilation, and murder

—Gans was a human monster of the worst kind, the kind who enjoyed killing slowly and personally after taking all hope, all freedom, from his victims.

Dubykky backed out and shut the door silently. Mildred was sobbing and retched once more.

"Oh, Will, that little girl's mouth is slit just—" She gulped and paused. "It reminds me so of that little boy who came into my library. The one we saw during the picnic."

Dubykky was still stunned by the sight of the corpses, and that was extraordinary indeed. There were very few sights that could leave him stunned. So much deranged cruelty, so much perverted desire—how could a human go so wrong?

It was the brazen audacity of monsters like Gans that particularly unnerved him. To leave the corpses where they eventually would be discovered, their decay slowed in the dry air of a sealed room—it was like a display of trophies, just so that sometime someone would find them and guess that Gans was responsible. That, to a monster, was appealing. Just the prospect of discovery sweetened his murderous appetite.

"Will, it's getting awfully stuffy in here." Mildred's voice was broken.

He sniffed. Oh.

So wrapped up was he in the charnel-house sight of the bodies, he had not paid attention. With the passageway door closed, two breathers, two smoky candles, and the fetid odor from the bodies, the air in the shelter was getting rank. "Put out your candle, Milly. And follow me." Crouching, he led her through the passageway to the shaft. There he handed his candle to her and climbed. It didn't occur to him until he had positioned himself to push up the trapdoor with his shoulders that someone might still be waiting in the basement.

"Milly," he whispered. "Step into the passageway and block the candlelight from the shaft."

Her face, bathed in the light, frowned. Then she understood and complied. Dubykky went silent once more, pushing his awareness outward for any living presence besides Mildred. And sure enough, there it was, above and to the left. But who? Dubykky doubted that a police officer had remained behind on the off chance of catching someone besides Cledge. He was confident that Cledge wouldn't reveal their presence. So, if not a police officer, then a neighbor. Almost surely that meant old Sanderman.

He probably had his pistol with him—and was eager to find someone the police had missed. Both feeble and jumpy—in other words, trigger-happy. What a silly predicament for Dubykky. He didn't relish getting shot, but he was worried about Mildred above all.

Climbing back down, he whispered into her ear that someone might be waiting for them in the basement and not to come out of the passageway until he called for her. He made her promise to stay put. Twice.

"Okay, okay." She was growing testy. "But hurry, Will. It's getting hard to breathe, and the candle will burn out soon."

What to do about Sanderman? Reasoning with him would be futile, especially when he saw it was Dubykky emerging from the hole. Going into stony stillness again after getting past the trapdoor wasn't likely to help either. In a concrete basement, even a poorly aimed pistol shot might ricochet and hit him. So, it had to be surprise and direct assault. Dubykky disliked having to jump people, even an idiotic Commie-baiter like Sanderman. Reckless interference, nuisance, wasted effort—that was all old fools like him accomplished. If Mildred hadn't been with him and Milt hadn't been in need of rescue soon, he would simply have breathed shallow and waited Sanderman out. Yet there was nothing for it now. He had to move.

Returning to the trapdoor, Dubykky braced his feet securely, hooking his shoe heels on the third rung down. He took a slow, deep, steadying breath and shoved his shoulders upward with all his might. The trapdoor tilted upward, he pushed a foot against the opposite wall of the shaft for more leverage and lunged backward, and the washing machine hit the floor with a crash. Pivoting on his hands, Dubykky swung his feet up and out of the shaft and then stretched flat and rolled sideways.

Suddenly, Dubykky was tired, sick of bodies and fools, annoyed almost beyond endurance. Yet once again Mildred had routed his patience. What would happen, he suddenly wondered, had he not killed rogue echoes, and they all lived on and on, producing generation after generation of offspring like Silly Milly? Dozens upon dozens of them without Dubykky to curb their waywardness. He shuddered and forced the thought away.

Sanderman shouted, "Got you, you bastard!" A flashlight snapped on, and almost at the same time a loud, scratchy boom rang out. It was Sanderman's .45 pistol, its report magnified by the concrete walls and floor. Clang! The bullet struck the washing machine, missing Dubykky by inches. Dubykky dismissed all caution. Vaulting to his feet, he charged at Sanderman.

He needn't have bothered. Before he got two steps, the flashlight fell to the floor, followed by the pistol. Sanderman staggered. At first Dubykky thought the old man had been struck by his own bullet, but it would have had to ricochet at least twice off concrete, and there would not have been enough momentum left to do any damage. He grabbed up the flashlight and shined it on the old man. He had gone down on one knee, looking both surprised and angry. He blinked heavily a couple of times while his lips writhed as though trying to grasp something slippery. Then he pitched sideways and was still.

"Will? Will! Are you okay? What happened?" Dubykky swung the flashlight beam around to Mildred, who was already climbing out of the shaft.

"Milly, you gave your word!" He was outraged. Would she never have the sense to keep herself out of harm's way?

"But—Will, oh, I thought you were—!" A sob followed.

Dubykky blew out a breath theatrically and examined Sanderman. Stroke, heart attack, he couldn't tell. But the eyes were fixed, and there was no pulse. Dead is dead. "Well," he said softly to the corpse, "you saved me the chore."

"Who's he?" Mildred gaped at Sanderman, fascinated.

"The next-door neighbor," Dubykky explained. "And we can't leave him here."

"Why isn't he moving?"

"He's dead, Milly."

"Did you kill him?"

Suddenly, Dubykky was tired, sick of bodies and fools, annoyed almost beyond endurance. Yet once again Mildred had routed his patience.

"No," he seethed. "He had a heart attack. He frightened himself to death with his own gun. And you're about to give me a heart attack with damn fool questions and total disregard of doing what you're told for your own good. Now take the flashlight, pick up the pistol—don't touch that trigger!—and follow me."

When Dubykky pulled Sanderman over his shoulder and stood, the weight was unexpectedly slight, but any relief Dubykky might have taken from that was canceled by the long fart that sputtered from the body. Mildred giggled from fluster.

In half a millennium, he groused to himself, this has got to be the most revolting, absurd day ever. Humans! Who needs them! He followed Mildred up the basement stairs, lugging the body. As he trotted across the driveway, snuck into Sanderman's house, and tucked the body neatly in bed, instructing Mildred to stow the pistol in the back of a cluttered closet, he indulged in longing for his favorite respite from this sort of witless human folly. War and its—by comparison—simple, lucid, incisive rationality.

Nine

Halfway back to the motel, Mildred finally got the jitters. She jerked up in the car seat as if awakening from a trance.

"My God, Will. Those poor children. It's like they were butchered! How could anyone do that? Could Matt Gans have actually done that?"

Dubykky no longer felt the need to be cautious. "Yes," he said. "All four." He no longer had to pretend to himself that Gonzales should remain a suspect.

"Who knows how many more!" she wondered.

"None."

He felt her eyes on him. "How can you be sure?"

"Think, Milly. The news stories you got for me, the map, the timing. We can rest assured there are no other victims," he replied. "So far." But that was not what made him so confident. Four murders of exactly the same sort—the threshold for an echo. Junior, who would contrive to be the fifth. Though that was proof enough that Gans had killed no more in Los Angeles, Dubykky would keep it to himself.

"Who's going to stop him?" Again, Mildred spoke as if talking to herself.

"He'll be stopped. Don't you doubt that. I'll—we'll—make sure."

Mildred gaped. "And that poor old man. Who was he?"

"A fool at death's door."

"Will! What a nasty thing to say."

"But true. He was a man blighted by loneliness, narrowness, and a disposition to magnify threats. The world will not miss him."

Mildred spluttered, "That's—that's unfeeling and cynical. Every man has some good in him."

Unfeeling—true. Dubykky had long ceased to offer compassion to people petrified by hatred. As for the goodness in every person, he couldn't judge. Evil arose with humanity. *That* he knew. It was latent in all humans. That so many lived their lives without it manifesting might be considered a sort of collective goodness, he supposed. But he was not prepared to acknowledge it.

"What the world needs is more Milton Cledges," he said to divert her.

She nodded. "Milt was so brave and quick-witted. He kept us from getting arrested. That's a good thing. But then if we had, we wouldn't have found those hideous bodies. I wish we hadn't." She wrapped her arms around herself. "I'm so confused, Will."

He was glad she recognized it, though he doubted—with half his mind—she would remember it for long. The other half was still preoccupied with Junior. Where was he at that moment?

The answer would have dumbfounded even Dubykky. That very moment, Junior was lying in the bed of Judge Dorothy Younger's guest room. He was staring at the shadowy ceiling and the languid reflections of moonlight there, holding still as she had instructed him in order to "get a good night's sleep." What made a night's sleep good? Her motivation for bringing him into the house was beyond him. Somehow, he concluded, she was acting on behalf of Kind Sir. It didn't matter anyway. The bed was softer than the floor of his tent, and she promised to feed him in the morning, which would save him time and trouble. Jurgen was perched on a bedpost, rumbling faintly in his sleep. Junior was content, even though he sensed that his life was rapidly drawing to an end, an all-important end.

THE MANAGER had left a message pinned to Dubykky's door at the Musketeer Motel. It told him to expect a phone call at 6 a.m., two hours from now. Nothing more, yet it could only have been a message forwarded from the police trying to set up Cledge for his one phone conversation. Dubykky shooed Mildred off to her room to get some sleep and settled in a chair to wait.

Although he could do little about Gans so early in the morning, there was much to think about. Not about Gans. That issue was settled as far as Dubykky was concerned. A crux was coming. He sensed it. When Gans was on the verge of striking again—and by Dubykky's estimate that would occur soon—Junior would be drawn to him. Only after they met, should Gans survive, would Dubykky have to act. Or if Junior survived.

That second possibility made him unhappy. Junior was such a quick-learning, demure, appealing young echo. But it was the natural course of echoes, however likable, to die with their victims. It was better that Junior meet that fate, for otherwise Dubykky would have to end Junior's life himself.

Yet what compelled him? Of all the echoes he had encountered, including the few he had had to dispatch himself, not one showed the depravity of their creators. Apart from killing that one person, a single act of balancing justice, each echo was as careful of other people as were real humans—more so, really. Think of Victor Warden: a loving husband and father, hard working, and selfless enough to volunteer to defend his country in two wars. Though spawned by evil, did Warden really add evil to the world? He killed, yes. Out of compulsion. Did that condemn him, or did it counterbalance his dark origin and destiny?

As for Dubykky, the human immune system provided an analogy. After the response to an infection, when the body's various killer cells attacked and destroyed the invaders, a small subset remained to deactivate the others lest they turn on the body itself and create disease of their own. Autoimmune disease. Dubykky liked to think of himself as a deactivator. He protected the body of humanity from the aftermath of evil. Analogies proved nothing, of course, and he wondered whether he really understood anything of evil at all. Yet the notion gave him heart.

The simple truth was that, however ineluctably, he was driven to destroy rogue echoes, just as he was willing to help any offspring they produced. He wanted to protect Mildred and now Dorothy Younger. That compulsion was not so mysterious. He had no duty to kill them, and they shared something of his nature. Cousins in evil, if many times removed. So why not help?

The thought of Younger brought to mind her grandmother, Hortense May. Was she still alive? Was she like Dubykky? Or did she follow a different path? Might a rogue evolve an evil all her own? He could not think of her as a distant relation to protect, in any case. A rogue echo had to die.

Echoes would damage human society, perhaps irreparably. Good-natured, attractive, selfless? Immortal? Humans would regard them as gods. Cults would arise, manipulated by the power-hungry. Established religions would denounce the echoes as evil, correctly so. Conflict would follow, then division, war, and chaos, because nothing was more inimical to a heavenly god than godlike creatures in the flesh.

Dubykky slowed his breathing and calmed his mind. He was drifting from the practical matters at hand, which were Dubykky-Gans, Mildred-Cledge, and Younger. Maybe Younger-somebody. He would fill in that blank later, as needed. For now there was nothing he could do. A look at his watch told him he had an hour more to wait, at least. He let himself pass into a light doze.

UNLIKE HIS BROTHERS, George Patton and William Halsey, Douglas MacArthur Gans was never comfortable with his parents. George had a cruel streak like their father and was otherwise cold-hearted like their mother; he got along fine. Billy largely ignored them, giving his all to sports. For some reason, Dougie couldn't stand cruelty. It made him sad, not powerful. And though he liked sports, they didn't occupy his mind as they did Billy's. His parents were still the foundation of his life, he couldn't ignore them, but they kept him confused. Guessing. His mother might pay almost no attention for two solid weeks, and then, in a complete turn-around, she would be hugging him and asking him how he was and feeding him his favorite foods for a whole day at a time. The next day, back to frigid disregard.

But it was his father who made him really uneasy. He was always friendly and smiling but did mean things. Like painting Dougie's Schwinn yellow so it would be easier to see. For safety, Dad claimed. But it made the other kids laugh at him. Dad enjoyed that. Or for instance, if Dougie didn't clean his plate fast enough, making him take it to bed with him. Or like making Dougie watch as his father killed their dog's puppies with a paring knife. Dougie had to be sure never to cry and always, always to answer questions right away.

Even if he was afraid to. Twice in the last week, his father had asked him about Sarah Muni. Sarah was a nice girl, popular in class, and smart. Dougie was a little sweet on her, from a distance. They weren't close friends. Not going-to-each-other's-birthday-party friends. Certainly not, since his parents would never let an Indian into the house. Still, he didn't want her to be subject to his Dad's attention. When his Dad asked about Sarah, something came into his eyes. It was like the look that came to George's eyes when he saw a very fancy sports car—an intensity that made Dougie afraid. He was afraid for Sarah. He was afraid as he had been afraid after his sister, Lucy, disappeared. Why had his parents not seemed to care much?

Dougie had answered his father's questions, and right away. But he hadn't said a lot. Just enough so that Dad didn't pinch him on the ear more than once.

Now, standing out of sight in the hallway well past bedtime, he was listening in on a conversation between his father and mother. He had heard similar conversations before. They always spoke of vacations, but Dougie worried that they weren't really talking about vacations. They were talking about something else while seeming to talk about vacations.

"I'm restless, Misty. I need a small adventure." His father's voice had a strange overtone, almost as though he were teasing his wife.

"You just had a vacation before we came to Hawthorne. It's too soon. We have to be careful about expenses. And there's the boys to think of. It's not as if they could come."

His mother's voice was wheedling, thin. He heard a chuckle from his father.

"No. True. A vacation isn't for them. Well, maybe George, huh?" His father mused, then continued, "But everything's fine and dandy. We're safe and sound. In the pink. Best of all, my campsite is all set. It would be a shame for it to go to waste. Just one short adventure there. That's what I need to calm my nerves. Besides, you like a little fun as well as I do."

There was a silence. His mother sounded as though she didn't especially care now. She said softly after a pause, "Do you have any particular theme in mind?"

"I do." His father sounded pleased. "A perfect theme. Local. Exactly the right way to get to know the culture." He laughed. "Did you know that Indian tribes have lived around the lake for thousands of years?" There was a rustling of paper, then his father said, "See how my campsite would be perfect? It even looks like an Indian cave. We're all set."

His mother didn't answer. His father went on, "It won't last long, probably. You know how these things go. A person can only take so much adventure. Besides, I'll have to get back to work Monday." There was another chuckle.

Dougie didn't like that chuckle and suddenly was terrified for Sarah Muni. But what to do? He couldn't bear to hear any more and crept back to his room. Billy was asleep, breathing roughly. But he felt George's eyes on him from across the hall as he slipped through his door. And though George said nothing, Dougie expected there would be trouble in the future. Whatever he did for Sarah, it would have to be soon.

The next morning, Dougie set off walking to school instead of riding with Dad and his brothers. There was nothing unusual about this. The middle school and high school were side by side on the edge of town, whereas his elementary school was near the center. His father did not begrudge him rides but let him walk if he wanted to. So Dougie informed his mother, who glanced at him coldly, and rushed out the door.

It was all to avoid George, or more questions from Dad, but beside that Dougie liked to walk through town. Hawthorne was better than Los Angeles in important ways. Most important were the dogs. In West L.A., around his neighborhood, dogs were uncommon and were either kept inside the house or in the backyard. In Hawthorne, dogs were everywhere and happy. He liked dogs. And they liked him. As he went down the street, Hawthorne having few sidewalks, dogs took up the morning hello to him in yips, barks, howls, and woofs. Many came running out for a sniff and pat; even the mean dogs grrred just a couple of times, for the sake of show, before trotting up to him.

The second biggest point of improvement was that in Hawthorne all the kids were about the same. There were bullies, to be sure, and pretty girls and doofuses and whizzes, but they were poor bullies, poor pretty girls, poor doofuses, and poor whizzes. They belonged together. Nobody pretended not to see another person because there was too much difference in their parents' size of house or type of car. Dougie fit in with them, even with those who had a notion to beat him up.

So it was eerie that the dogs stopped barking after a couple blocks. Not a single one was to be seen either. He cut down an alley because the dogs were usually livelier in the alleyways. Nothing. Neither dogs nor barking.

Halfway through, Dougie froze, for a person stepped out of a backyard gate, a person who unmistakably did not belong in Hawthorne.

It was hard to figure exactly why, but the first sign was the bird. It was a boy with a crow on his shoulder. That was exceptional anywhere. The boy stopped ten feet away from Dougie and stared. His clothes were new and fit well, a bright white shirt, plaid bow tie, and tan trousers. Too classy for normal school clothes. Yet those weren't the main difference. It was his face. It did not belong to a boy's body. It was square and had a lot of brown hair badly plastered down, and there was a small, ugly scar in a corner of the mouth, but above all it was the expression. Level, patient, unconcerned, passive, appraising—something like those perceptions passed through Dougie's mind in a rush.

"Hello?" he said tentatively. The boy's expression did not change. "Are you new here?"

"I am new everywhere," said the boy. His voice was deep, uninflected.

"Where do you come from?"

"Where? Oh, that I were where I would be, then would I be where I am not? But where I am, there I must be, and where I would be I cannot."

The answer reminded Dougie vaguely of poetry, but he wasn't sure. He was sure, though, that no boy he ever knew spoke in poetry. And it didn't tell him anything.

"My name's Doug Gans. What's yours?"

Finally, the boy's face revealed something. A slight narrowing of the eyes, a yet slighter lift of the brows. Signifying what? A glint of interest or a memory or a calculation or an intention? How to tell which?

"I am Junior. Jurgen is Jurgen." The boy pointed, and the crow rose up and flared its wings, at which Dougie took a step backwards.

"You have a pet crow?" Dougie was impressed that the bird seemed to recognize its name.

"I have Jurgen. Jurgen has me. That is where we want to be."

That answer didn't strike Dougie as apropos either.

In any case, Junior barely paused before asking, "Do you know Kind Sir? Do you know Sweet Auntie Younger?"

To both questions Dougie shook his head no, mystified.

"Do you live in the house of Mr. Matt Gans and Mrs. Misty Gans?"

Dougie was liking the conversation less and less. "They're my parents. Dad's a teacher at the high school."

"Don't know much about history. Don't know much biology. Don't know much about a science book," said Junior.

Dougie recognized the lyrics from a popular song and ventured a smile. It was not returned. There was only the purposeful stare. Was he in for a fight? It was always a possibility. Being a teacher's kid, a TK, meant that Dougie sometimes had to fight another boy because of something his father did to the kid's older brother that Dougie did not even know about. He prepared himself. But Junior did not make a move toward him. He hardly did anything but breathe.

"Do you know my dad?" It seemed like an inane question, yet Dougie asked it for want of anything better to say. He considered turning and running, though if word got back to George or his father that he had backed down from a fight, he would pay for it.

"I know Kind Sir, I know Jurgen, I know Sarah Muni, I know Sweet Auntie Younger, I know the book lady." With a jerky movement, Junior raised one arm in the air and waved it about. "If wishes were fishes, we'd swim in the sea. I wish to meet Mr. Matthew Gans."

"You know Sarah? She's swell."

Junior only blinked at him.

Dougie wished that he could get away from the weird boy, and right now. He realized, too, that he was going to be late if he didn't set off at once.

He pointed past Junior, down the alley. "I have to get to school."

"I like Sarah," Junior said and stepped aside.

As Dougie walked past, relieved yet still on guard, the crow emitted a modest *grree-ik*. The sound made him quicken his pace. He kept his eyes straight ahead until he reached the end of the alley, then glanced back. It was empty.

AFTER THE PHONE CALL, Dubykky did not go straight to the county jail, where Cledge was waiting in a holding area until he was processed into the jail proper or bailed out. He agreed that Dubykky should call Assistant District Attorney Boyden Smoot first.

On the phone Smoot started off brusque, as might any public servant when telephoned early on a Saturday about something related to his work. Then he was incredulous when told that his old friend had been arrested in West Los Angeles for breaking into the basement of a house.

"Milton Cledge? An impossibility. He wouldn't even jaywalk," Smoot insisted.

Dubykky convinced him that it was true nonetheless and that moreover Cledge's appearance in jail was due to an investigation that Smoot would find of great interest. Smoot could sense that he was being lured into something but still agreed to meet Dubykky at a café for Cledge's sake.

Dubykky considered taking Mildred along but decided against it. She was still asleep in her room and needed to make up sleep after the last couple of days. More than that, though, he worried she would prove a distraction to Smoot when they met to discuss Cledge.

Why did the offspring of evil have to be so attractive? It was nearly always an inconvenience. Dubykky left a note and drove into downtown L.A.

To Dubykky's delight, the café was chic and lively, a refurbished 1920s-era railway dining car. Not what he expected a bureaucrat to choose. The interior was cool and shadowed, swing jazz playing in the background, and the booths were crammed with loud-talking professional people in their twenties and thirties. Dubykky fit right in. And so did Smoot, even if he was the unlikeliest of the up-and-comers there.

As instructed, Dubykky sought him in a corner booth. Smoot rose to shake his hand and gestured for him to sit opposite. In several ways, he was Cledge's opposite. Smoot was short without seeming small, stocky in the way of a weight-lifter, and thoroughly measured in demeanor. His head was large and looked wider than it really was because his ears stuck out. That might have looked comical on another head, but Smoot's brow was heavy and dark, his brown eyes peering from deep sockets, guarded and intense. He had a bald pate and heavy beard shadow on his jaw and cheeks. But, unlike Edward G. Robinson, who otherwise might have served in a comparison, Smoot had thin lips and a slight overbite. He projected easy competence and moved with a contained, graceful confidence. When he leveled his eyes on Dubykky, after they made their orders, there was no pretense of chumminess or patience. He was simply receptive. No one could but mark him as a man who fully expected to succeed in life.

It seemed unlikely to Dubykky that Cledge should regard this man as a close friend, an alter ego. He wondered if perhaps Cledge had simply deluded himself. That turned out not to be the case.

Dubykky opened the conversation, "Being in a law practice with Milt is like having the town crier for a partner."

Smoot nodded, grinning slightly. It was an affectionate reaction.

"But Milt is smart, trustworthy, and braver even than he realizes."

Another nod. "You're here to tell me about the 'braver' part," Smoot said. He leaned forward on his elbows.

"I am. There are two reasons for it. The first you'll just have to make a note of for now. Milt is in love." At Smoot's astonishment, Dubykky raised a hand to check questions. "The second is that he and I—with a certain pretty girl's help—believe we've uncovered evidence of a serial murderer living in our town. That's Hawthorne, over the border in central Nevada. A murderer who recently moved from this area."

"And in whose former house Milt was just arrested?"

"Yes."

Smoot pressed back into the seat cushion when the waiter arrived with their coffees and donuts. Stirring cream into his cup, he broke off an arc of donut and nibbled at it.

He said, "Milt is no fool, despite his quirks. And he wouldn't lightly undertake anything dishonest even if he is head-over-heels in love. So it's only because I am confident it's true that I'll continue to listen to you for at least two more minutes, so long as you tell me something that I can accept as just as true. Keep in mind, also, that I am a sworn officer of the court. Lie to me, mislead me, withhold facts from me at your peril. Your relationship with Cledge will not protect you. Got it?"

Dubykky gestured two palms up, *of course*. "The man we're investigating is named Matthew Gans. Last August, he moved from Paisley Street in West Los Angeles to Hawthorne to take up a job as auto shop teacher at the high school. He previously taught the same subject here in L.A., at University High School. His former house lies at almost the exact center of a triangle formed by the residences of three young girls who disappeared in the last two years." Dubykky recited the names. "He kidnapped and killed them. He killed his own daughter as well."

Frowning, Smoot peered doubtfully at Dubykky. "How do you know that? Speak precisely."

"By the fact that four decomposing corpses of young girls are hanging in a converted fallout shelter in the backyard."

Smoot stiffened and said, low and urgent. "Keep your voice down!"

"Why?" asked Dubykky innocently. "Do reporters frequent this place?"

Smoot made a dismissive, chopping motion with one hand. "This is not a matter for levity, Mr. Dubykky. You saw these bodies yourself?"

"Yes. When the police arrived at the house, Milt closed the hidden entrance to the fallout shelter and pretended he had broken in on his own. He was protecting me and the girl he's in love with."

Because of Smoot's incredulous reaction, he rushed on, describing the hatch below the washing machine, the tunnel to the shelter, its layout, and what he had found behind the larder door. He tried to pass quickly over Mildred's role. Smoot was already a seasoned prosecutor, however, and questioned Dubykky until he was satisfied about her presence. Satisfied but disapproving.

"How did you learn that there would be bodies in the shelter?"

"A surmise." Dubykky described Mildred's research and their mapping of disappearances in the L.A. area.

"Mr. Dubykky, you surely realize that you can't avoid the most important question for long. Out with it."

"Why did I suspect Matthew Gans in the first place."

Smoot nodded once, a sharp, vehement yes.

A good prosecutor doesn't care about the substance of lies so much as the motive for lying. Dubykky considered carefully. What he couldn't tell Smoot, because the man wouldn't believe it, was the truth: you live in a world where human evil creates a backlash, and I am an example, an echo of evil; I suspect Gans of being an evildoer who has created an echo like me. It wouldn't do. Nor would it work to be evasive with Smoot. He would sense that something was being hidden from him. The result would be at best wasted time and at worst legal trouble for Dubykky. So he suppressed his natural impulse—a clever lie.

"I'm going to tell you only what I want you to know, and if that's unacceptable, so be it. I am a lawyer in a small town. I pay attention to those around me, both for professional and personal reasons. I have a particular sensitivity to people who are hiding something important. Why I have this ability I won't go into. But I sensed something devious and sinister in Gans, so I looked into his background. What I found worried me. It still does. I'm worried about the safety of local children. So I came here to discover if my worries are merited. I came with Milt Cledge because he is familiar with Los Angeles. I came with Mildred Warden because I want her and Milt to fall in love and get married, a secondary motive but a real one."

Smoot's glower told Dubykky that not all of his statement was acceptable without further explanation.

Dubykky was not about to give it and went on, "Make of all that what you will. The important thing is that I was right. Gans is a serial kidnapper and murderer of children. Possibly for sexual reasons. I can lead you to the bodies. I am telling you all this mostly because I want your help getting a warrant for Gans's arrest so that he can be detained pending extradition and thereby remove a vicious threat from my community."

When Dubykky started the last sentence, it was as a matter of course, something he would be expected to say. Saying it, though, it sounded like an excellent idea. Get Gans locked up and away from children. Junior would track him down wherever he was, even in jail.

Smoot said, "You've already told me where the bodies are. Why do I need you to lead me there?"

"It'll save time. And if we take along the police, it'll provide you with an excuse to get Milt released from jail. You can cite him as a confidential source who led you to the find. With all the attention that the discovery will make in the newspapers, radio, and TV, his presence can easily be swept under the carpet. Isn't that the best thing for your old friend? Besides, he'll want you to get all the credit."

Everything that Dubykky had said aimed at ending with those last three words, all the credit. Although Smoot appeared uninterested, Dubykky could almost feel the dart of credit thunk home in his soul. Smoot finished his coffee and donut without replying.

"The average interval between kidnappings has been seven and half months. Nine months have now passed. Gans is about to strike again. I'm sure of it. So time is of the essence, Mr. Smoot. Let's get going."

Smoot grunted and shook his head slowly, but it wasn't a refusal. "Mr. Dubykky, I'm going to take a chance on this, only because Milt is my friend. You obviously think I'm just another ambitious legal functionary who will rise to the bait of 'credit.' And to an extent you're right. But friendship counts with me. If Milt weren't involved, I'd simply have you arrested for suspicion of murder and let things work out through the judicial system. You, I don't care about. But Milt doesn't deserve the trouble you seem to have led him into. You just keep that in mind during the next few hours. So then, let's go to the county lockup."

"No. First I want to pick up his girlfriend. You'll see why."

Smoot followed him to the Musketeer Motel. As Dubykky drove he reviewed their conversation in his mind, an unsatisfactory performance on his part. Whatever credit should come his way for the Gans affair, however much he helped out Cledge, Smoot was not the sort of man to let matters rest. He would remain interested in Dubykky, and that could not be good. It was one more reason why Dubykky had to disappear from Hawthorne after Junior fulfilled his destiny and Gans was dead. Leave and become a new person in a new place. It was a wearisome prospect, although he was long accustomed to moving on every twenty years or so. It meant, moreover, that he would have to leave Mildred in good hands. To ensure that, the upcoming meeting between her and Cledge at the jail would be pivotal.

The introduction between Mildred and Smoot was everything he hoped for. When Dubykky knocked on her motel room door, she flew through it, angrily demanding, "Where's Milt?" Then she saw Smoot and checked herself. His eyes popped at her. Yes, Dubykky said to him silently, this is the woman who's falling in love with Milton Cledge. Or so I intend.

When he introduced them, Mildred bestowed on Smoot one of her breathtaking smiles. "Milt has told us so much about you," she lied. He practically purred. Knowing Mildred, Dubykky fully expected she could have stood there chatting to the bedazzled Smoot for an hour, Cledge all but forgotten, unless he asserted himself.

"And right now Milt is rotting in jail," he said to them.

Smoot started, then snorted at "rotting."

"The county jail is a fine facility," he grumbled, then grumbled some more when Dubykky insisted that Mildred ride with him. But at last they were in their cars and on their way.

MATT GANS had made his choice. The bright-eyed little Paiute was the winner of Maybe You. Hands down. No doubt about it.

Of all the girls he had studied in Hawthorne, she showed the most exotic spirit. And she was open, curious, which made things easier for him. The question now was exactly when. Soon. And exactly how. That was trickier.

Sarah Muni walked home after school, sometimes stopping at the Fish and Wildlife office to see her father, but more often not. Home was an eleven-block walk. Somewhere during it he could make his move, but he would have to be careful. Morning before school? After school? The morning would undoubtedly be safer. Other adults would be occupied in typical morning preparations for the day or already on their way to work. Pursuing a goal, especially one that was routine, made people unobservant.

Yet the morning was out. His absence from class at the high school would be noted. He couldn't have that. So, afternoon. But that meant waiting till Monday, and Gans didn't want to wait. It was feeling urgent in him, the need, now that he and Misty had made the decision.

Gans did a lot of waiting and normally didn't mind all that much. At that very minute he was sitting in his car waiting for Misty and Dougie to emerge from the elementary school. His other sons were at home watching baseball on the television. Gans could not remember the nature of the special Saturday afternoon assembly here, only that a parent was invited to be in attendance for some kind of performance. Wanting another opportunity to study Sarah Muni, he had offered to be the parent, but Misty surprised him. She was in one of her increasingly rare lovey-dovey moods and insisted that she accompany Dougie. That was fine with him. Anyway, he had stopped paying much attention to her mood swings. He claimed that he needed the car that morning, a self-contradiction she didn't notice, and so drove them to the event. It was for all six grades, apparently, because now that it was over, people were streaming out both the building's entrances. Gans watched.

Sarah came through the front door just ahead of Dougie. He caught up with her and tugged at the sleeve of her pretty yellow frock. Turning, she smiled at him. He said something that made her smile widen. Then Misty came out, saw the two children talking, and taking up Dougie's hand, yanked him away.

It was obvious, once she pushed Dougie into the back seat and then slammed the door, that Misty's lovey-dovey mood had evaporated. Her voice was ice hard. "Dirty little Indian girl! You're to stay away from her, Dougie. Hear me? Don't ever touch her again. Insufferable showoff! I thought Indians had to go to the Indian school."

Gans laughed at his wife. When she threw him a dark look, he winked and nodded toward the girl, which made a corner of Misty's mouth rise. She turned away then, and watched Sarah skipping lightly down the sidewalk. Dougie pressed his face to the window to watch her go, too.

He was very afraid for her now. He couldn't say exactly why. Just that he had seen his parents have the same expressions on their faces before. It was the way they looked before Dougie or Billy got a beating. But it wasn't him that they were looking at now. It was Sarah.

HOW PERFECTLY THE RECITATION had gone for Sarah! The whole crowd in the multipurpose room had clapped, happy smiles on every face, after she piped out the words with so much feeling. It made her happy to make others happy. She had been assigned a section of Longfellow's "Hiawatha," which made her father grumpy, but she enjoyed it. The words and rhythm were so beautiful together! Sarah loved the sound of it. Too bad her parents had refused to attend. She wondered if it was really because they disliked being around the other parents. Sarah couldn't understand that either. It was so natural and easy, getting along. All she had to do, she had discovered, was be happy around others, and they would be happy around her.

As she skipped along, avoiding cracks in the sidewalk, she began reciting the passage again, for fun:

> And Nokomis warned her often,
> Saying oft, and oft repeating,
> "O, beware of Mudjekeewis;
> Listen not to what he tells you;
> Lie not down upon the meadow,
> Stoop not down among the lilies,
> Lest the West-Wind come and harm you!"

She imagined herself as the beautiful Wenonah, lying in the meadow while the West-Wind wooed her with words of sweetness and soft caresses. How thrilling! Although she was a little vague on what wooing entailed. Yet clearly enough, it had something to do with boys, since the West-Wind was male, and that brought to mind Dougie Gans.

She was blocks away from the school and round a corner and just entering the courthouse park, still reciting flawlessly, though a little out of breath now, when the strange boy Junior stepped in front of her from behind a cottonwood.

"Oh, hi!" she squeaked, then giggled. "You startled me."

"I am Junior."

Sarah imitated his deep, flat voice. "And I am Sarah." She smiled, so as not to appear mean, and was about to ask where his crow was when a dry whooshing of feathers announced its arrival. Jurgen settled on Junior's right shoulder and regarded her with one eye. Recognizing her, he folded his wings and began nuzzling Junior's earlobe.

With a move so swift that it startled Sarah, Junior plunged his hand in his pocket and pulled out a short strip of raw bacon. It glistened in the sun for a second as he held it up to the crow. Jurgen gobbled it down. Sarah laughed. What fun to have a bird to feed!

Junior reflected carefully on everything he had learned during the last weeks. Something about this girl made him hesitate, uncertain. Why? For the first time he wished something just for himself. He wished Kind Sir were standing next to him, telling him how to think. Even Sweet Auntie Younger might be of help, for Junior felt conflict. He understood what he must say but did not want to. Sarah waited, watching him with an odd expression.

"You know," she said, leaning her head sideways, "if you combed your hair better, and had a face that was a little skinnier—and didn't have that scar—you'd look like Dougie Gans."

This interested Junior, yet he had no idea what to make of the interest. When Jurgen pecked at him, hoping for more bacon, he lifted a forefinger to his ear to stop him. And decided.

"If Dougie's father asks you to ride, don't go. Go hide. Home again, home again, jiggety-jig."

Sarah clapped her hands. "From Mother Goose, right? That's so sweet of you." Sarah, stepping up to Junior, gave him a quick peck on his cheek, then ran away, laughing.

Slowly, Junior moved his hand and touched a finger to the spot. He wanted to smile. But did not. It was not his place to enjoy a girl's kiss.

He blinked twice. "I am here to tell you," he said to no one.

Ten

So much for patience, the primary virtue. Dubykky's was entirely obliterated. He was nearly beside himself with anxiety. He felt it deep down, beyond the realm of explanation. Time was running out. There had been too much delay. They had spent too much time in Los Angeles. Events were coming to a head, and here he was with Cledge, sullen and quiet beside him, and Mildred, in a funk in the rear seat, speeding through the Mojave desert as fast as Cledge's car could go, which wasn't fast enough.

Still, Dubykky could not imagine how he might have acted faster.

After he, Smoot, and Mildred had gone into the county jail, Smoot took charge. He was determined to handle matters his own way and turned a deaf ear to Dubykky's suggestions. In short order, he had the duty police lieutenant issuing orders for cruisers to investigate the Gans house: search for bodies of kidnapped children. An anonymous tip. A hidden chamber. A slaughterhouse tableau. Look under the basement washing machine.

The lieutenant was excited, repeating into the radio almost word for word what Smoot claimed to have gotten from the tip. The lieutenant anticipated that he could clear the books on four—at least four!

—outstanding cases, all at once. He foresaw a commendation, maybe even a promotion. The cruisers were dispatched, the lieutenant poured himself a coffee, with a little slug of something added despite the hour, and Smoot opened the subject of Milton Cledge. He began to explain that Cledge was a colleague whom he sent to look into the tip.

And Dubykky's attention was pulled away. He glanced out the office door to see Mildred chatting happily with a sergeant and two clerks, all transfixed, and went out to stop it. This was no time for her to dazzle random men, not when they needed to spring Cledge in haste.

She was in a state of high excitement, which made her face glow. This both pleased and distressed Dubykky. The excitement was at least partly because of Cledge, and that was good for romance. He dragged her into the office, but then the lieutenant and Smoot began throwing covert glances at her and stumbling in their conversation.

Dubykky took her by the arm and led her outside.

"Milly, stop being so pretty!"

She raised her eyebrows. "Oh, don't be such a fuddy-duddy. I'm not doing anything that Mother would disapprove of."

"You're distracting people. We have to get Milt and head back to Hawthorne as soon as we can."

That made her worried. "What have you heard, Will?"

He shook his head absently. "Nothing yet. But I'm concerned. Look, Milly, just do me this favor. Go sit in the car and don't talk to anybody until I get there. I have to make a phone call. Do you have any change?"

He found a pay phone in the foyer to the police station that fronted the jail complex. Why, he asked himself out of annoyance as he went through the awkward dialing, dealing with the long-distance operator, receiving the price for the first three minutes, thumbing coins into slots, and tapping his toe as the phone rang and rang, is it that improved communications increase impatience? At last he heard the receiver lift.

"Hello, Dorothy? Listen to me carefully—"

"Will? Where the hell are you? I've been calling you every hour for the last day and a half! Jesus, Will, I need your help."

"Wait, Dorothy—"

"No, you wait, William Dubykky." She spoke in the from-the-bench-tone that meant there would be no getting through to her until she had vented her mind. Dubykky puffed out his cheeks, exasperated. The human race would be better off, he sometimes thought, if one of the sexes lacked vocal cords; it didn't matter which.

She said, "Friday morning I took time off from my busy court schedule to perform the errand you so mysteriously demanded of me. I drove up to the reservoir—almost wrecked my car doing it—to deliver food to that boy. Well, he nearly gave me a heart attack. Suddenly, poof, there he was. And what a mess! Hadn't changed his clothing, hadn't bathed—hadn't behaved like a real person in who knows how long."

"Dorothy—"

"Quiet. Do you know that the boy has a pet crow? A crow, for God's sake. Sinister-looking thing." Her tone moderated. "Though charming in its way. It sounded as if it said Junior's name once. But anyway. Look, Will, I don't understand what you're up to letting that boy roam the hills out in the open like that. He needs a lot more than cans of beans. So I brought him home with me. The crow, too. I gave him real food, bought him new clothes, gave him a bath, cut up raw chicken for Jurgen, tucked him into a clean bed, told them a nice story about how good boys behave—And now they're gone! I got up in the morning, and no Junior." Her tone, though affronted, held something more. Concern, even fear.

Uh-oh. She's bonding with Junior. Dubykky rapped a knuckle on his forehead for thinking Younger incapable of it. Junior was an echo. Their common heritage was a bigger attraction than he'd thought, strong enough to overcome Dorothy Younger's fastidiousness about children. She had taken him in.

"That's one reason I'm calling. Junior may be in danger. That's why I'm in Los Angeles."

She erupted, scoffing at that, so he wasted precious seconds being patient with her while she ranted about how cold-hearted people were toward children nowadays. He lost patience.

"Save it for the campaign, Dorothy. Now listen to me. I need you to make out a bench warrant for the arrest of Matthew Gans and give it to the sheriff."

"Matthew Gans? The shop teacher? What do you mean a warrant? Are you presuming to order around the Mineral County Court?"

"Calm down, Dorothy. This is life or death, and it may affect Junior. I'm not ordering anybody to do anything, just trying to speed things up."

Now for the truth that strategically misled. "I'm in L.A. because Cledge and I had reason to believe that Gans is a murderer. And we found evidence of it in his old house. The corpses of four missing children, all brutally mutilated. I've brought in LAPD, and an assistant D.A. named Smoot will be calling you any minute now requesting the arrest and extradition."

"Wait a second, Will. Slow down. What made you think Gans is a murderer?"

"There's no time for spelling out things now, Dorothy. I *will* explain. But we also have cause to believe that Gans is about to strike again, in Hawthorne, and with Junior roaming around, he's in danger. We have to nab Gans *now*."

The phone was silent a moment.

"You have some big talking to do when you get back."

"And you'll have big thanks when the publicity for helping catch a serial murderer gets you elected. I'll be there sometime tomorrow." He hung up.

He started dialing the Mineral County Sheriff's office to give the wheel of justice another boost, but the coins remaining weren't enough. It didn't matter, anyway, for at that moment Smoot walked into the foyer with Cledge at his side, the pair talking animatedly as they moved slowly over the shiny granite tiles. At Cledge's side Smoot looked a different man entirely. Gone was the tough, professional aplomb. He was hanging on Cledge's every word and laughed merrily at something Cledge said. There was no mistaking that they enjoyed each other's company. Dubykky went absolutely still, hoping to eavesdrop as they passed by. They stopped in front of the entrance, just steps from the bank of telephones, scanning the wide foyer. Their eyes swept past Dubykky twice.

"Your partner said he would meet us here," Smoot complained.

"Oh, that's Will for you. He has this way of materializing out of nowhere when you least expect him. He'll be along soon." Dubykky's heart warmed to Cledge, who was more observant than Dubykky had given him credit for. Cledge went on, "Anyway, so the sergeant says to me, 'You don't need a defense lawyer, mister,' he says, 'you need a bag over your head.'"

Smoot chuckled affectionately and replied, "Truer words were never spoken, Milt." They laughed together.

As if to provide another test of Cledge's complete inability to dissemble his feelings, Mildred came charging through the door at that instant. She looked around frantically and spotting him smiled like a spring sun. In turn, Cledge's face flexed from relief to desire, to wonder, to transcendent hope, seamlessly and so powerfully that Smoot took a half step backwards, as if for safety's sake.

"Oh, Milt, you're okay!" Milly called out and flew to him, hugging him close and hard. He returned it, somewhat stiffly, but his face sang his joy. Dubykky decided it was time to end the love-o-rama.

"Milly," he said, making a show of being put out, "I asked you to wait in the car."

The three of them jumped and turned to him.

"Where did you come from?" Smoot demanded, chagrinned.

Cledge elbowed him. "Told you."

"Never mind," Dubykky answered Smoot. "Time's short. We must start back for Hawthorne right away."

But that turned out to be impossible. There were more formalities to be observed, Smoot insisted, before Cledge could be fully at liberty. These formalities had to be taken care of at Smoot's office. It was a ploy, Dubykky saw, because Smoot did not want them to leave his jurisdiction before a thorough site investigation had been completed at Gans's house.

They drove to the Office of the District Attorney, Dubykky alone in Cledge's car and the other three in Smoot's. When the call came through from the police, confirming everything that Dubykky had claimed, Smoot cleared up the remaining red tape in minutes. It was nearly three o'clock, too late, he argued, for them to drive all the way back to Nevada that night, so he invited them to dinner.

Dubykky's impatience tormented him, but Cledge and Mildred took no notice, accepting the invitation gladly. Dubykky borrowed coins and made two calls to Hawthorne. Younger did not answer her phone. The phone at the sheriff's office was answered, but to no real advantage. The weakest link of the whole force was on duty that evening, Deputy Sheriff Dodd, known as Deputy Dog because of his fondness for chasing cars. He knew nothing about a warrant and warned Dubykky not to create mischief with hoax calls. When Dubykky insisted that he get in touch with Younger, Dodd hung up.

The dinner at Smoot's was interminable to Dubykky. Everyone else, including Smoot's wife, Karen, had a famous time. Sturdy like her husband, Karen Smoot had fine Hispanic features, an altogether pleasant and comfortable face. She would do superbly as a politician's wife. She also had a flair for narrating anecdotes, about Cledge in particular. Dubykky could tell that she approved of Mildred and, assuming that Cledge and she were a couple, was happy on his account. All this pleased Dubykky but did nothing for his anxiety.

As they were, *finally*, leaving to return to the Musketeer for the night, Smoot drew him aside. "Someday, Mr. Dubykky, you're going to explain to me in full just how you came to suspect Matthew Gans of these murders."

"Someday," he shot back, "when you're attorney general, Milt is going to move back to California with his family and be your chief administrative law officer, and you'll be a team like no other, providing only that you give him plenty of time to go rockhounding. Then nothing more than you already know will matter to you. Or should."

Smoot regarded him humorlessly, then nodded. "I telexed the request for an arrest and extradition. I was to be called when it was acknowledged." There had been no calls interrupting the dinner party. Smoot held out his hand. "I have a feeling it's a good thing that you're Milt's partner and friend. And a good thing that you don't live in L.A. County." Finally, he smiled, if wanly. "Good luck, Mr. Dubykky. Take care of him. Milly, too."

Back at the motel, Dubykky tried again to call Dorothy Younger, to no avail. Next, he dialed Loretta Lurie's house. The phone was picked up after the fourth ring.

It was O'Faelan, who wasn't in a mood for pleasantries. "What the hell do you think you're doing, calling at this hour?" Dubykky checked his wristwatch. It was 10:30. O'Faelan adhered to Benjamin Franklin's advice about early bedtime, health, and wisdom.

"Sorry to wake you, General. I'm just concerned to hand you the biggest news story of your long, distinguished career before another paper gets hold of it."

"Don't be a goddamned smart-aleck, young man. Were you really calling for Lorie?"

"Either of you will do, but you'd better have her follow up the lead. There could be a lot of legwork, and some danger."

O'Faelan was silent a moment, assimilating Dubykky's tone, which had turned dead earnest.

"Spill."

"On the condition that you embargo the story until I get back to Hawthorne. I'm in L.A. right now."

O'Faelan didn't like restrictions but was too curious now to refuse. Dubykky laid out a sketchy version of the suspicions about Gans, that he may have been involved in a serious crime, or series of crimes, in Los Angeles. Dubykky said that he was in L.A. to assist in the investigation. And LAPD was very interested in Gans. He recommended that O'Faelan talk to Dorothy Younger for specifics.

O'Faelan was immediately suspicious. "You're doing everything you can to get us together, aren't you. Now just why is that?"

Dubykky let out an exasperated huff. "Just leave room in your next edition for a huge story. And it'll only be huge if you talk to her."

He hung up, thinking, children! Even while others are in deadly peril, they still think about their own little peeves.

He turned off the lights in his room, preferring to think in darkness. He preferred thinking in silence, too, but the city did not accommodate him. Traffic growled past on the boulevard, and the final crowds of the night were leaving Disneyland amid fireworks and music. He tuned all these out, concentrating on how events might unfold during the next couple of days, and about his priorities.

At last the general ruckus outside subsided, but then his thoughts were interrupted by the sound of the door to Mildred's room opening and then closing softly. Her silhouette passed by the window to his room. She tapped lightly on Cledge's door, waited, then rapped louder. His heavy steps crossed the floor, and his lock was undone. The door opened.

Dubykky moved to sit close to the window, focusing on every sound that came from next door.

"Milly!" Cledge's soft exclamation was smothered, and a short silence ensued.

Good. Finally. A heartfelt kiss, Dubykky told himself.

But Cledge let him down.

"Milly, no."

She made a sound of surprise, then, "Oh, Milt, I was so worried about you sitting there all alone in jail. I had all sorts of nightmares. Criminals attacking you. Police beating a confession out of you—"

"Milly, I was perfectly fine. The only thing the police used on me was sarcasm."

Mildred tried another tack. "Oh, Milt, I feel that I owe you so much for protecting Will and me. You shut the trapdoor and didn't tell on us! You saved us!"

"And because of it you were left to find those bodies," Cledge replied sadly. "I'm sorry that you had to face that." Dubykky had described the scene to him in detail.

There was a rustle of clothing, which Dubykky interpreted as Mildred snuggling in close. "I owe you so much," she repeated. "Milt, you shouldn't have to spend another night alone like last night."

Dubykky bit his lip. But if Mildred was unsubtle at seduction, then Milt was equally obtuse, because he answered, "There were forty other people in the holding cell last night."

Mildred sounded a little exasperated now. "I mean, alone among strangers."

More silence, and then a quick intake of breath from Cledge. Dubykky imagined that Mildred's hands were doing the talking now. "Oh," Cledge said, understanding at last. "But Mildred—"

"Don't you like that, Milty?" Mildred crooned softly.

"Yes. I mean. Oh, Milly! But—"

"But what?"

"Uh, with Will right next door—I don't know."

"Will's asleep."

"But out here on the sidewalk! In plain view!"

"Then take me inside, Milt." Mildred's voice had taken on a husky edge.

"In my room?"

Mildred's foot stamped the concrete. "Yes, of course inside your room. Where do you think, Milt?" She softened her voice again, adding reasonably, "We can't stand here making out right in the open!"

"But in *my* room?"

"Would you rather it be mine?" Mildred sounded pleased by the idea.

"No! I mean, what would your mother say?"

"About my room or yours? What would she care?" Mildred was now segueing to impatience.

"No, no. About us doing—being together like that."

There was the sound of a light scrape on the sidewalk. Mildred had stepped back and sounded outright angry now. "Mother is in Hawthorne. We're here."

"Of course, I'd like—But before marriage? She might not think well of me."

"What about what I think?—Wait! Did you just propose marriage to me?"

Cledge hesitated a little too long. Mildred spat out an enraged growl and stomped off. When she slammed the door to her room, Dubykky's windows shook. He continued listening, hoping Cledge would come to his senses and follow Mildred, but he didn't. After a long minute, his door closed, too, with a slow click.

AND NOW IN THE CAR, as they passed through Lone Pine, Cledge and Mildred weren't speaking to each other. They hadn't spoken during their hasty breakfast. They had hardly glanced at each other the whole trip, their faces set.

As far as Dubykky was concerned, it was just as well. It gave him time to think some more. No new ideas came to him, though. The black strap of the highway led gradually upward through dry, sandy flats, ancient lake beds, desert valleys, and into sparse forests, and all that fixed in his mind was the certainty that matters were approaching a crisis and that there was no avoiding his duty—though, he had to admit, he wanted to. He wanted Junior to survive his destiny. He wanted Junior to enjoy a life, were it possible. But one big, ruinous fact stood in the way.

Echoes did not age. Not at all. The Dubykky of 1960 was a twin of himself in 1460. And there was no reason to doubt that it would be the same for Junior. He would forever have the appearance of a six-year-old. Eventually humans would take note of the everlasting boy. Impermissible.

His intention to leave Hawthorne after Mildred was paired to someone who could curb her dark side also seemed to be stymied, judging from his two passengers. Cledge stared forlornly out the window. Mildred was now pretending to doze despite the noise and rush of air from the open windows. It was a hot day. Dubykky drove the whole way, exceeding the speed limit despite occasional reproachful looks from Cledge. Now as they climbed up to Montgomery Pass, he was forced to slow down because the engine's temperature gauge was creeping into the red. A couple of miles before the pass he pulled over onto the shoulder to let the radiator cool. He explained this to Mildred and Cledge. Cledge immediately got out, murmuring that he'd be right back. Struggling against gusts of wind, he made his way diagonally down a slope and out of sight behind a rock outcropping. To pee, obviously. When Dubykky turned round toward Mildred, her eyes were open but evasive.

"Milly."

She did glance at him then, her face troubled. He recognized the sequence, having seen its like so many times. She had gotten over her tantrum and was feeling uncertain, misunderstood, and probably on the verge of tears. She would be receptive.

"Milly, you have to be patient with Milt. He's kind of a square."

The corners of her mouth twitched upwards at that, then she was distressed again, saying nothing for a while. Suddenly she straightened, affronted, demanding, "What? What do you mean be patient? Did you hear us last night?"

"Probably everybody staying at the motel heard you two, Milly."

A furtive, mischievous delight crossed her face before she returned it to disapproval. "Well, you had no business eavesdropping. Shame on you, Will. Whatever you thought you heard, it wasn't what you think."

"What do I think?"

Mildred tossed her head.

"When you slammed the door to your room, it nearly toppled one of the towers in Disneyland."

"Oh, pooh." But she smiled, hugging herself.

"Just give Milt another chance, will you?"

"A chance at what?"

Dubykky ignored that, knowing what rankled Mildred more than anything. Cledge had remained silent when she used the word *marriage*. "He's worth it. You'll be glad you did."

"He doesn't want me."

"Milt Cledge is strongly attracted to you, almost overpoweringly attracted. And he *wants* you to be his wife. But you simply cannot expect him to respond coherently when you attack him like you did last night. In public."

"It was just one kiss."

"It was more than a kiss, and you know it. But the one kiss was enough. There were explosions and clanging bells and tornadoes and roaring crowds in his head. The poor man couldn't get a sane thought through to his mouth for all that."

Mildred's shoulders shook, and a low giggle leaked out. "You should have seen his face and his—" She cut off when the man in question emerged from behind the rock formation and labored upslope toward them.

Dubykky got out of the car and felt around the hood until he released the catch. Lifting the hood, he took out a handkerchief and covered the radiator cap, then twisted gently. The radiator was still hot, but no steam jetted out, and he was able to unscrew the cap all the way. Cledge got a can of water from the trunk and topped off the reservoir. Only when he was finished did he glance shyly at Dubykky.

He reached into his pants pocket and pulled out a flattish rock with a segmented, tapering black bulge along the center. "An ammonite," Cledge whispered, his expression suddenly writ large in pleading and hope. Dubykky pointed with his chin toward Mildred, then lowered the hood once more. Cledge poured water over the rock, cleaning it thoroughly and drying it on his pant leg before climbing back into the passenger seat. Dubykky hung back. When Cledge twisted around and held out the rock to Mildred, she accepted it gravely, asking what the bulge was. Cledge explained, his face Technicolor with relief. She accepted his explanation just as gravely, making her eyes widen at "fossil" and finally awarding him a small, bashful smile.

Well, good. Dubykky mentally clicked his fingers.

Eleven

"HelloWillhowareyouIamfinetoo, you bastard," Loretta Lurie yelled, "and thank you for finally answering the phone. So now tell me why you're trying to destroy my health, happiness, and career?" There were raised voices in the background.

They had reached Hawthorne early Sunday evening. Dubykky dropped off Cledge and Mildred at her house, to a barrage of questions from Gladys as she let them in the door. Then he rushed straight home. He heard the phone ringing as he approached and continue ringing as he walked through the door.

He cut in on Lurie. "Cool down, Loretta. Now, let's get serious. Did the General tell you about Matthew Gans?"

"Yes, but—"

"Well, I have new information from the L.A. police, but let's come back to that. Did Dorothy receive a request for a warrant for his arrest?"

"No, but—"

"What? Why not? Is Dorothy there? Let me talk to her."

A shout rang out in the background, Younger's voice: "Put that thing *down*, you knucklehead."

"What's going on, Loretta? Has the General pulled a gun on Judge Younger?"

"Of course not. He pulled a microphone on her. Dorothy doesn't want to be interviewed on tape." An outraged bellow came from O'Faelan. "What now?"

Lurie sighed. "Look, Will, you tricked them into getting together, so you can calm them down. Get over here." Lurie slammed down the receiver.

He got there in five minutes, by which time O'Faelan and Younger had already calmed down. Some. They were seated at either end of a long table, glaring at each other. In the middle of the table was a reel-to-reel tape recorder, but without one of the reels. It lay in a corner of the dining room, trailing tape across the floor and through the branches of a potted ficus. O'Faelan held a tissue to his nose. It was spotted with blood. Younger's arms were crossed over her chest, her hands fisted and knuckles white.

They started in on him at once. Talking at the same time, shouting over each other, they jumbled together complaints and accusations until they realized that he was watching them with the look of a high school principal who had caught two students necking. They fell silent.

"You know," he commented, "whenever you two are together you look years younger. About ten years old, in fact." Lurie snickered, which earned her a sharp glance from her father. "Just to save time, Loretta, why don't you summarize?"

"I'll start with Dad," she agreed and holding up a hand stuck out a finger with each assertion. "Dad is just trying to follow up *your* lead on the big story about Matthew Gans. Dad only wants to interview Judge Younger as a source of information. The judge refuses to be interviewed by him just because of an old grudge. The judge is a brutal hellcat who broke his tape recorder and gave him a bloody nose when he tried to explain how important newspaper coverage will be.

"Now for Judge Younger." Lurie held up her other hand. "The judge is just trying to follow your advice that she work with Dad. As a potential agent in the prosecution of Gans, she cannot make any official statement at this point. She certainly has no intention of having her remarks recorded. Who knows what might happen with the recording later? Dad is a bullying jackass for shoving the microphone under her nose and accusing her of being too full of political ambitions to do her job."

"I see." Dubykky trained his most disgusted expression at them. They had regained enough self-possession to look abashed. "Forget the quarrel. Return to what you are: two of the most distinguished, responsible people in Mineral County. Now, Dorothy did you receive the request for an arrest warrant or not?"

"I've heard nothing from the sheriff's office, or from anyone else since you called me. Except Mr. Microphone here." She jabbed a thumb toward O'Faelan. Dubykky half expected them to stick their tongues out at each other.

He said, "Then the three of us are going to the sheriff."

"You pup, who do you think you are to order us around like your personal dogsbodies?" O'Faelan snapped. For once, Younger looked as though she were in complete agreement.

In any case, Dubykky ignored them. "Loretta, I would gladly repay you if you do some research for me." He handed her a sheet of paper. "Here's a list of abandoned buildings in the vicinity, to my knowledge. I need to know if there's any sign one of them has been used recently. Oh, and call the Officer of the Deck at the ammo dump to see if there are any abandoned structures there."

Lurie frowned. "I'll need more to go on than that, Will. What am I looking for?"

Dubykky described what he had found in the fallout shelter at Matt Gans's house in Los Angeles: a torture chamber and a corpse locker. They needed to find where Gans was preparing something like it.

The mood in the room shifted dramatically. "He killed children in a *fallout* shelter," O'Faelan gasped. But it wasn't as though the location made the killings worse for him. He was so shocked that he spoke distractedly. Younger, who had stood up as Dubykky related the details, now plopped back into the chair, her knees weakened. Lurie was ashen.

"What else can you tell us?"

"Not much. There was a seven-and-a-half-month interval between killings, on average, and at least that much time has passed since the last one. Now do you understand why I'm in such a hurry? I think that Matt Gans is preparing some well-hidden place for his next victim."

"What has Junior got to do with this?" Younger had found her voice.

"That's a side issue, Dorothy," Dubykky lied. "We need to go personally, all three of us, to the sheriff's office to see why nothing's happening to arrest Gans."

While Lurie started on her round of checking abandoned buildings, Dubykky, O'Faelan, and Younger rode in her Chrysler to the sheriff's office. It was well past nine when they got there.

Deputy Owen Spezze was definitely not happy to see Dubykky. "Mike Dodd warned me you've been pestering him with some nonsense or other," he said, eyeing Judge Younger and O'Faelan nervously. "Evening, Judge, Mr. O'Faelan, sir."

"We're expecting a telex from the Los Angeles District Attorney's Office," Younger said tightly.

"Telex's been broken for the last two weeks."

"Why hasn't it been fixed?" O'Faelan demanded.

Deputy Spezze shot him a nervous look. "Takes a while to get a repairman from Reno."

"And what about the phone?"

"Works fine."

Younger broke in impatiently, "No, no. We mean did you get any calls?"

Growing sullen, Spezze shrugged. His voice when he replied had a defensive whine to it. "I've been on my rounds a lot today. A lot happens on Saturdays."

They all knew that to be baloney. Spezze had surely passed a large part of his time sitting in Kathy's Kafé drinking coffee and shooting the bull.

"And what about Debbie Donnelly?" O'Faelan's tone was growing ominous. Donnelly was the dispatcher who worked weekend shifts.

"Called in sick."

O'Faelan was reddening toward an explosion. Younger was glowering coldly.

Deputy Spezze looked uncertainly from one to the other and said, a little truculently, "I'm the only one here, and I have to cover the whole town."

O'Faelan detonated. "Bullpucky! Young man, the criminal's best friends are lazy cops. Incompetents, tough guys, know-it-alls, opportunists, even corrupt cops—we can survive them. But when a cop spends his time loafing at a coffee counter, when he shrugs off calls, when he 'patrols' in a parking lot, then criminals know that they are free to do whatever they want. Then property disappears, then women are molested, then people die. Deputy, I promise you this, if a child ends up killed because you couldn't be bothered to do your job, I'll make such a fuss in my paper you'll be lucky to get that Nazi's job policing the garbage dump."

His anger drove Spezze behind a desk. Dubykky had to admit it—the General had made a fine little speech. It would probably appear on the *Independent-News*'s next editorial page.

Now it was Younger's turn, and she was already in motion, advancing on the deputy. Dubykky held up Boyden Smoot's business card. She swiped it out of his hand in passing. "Call this number *now*," she ordered. "Identify yourself. Ask to be connected to Assistant District Attorney Boyden Smoot. Move."

Thoroughly alarmed now at the two angry town stalwarts upbraiding him, the deputy tripped backwards into the desk chair and banged his head against the wall.

"God in heaven, what a Keystone Kop you are!"

"Never mind Spezze, Charlton. I'm calling this Smoot fellow myself. We're wasting time."

Pressing a hand on the back of his head and wincing, Spezze objected, "Your Honor, I don't think you should—"

"Shut up!" the three of them said. While Dubykky, tickled pink, went over to the General to put a restraining hand on his shoulder, Younger began dialing. As she waited for the call to get through, her eyes met O'Faelan's, and what passed between them, a grim agreement and solidarity, pleased Dubykky even more. He loved it when humans danced to his tune.

DESPITE THE MILD EVENING, a chill spread through Paul Muni when he answered the doorbell. There on the small concrete porch stood a strange creature, like the boy Sarah had described seeing at Walker Lake two weeks earlier. And on his shoulder was the crow she spoke of, its head tilted forward, as though it were asleep.

Eerie boy, black bird—it was like a vision from the spirit world.

Before he could respond, though, the boy said, "Z and ampersand—go to school at command. No school for Sarah tomorrow!"

He held up his hand, fingers splayed, and the sight choked off Muni's retort. The boy had four fingers! He blinked and looked again. Three fingers and a thumb. Stranger yet, there was no stump from a missing finger. A deformity. But instead of feeling pity, Muni was repelled.

"I am Junior. Jurgen is Jurgen. We like Sarah," said the boy. He turned, walked away, and passed out of the porch light into the night as though he were dissipating smoke.

Deep unease awoke in Muni. He was shaken, as by an apparition, but when his wife asked him who was at the door, Muni pretended that it was a mistake, someone at the wrong address. Through the rest of the evening he wondered if he should heed the child, that Sarah should not go to school, that malign spirits were gathering, the dwarfish *nimerigar* of Paiute legend. He had never wanted to believe they existed. He never wanted that more than now.

Junior walked across town and stationed himself near the Gans house. As Jurgen continued to doze, Junior let his mind empty and simply watched. Or not quite empty. It occurred to him that when his time ended, as he knew it surely must, there would be one last instant when he would still be aware of something, a last odor or sound or sight. What would it be? And where would it go when he stopped being aware? And what of Jurgen, Kind Sir, Sweet Auntie, book lady, and Sarah Muni? Would they disappear with him? "All the King's horses and all the King's men cannot put Humpty Dumpty together again," he whispered.

The telephone rang in the Gans house. Mrs. Gans answered. Although Junior could hear the words, many of them he did not recognize. One thing was clear, though. Mr. Matthew Gans was not in the house. After Mrs. Gans hung up, there was commotion. Her voice was icy and fast. She was answered first by an uncaring voice, then by a frightened voice, which he recognized as belonging to Dougie Gans, and finally by an excited voice.

The side door flying open, Mrs. Gans and her tallest son, the one who was excited, bustled out. They got into the station wagon and left in haste. As they did, Junior felt a spark deep in his mind, as faint as the flash from a single sequin in a gloomy room, but plain enough. It came from Mrs. Gans. The car soon disappeared down the street and round a corner into the night. Something had started.

Why? He wondered. Then, what was the reason they did go? I cannot tell, for I do not know.

The commotion had awakened Jurgen. He murmured discontent-edly into Junior's ear, Junior nodding. Jurgen also sensed evil.

This little boy is the bad little boy. And so are some adults. Junior started after the station wagon at a steady, unhurried pace. He would track Mrs. Gans, her trail marked by the spoor of depravity. Jurgen took to the air to find the most efficient route of pursuit, as the crow flies.

DEPUTY SPEZZE hung up the phone hoping he'd done the right thing. He had clearly screwed up in the eyes of Judge Younger and Charlton O'Faelan. And that asshole lawyer, Dubykky. Spezze still shuddered when he recalled the ass-chewing from the old man.

But what if Gans was not in when the sheriff called at his house? That occurred to him after Younger, O'Faelan, and Dubykky left.

Spezze knew Matt Gans slightly. Both their boys were on the high school track team, and fathers naturally get to know one another in Hawthorne during sporting events. To Spezze, Gans was a pretty straight-up guy even if he was new to town and from California. So this whole rigmarole about him was clearly some kind of mistake. In the meantime, he had to look on the ball. That was why he had called the Gans house. To make sure that Matt Gans was there and would stay there until the sheriff arrived.

Matt Gans was at home and *would* wait for the sheriff. That was what Misty Gans told him. So, good, Spezze hoped. On the other hand, Matt himself had not been available to come to the phone, which he had to take Mrs. Gans's word on. Something about her voice made Spezze unsure now, a small hesitation before she answered questions. And then she spoke a little too brightly. Had she lied to him? He really hoped not. If getting chewed out by Charlton O'Faelan was bad, it was nothing compared to what the sheriff was capable of, given a real bad screw-up. Like warning off a deadly criminal.

At the duty hooch for the Navy Ammunition Depot's Officer of the Deck, Lieutenant Parselknapp hung up the phone wondering if he'd said too much. He had to stand the watch once each month, which involved staying awake through the night and supervising the marines who guarded the sprawling base and its ammunition bunkers. Being OOD was like going for a check-up at the dentist's: you sat around waiting and waiting, bored except for the anxiety that something bad might actually need attending to. Almost nothing ever did, aside from angry calls about drunken sailors.

So Loretta Lurie's call had been a welcome diversion. He remembered her from the picnic at Walker Lake. Angular and probably on the wrong side of thirty, she was okay looking. But clearly smart and aggressive. Intelligent, ambitious women made him shy. Then the shyness exasperated him. Wasn't he a line officer in the world's greatest military outfit? A man's man! He preferred slightly plumper, more compliant women. Like Angie Ottergol, or so he had thought. He went out with Angie after the picnic, and it was a bust. She was about as exciting as a supply inventory. His thoughts returned to Lurie.

And that phone call. Despite Lurie's friendly manner, her questions were very strange, abrupt, edged with impatience. No, not impatience —apprehension.

After cursory pleasantries, she inquired about abandoned ammunition bunkers.

"What about them?" he replied. The subject wasn't exactly top secret, yet no responsible military official liked doling out information to the press for no reason.

"Look, Lieutenant—"

"Harry."

"Okay, Harry, I don't mean to be alarmist, but if there are unused bunkers on the edge of your base, or fallout shelters, there's some reason to believe one might be used for criminal activity. I'm just checking. If everything on the depot is all secure, then no worries."

"Fallout shelters? No. We don't need them. We'd use the bunkers," he answered, amused.

"Well, what about them, then? Time's important."

Parselknapp mulled this. He had learned early in his naval career that vagueness and rush from others meant dissembling. When he pressed her on the type of criminal activity, she only repeated that she was just checking. He knew he should just hang up on her with a bland reassurance. But he didn't want to. Nothing else was going on. Talking to her was at least better than trying to talk to the marine corporal of the guard, whose vocabulary was fifty-percent composed of *sir*.

"Well, then," he told her, "you needn't worry. There is a group of bunkers at 38 degrees, 27 minutes, 45 seconds by 188, 35, 44 that were emptied about a year ago, but hard to get into." The use of coordinates was a tease, of course. He enjoyed the response.

"Where? I'm not a navigator, Lieutenant."

"Harry."

"I'm a civilian, Lieutenant Harry. Talk compass directions and miles."

"About four miles from town, south by southeast. That's off the highway a half mile or so after the second bend out of town. But, as I said, you don't have to worry about them. The bunkers have steel blast doors that would take an acetylene torch to cut through."

"Like a shop teacher would have."

"Pardon?"

"Never mind. Thanks, Lieutenant Harry, that's all I needed to know."

"Wait a second. This won't be in a newspaper story, will it?"

She had already hung up.

The more Parselknapp thought about that phone call, the less he liked it. Something was up. Damn. The next highest authority was the base executive officer, Commander Tuleg. But a call to him late in the evening over something so indeterminate as Lurie's call—he would look like an idiot. Bugging the XO over nothing was the sort of thing that got remembered when time came to make out fitness reports. His career couldn't afford a bad fitness report. Should he call the marine captain in charge of security? No. Captain Appleton was an all-right guy, for a marine, but what could he do that Parselknapp couldn't? *Double damn.*

The corporal of the guard was dozing at his desk in the front half of the hooch. He snapped alert when Parselknapp emerged from his cubicle.

"Yes, sir," he said thickly.

"Corporal, call in the security jeep. I'm going to make the rounds."

The corporal's eyebrows went up fractionally. It was not standard operating procedure for this time of night. Seeing the marine's badly disguised annoyance piqued Parselknapp. Immediately he was eager.

"Yes, sir. But it will take awhile, sir. The patrol is scheduled for Area Seven right now, sir."

Area Seven was about as far across the depot from the empty bunkers as it was possible to get.

"Then get on the horn, Corporal. I want to do this ASAP."

O'FAELAN, YOUNGER, AND DUBYKKY drove to Sheriff Yarborough's house and then followed him as he drove his patrol car to Gans's house. Though the sheriff arrived first, Dubykky hustled ahead to be first on the doorstep, at which Yarborough bristled.

But Dubykky didn't knock. Instead, he waited, looking carefully around for any sign of Junior. There was none. He didn't know what to think about that.

"Nice of you to wait for me to do the official honors, Counselor," Yarborough said, heavily sarcastic, when he caught up. He had nothing against Dubykky. It was just his manner. Yarborough was a tall, potbellied, plodding man of sixty-two, grizzled from spending his life in the high desert and driven to irony from a career policing the follies of locals, tourists, and sailors. Followed closely by O'Faelan and Younger, he stepped to the door.

"Mind if I ring the bell?"

Dubykky made a small bow and gestured to the button by the screen door.

Yarborough pressed it. Nothing happened. Yarborough let out a heavy sigh and knocked, banging the screen door against the jamb. Silence followed. After a moment, Yarborough huffed to himself and knocked again. More silence. He turned to Younger, raising an eyebrow.

"Is oral permission to enter the house enough for you, Sheriff?" she asked. He nodded wearily, and she said, "Then you've got it."

The front door was unlocked. This was not unusual. The Gans house lay in the sprucest quarter of Hawthorne. Neighbors here typically left their doors unlocked, even at night.

Yarborough stepped inside, flipping on the light switch. Huddled on the sofa against the far wall sat Dougie Gans, his face tear-streaked, his eyes large. Though he was crying, no sound escaped him.

Younger and O'Faelan followed the sheriff into the living room, while Dubykky hung back in the doorway.

"Where are your parents, young man?" Yarborough demanded.

Dougie only shook his head.

"What about your brothers?"

The boy made no sign that he'd heard.

Dubykky said, "He's in shock, or scared. You're not going to get anything out of him being so brusque, Sheriff."

While Yarborough turned ponderously to give Dubykky a "why don't you just shut up" look, Younger went to the sofa and sat next to the boy. She put her arm around his shoulders, murmuring to him soothingly. His body, tense as a piano wire, relaxed and slumped, and as it did he sobbed, the tears coming faster. Younger crooned in his ear that everything would turn out fine, but he shook his head hard.

"No, it won't," he managed to get out. "It's going to be one of the real bad times. I *know* it."

Dubykky was growing increasingly impatient. They were wasting time. And the crisis was imminent. The feel of it was almost like a headache. Neither O'Faelan nor the sheriff was willing to interrupt Younger to hurry things along, so Dubykky stepped closer to the boy.

"Dougie," he commanded in a firm but low voice. The boy's sobbing subsided, and his eyes raised to Dubykky's. "They're not going to hurt anybody this time. We'll make sure. But we have to find them."

Dougie stared at Dubykky as if fascinated.

"Where's your father?"

"Gone." Pausing to swallow, he added, "After dinner."

"Where's your mother?"

"Gone right after bedtime."

"Where are your brothers?"

"George went with Mom. Billy's asleep."

O'Faelan stepped into the hallway and entered the first room. He returned, nodding. William Halsey Gans was sleeping peacefully. Sheriff Yarborough, who looked as though he were watching a tedious television program and wanted to change the channel, spoke up again.

"Where? Where did they go, boy?"

Younger frowned at the tone, and Dubykky said, "He and his brother don't know. We'll have to go out and find them ourselves. Tonight."

Yarborough snorted. "Look where? They could be halfway to Vegas by now." He gestured at Dougie. "And this kid is in a state. He might be just saying things."

Younger looked outraged, but he ignored her. "I'm betting that in the morning Mom will be fixing breakfast, brother George will join everyone at the table, and Dad will be about to set off for his first class of the day."

Dubykky moved close to Yarborough. "Exactly *what* are you betting, Sheriff? And against whom?"

Briefly, the irony disappeared from Yarborough's face, replaced by a dangerous look. "Time for you to go home, Mr. Dubykky."

Without taking his eyes from Yarborough, Dubykky said, "General, Dorothy, see that those boys are safe, won't you. Sheriff, here's hoping you win that bet." He left quickly. Breaking into a jog when he reached the sidewalk, he headed for his house.

Essentially, he agreed with the sheriff. Yet, it wasn't because he believed, as the sheriff clearly did, that nothing would be gained by a search during the night. The sheriff's way was to follow procedure, leaving someone to watch Gans's house, informing nearby jurisdictions of his interest in the man, and otherwise waiting. It usually worked.

Anyway, Dubykky was not in favor of a large, noisy, comprehensive search of Hawthorne and its environs. It was likely to make matters worse. Alarmed, Gans might flee entirely, or rush into another murder. Neither was tolerable.

Besides, had Dubykky insisted on immediate, concerted action, Younger would have seconded him, and the result would have been a standoff, the two leading local government legal figures in the area at odds, while the leading media figure looked on. Nothing good would come from that, only wrangling and delay. And ruffled egos. So it was better that the sheriff followed his saturnine disposition, believing the whole business was being exaggerated and routine procedure would sort everything out. That is, let humans act like humans, while Dubykky did things his way.

The phone was ringing as he reached his yard and kept ringing while he hurried into the house.

"Well, finally!" snapped Loretta Lurie when he answered it. She didn't wait for him to speak. "Did you find Gans? Well, I haven't found anything either on that list you gave me. So I called Joe about empty houses in the area." Joe Wells was Hawthorne's biggest realtor. "But there aren't any of the kind you asked about, just some old shacks out on the fringes of town."

"Gans wouldn't use one of those."

"You sure?"

"Trust me."

"Then I called Herb to see if he had any suggestions." Herbert Duggart was county clerk. "This all better be worth it, Will, because both of them were pretty cross about being phoned late on a Saturday and grilled by a reporter. I had to call in some favors to get them to answer at all."

"Did Herb know anything?"

"No. Then I called the ammo depot. Lieutenant Parselknapp was on duty. He said there are no fallout shelters on the base because they don't need them. But the ammo bunkers are sort of like fallout shelters, aren't they? There are some empty ones way out on the periphery. He made it sound as if they would be just about impossible to break into. But do you think Gans could do it?"

"Loretta, can you come right over and pick me up?"

"So that means yes. Where're your truck and car?"

"Just come pick me up. I may need more help from you."

Lurie pulled into his driveway only minutes later. He was waiting there for her and climbed in the passenger side.

"Where's Dad?" she demanded.

"He's with Dorothy at the Gans house. They're babysitting the sons."

Lurie was silent awhile, parsing that out. Finally she said wryly, "Just like you," and began backing out into the street.

"Beg pardon?"

"You've been maneuvering them together for a long time now. Really, Will, what do you think you're doing? First it was Milton Cledge and Mildred. Okay, fine. But now it's Dad and Dorothy Younger. Not so fine. Are you an attorney or a matchmaker? I suppose you have someone in mind for me, too."

"You're not getting any younger, Loretta, and soon you'll be running the *News* all by yourself. You should have some nice romantic fun while you still have the time to be chasing after trousers."

"What about your trousers?"

"The zipper's jammed. Seriously, after all this is over, look around you with a clear eye. Take that Lieutenant Parselknapp, for example. Out of the navy and with the right partner, he could go a long way."

Lurie turned left onto A Street, her face passing in and out of the light from a street lamp. Her mouth was set in a sardonic grin, her eyes sad. "And be called Mrs. Parselknapp?"

Despite his anxiety, Dubykky couldn't help himself. He snickered, and she began chuckling too.

"I'm saying, just keep an open mind, Loretta. In the meantime, head for Bowser's."

"I don't need gas. The tank's almost full."

"It's intelligence we need."

"Well, you won't find it there."

Dubykky made a face. "I mean the military kind."

Pete Bowser operated the Texaco station at the intersection of Nevada 362 and US 95 in the center of town. He was a gentle, gossipy, snoopy, lethargic, blocky, middle-aged man, reputedly the ugliest person in the state. He always worked the late shift at the station because he liked to sit by the pumps in a swivel chair and watch who drove by after the working day, and with whom, and who was out on the streets, and who came out of the El Cap or the Hawthorne Club and whether they would make it home in one piece. He was a watcher. Just what Dubykky needed.

When Lurie came to a stop beside Bowser, Dubykky leaned out the window, motioning for him to stay seated, which he appeared already to have decided on doing.

"I just filled up Loretta's car this morning, Will," he drawled. "But nice of you to stop by. How's the Manhoffer case panning out? He going to woozle some money out of the county?"

"You're welcome. Pretty well. Probably, but not more than a couple thousand," Dubykky replied, winking heavily for Bowser's amusement. "You know Matt and Misty Gans, don't you?"

"'Course I do. Handsome couple."

There were many reasons not to rush Bowser, but the main one was the need to keep him on the right subject. Dubykky said, "I couldn't agree more. And a fine shop teacher. The oldest boy runs the four-forty, I hear, and the youngest is quite the student."

Bowser kept nodding. He knew these things. Everybody did. They weren't gossip-worthy. But Bowser knew something that might be. "Saw Misty and that oldest boy go by in their station wagon not a half hour ago."

"Oh?"

Bowser nodded, significantly. "Didn't look left nor right. Headed south on the highway like they's going someplace important. Now why would that be?" He waited, hoping for an explanation.

"Shoot. I was hoping to catch her or Matt tonight. Nobody's home and I have some papers that need signing."

All ears, Bowser perked up, eager to hear more. "On a Sunday night?"

Dubykky asked pointedly, "You sure that Matt wasn't with them?"

"Sure as taxes."

"Have you seen his pickup out and about?"

"Nope. What kind of papers?"

"Now, Pete," Dubykky grinned. "You know I can't tell you that." He winked again.

As they drove away Lurie asked, "What was that about papers?"

"A diversion. I had to sidetrack the Bowser gossip express. If all this business about Gans does turn out to be a false lead, there's going to be marital trouble for him. By sundown tomorrow it'll be all over town that the Ganses are getting divorced. It's the first kind of papers that would occur to Bowser."

Lurie shook her head in disapproving admiration. "How you do maneuver people! Have you no shame?"

"Shame is a luxury for people without a purpose."

Lurie didn't like that either. She asked, "Okay, so where to? The bunker complex?"

It lay in the direction that Misty and George Gans had taken. Dubykky nodded. "To the bunkers. Misty must be trying to find Matt and stop him. She's got to have some idea where he'd go."

WHILE HIS WIFE was taking the phone call from the deputy sheriff, Matt Gans was finishing the setup for his Injun Dazzler. He had waited what seemed like hours hunkered down in bushes by Paul Muni's house until the lights finally went out. Now he moved the pre-made mini-tepee into position on Muni's doorstep, taking care that no neighbor saw him.

There was little danger of that anyway. The Munis lived in an old neighborhood of Hawthorne. The houses were small and, unlike Muni's, mostly ramshackle, surrounded by slatternly bushes in large, sandy lots filled with vehicles. Still, hiding behind the neat, waist-high boxwoods around Muni's front yard was a comfort. A man couldn't be too careful.

A yard away from the tepee he set down the noise-maker, a whistling cone that he had saved from Fourth of July fireworks for just such a purpose. He attached long fuses to both the noise-maker and the tepee. He lit the first, counted to five, and lit the second, then ran back to his hiding spot. Just as he was crouching behind the boxwoods, the cone fizzed, gave a loud *pop*, and began emitting a screeching whistle that faithfully replicated the brakes squealing from a skidding car. *How appropriate*, Gans thought. Even as he thought it, the tepee started gushing smoke, growing flames a moment later. He watched eagerly, whisper-singing to himself from a popular song he had heard earlier in the day:

> You got the lips that I'm mad about.
> I got the lips that'll knock you out.
> C'mon, little one, be wild with me.

Inside, Paul Muni had just returned from getting Charlie, David, and Sarah to bed. As usual, Charlie and David had fallen into a deep sleep almost at once. He always settled them in for the night first because they were easy. Also, as usual, Sarah had charmed him into another and another and another bedtime story-poem until her lids drooped despite herself. Now Paul was standing by his own bed pulling the pajama top over his head. Judy was leafing through *Look*. A loud *pop* from the front of their house made them both jump. Then a demonic tocsin started. Judy sat bolt upright, frightened.

"Paul," she stammered, "it's a car accident right outside!"

He grabbed a bathrobe and headed for the front of the house, dubious.

The horrible screeching just kept on going. When he threw open the door, he nearly stepped straight into the tower of flames on the step. The heat drove him backwards, scorching his robe. He shielded his eyes with an arm, but even so he recognized the structure beneath the flames. And surprised himself by bursting out in a Paiute curse.

Living among white people, Muni and his family had occasionally been the victims of anti-Indian harassment, but never anything like this tepee. Bias, unyielding mistrust, and ignorance—only an idiot white would attribute tepees to the Paiute tribe. Their traditional structure was the wickiup, entirely different in shape. He slapped at the smoking fabric of his bathrobe and yelled for his wife to call the fire department. The dry wood of his door jamb was already sprouting little flames. He ran into the kitchen to fill a pitcher with water.

Gans only waited to see the angry bewilderment on Muni's face (satisfyingly dramatic) before scuttling in a crouch around back of the house. He stopped below a window and hopped up for a look. Two boys lay in bunkbeds in a room hardly wider than a bathroom. No. The next window over and another hop up, and there she was, his Indian girl. In the distance, neighbors were calling out to Muni as they rushed toward the house to see what was going on. Gans knew that none would think of coming round to the back.

The window slid upward with a little scrape that no one would hear over the racket. He scrambled through into the bedroom, a velvet hood in his teeth and sturdy medical tape ready in his hand.

Sarah Muni was just raising her head from her pillow, blinking in sleepy confusion at the noise that seemed to come from everywhere, when Gans got to her. He deftly flipped the long black hair from her cheek and slapped the tape over her mouth.

All she saw was a large hand. Then her mouth was covered, and for a second she couldn't breathe, until she drew in a shaky breath through her nose. As she did, soft thick fabric slid over her face, and the world went utterly black. It was harder yet to breathe, the air suddenly stuffy.

She felt strong hands force hers together and cords dig into her wrists. Suddenly her whole body left the bed. She was flopped on her stomach over a shoulder. She struggled and stiffened out her legs, but the hands on her were far too strong, and the motion of being carried dizzied her. She drew in a long slow breath to scream, but that too was useless. All she could produce was a groaning whine deep in her throat, and as she tried even harder, the back of her head struck wood, and her thoughts dispersed in a sparkling cloud.

Twelve

Jurgen disliked flying at night. He did it only because his friend Junior wished it. Night flying was confusing. There was light from a diminished moon and from the great nest of stars overhead and from the artificial lights below. But taken together, it was nothing like sunlight, the nice steady downpouring generality of illumination. At night, shadows were cast in every direction, contradicting one another, and some lights moved in random ways or stopped and started or went off and on. Yet still Jurgen was able to follow the car that Junior had pointed out. Jurgen had grown to dislike cars, too. Noisy, smelly, unpredictable, awkward, thoughtless, dangerous, and ugly. At least he wasn't on the inside of this one. The inside of a car was like a metal belly that tried to digest him with rumblings and shakings and sudden swerving.

From a couple hundred feet up this car did not look so brutal. It looked like a box moving in a straight line on a straight black path, keeping strictly to one side of it. That consistency, to Jurgen, was impressive. There was an appreciation among crows about the ideal route between two points—as the car crawls. Now he could see the wisdom of it. The car never deviated from its course. It left the town, accelerating out into the desert.

Jurgen flew as fast as he could, climbing all the while, but soon the car was far ahead. In the distance, it angled slightly when the black path angled. Then after a few minutes its lights disappeared behind a mountain slope and did not reappear. Jurgen executed a sharp turn back toward Hawthorne to report to Junior: the car was running away.

Junior was walking swiftly now. By the time Jurgen found him, he was nearly to the edge of town. Feeling a little foolish doing it, because crows did not normally speak loudly at night, Jurgen shouted a *grrgk* and circled downward until he was close enough to splay his wings and alight on Junior's shoulder.

"You are Jurgen. Good."

Jurgen cooed a quick hello and nuzzled the boy's hair, then got to the point. It took some time, but finally Junior understood that the car was far away and getting farther. He paused, squatting in the shadow of a placard advertising Farmer's Insurance, silent, thinking.

And then not thinking, for there was nothing to think of. He could not catch the car. He didn't know where it was going. He wasn't sure that it was right to follow it anyway, because Matthew Gans was not in it, only the wife of Matthew Gans and a boy who was not the boy that Junior had met, Dougie. Kind Sir had taught him that when there was no obvious course to follow, he should wait and watch. Patience would provide. A course of action would present itself. Junior wished that Kind Sir were with him right then. He had questions that needed answering. But Junior was alone. He watched.

To his satisfaction, a course of action did present itself after a while. A car passed by, and inside was Kind Sir, as if in response to Junior's wish. Junior jumped to his feet, prompting an irritated squawk from Jurgen.

Kind Sir was sitting in the passenger seat. It seemed to Junior that the man's head turned ever so slightly in his direction. Had he seen Junior? There was no indication. But Junior knew Kind Sir to be a being of unfathomable understanding who always had a purpose.

Wherever Kind Sir was going was the necessary place to be. Whatever was happening, Kind Sir would know how to act. Junior would follow. He sensed his destiny was near.

Junior whispered to Jurgen, "Run, run, run. Let's all of us run. We ought to be inside before the day is done." The crow leapt aloft to follow this car, too, while Junior set off after it in the same direction, trotting.

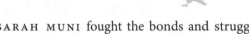

SARAH MUNI fought the bonds and struggled to toss off the hood and work the tape off her face until she went limp with exhaustion. Wet stains grew on the hood from her tears and mucus.

This was not Gans's favorite part of an adventure, but he still enjoyed it. His only regret was that he couldn't see her face. He imagined well enough what it would look like, though, and he'd see it soon enough. It would have an expression like that of lazy or stupid students when he gave them a pop quiz. Bewilderment first, then growing resentment at the unfairness, and on to puzzled resignation, because there was nothing they could do to pass the test. It would affect their grade, which meant they would have to work harder and suck up to the teacher more. Of course, Sarah's experience would be so much more intense. Briefly she strained and flopped once more, then stopped again, her little chest heaving for breath. She was a feisty one, all right. Gans had foreseen that. It was a big part of the reason for choosing her. A powerful spirit dwelt in her. His eagerness swelled.

The only danger now was that she might vomit behind the gag and drown. He watched her closely for any sign of convulsions, his eyes swinging between her and the road.

It was a narrow, rocky dirt road. He permitted himself only his parking lights to see by, so he had to drive tediously slow. The roundabout route was a necessary precaution. People were so snoopy in tiny Hawthorne, unlike L.A. where his neighbors had seemed to go out of their way not to notice anything he did. In Hawthorne, if he, say, took a quick trip to the supermarket after dinner, sure enough someone would see it and say something about it to him the next day: "Run out of beer last night, Mr. Gans? Haw haw haw haw." That's probably why it's called Hawthorne, he quipped and chuckled. Nosy, silly, gullible people. Inferior. They were so dense that Gans figured he and Misty could safely stay long enough for George and Bill both to finish high school.

Probably not Dougie, though. In fact, Dougie was probably not going to finish anything. Gans was coming to that conclusion. Dougie was too much like his little sister. He knew Misty agreed. Her periods of motherly warmth toward their youngest son were growing shorter and less frequent. The boy was repellant to her. Unlike his brothers, that fact upset Dougie. He wanted to cling. He would have to be gotten rid of soon.

Caught up in these thoughts, Gans did not notice Sarah slowly twisting in the seat so her back was to him. Her hands were still tied to the arm rest on the door, but her legs were simply bound to one another under the calves with clothesline. Her struggles had loosened the knots. The clothesline slipped down enough that it was now looped over her ankles.

Gans was thinking about the day his daughter was born, when, after Misty came out of the anesthetic and learned it was a girl, she became hysterical and had to be re-sedated. She refused to nurse, absolutely refused, and would only agree to hold the infant when one of the nurses was in the room watching. The hospital released her after a week, and when she got home he and Misty had had the most spectacular fight of their marriage. A real lamp-smashing, toe-to-toe, flailing slugfest. Gans smiled at the memory. He had to give it to her—Misty was a clear-headed scrapper. And she had won that one. Her face bloodied, one eyelid swelling to plum size, she still had the presence of mind to deliver a kick to his groin that left him in a fetal position on the floor. On her knees, punching his kidneys and neck, she screamed obscenities for putting a girl into her.

He was sore for a week. But real good came out of it. The upshot was that he had to bottle-feed Lucy and gradually found himself quite attached to her. The little tyke returned the affection. The more her mother alternately mistreated her and ignored her, the more Lucy clung to him. All that closeness stirred him. From it, he evolved the idea of adventures.

For her part, Misty carefully watched her husband's attitude toward the girl. She suspected what was going on in his head because to her all men had the same mental processes as her own father. Misty expected that Gans would become to Lucy what dear old Daddy had been to her. She seethed and erupted in anticipation, promising to do many horrible things to him if it happened.

In spite of the drama, he could tell she wanted it to happen. She hoped he turned into Daddy. Needed him to. It would confirm her expectations: fathers abused daughters, plain and simple. Her abhorrence of girls, weaklings and clingers all, would be justified.

But about one thing she did not dissemble. She promised to cut his throat while he slept if he ever got her pregnant again. Matt chuckled, imagining her inflating with another pregnancy and growing more enraged by the day. He laughed out loud.

Reverting to his kids: they were so varied. Funny thing, that. Same parents, same household, community, yet they reacted differently. Take George, for instance. He thrived under the good mother/bad mother treatment. He could deal out as much pain as he received, just as he could deal out affection and even brotherly love when it was useful. A promising kid! So was Billy in his own way. Billy had poured himself into sports. Perfectly respectable. Gans had no doubts that Billy would be a success at one of them. But Lucy? She always wanted something from her mother that would not be offered. And she thought she recognized that something in him. But her need deceived her. His affection was never anything but a pretense. In the end, that made her puzzlement all the more delicious. Dougie was subtler, more controlled, yet it was now clear that he too cared about what others thought or felt. A pathetic vulnerability. Gans wondered, how could *that* come to happen? To prepare yourself to be a victim! Wacko.

Suddenly, Sarah twisted one foot free of the clothesline and kicked out at Gans. It was completely blind, the kick, yet it struck home. Her foot gave him a glancing blow to the knee. It didn't hurt much but did knock his foot off the gas pedal. The truck slowed, stalled, lurched, and came to a stop, the engine dead. The motion threw Sarah onto the floorboard, hanging by her hands from the arm rest. Initially blind with red rage, Gans calmed at the sight of her hanging there painfully and resisted the urge to kick her in return. She would be hanging like that, even more so, soon enough, her toes straining to reach the ground to ease the agony. Gans smiled at the image before pushing in the clutch and restarting the engine.

By the time he did, he realized he really didn't need to have the parking light on. Though the moon glow was feeble, the stars provided enough illumination for him to make out the road well enough. This was better than ever! Gliding through the dark in the blank desert under hulking mountains, far out of sight. He had to go a little slower, but that didn't matter. He and Misty had coordinated their runs. There was plenty of time to beat her to their fun room.

MISTY DROVE AT THE SPEED LIMIT, even below it, to eat up time. She suspected that Matt would dawdle. The pace made George restless in the seat beside her, so she talked to him. She told him what a filthy, vile creature he was, little better than an animal. Crude, stupid, deformed, masturbatory, doomed to insignificance and futility. She said it in her sweet voice, using filthy words. That made him grin as if they were in on a big joke together. He said nothing back, of course. He never would. But he leaned forward in his seat, anticipating. She could see his mind working. Another version of Matt. Of old Daddy himself. These adventures were her way to expose their true nature as males. Their degradation was her fulfillment. She was glad Georgie was participating this time. Her ecstasy would be twice as keen.

The distance from Hawthorne to Mina was only twenty-five miles, the road flat and easy. Still, Misty used up half an hour getting there, and spent nearly as much time picking her way down a rutted road. Their destination was a shed made of beams nearly as stout as railroad ties, nestled in the crook of a hill. Though gray, split, and in places warped, the exterior wood was still solid. Who knew what the shed was built for?

Nevada's official nickname was the Silver State, but it might as well have been the State of Abandonment. In Nevada's century, its citizens had walked away from cabins, houses, farms, ranches, mines, whole towns—just up and left. Whatever the reasons, the underlying attitude was the same: it's a big, dry, empty, harsh land; if something doesn't work here, try somewhere else over there. Structures in various stages of tumbledown lay among the brush of a desert slope or the cotton-woods of a seasonal stream's flood plain or scattered along a gulch, and few people knew much about them, except maybe the name of a ghost town, and fewer cared. Misty herself had asked a local about a group of derelict buildings near the Paiute reservation, and the woman only gave her a curious look and shrugged. To Misty, that meant *dumb hick*. That was just the problem moving to a small town. All of Mineral County could hardly boast six thousand people, if even that, less than one percent of her home, Los Angeles, and they were all of a piece, clods. She had never troubled herself to ask another.

In any case, all that mattered about this little blockhouse was that it was stout and lay out of sight.

It was part of Matt's adventures that the preparations be separated, in steps, elaborate, and Misty approved. There was safety in that—not putting your eggs in one basket. In L.A. it had been difficult to distribute their props and traps and still maintain coordination. Traffic was always an obstacle. So Matt was forced to restrict their activities to a small area. Risky. Hawthorne afforded far greater scope. She had enjoyed their explorations of dirt tracks through the desert. Pleasant, languid, healthful outings in the wilderness. She liked the high desert, even if the people who lived in it were jays.

When she parked the car, George stared at the shed blankly. He was lost in an anticipatory fantasy, she could see. She pinched him hard to bring him out of it. He flinched, laughed, and wiggled away from a second pinch. They got out.

The shed door swung open with a magnificent screech. George laughed again and exclaimed, "Like a cell door!" She told him to shut up, but without feeling. When he smiled in return, he looked very much like her husband. George carried the big chest with the toys and the small chest with the costumes out to the car and stowed them in the trunk. While he was at it, she scurried to her secret place under a floorboard and removed the Instrument. It was wrapped in a pure white cloth that she had ripped from her First Communion dress. It was thin enough to tuck into the interior pocket of her jacket. Having hidden it carefully, she walked out of the shed. George was closing the trunk.

"Jeez, Mom, I'll bet Dougie and Billy wouldn't get how neat this is!"

Misty considered. "Billy maybe, but Dougie, I'm afraid, is a wimp." Just like his sister, she said to herself.

George laughed darkly, nodding. They drove just as carefully on the return trip. There was still plenty of time before she was due.

Then Misty thought of the phone call from the idiot deputy sheriff. The trip out for the toys and George's chatter had pushed it out of her mind. She grunted angrily and punched George hard in the shoulder. He grinned back at her.

Misty did not try fooling herself. The deputy knew something about Matt. That could not be good. There was nothing innocent about them to be known. Maybe the stench from their dungeon in L.A. had gotten noticed. Something bad was going on.

Back on the highway, she pressed on the accelerator. The car shot forward. That horrible feeling of being followed, which had plagued her youth, was back. Matt wouldn't like her showing up before her turn, but too bad. This adventure would have to be a rush job. Her eyes darted everywhere in search of police cars. The stars overhead, and the moon, they were watching her, too. And the mountains—their jagged teeth rimmed the skyline like a bear trap.

Anxiety mounting, Misty fought for control. Be sensible. They had at least eight hours and probably as much as a day before the cops got started on a proper search. That would give her, Matt, and George plenty of time to hide the car and switch to the one cached near Tonopah. They could be in Utah by midafternoon. From there it would be no trick at all to vanish.

It would mean abandoning Dougie and Billy in Hawthorne. They couldn't risk returning home for the boys. A pang of regret took her by surprise, but she dismissed it. Dougie wouldn't have lasted long anyway. Billy could take care of himself.

DOUGIE AND BILLY were just then sitting in Dorothy Younger's house, both bedraggled and sleepy. Billy was also bored and sat slumped with a glass of milk in one hand and a cookie in the other, which Younger had given him. But Dougie looked around with interest despite his fatigue.

Mrs. Younger had told him that Junior lived here now, the mysterious boy he had met in the alley and half feared. Dougie imagined Junior walking through these too-white, uncomfortable adult rooms. But Junior was not yet home for the night, which was strange. Mrs. Younger's face went unhappy when she told him that, while Mr. O'Faelan looked at her curiously.

"Well, boys," he said, rubbing his hands, "we better get you bedded down until your parents can pick you up. There's school tomorrow, you know."

Mrs. Younger nodded as he spoke, and they led Dougie and Billy into Junior's room. Mr. O'Faelan set down cushions on the floor, along with blankets and a pillow for Billy, who fell asleep almost immediately. Dougie got into Junior's bed and pulled the covers up to his lower lip. The sheets had a strange smell he couldn't identify, faintly sweet and earthy, but nice.

Mrs. Younger leaned over and swept back his hair, staring deep into his eyes. Hers were sad when she said, "Everything will turn out fine, Dougie. You're such a good boy." She touched his nose with a forefinger. "Keep that in mind. Now, close your eyes, relax, and go to sleep."

Out in the living room, O'Faelan grinned wearily. "Dorothy, I'm not the least bit sleepy. Why don't you toddle off to bed while I stand watch by the phone in case Will needs us."

"Aren't you hungry? Do you want a bite to eat?" she answered, a little disconcerted. The situation was unfamiliar, being host to a man in the evening. Moreover, an obliging O'Faelan seemed an oxymoron.

"No. Can't say I am. But a sip of bourbon would be welcome. Perk me up."

Younger went into the kitchen to pour him a tot of Jim Beam. When she returned, his head was tilted forward and breathy gurgles came from his mouth. It occurred to her that he sounded a little like the crow Jurgen. The thought made her smile, and she sat down beside him on the sofa to sip the bourbon herself.

Dougie did not go to sleep right away. He pondered being in Junior's bed. Was Junior like him, or was Junior like his father? There were only two ways of being, his father and mother had long preached. You were either a master or a slave; a predator or prey; a winner or a loser; a doer or a done-to; a victor or a victim. You proved you were not a victim by getting what you wanted out of others. It was simple, they said.

Dougie knew he was a victim, and he had enough experience of victors to recognize that most other people were like him. But what about Junior? Their brief conversation did not clarify Junior to Dougie. The eerie fear he felt toward Junior was different from his reaction to victors like his parents and George. And what about the crow, Jurgen? Was the same distinction true for crows? Crows were scavengers, he'd learned in school. What did that make them? But this Jurgen was a friendly bird. He couldn't believe that a friendly bird would live on the shoulder of a victor. So, Junior had to be a victim.

Dougie opened his eyes. And where did Jurgen sleep when Junior was lying flat on the bed? On Junior's stomach? Uncomfortable for them both. A leg? Then Dougie noticed scratches on one footboard post. Oh, sure, he sighed to himself, and slept.

JURGEN WAS ON HIS WAY BACK to report when he detected distant motion where motion should not be. What large animal would be roaming the desert alone at this hour? Intrigued, Jurgen banked left to investigate. It was a truck, creeping along without the usual bright lights that vehicles projected from their snouts. Jurgen swooped low to see what could be seen through the windshield. There was a figure behind the steering wheel, and he glimpsed another person, just the hands and the top of the head.

The sudden streak of black right in front of the car startled Gans. He jerked backward, pressing his legs forward to brace. The motion depressed the throttle, the engine roared, and the truck bucked forward, smacking Sarah's head against the seat. A low groan came from her.

Gans cursed and stopped the truck, shifting into neutral. All this jostling around, he worried, was going to damage the girl too much. He pulled her up so she was sitting on the seat again, slouched sideways. He shook her. She was unresponsive. If she was dead or dying, she would be of no use to him. Or unconscious. That would ruin the fun. He pulled the hood from her head to check her out. Her eyes were closed, her lower face covered in a gooey sheen. He peeled back an eyelid. The pupil was large, but he didn't know what to make of that. When he let go, the lid drooped closed again.

"Shoot."

Carefully, Gans pulled loose the tape. Immediately she drew in a deep, rattling breath and emitted a piercingly pitched, warbling scream that dug into Gans's ears like a corkscrew. He wadded up his handkerchief, stuffed it into her mouth, and pressed the tape back.

Jurgen heard the scream behind him. A sound like that, whether from a wind, an animal, a bird, or a human, wasn't good. It frightened Jurgen, the more so when it suddenly cut off. Jurgen angled lower to the ground and flapped harder. There was panic in the air. He felt it. It hastened him to his Junior.

Intent upon finding him, Jurgen committed a careless faux pas. He flew low and fast over the cottonwood that was the town's biggest rookery. The rapid whooshing of his wings alarmed the lookout. "Grawwkgk," she scolded him, as if to say, what are you doing flying at night like some demented nightjar, you fool? Find a branch and settle down. Then in a low gripe, "Mnrk": nincompoop fledglings nowadays.

Jurgen felt uneasy. He realized that he was rapidly getting a reputation: consorting with humans, learning some of their sounds, eating food from a hand. That was all definitely infracrow in Hawthorne. Already some adults turned their backs to him if he lighted nearby. Now, flying at night—another eccentricity. But he flew on.

He located Junior a half mile out of town and landed on his shoulder. There was a lot of complexity to convey, and it took awhile. Car disappeared. Strange truck in the desert with one man and an extra pair of hands inside. Scream. Other crows mad at him.

Junior did not comprehend it all. It didn't matter. He understood enough and had already veered off the road and onto the sand. It was slower going away from the blacktop, so Junior picked up the pace, dodging clumps of greasewood and sagebrush. To maintain his balance on Junior's shoulder, Jurgen dug in his claws. It was uncomfortable for them both so Junior ordered Jurgen to take wing again and follow the truck. Jurgen made a wide detour to stay well out of sight of the rookery.

DUBYKKY WAS FLUMMOXED. There was no sign of Misty Gans. He asked Lurie to pull over when they were as far south as the farthest bunker complex, and waited. He suspected a simple ruse, yet they sat ten minutes in increasing frustration. Nothing.

Dubykky felt Lurie's eyes on him, wanting to know what was going on, what to do, where to go.

He wasn't sure. Had he been wrong entirely? "Loretta, look away from me for a few minutes, please."

"Why?"

"*Please.* I have to do something . . . personal. Right away."

Her brows shot up. "In my car?"

"Of course not." Although he hadn't intended to get out, now he did. He turned back to peer through the side window, making sure her face was averted. It wasn't. Then she wrinkled her nose and turned away.

He drew in a long breath and silenced every part of his body and mind. His awareness ranged outward. He didn't expect to detect a presence, or even a vital spark, however feeble. He was only hoping for some variation in the mood of the landscape, however infinitesimal, some tweak in his mind that would suggest a direction. It was all very impressionistic, and he was well aware that impressions could be influenced by desire, so he did his best not to want anything.

Time dripped on. Nothing, nothing, nothing.

Something?

Hmm. Maybe. Or not. So fleeting.

Dubykky couldn't feel it for sure, frustratingly. He let his mind back into his eyes, and suddenly there *was* a hint. A small movement up in the sky. He scanned slowly. There! A thin linear occlusion of stars. He focused. A bird? He watched. A tiny, frayed silhouette cutting across the Milky Way. A crow?

Dubykky fairly jumped back into the car. A snide remark was on its way out of Lurie's mouth, but he cut her off with orders to get moving.

Jurgen. Junior. It had to be. Jurgen was flying at Junior's behest. Dubykky was sure of it. He mentally estimated Jurgen's course, then peered into the night.

"Drive to just beyond that bend up ahead and pull off," he directed Lurie.

"But I'll get stuck in the sand, Will."

"Just do it. I'll buy you another car if it makes you happy."

Dubykky's tone alarmed her. She complied, swallowing her resentment.

When the car, crunching gravel on the soft shoulder, came to a stop, he shouldered out the door again, then leaned back in. "From here I hike. If you want to witness the climax of this whole wretched affair, you can come too. Otherwise, go back to town and alert the General and Younger that it's going to happen somewhere in that complex of ammo bunkers." He pointed.

"What's going to happen?"

"Come and see." He started off without waiting for a response.

Lurie hesitated. She had on peddle-pushers and flats, hardly suitable for tramping across the desert. But she was a journalist above all things. Curiosity won out. Climbing out of the car, she called Dubykky a jerk and meant it.

AMMUNITION BUNKERS, or igloos in navy parlance, come in various sizes and designs, though the basic shape is like an angular loaf of French bread. Those that Dubykky was now striding toward, while Lurie struggled to catch up, were built in 1931 and looked like loaves with a slice cut out between one heel and the rest. This heel was an earthen barricade faced with a concrete wall. Opposite was another thick concrete wall through which was the only entrance, a depressed iron blast door. Behind that was the main igloo, eighty feet long and twenty-five wide, a reinforced concrete structure covered by earth. Over the sunken floor, under the arched ceiling, there were twenty feet of clearance. A lot of room. Enough to store mayhem capable of killing tens of thousands, leveling towns, realigning nations.

The group of forty bunkers, each separated by six hundred feet, had gradually been emptied of their naval munitions following the Korean War. The Pentagon was preparing for new types of warfare, new tactics, new armaments, but had not yet decided what to put in these particular bunkers. They were empty, musty spaces whose electric lights had been disconnected. Like dungeons.

Just what Matt Gans appreciated. The bunkers attracted his interest as soon as he moved to Hawthorne. He spent the first semester covertly examining them, learning which were unused, the timing of Shore Patrol checks of the various areas, and the best access via back roads.

He settled on the southeastern bunker of the cluster farthest from the depot and town, and set to work. Breaking in required first the construction of a portable shed to hide the light from his principal tool, an acetylene torch, and five nights of intense bursts of work. Finally, though, he was in.

The space was too cavernous for his tastes, but with a little alteration quite suitable. He built an interior wall that created a room about an eighth of the bunker's length. Though he felt more comfortable in the smaller space, that was not the biggest reason for the wall. Large spaces diffused sound, and the sounds his girls made were central to a proper adventure. Worse, a space the size of the full bunker tended to produce echoes. Gans had a phobia of echoes. The alteration had taken up another couple of weeks of sporadic work. Yet another month passed before he moved in the basic furnishings. He had been ready since mid-April, but it was so bitterly cold inside the bunker that there was real danger of hypothermia. So his dungeon awaited warmer weather.

He pulled to a stop on the bunker side that faced away from Hawthorne, then checked Sarah's bonds. They were good and tight. He lifted the hood to check her face too. Her eyes immediately opened and she tried to grimace past the tape, but it was a feeble effort, and she did not make any violent movements. Spirited still, but she was exhausted. He tugged the hood back down.

Satisfied, he got out of the truck and went round to the entrance. One of the most difficult tasks of his alteration had been to disguise his work on the door so that a reasonably close inspection would reveal nothing unusual. This meant he now had to spend five to ten minutes unscrewing plates and removing false handles so he could insert a square-tipped metal bar that would engage the lock mechanism. Turning it, moreover, required a good deal of muscle power, which forced him to rest a couple of times.

Gans was still in the preliminary removal of screws stage when back in the truck Sarah felt a gentle tug on her wrists. The door was opening very slowly and quietly. She let out a muffled groan. The motion stopped. The door clicked closed. Though sick, hurt, woozy, and scared more than she had ever been before, Sarah had not entirely lost hope. She tried to shake the hood from her head so she could see. But it was no good. Was the bad man coming back for her? She didn't think so. She hoped not. Why would she not just be grabbed and hauled out if it was the bad man again? She held her breath and listened.

The driver's-side door opened with a low, slow creak. It seemed that whole minutes passed before the sound stopped. Then she felt the seat cushion sway as someone climbed onto it. All agonizingly slow, yet Sarah perceived it with refreshed hope.

Fingers closed around the loose fabric of the hood at her neck. The hood was drawn upwards. Even when it cleared the top of her head, though, Sarah kept her eyes closed for a few seconds, willing with all her might that this development might save her. Then popped them open.

And someone wholly unexpected it turned out to be. She looked into a squarish face, and even obscured by shadows she knew at once who it was. The strange boy Junior.

"I am Junior," he whispered in his odd flat way. "I like Sarah Muni."

Sarah made gagging noises in response. He removed the tape and cloth wad from her mouth, leaving a finger on her lips to warn her to keep quiet. "Speech is silver, silence is golden," he said. "We must be mute as a solid gold flute."

He untied her bonds, then pushed open her door so she could step out of the truck. She stood trembling on the ground, sore and weak at first, breathing in long gulps of air.

When he began to unbutton her pajamas, her strength returned in a rush, and she batted away his hands. But, gently, he resumed, saying, "I must be you, you must be me. It's the very best way to be."

He quickly removed her pajamas. For a brief time she stood in only her underpants under the bright, bright stars, listening to a thin, intermittent whine of metal scraping in the distance, until he had taken off his own clothes and dressed her in them. He was murmuring to himself, "I wish I may, I wish I might, have the wish I wish tonight."

When he finished, he picked up the velvet hood from the truck seat and said to her, "Ladybird, ladybird, fly away home. Find Kind Sir. Find Sweet Auntie. Now I must be you." He climbed in the passenger side of the truck and closed the door with a soft *tunk*.

Sarah didn't want him to go away, but far more she didn't want to stay put. She looked around wildly. A harsh scraping from one end of the bunker made her jump. She set off running in the opposite direction, toward the distant glimmer of Hawthorne.

She ran and ran, stumbled because of the unfamiliar clothes, got her balance, and kept running, not caring when her bare feet landed on the gnarly stem of a sagebrush or how the course sand slipped under her and scraped her soles. She got quickly out of breath and had to stop, hands on knees, feeling weak and dizzy again. The lights of town were just too far away, she realized. She turned in a complete circle. Where to go? Then the headlights of a car slid by in the distance. The highway! She started off toward it, running again for a dozen steps but then having to slow to a walk. The sound of her name came to her in an urgent whisper and froze her mid-step, dread welling up again like the reflex to vomit.

"Sarah," a man's voice repeated. "It's all right. I'm with Junior."

She breathed out slowly, forcing herself to look around. The dark shape of a man stood next to the nearest bunker, beckoning at her. He was joined by the shape of a woman who limped to a stop beside him.

"Come here, Sarah, we'll take you home."

Could she trust them? Did she have a choice? The man's voice was kind, reassuring, and when he dropped into a crouch, so that he and she would be at eye level, Sarah went to him. He held out his hand. When she took it, she looked hard into his shadowed face and recognized him. She had seen him at Walker Lake, too, on the same day as Junior. Was he *Kind Sir*? The woman watched silently, her face hawkish but unthreatening.

Sarah burst out, "The bad man grabbed me out of bed and tied me up so it hurt and we were in a car or something for a long time and my mouth was stuffed so I couldn't breathe and I almost died and couldn't see anything and Junior found me and untied me and took my pajamas and got in the truck and told me to run fast and the bad man's going to take him—and—and—" She gulped a breath.

The man lay his hand on her shoulder. "Sarah, you can take it easy now. It's going to be all right. I'm Mr. Dubykky, and I'm here to help Junior. This is Miss Lurie, and she'll make sure you get home to your parents."

"What?" the woman said crossly. Mr. Dubykky shushed her, so she lowered her voice. A rapid argument followed. Miss Lurie said she was not a babysitter, was here for "the story." Mr. Dubykky insisted that

Sarah had to be protected. Miss Lurie refused to go tramping back through the desert at night with a barefoot kid. Ridiculous.

"Fine," Dubykky replied, impatient. "Stay here, just—" But then he froze and motioned for Sarah and Lurie to hug the wall of the bunker.

From the highway came the distant sound of a car gearing down. Dubykky peered around the bunker wall. The car turned off the road and doused its headlights but kept on the parking lights. It approached at a crawl.

And *that*, Dubykky surmised, must be Misty.

Was she here to stop her husband or help him? He feared the latter and kept his eyes on the car, musing on the preposterously elaborate subterfuges of evil.

JURGEN'S FEELINGS WERE RUFFLED. His boy had literally forced him—forced him!—to fly away. He was not used to such treatment, and it stuck in his craw, even if there was a task for him to do. He was supposed to circle over the strange buildings and watch. Watch for what? He didn't know. All he was sure of was that he was tired and sleepy and a little hungry and peeved by his boy and generally fluffed about everything. So instead of doing as he was told, he glided down to the bunker. By it stood the vehicle that Junior had disappeared into. He perched on one edge of the bunker's big slot. In landing, his claws scraped on harsh concrete, which he had mistaken for something softer, like chalk or gypsum. Below a man emerged from the bunker and looked around, paused, then went back inside. He came out again once more after a minute and walked quickly to the truck. Jurgen followed his every move.

Gans had a sensibility highly attuned to trouble, so highly attuned in fact that often he could not discover the source of disquiet. As soon as he opened the truck door to get the Indian girl, he felt something wrong. He fought his lust to hurry on with the adventure, to get to the joyfully, liberatingly painful climax. Concentrating, he inspected the cab. What was different?

The Indian girl had shifted slightly on the truck seat, but that was not important. He ran his finger over the knots holding the clothesline around her wrists and the armrest. Loose again! She must still have had enough energy to struggle. Well, that was it then. The little minx. Nothing to worry about after all. And besides, he was pleased that she had enough vinegar left in her to fight. He didn't like his prey to be passive. Real joy came from struggle and conquest.

He untied the clothesline, pinning her wrists together with one hand, and grasping her under the arm with the other, rolled her over onto his shoulder. She did not resist, although an odd little deep grunt escaped her when her stomach was pressed against his clavicle.

Inside the bunker, Gans flipped Sarah off his shoulder and onto the mattress. She landed on her side and was still. After dimming the Coleman lantern that provided the room's only light, he hurried back out the entrance to check on something he'd noticed while carrying in Sarah. Sure enough. Damn. He could see parking lights juddering in the distance. A car was following the narrow twin tracks from the highway that he had hoed out a month ago. Only Misty knew the way. She was early.

Damn. He rushed back inside, unlatching his belt. He'd have to hurry. But then, Misty was sensible. She'd probably wait to give him plenty of time before it was her turn. But then again, George was with her. His first time. He'd be antsy. Gans wondered if their planning had been insufficient, then pushed the worry out of his mind. There would be time for a critique later. He had his loafers and pants off, kicking them beside the door as he passed through, and was peeling off his jersey when he heard the strangest thing of his entire life. A voice, almost like his own in timbre but lacking expressiveness, said, "I am Matthew Gans."

He flung away the jersey, leaving himself in socks and jockey shorts. He was ready.

But everything else was wrong. This wasn't how his adventure was supposed to go. There on the mattress was not pretty little Indian Sarah, but a boy. He wore her pajamas. He held the hood in his hand. The clothesline lay in a tangle at his feet.

Gans goggled, dumbstruck. A boy, not a girl? How?

And it was an ugly boy with a mess of dark hair. An ugly scar by the mouth. Like the cuts Misty had made in the other girls. Gans blinked in astonishment, then looked around wildly. Where was his prey? What had happened to her? Disappointment stabbed him. He had been cheated! There had been a switch. How? Only Misty knew he was here. And she was just now arriving. Nothing made sense.

"I am Matthew Gans," said Junior.

A sour, silent keening of fear and injustice started filling Gans's head. He needed little girls, not little boys. How could he be cheated like this? When the boy opened his mouth to speak again, Gans shouted, "Shut up, you little shit!"

This adventure was a bust. All the work and late hours and enduring the cold, all for nothing. Now how was he going to handle the hunger, which with all the delay, on the very verge of satisfaction, was bursting in him? Hatred seized and shook him. It only made it worse that the boy looked like a thicker version of his pathetic son Dougie.

But the boy was unperturbed. For a third time he made his ridiculous claim. "I am Matthew Gans."

"*Shut your mouth*! I *am Matt Gans*." He was screaming at the boy, his hatred like the froth on his lips, and yet part of him experienced something like recognition. It was like the déjà-vu feeling, the perception of something as familiar that cannot be familiar.

"We are Matt Gans," said Junior. "What is the reason we must go? I cannot tell, for I do not know."

At that, Gans's hatred deflated. In its place, dread chilled him like a cold electric shock, to the bone. He longed for his toys so he could protect himself, but that part of the adventure, when the toys were wielded, he always enjoyed with Misty, and she kept them to bring with her for the dramatic entrance. How could he deal with the crazy boy without them? He glanced around the room. Of course! The hammer. He had neglected to take it home after building the false wall. Lucky oversight! He leapt to where his carpenter's belt lay on the floor and pulled the hammer free.

But the boy was also in motion. By the time Gans straightened up, hammer in hand, Junior had clambered up on his shoulders. Teeth clamped onto the nape of his neck, a wide powerful bite. Gans bellowed at the pain. He swung the hammer backward over his shoulder. It struck flesh, but the bite only sank deeper. Junior began chewing at him. Gans swung again and again, yet the boy clung there silently. He would not let go. Gans felt blood trickle down his back and realized it was his own. He panicked, whirling to throw off his attacker. That didn't work either. So he dropped the hammer and leaped backward, landing on top of the boy. That did it. Junior's grip loosened. Gans threw himself into a roll.

As he did, there was a powerful pull at his neck, then a sudden and sickening release. The pain was terrific. His throat was raw with roaring, and tears blurred his eyes, yet when he did manage to get a look at the boy, it was even worse. In Junior's mouth was a chunk of Gans's neck muscle, the size of one finger. Around that chunk Junior's teeth ran with blood. It smeared his chin, and bubbled from his nose.

Gans screamed, clasping his neck with one hand, using the other and his heels to propel himself away. Where was Misty?

"Misty!" he screamed as Junior spit out the bloody mouthful and started toward him on hands and knees.

But no sounds passed through the thick concrete walls or the stout iron door of the bunker. Misty Gans heard nothing. In any case she was occupied with giving her son strict instructions.

"You stay behind me," she said. "And do nothing. *Nothing.* Until I tell you. Now here, hold this." She passed over a three-foot cudgel with a coarse rag wrapped tightly around one end.

Misty had gotten the idea at Disneyland. It was while taking her younger boys there a year ago that she saw tiki torches for the first time, and it gave her pause. Why not? How perfect, really. She had not told her husband about the idea, wanting it to be a surprise. And she knew at once that it would work. What would suit a dungeon better than a torch? And for more than just light. Torch . . . torture. That was proof of concept! She had experimented and found that canvas with the right amount of paraffin soaked in, tied around an oak stick, produced a reliable and thrilling new toy.

It irked her having to waste time explaining to George. She spoke viciously. But he didn't mind, he was so excited, and seeing it she felt the excitement heat up in her, too. They got out of the car.

Dubykky and Lurie, with Sarah Muni shielded behind her, watched them. The car doors opened, the overhead light illuminated the maniacal faces of Misty and George Gans, the doors closed, and the two were hulks in the darkness gliding toward the bunker entrance.

"Will," Lurie whispered. "You have to stop them. You have to get the boy."

No, I don't, he thought, I mustn't. But he was arguing against himself. He wanted to intervene. And it wasn't because of George Gans's presence, although that surprised Dubykky and worried him—George was an innocent. No, it was because he badly wanted to rescue Junior. It was perverse, it was wrong, but the feeling was undeniable. Had he developed paternal affection for the young echo? Nonsense, yet here he was taking a step in pursuit of the Gans duo.

Then fingers clutched at his jacket. It was Sarah. She had ducked under Lurie's hand and grabbed, not wanting Dubykky to leave them unprotected. She didn't speak, but she didn't have to. Terror craves company. Lurie also looked afraid, torn about being left alone with the girl.

Go? Stay? Save Junior as he wanted, or leave him to his fate as he ought? The decision was made for Dubykky when a flash of light appeared in the hand of Misty Gans. He sank into a crouch, as did Lurie.

Misty let the match bloom fully, then touched it to the head of the tiki torch. Blue flames spread over the cloth like oil over water. Then with a flare the torch was ablaze good and proper, and she handed it to George. She drew out the bundle from her jacket pocket and unwrapped it. In the torch light the metal of the butcher knife seemed to sparkle in its depths, seemed as charged as she was. She slipped on her mask, then took the handle in her fist, blade down, and descended to the bunker door. She leaned into it, shoving it open with her free hand, the snarl already rising in her throat. She nodded without looking back. George, smiling and wide-eyed, held the torch up high.

Then Misty pushed all the way in, shouting through the mask of Minnie Mouse, "You filthy little bitch, I've caught you at it this time. It's the last—"

And choked to a stop.

Everything was wrong. In the dim lantern light nothing looked as it was supposed to. She reached back and pulled George farther into the room so the torch lit everything better, and as she did, her husband cried out in panic, "Kill him, Misty, kill him!"

Matt was doubled up, back against the wall, blood seeping between the fingers pressing on his neck. A boy in pajamas—not a naked whimpering girl, as she expected, but a boy—was crawling toward him. And the boy didn't look afraid. He looked like a demon, his jaw covered in blood. He paused, swung his head round toward Misty, his bloody, toothy mouth spreading in a hideous smile.

Her hand still holding onto George's sleeve, Misty lurched forward, raising the butcher knife. She stabbed down at the boy, hard, but he twisted out of the way, rolling onto his back. The momentum of the blade carried past him and, just as George stumbled to her side, nicked her son's thigh.

George yipped in pain and tore loose from her. Misty, urged on by her hysterical husband, raised the knife again. The diabolical little boy would not escape her.

By then Jurgen had heard enough. He knew that his Junior was inside the building and was afraid for him. Now it was worse. Two more humans had just gone inside. He couldn't hear Junior's voice, but there was an insane racket. Worrisome enough, but a ball of flame on a stick had gone into the room as well. Jurgen hated fire. It terrified him. The thought that it might be used on Junior, however, propelled him off his perch above the door. He executed a pinwheel pivot and streaked into the bunker.

The apparition, out of nowhere, of a squawking, flailing crow flashing by her and stretching out its claws at Matt unnerved Misty Gans entirely. When it swooped around, she slashed wildly at it with the knife, missing again, but felt the blade nonetheless meet resistance. George now was squawking, too. His eyes were wide and unseeing, one hand rising to the deep cut in his neck and the blood that was gushing out. The tiki torch fell to the floor.

Misty, irritated, scowled at her son and went for the torch. Her husband crawled for it, too. But it was Junior who got his hand on it first.

Overhead, Jurgen executed tight circles, seeking a way to help his boy. One of the other humans, a muscular young one, fell onto his side, a pool of red spreading from his neck. Jurgen discounted him. The other two were reaching for the fireball stick. Jurgen dived.

Junior was no match for Matt Gans in strength. The man wrenched the torch from his hand. But just as he shoved it at the boy's face, the crow was scratching at his. Jurgen was no match for Gans either, not in strength or agility, and the claws did nothing more than distract him. Confined in the room, Jurgen could not fly away quickly either. And so when Gans waved the torch over his head, the haft struck Jurgen a blow in the tail that sent him tumbling to the floor.

Junior's hair was singed and smoking, one side of his face burnt, and he lay panting. While her husband was busy swatting at the crow, Misty aimed another stab at the boy. Her mask had slipped awry, though. She didn't have a clear view, so the point of the blade hit straight on the concrete floor just a quarter inch away from Junior's knee. Her hands, already slick with George's blood, slid down along the blade at the impact, cutting deeply into her palm, and with a howl she let go. Tucking the injured hand into her armpit, she swept off the Minnie Mouse mask with the other and reached for the knife.

But Junior kicked it away. He was scooting backwards on his rump away from Gans when the man swung the torch at him again. It was a wide sweeping attack, and Junior was able to lie flat at the exact right second. It passed just over him. Centripetal force caused the flaming fabric to slip off the end of the cudgel. It flattened against the wooden wall, splattering little daubs of fire. Soon fire was sheeting up the plywood. Its glue began popping and smoking, filling the small room with choking heat.

When Misty Gans pulled open the bunker door to get out, Jurgen launched himself at the opening, bounding off her head to get more speed. At the needling impact of his claws, she recoiled, striking her shoulder against the frame. She paused, looking back into the room, first at her son, dying or already dead on the floor, and then at her husband. He was struggling to get to his feet, but the boy had his arms wrapped around one leg, so that Gans alternately hit at him and dragged him over the floor, desperate to get away from the fire and out of the smoke. For a second Misty was torn between the urge to flee and the desire, unexpectedly powerful, to help her husband. She went to him just as Junior gave Gans's knee a violent yank backward. Gans yowled and tipped over, buckling his shoulder against the wall. He flailed to get away from it as the flames spread to his hair, but Junior still held on, and he ended up falling against the wall once again.

Misty kicked at the boy. It made absolutely no impression on him. He hugged Matt's leg just as tightly. So she grabbed up the knife with her uninjured left hand and lunged forward with it. The blade sank into the boy's thigh and cut a gash toward his hip along the bone, but then her left hand also slipped, although, immediately releasing the handle, this time she was not cut.

Enough damage was done to the boy anyhow. Finally, he let go of Matt to hit out at her. Screaming, Matt pressed his palms over the blistering scalp. Misty fumbled for the knife, got a firm hold, and drew it back for a another stab, this one aimed straight at the boy's heart, her hand tightening on the handle until her knuckles blanched. Her grip would not fail her again.

When the bunker door opened and smoke gushed outward and then Jurgen exited squawking and flapping like an angry black asterisk, Dubykky pushed Sarah into Lurie's arms and ran. He did not hesitate at the steps, ignoring everything, even the smoke, but took a deep breath and plunged in, halting just beyond because of the heat. Through the smoke he saw Misty Gans, looming over Junior, pull back her arm, her hand holding a long bloody knife. Junior held out his hands to ward her off. Behind him, Matt Gans rolled on the floor at the foot of a makeshift plywood wall. The revolting odor of burnt hair and flesh penetrated the smoky pall.

"*No!*" shouted Dubykky with all his might.

Misty Gans hesitated, looked back at him, grimaced, and swiped at him with the knife so he had to flinch away. Then she stepped toward Junior, raising her hand high for another stab.

Dubykky hunched to jump at her, but a hand on his shoulder pushed him to his knees as a great *Boom* rang out over his head. Misty's body arched forward so fast that her head and arms flew backwards and for an instant she looked as though she were executing a swan dive, while a spray of blood splattered Junior and the floor. She collapsed onto Junior. With a creak and groan, the wall bent forward over them, enclosing her and her husband, as well as Junior beneath her, in a fiery tent.

Choking, his ears still roaring from the explosion, Dubykky found himself hauled backwards until he was sitting on the step in front of the bunker door, side by side with Lieutenant Parselknapp. The lieutenant's eyes were large as fried eggs. In his hand was a .45 Colt automatic which he stared at with astonishment. Behind them, a hand on the collar of each, a very large marine wearing a big white cap and a Shore Patrol armband sat on the next step up.

The lieutenant shook himself and yelled at Dubykky, "We've got to get away. *Now!*"

Dubykky shook his head violently and twisted out of the marine's grasp. "No, there's a boy in there. I've got to get him out."

Both the marine and lieutenant made grabs at his arm, the lieutenant shouting, "These igloos have enough residuals to explode in a fire."

But Dubykky was already back inside. He dove flat over the floor, which was now so hot to the touch that his palms stung. Grabbing Misty's ankles, he levered her into a sideward roll against the burning plywood. Just enough space opened for him to reach in past her and close his hand over the hem of a pajama leg. He rolled it over his fist just as he felt his own legs taken up, and he was dragged backwards once more, pulling Junior out from among the bodies in the process.

Lieutenant Parselknapp reached past and took Junior out of Dubykky's hands, hustling up the steps, while the marine, having heaved Dubykky over his shoulder, followed. They ran some five steps before a deafening *Wump* came from behind, and all four were thrown to the ground.

Thirteen

Lieutenant Parselknapp was a hero. So was Dubykky. Loretta Lurie saw to that personally. A special edition of the *Mineral County Independent-News* hit the stands late afternoon Monday.

SERIAL MURDERERS FOILED!!!

Naval Officer Slays Rapist-Killers in the Attempt!!!

Predators of Children Bring Horror from Los Angeles to Hawthorne,

But Local Lawyer Saves Victim

By Loretta Lurie, Executive Editor

BABBITT—A crime of unimaginable cruelty and horror was stopped just seconds before it happened late last night in the Navy Ammunition Depot. Based on a tip from the Los Angeles County District Attorney, the Depot Officer of the Deck, Lt. Harold Parselknapp, reached the outermost bunker of the facility in time to shoot Misty Gans as she and her husband were preparing to stab to death six-year-old Junior Szellem.

What followed was a series of facts, half-truths, misdirection, outright errors, and quotes used to distract readers from obvious holes in her story. It made Dubykky grin appreciatively. Lurie had produced a first-rate narrative. Soon it would be printed throughout the nation, because she had phoned in a version to the Associated Press office in Reno. Months of updates, elaborations, and revelations awaited her as problems were noticed.

Just for instance, who was this Junior Szellem? It would soon become apparent that nobody in Hawthorne had ever heard of him. Dubykky doubted, moreover, that anyone among the readership spoke Hungarian, and if one did, would he inquire of Loretta why the injured boy's name was Spirit? Not likely, but what if someone did? The prospect amused Dubykky. It was always a good idea to leave confusion behind him.

He had a lot to thank Lurie for. Most of all, Sarah Muni's name did not appear. Lurie took her home while Dubykky accompanied Parselknapp to the hospital with Junior. Paul and Judy Muni were effusively grateful to her, the more so when she voluntarily promised not to mention Sarah. A promise that Dubykky had bullied her to make.

Dorothy Younger was quoted as saying that the county and state had to do more to protect today's youth and prepare them for modern life. A solid preview for her state senate campaign.

Good.

Cledge's name appeared only in passing as having assisted Dubykky's investigation, which in the long run would help his career.

Good.

Mildred was not in the story at all.

Very good.

When Cledge walked into the office on Monday morning, Mildred was on his arm. As soon as she saw Dubykky, she rushed to give him a hug. A garbled version of events had already reached them. Dubykky straightened the story out, watching their faces carefully. When Mildred looked at Cledge, which she did frequently, there was a hint of smug triumph to her face. For his part, Cledge was bashful around her, but his face when he met her gaze was completely beguiled. It was plain enough what had happened while Dubykky was away saving Junior.

She had succeeded in bedding Cledge, and he had pleased her. An experience like that for an echo's child was a turning point. Mildred and Milt were a couple, now and always. Dubykky need worry over her no further. His obligation to Victor Warden was discharged.

Yet despite these neat turns of events, the article left Dubykky profoundly unsettled. He had failed. Junior survived. Worse, he survived because Dubykky had ignored his duty and saved him from the fire.

All that Dubykky's long life had taught him about the order of nature was violated. He had kept alive an echo of evil when it should have expired naturally. Nothing but more evil would come from that. His affection for Junior, his moral weakness, would endanger others. Only of that could Dubykky be positive.

Yet his feelings about the boy continued to argue with him. Odd as he was, Junior listened, learned, made friends, helped, and liked and was liked. Even Dorothy Younger, a woman with no maternal impulses, was drawn to him. He had made friends, of a sort, with Dougie Gans and Sarah. And—the clincher for Dubykky—there was Jurgen. The crow was bonded to the boy. Junior might have sprung from evil, but there was a natural purity to him. Irresistible. For now—maybe, said Dubykky's voice of duty. Contact with humans would change Junior, just as it had changed Dubykky. The nature of the changes could not be foreseen, or guided. Meanwhile, whatever happened to him, wherever he was, Junior would be an aberration. The unaging boy.

It could not be allowed. And yet Dubykky still resisted his clear duty because a revelation had come to him. First Victor Warden, and now Junior, had awakened feelings that had never touched him before. Vitality, wonder, captivation. Life felt different, appealing.

So Dubykky daydreamed, if only I could get Junior away from people. Some special arrangement, precautions . . . He was startled out of it when Cledge walked into his office. There was work for them to do. Cledge, beaming like a spotlight, opened discussion on their most pressing case. Though his indecision oppressed him, Dubykky immersed himself in the details.

EVERYTHING turned wrong for Jurgen.

After he fled the strange, disgusting house-cave on the desert floor, so frightened his tail wouldn't stop twitching, he soared overhead in wide circles, waiting. Junior did not come out. Then his oldest human, Will, went in too. From above, the angle was bad. Jurgen couldn't see well. Nothing was clear. Then came a terrible loud noise, like a monstrous wing beat, and a flash of light. Doubly frightened, Jurgen flew away as fast as his wings could carry him.

What about Junior? What about Will? Did they escape the terrible noise? Or was that what humans did to die—go into a cave? Jurgen did not know and trembled.

Matters only got worse.

Calming, he headed to Hawthorne, seeking the comfort of fellow crows at the rookery. Dawn was breaking by then. Crowdom was stirring, wings stretching out, croaking murmurs passing through the sleepy community.

But as soon as Jurgen alighted, the sentinel blurted a stentorian alarm. Suddenly, the crows lofted almost as one and, landing, positioned themselves facing him. What then happened was entirely shocking, something, young as Jurgen was, he never imagined. The crows began screaming at him. Awful things were said, devastating things. To them, he was worse even than humans. He was a pet.

He fled again, driven away not just by their rage but by the stinging realization that in part it was justified.

Crows are gregarious. Solitude distressed Jurgen nearly to panic. He sought out the one place he was sure to be accepted, whatever his transgressions. With a lightened heart he flapped across town to the park beside the courthouse.

He settled a polite five feet away from the nest and crooned his special call to the mated pair who had raised him. And waited.

And waited.

The mated pair kept their backs to him. Were they angry with him for staying away? They must have known what he was up to. Still, it occurred to him, an explanation would be a civil gesture. He had an idea for that. He launched himself from the cottonwood swooping low over the ground. Humans had a way of casting off perfectly beautiful things wherever they went. If he brought back a beautiful thing, it would please them, as well as explain his recent experiences. He searched, keen for the right thing.

There it lay! Shiny and orange and perfectly round. Just the thing to entrance a crow. Jurgen landed, delicately flipped over the bottle cap, then taking it in his beak he returned to the cottonwood.

He deposited the cap in the nest, squawking cheerfully. The mated pair, startled, gawked.

The female canted her head to study the cap. But only for a second. Then with an angry *kgrank* she was speeding away. Her mate reared, flaring his wings, and he too launched, passing right over Jurgen and giving him a sharp peck on the head.

Stunned, humiliated, Jurgen took off, flying blindly. Rejected by his community and family, his humans dead, where could he go? He flew with misery, his only companion.

TWO DAYS LATER, Hawthorne's only general practitioner and surgeon admitted that Junior needed more sophisticated care than could be given at a rural hospital. The stab wound had been stabilized, but the burns to his face and neck were trickier and required a specialist's attention. Doctor St. Claire admitted these things to Dorothy Younger, who was assumed to be responsible for Junior. She had called Dubykky to accompany her to a meeting with the doctor at Mount Grant General Hospital, but a surprising number of others showed up, too.

Lurie was there in her capacity as a reporter, pad in hand, pencil poised to take notes. Also in his official capacity, representing the navy, was Lieutenant Parselknapp. He was a happy man. His commanding officer was recommending him for the Navy and Marine Corps Medal, also known as the lifesaving medal. But even more important for his career, scuttlebutt had it that he was the first member of his Academy class to shoot and kill someone in the line of duty. His reputation was made.

Doctor St. Claire led the group to the hospital bed. He took Junior's pulse, listened through his stethoscope, turned back an eyelid, and muttered a professional hmm. No change. Junior was sedated. Half his face, neck, and one shoulder were swathed in bandages. He looked like some strange organism emerging from a cocoon.

Knowing there was nothing he could do about Junior just then, Dubykky stepped back to observe. The General had come with Younger, the Gans boys in tow. O'Faelan, Younger, and the boys stood together in a way suggesting a nascent family group. Were he and Younger planning to be their guardians? She could arrange it easily enough. Would that work if she took a seat in the state senate? Dubykky decided, relieved, it was no longer his lookout.

Doctor St. Claire cleared his throat. Junior, he told them, could be moved the next day. He would order an ambulance to drive him to Reno. Which hospital was to be the one to treat him, St. Mary's or Washoe County Medical Center? He addressed the question to Younger, but Dubykky spoke up.

It was with an inward sigh that he said, "I'll take him myself, if it's all the same to you."

Though surprised, the doctor was relieved that his hospital would not have to bear the expense of transportation. He allowed that the boy would be able to travel with a nonmedical person, promising to give Junior enough sedation to make him comfortable during the three-hour drive. When he asked about the hospital, Dubykky chose St. Mary's. He preferred taking evil to a Catholic institution.

THE RULES FOR DISAPPEARING WERE: give no sign, take nothing, leave no trail; go fast, don't do as Lot's wife, stay gone. Dubykky
was thoroughly practiced. How many times had he done it? Dozens,
probably. He never kept a count. He didn't like to think about it. Each
time was much like the one before, identical imps tagging behind,
dragging at his soul.

If he had a soul. It was times like these that he understood the concept to be a moot point for him. If he did not have to die, ever, there
was no need for a soul. That is, if he thought of a soul as like chalk on
the eraser—what remained when death wiped your slate.

Dubykky angled down the rearview mirror of his Edsel and glanced
at Junior, lying in the back seat. Did he have a soul? He had awareness,
and he was supposed to die. Wasn't that enough? Junior had something
to lose. Wasn't that how humans thought of their soul?

Early that morning as the eastern sky was brightening, Dubykky
had tucked Junior in the back seat. Nurses helped, bringing out blankets and pillows from the hospital. Movement was painful for the echo.
He came awake, despite the nurses' gentleness. Dull-eyed and distant,
but awake. While being made comfortable and lashed down snug so he
wouldn't roll onto the car floor, he kept his eyes on Dubykky. The two
did not speak, but there was trust and understanding in Junior's eyes.
And resignation. His purpose was fulfilled. He was done and knew it.

Doctor St. Claire got there just as Dubykky was ready to start off.
The doctor was brisk, examining Junior carefully to make sure he was
tied down securely but not too tightly. Because Junior was conscious,
St. Claire administered another small injection of phenobarbital. Then
he trained his sternest professional stare on Dubykky and made him
promise to stop every half hour to check on the boy and give him a
little water if he was awake.

"And avoid those potholes outside Fallon," he finished.

"He'll feel nothing," Dubykky replied, slapping the doctor on the shoulder, which earned him a haughty glare.

Now, only twenty minutes later, he came to the sharpest curve above the steepest hillside over Walker Lake. He pushed the accelerator to the floor, and the car shot forward until, just yards from the curve, he stomped on the brakes. The car skidded, tires screeching. Dubykky juked the steering wheel to make the car fishtail once to the left and once to the right. He nearly misjudged the distance. The car juddered to a halt with the rear wheels still on the pavement but the right front wheel free of the dirt on the shoulder, hanging above the slope.

The braking and skidding had jostled Junior too much. When Dubykky opened the rear door to check on him, the echo's eyes were open again. Just as Dubykky had suspected, Doctor St. Claire, assuming Junior to be a standard human child, had injected too little sedative.

Dubykky was prepared, though, having picked the doctor's smock pocket when he slapped his back. He took out the syringe and filled it from the vial of phenobarbital. At first Junior did not react when Dubykky freed one of his arms and gave him an injection. Enough to knock out a horse.

But while Dubykky was tucking the arm back under the blanket, he whispered, "I am Junior."

"Yes, you are. You are uniquely you. And pure, free of all evil association, past or future." Dubykky said it as much for himself, almost envious.

Junior still did not react. His eyes remained fixed on the car ceiling for a moment, then rolled slowly counterclockwise in a full circle, the space between his brows bunching in worry.

"Jurgen is Jurgen," he said, barely audible.

Dubykky had not caught sight of the crow since the incident at the ammunition bunker and had no idea whether he was still in the area, or even alive. But there was no doubt about one thing: heedless honesty would be cruel.

He lied, "Jurgen is safe and well. I'll bet he's flying overhead right now hoping to get a peep at you."

Junior's face relaxed, his eyelids lowering halfway. He mumbled, "This little boy . . . ." but trailed off unintelligibly to a slow, rough release of breath, his eyes fluttering all the way shut.

"Is the good little boy," Dubykky finished for him. "You are a good echo, Junior. The best."

He was also the youngest echo Will had encountered, and he had faced the most complicated task. Junior's target was larger and stronger, and he did not even realize that his quest had involved two adults. Their names were so similar, their evil so intertwined, that no distinguishing pronunciation had accompanied Junior's creation to guide his search.

He brushed a lock of stiff hair from Junior's forehead and, bending over carefully, kissed him once on the left eye and once on the right, then touched a finger to the flattened tip of his nose.

For a moment Dubykky remained bent over, breathing in the young one's breath, flavored with sage and ozone, as the events of the past month flitted through his mind. He shook Junior's shoulders gently, but the eyes did not reopen. Heaving a sigh, Dubykky backed out of the car, pushed down the lock knob, and eased shut the door as readers might do with the cover of a book they think has ended too soon.

For a second he stood still, downcast, unfocused, unwilling. A breeze washed around him, soft as alpaca and bearing the faint, sad odor of decay as if from far away.

How odd!

The desert air typically held still early on a cloudless spring morning. Dubykky glanced down at the lake. It was glasslike.

What?!!

Underfoot the ground shuddered, or seemed to. Dubykky, already puzzled by the wind, wondered whether he was imagining things. But no. On the hillside across the road a trickle of gravelly sand slipped a few feet downward.

Ah. Yes.

A polite nudge. Get on with it, nature urged.

He went round to the driver's side and got in. A turn of the ignition, a jab at the drive-gear button, a stomp on the accelerator as he rolled out the door onto the shoulder, and it was done. The car jumped forward and over the edge, accelerating down the slope. The fender hit an outcropping thirty feet below, and the car turned a ponderous forward somersault into the lake. Dubykky watched it plunge under the surface, then bob up again, the trunk in the air, its lid swinging open. Big belches came out a window, and the car rocked sideways.

Unlike the mountains, the lake had no stolid subtleties; unlike the capricious air, it was self-contained. It was quite ready to receive the car, a sacrifice that buoyed it ever so slightly after decades of losing territory to humanity.

Another burp of air, this time from the engine compartment, and the lake wrapped the car in its loose embrace and pulled it down. The spot was deep, more than thirty feet. A second later the car faded to a ghost in the bright blue water and then disappeared. Its trail of bubbles petered out like a bitter chuckle.

There were times in his life, precious few, when Dubykky wished that he could weep. He had witnessed riots, mass executions, chaotic battles, grizzly deaths, charnel-house scenes of mayhem and cruelty, yet none of it had moved him as did the sight of his car disappearing into an obscure desert lake carrying with it an echo only one month old. Yet no tears came. Just futility and loss.

And the future.

He walked off down the blacktop, hiding from the two cars that passed minutes later, until he came to a place where he could set off into the desert, out of sight and alone. He tried to cheer himself by imagining what headlines Loretta Lurie would write for the next edition of the *Independent-News*:

Local Hero Dies in Accident.

William Dubykky Plunges into Walker Lake

En Route to Reno with Injured Kidnap Victim.

Only Boy's Body Found.

The story would tell of a skid, a desperate attempt to keep the car on the road, and the deadly plunge to the lake. Lurie would have a grand time with the follow-up: the car winched out, no trace of Dubykky, mourning friends, their resolve to carry on in directions that he had pointed them. Picturing it made him grin.

He skirted the northern end of the lake until he met a dirt road that was the back way to Schurz and turned north. His spirits lifted as the sun rose high and the desert came alive.

He would go into the army again, he decided. There was a war on the horizon, a big one. The prospect buoyed him. Wars had clarity; there were defined sides, friends and foes. Wars were refreshing, chances to redefine himself. It was peace that was foggy. It was peace that was agonized by conflicting obligations, unaccountable tasks, and the duty to hunt down creatures like himself. The straightforward brutality of war, wherever, would take his mind off Junior and the evil, intimate and shadowy, that had brought them both into existence.

And he could change his name. That almost made Dubykky laugh. He used to concoct such glorious names! Le Comte Vilmos Damiani de Foîtu. Graf Uil'yam d'Yavola. Sir William Lucius Raddinghouse Demond. And his particular favorite, William cú Diabhal, Sciúirse-Casúr. Those were the days! He would make up something really debonair for the next war. Now what should it be?

But he didn't get the chance to think. There was a swish and whoosh, and claws dug into his shoulder. "Kind sir," said Jurgen and nipped his earlobe.

Dubykky could not bear being called that now. "Will," he said.

"Will," Jurgen echoed.

Dubykky sighed and *tsk*ed and, reaching up, lightly ruffled Jurgen's chest feathers, which made him raise his beak and clack happily. Dubykky never for a second considered shooing away the crow. As soon as claw touched shoulder they were partners. He had been the crow's first friend, and he would be the last. Junior had only had him on loan.

Dubykky's fantasy of yet another brisk military vacation faded away. No army would accept a recruit with a crow on his shoulder. And, it seemed, he would have to remain Will. That's how Jurgen knew him.

"All right, Jurgen, my friend. We've got a mission, you and I. Highly difficult, probably dangerous, undoubtedly necessary. There's a rogue at large somewhere out there in this sad, flighty world, and we're going to find her."

In fact, there was more than the rogue to concern him, there were deep mysteries, but he didn't tell Jurgen so.

Why had Junior been made a boy rather than a girl like the victims? Did he look like Dougie Gans because Dougie would have been the next in line to die? Then there was the matter of his target. Matt and Misty. Two evildoers. It had happened before, a monstrous duo, but only once that Dubykky knew of. Victor Warden's brother-sister target. Maybe evil was somehow changing the way it conducted its business. Dubykky shied from the thought. Evil's steady orthodoxy had always been a comfort.

Ah, well.

For now, what else could he say?

He took the gris-gris bag out of his inside coat pocket and hefted it. It was callous to steal it from Dorothy Younger, sure. She treasured her only memento of her grandmother, Hortense May. Yet his duty trumped her nostalgia.

ACKNOWLEDGMENTS

Echoes owes its gestation and birth to the Baobab Press editorial team: Christine Kelly, Karen Wikander, Molly Albert, Curtis Vickers, and Margaret Dalrymple. It was a heartening surprise to find my story taken seriously, even liked; it was a deep pleasure to attend the editorial sessions and read their comments, which embodied the good nature, considerate scrutiny, and meticulousness that only true literature lovers can offer. They have my admiration and gratitude.

Friends and family also critiqued *Echoes* in its permutations and endured my fixation with it: Bill Wilborn, Whit Draper, Corinna Wilborn, and Matt Giraud. My thanks goes to them too, and particularly to Matt for acquainting me with social media marketing. And thanks to my wife, Sandy Wilborn, I enjoyed a calm place to work, commonsensical encouragement, and an adamant refusal to put up with silliness in my writing.

Rogues

ROGER ARTHUR SMITH

Keep reading for a special excerpt from
the next exciting novel by Roger Arthur Smith

To be published February, 2019
by Baobab Press

Prologue

Stewart Street. Carson City, Nevada. The blacktop wet from spring showers, the night air cool and acrid with ozone, the silver-domed hulk of the Capitol a block away. Beyond it, the great ragged, snowy rampart of the Sierra Nevada. Two women approach each other on the sidewalk.

There was an oddity about them, the streetlight revealed. Each wore platform shoes and black hose, a miniskirt, and a form-wrapping elastic top that left the navel and shoulders bare. Both were brunettes, their hair fluffed out on the crown and long feathery cascades over their shoulders. One was tall, five-ten, the other about two inches shorter, yet from a distance they appeared identical. The same vermillion skirt, the same black bodice, the same outsized brown leather handbag slung over the right shoulder, the same eyes shadowed in heavy makeup, the same glistening lips.

If they suggested the illusion of one woman walking toward a full-length mirror, they didn't quite act that way.

The taller one approached the streetlight in measured, purposeful strides, head held high and expression set firm, one hand grasping the handbag strap, the other swinging stiffly. The shorter one was pacing, just to keep warm, within the wide cone of overhead light, humming Blondie's "Call Me." She was stepping past the lamppost when she became aware of the other. She halted, reaching into her handbag.

Esmeralda, her work name, was already nervous. She was waiting for her date to pick her up, or at least her date's representative. There was nothing particularly strange about the pick-up occurring on a street. She had done it before, although she preferred meeting in a casino hotel room. Stewart Street, after all, was well-lit, had a blocks-long clear view, and ran parallel to U.S. Highway 395 on the other side of the Capitol and Legislative Building. The hour wasn't so strange either. 1:30 A.M. The majority of her dates started between 11 P.M. and 3 A.M. Moreover, her handler was waiting just a block away in the escort service car, a brand-new Lincoln Versailles, until after the pick-up. Esmeralda didn't like him. He was just a foulmouthed ex-army thug, but he could handle trouble if the pick-up went wrong.

Esmeralda should have been relaxed. She wasn't.

When Helen's Ready Girls had called to arrange the date, the details surprised her a little. The client asked for her specifically. And paid the first asking price. Esmeralda never went out for less the five hundred dollars, her usual, but when Mother Helen asked for seven hundred, all up front, the man agreed without a murmur. Just a little weird (not that Esmeralda minded getting more money from her cut), but it was the larger context that really put her on edge.

Three women had been murdered and mutilated during the last month. All early in the morning, all on well-lit streets. None of them on Stewart Street, true, or even in Carson City. One in Reno, one in Sparks, and one in Stateline up at Lake Tahoe. And though all three victims were in the exotic entertainment industry, like Esmeralda, they had not been in her class. They were mere call girls lent out by brothels.

But still, Esmeralda felt exposed.

So the sight of someone striding toward her sent a thrill of fear down her spine. Looking from the streetlight glare out into the dark,

Esmeralda could only distinguish a tall figure. Her first thought, a hopeful one, was that it was simply a late-night walker. They passed by now and then, even after midnight. In case it was a cop, however, Esmeralda felt for the work card in her purse. She had every right to be where she was; she wasn't a streetwalker, after all. She glanced back at the escort's car, a dark blob a block away. Suddenly, it seemed way too far.

It wasn't until the figure was a quarter block away that Esmeralda realized with relief that it was another woman. She had raised her arm halfway to give her escort the signal for trouble but now let it drop. A woman she could handle. And she definitely didn't want the thug to come gunning the Versailles up to her because of a false alarm. That would end in nastiness she didn't need.

What Esmeralda did need right then were her glasses. Of course, she didn't wear them on a date. *Men seldom make passes*, and so on and so forth. She carried them in her purse, though. Now she let go of the work card and felt for them. She had them out and on her face as the woman drew near.

With clarity came confusion. It was not only a woman. She was dressed like Esmeralda. Huh? was all she could think. Was her date picking up two women? Esmeralda never did doubles. It wasn't her style.

Then Esmeralda realized, not just like me. Exactly like me. Even to the hair and nail polish.

The woman was very close now.

"I don't know what the fuck you think you're here for, but back off. Now!" Esmeralda used the voice that said, I'm crazy enough to do anything, like shoot you for the fun of it. Now scared, she fished around in her purse for the little Armi Tanfoglio Giuseppe .25 pistol.

The tall woman only laughed. And it was a wrong laugh. It derailed Esmeralda's whole line of thinking, and she gaped. It was the deep, reedy kind of laugh that came from a skinny man with a baritone voice. A kinky joke? Whatever. With her free hand she made the signal for the escort. A frantic signal. Trouble!

No. Not a kinky joke. A word flashed to mind that her father liked to use in his endless maundering about Vietnam. Ambush. She fumbled to cock the pistol.

It was almost too easy for Stanfield to drop his purse, leap forward despite the platform shoes, and knock the pistol from the prostitute's hand. That was not significant to his performance, though. Struggle—this kind—was only preparatory, like stretching a canvas before nailing it to the frame. Nor was pain required, not really. If the whore suffered, so be it, it was a bonus for him, yet it wasn't the point, and in any case for it to be fresh, the raw material had to be prepared quickly, so lingering pain was counterproductive.

The whole time he approached he had had the knife handle cupped in his hand, the long, slender blade hidden behind his forearm. Now he grasped it in his fist, blade facing outward. One fast, hard sweep, and the prostitute's throat was sliced—carotid artery, esophagus, and windpipe all together.

Not enough left to scream with. Her eyes rounded, her mouth hung open, and her fingers scraped at the blood pouring forth. Stanfield noted, idly, that her eyes were an unusually bright green, emerald-like.

She fell, her eyeglasses clattering across the cement. Her legs kicked, slower, slower, slower. Still.

Stanfield waited for the last pulse of blood. Then it was time for the real work. He slit open her elastic bodice, her miniskirt, pantyhose top, and then down along each leg to the ankle. For a moment he paused to consider her naked body, though not too long. Who knew what benighted idiot might blunder by even at this hour? Just long enough to verify that the skin was suitable.

"Okay," he told The Arm, transferring the knife from his right hand, his only real hand, "it's all yours."

Bending over, he let The Arm, now tremblingly eager, take full control. Swiftly, gracefully as Jackson Pollack drip-painting his enormous canvases, it set the knife to carving.

It was a new, daring kind of art, and Stanfield adored it. The woman's body as canvas. An attractive young body, a canvas free of blemishes, wrinkles, stretch marks, or fat pouches. A purity that needed neither color nor texture added but only lines to discover a deeper inner beauty, a revelation.

He watched The Arm at work: a curving, deep cut here and a symmetrical one beside it, a lighter fluttery flaying down *there*, where the focus of vile lust was transformed into something entirely different, flowerlike. Now some delicate piercings and strokes to the head, and it was no longer strictly recognizable as female. Stanfield pondered. A mandala, in fresh blood, surrounded by a cloud of hair? Maybe. Or maybe an oculus. Celtic interlace? Hmmm, Escher-like in all events.

The Arm flourished on. Stomach, breasts, legs. The smears and pools of blood added depth and contrast.

When it stopped, Stanfield straightened. He stood only a moment memorizing the finished work. Admiring.

True art brings death to life.

What was once just another nasty, grubbing, otiose, empty-headed prostitute was now unique. An aesthetic excarnation. A masterpiece.

Stanfield patted The Arm, almost affectionately. "Bravo," he told it. "Bravo." It was times like these when he could conceive of it as part of him. Almost.

Retrieving the purse, he pulled out a long shawl and wrapped his upper body. Then he walked away at the same pace he arrived, continuing down Stewart Street. In passing, he looked through the side window of the pimp's Lincoln. The man's head drooped on the steering wheel, still asleep, just as he had been when Stanfield peeked in before detouring around the block to begin his promenade.

Some lookout! Stanfield laughed. But then, he had never had trouble from any of the other pimps either. It just went to show—his art was so profoundly transformative that it nullified mere human interference.

After that he never looked back. He quickstepped past the only other car within sight, an empty Volvo, and reached his hotel room ten minutes later. He would pass the rest of the night sleeping in the prostitute's get-up. He would burn the clothes in the morning. It was a necessary precaution but an awkward, vexing one, because by morning The Arm would no longer be cooperating.

That was another side to art, and Stanfield just had to put up with it. Art demanded suffering. That was what made it more than mere self-expression, made it moral. Beauty and innovation had to be balanced.

Worth it, though.

He smiled to himself. The image of the night's masterpiece hovered fresh in his mind, and would continue to do so. It gave him profound satisfaction. That, and he had the pleasure of anticipating how his critics in the newspapers would react.

Yet even as Stanfield was walking away from the dead Esmeralda, his fourth execution, something was stirring that he, by killing her, had unknowingly invoked, something that would seek him out as relentlessly as his reflection in a mirror sought him. Something visceral, primordial, artless.

One

The man now known as William Damone tossed the *Oregonian*—April 1, 1980, morning edition—onto his desk. He leaned back in his swivel chair, considering the article he had just finished. He had read one similar two weeks earlier. It, like the new one, had been tucked into the police blotter columns of the newspaper's Region section. That first article disquieted him. It reported the third murder and ritual mutilation of a young woman in northern Nevada. This latest article deepened his concern. A fourth victim in the same general area.

It wasn't the death of a human that bothered him. He didn't relish killings, but he didn't shy away from them either. In the course of doing his duty, he had killed people himself. Only out of necessity, though. It was nothing personal. That duty had once been so clear and simple, but something about it was changing. Damone was not particularly given to reflection, yet it seemed to him that an incident in 1801 marked the beginning. Specifically, an unsettling question had been asked of him.

Willem Dagón, Damone's name at the time, had sensed that an echo of evil had come into existence, and contrary to the rules by which evil operated it had lived past its purpose. It was on the loose. The rules allowed no such freedom, and they governed Dagón as well. After a human exploited and then murdered four others, purely for self-satisfaction, the lingering malevolence created a disturbance in that small portion of nature that was exclusively human, and rebounded. An echo. The echo of evil assumed a human form. Its mission was to tempt, lure, and trap the human monster. The echo killed that monster and, if all went in accordance with evil's intent, died in the process. That was a given, the way of things. Nice and simple, without the nice.

It was Dagón's responsibility to find echoes who somehow managed to survive, but he got a late start tracking this one. Some months had passed before he finally caught up with it in a White Russian farmstead, only to discover that the echo had no desire to evade him. It perceived in Dagón its own doom and was relieved, as if it were being shown a kindness, as if what little it had seen of life among humans was more than enough.

When Dagón entered the stables, saber in hand, the echo, a female in form, was sitting on a three-legged milking stool. Morning sunlight seeped between the wall planks, spreading pale yellow fans through the hay dust and tangling in the echo's wiry black hair. Though the air was cool, it wore only a flaxen shift like a nightgown. It appeared insensible to the door's creaking, its elbows on its knees, its head in its hands. Finally, it looked up—as was usual of echoes, its was an open, winsome face—and asked the question: does goodness exist?

Dagón felt obliged to speak, considering what he was about to do. "No," he told it, "good does not exist in its own right. Only shadings of evil."

Then Dagón decapitated it, the swiftest death within his power. There was nothing personal about the slaying. It was simply a question of natural equilibrium, as Dagón was given to understand it.

Yet the question lingered and nettled. Was he right? What did "shadings of evil" really mean? It had popped out of him without forethought. Why did he bother answering in the first place? What did he, who represented evil, understand of goodness? Why, after almost four hundred years of supervising a narrow part of evil, should these concerns come up? The sense that change was in the air had only increased with the passing century and three-quarters. To his dismay, he caught himself thinking of the Russian echo as a *she* and not as an *it*, as if it were a person, a human. That was another change for him, and he could not undo the habit.

One thing did not change. Humans still preyed on other humans. Echoes continued appearing to stop a certain type of evildoer. Damone still had his duty. The killings he read about in the *Oregonian* demonstrated that. He was certain another echo would soon be created, another confrontation, another pair of deaths, or, if not, another mess for him to clean up. Duty was truth—although, he could not deny, duty was growing increasingly burdensome to prosecute.

Designed by Baobab Press.
The typeface, Minion Pro, is inspired
by late Renaissance-era type and
designed by Robert Slimbach in 1990
for Adobe Systems.

Printed and bound by Thomson Shore, Inc.

ROGER ARTHUR SMITH passed much of his youth riding in the back seat of the family station wagon to and from Hawthorne, Carlin, and Yerington. After graduating from the University of Nevada, Reno, he lived in Reno and Carson City, variously writing for the *Reno Gazette-Journal*, *Nevada Magazine*, and Carson City bureau of the Associated Press. He and his wife make their home in Portland, Oregon. *Author photo by Sandra L. Wilborn.*